The
CAPE
ANN

ALSO BY FAITH SULLIVAN

Repent, Lanny Merkel
Watchdog
Mrs. Demming and the Mythical Beast

The CAPE ANN

FAITH SULLIVAN

CROWN PUBLISHERS, INC.

New York

Published by Crown Publishers, Inc., 225 Park Avenue South, New York, New York 10003 and represented in Canada by the Canadian MANDA Group

CROWN is a trademark of Crown Publishers, Inc.

Manufactured in the United States of America

Library of Congress Cataloging-in-Publication Data

Sullivan, Faith.
    The Cape Ann / Faith Sullivan.
      p.   cm.
    I. Title.
    PS3569.U3469C3   1988
    813'.54—dc19   87-30555
                                 CIP

ISBN 0-517-56930-2

10 9 8 7 6 5 4 3 2 1

First Edition

For Maggie, Ben, and Kate

The
CAPE
ANN

1

"NEXT YEAR at this time, I want carpenters working on *our* house," Mama said.

Papa said nothing. He was reading the paper while Mama made supper. We were having fried pork chops, mashed potatoes with gravy, and Monarch brand canned peas. Mama had baked a couple of apple pies that morning. She never made fewer than two. Papa could eat almost a whole pie at a sitting.

Mama liked to bake pies, and everyone said she was the best pie baker in Harvester, Minnesota. "That's because the crust is thin and crisp," she had explained to me, "and the filling isn't runny." She'd added quickly, "But I never use tapioca or cornstarch to thicken up the fruit pies." Her tone implied that moral turpitude was responsible for pies with tapioca or cornstarch.

Mama's hair was in pin curls because she was going to her bridge club after supper. Bridge club met every other week on Friday. Tonight Bernice McGivern was hostess.

Mama carried the platter of chops and the bowl of peas to the table, then returned to the stove for the potatoes and gravy. Seating herself, she filled my plate, mashed potatoes first. I scooped out a well in the center for the gravy, and she took care to pour it into the depression. Mindfully laying my chop to one side of the potatoes, she spooned peas onto the other.

Papa folded the paper and put it on the floor under his chair. Taking up his fork, he reached across and dragged the tines

1

through my potatoes, laying waste to the dam. Then he laughed as though it were a great joke which only Mama and I would fail to see.

"Why did you do that, Willie? You know she likes to save the potatoes for last."

"For Christ's sake, Arlene. You gonna pick a fight over mashed potatoes?" he asked, continuing to laugh. Papa laughed a good deal, and everyone said he was a good-natured fellow. A real sport, they said. Mama set her jaw and passed him the chops.

With my fingers and my spoon, I shored up the ravaged well.

"Don't use your fingers, Lark," Mama admonished.

Mama had chosen the name Lark. Lark Browning Erhardt. Browning was Mama's maiden name. Papa had wanted to call me Beverly Mary; Mary after the Blessed Virgin. Mama said she wouldn't hang a name like Beverly Mary on a pet skunk. Where she got the idea for Lark, I don't know, although one time when I asked, she said that larks flew high and had a happy song.

When Mama told Father Delias that I was going to be named Lark Browning, he said it wouldn't do, I had to have a saint's name. Mama, who was a convert, didn't understand that but she went along. On my baptismal certificate I was Lark Ann Browning Erhardt.

Mama hated her own name, Arlene. "Arlene, Marlene, Darlene, they're all hayseed names," she deplored. Even more than Arlene, she hated "Lena," which she'd been called in school, growing up. Once when Papa called her Lena, just to get her goat, she threw a mustard jar at him.

Rising, Mama came around to my side of the table, took my knife and fork, and helped me to cut my chop. "Next year at this time, I want carpenters working on *our* house," she repeated. It was the same thing she'd said earlier, the same thing she'd said a hundred times. Returning to her chair, she warned, "I won't go on living in this place. If we don't have carpenters building our house next year, I'm setting a match to this dump." She rose to fetch the coffee pot. "There are plenty of people in this town who own their own homes, and they don't make as much money as you do," she told Papa, pouring coffee into his cup, then into her own.

"What do I care what plenty of people do?" he asked, stirring cream into his coffee.

Mama set the pot on the stove with a bang. "I'm serious, Willie. I want a house."

I didn't understand Papa's not wanting a house. It wasn't the way he was raised, Mama would say. Grandpa and Grandma Erhardt lived in a nice house with a pair of walnut trees in the front yard. Not a fancy or big house, but nice. We lived in the train depot, a few feet from the tracks.

Papa worked for the railroad. He was the clerk in the depot. He and the depot agent handled the coming and going of trains. They sold tickets and figured out routes and schedules for the passengers who were going far across the country. They accepted outgoing freight, weighing it and toting up the charges, and they unloaded incoming freight, and delivered it, too, if the party couldn't come down to pick it up. They dealt with mail, and sent and received telegrams. They saw to it that tracks were cleared or switched for trains requiring a siding. It was a busy job. There was a passenger train heading east in the morning, one going west in the after-noon. At least two freight trains came through each day, though these usually came through after supper in the evening.

The trains were big and noisy and dirty, and they smelled of coal, but Mama and Papa and I all loved them, each for our own reasons. I really couldn't imagine not living beside the trains, but I wanted a room of my own, so I supported Mama's campaign for a house.

Upstairs above the depot, in an apartment reserved for the depot agent, lived Mr. Art Bigelow and his wife, May, a taciturn, childless couple much devoted to stamp collecting and knitting, respectively.

When Papa came to Harvester, there were no living quarters provided for the clerk and his family. There was, however, a large, empty room at the east end of the ground floor. Its only door opened directly onto the station platform. Mama, who was deter-mined to save money for a house, saw in this room our rent-free living quarters for the next few years. I was a baby then, but she told the story so often that I seemed to remember how it looked.

A space twenty feet by twenty feet, with a fifteen-foot ceiling, it possessed three very tall, stern-looking windows, grimed with the smoke and steam of thousands of trains. The walls were of a narrow, vertical board, painted railway gray, and the floors were dusty, unvarnished oak. In one wall was a cold-water faucet, but no sink or drain. It was difficult to imagine for what purpose the room had been designed, unless the railroad had at some point envisioned it as lay-over quarters for train crews or section gangs.

Mama got in touch with the railroad company at once, negotiating a rent-free agreement for us to occupy this daunting, minimal housing.

Papa was daunted, not Mama. "There must be rooms over a store that we could move into," Papa suggested.

"If we live here," Mama pointed out, "we can save the rent money for a house of our own."

"There's no heat. What'll we do in the winter?"

"We'll have a coal stove put in. The railroad has lots of coal."

"And a bathroom? What about that?"

"We'll use the toilet off the waiting room. For baths we'll buy a big galvanized tub, and I'll heat water."

"There's no drain in this room. What'll we do with the water we run?"

"We'll carry it over beyond the tracks and dump it."

Mama had an argument for all of Papa's misgivings. He was stunned and displeased by her willingness to live "like hoboes." Mama, who had graduated from high school, whose parents had graduated from high school! (Papa had quit school after the tenth grade.) Mama who had grown up in a comfortable house in a town with paved streets and three railroads. How could such a woman insist that they live in this cold, empty room? And with a baby? In a few months, when the snow came flying, wouldn't she feel foolish coming to him to complain that she couldn't keep the place warm and that she was catching pneumonia hauling slop water across the tracks? Then he would have a good laugh.

But Mama didn't complain, not in the first years. We were going to save for a new house. In the meantime, she made the depot house as comfortable and attractive as her considerable ingenuity could manage. Linoleum in a tan and cream pattern covered the floor. The walls were painted ivory. A carpenter came with lumber and panels called compoboard, or a name very much like that.

With the four-by-eight-foot sheets of compoboard, he built partitions, and created a bedroom, kitchen, and living room. There were no doors, just doorways, and since the sheets were only four by eight, there was a two-foot gap between the floor and the bottom of the partition, and a five-foot gap between the top of the partition and the ceiling. Mama said the gaps allowed heat from the stove in the living room to circulate. Still, a lot of heat got lost up near that fifteen-foot ceiling, and once the place got cold, it took forever to heat it up again.

In the kitchen, which was the room with the faucet and the door to the outside, Mama had a sink installed, with a drain that went into a pail underneath. She sewed a pretty fabric skirt to hide the pail. As I grew into a child, emptying the pail—*pails*, actually, as there were three of them—became my responsibility, though Mama helped in the coldest weather. The bedroom held Mama and Papa's bed, a bureau, wardrobe, and my crib. You had to walk sideways to move around the furniture.

But, despite its shortcomings, once he'd gotten over the embarrassment of living as we did, Papa grew accustomed to our cramped quarters, and he could see no reason to go to the expense and disruption of building a new house. Mama, on the other hand, grew increasingly dissatisfied.

Clearing away dishes, she told Papa, "I went by the lumberyard this afternoon and got some more house plans I want you to look at."

Papa reached for the newspaper under his chair.

"Willie, I want you to look at them. We've got to get out of here. Lark can't go on sleeping in a crib. She's six years old. She needs a room of her own and a real bed. I've made as much of this place as I can, but I can't make it bigger."

Papa lowered the paper. "Where are you off to?" he asked, taking note of Mama's pin curls.

"Where am I off to! It's Friday. I'm off to bridge club. How many years have I been going to bridge club? You still have to ask." She poured boiling water from the tea kettle into the dishpan and added cold water from the faucet. "Lark, if you've finished your pie, would you give me a hand here? I'm going to have to shake a leg if I don't want to be late."

"Who's staying with the kid?" Papa asked.

"*You*," Mama told him impatiently, scrubbing an empty pie plate.

"No, I'm not."

"What do you mean?" she asked, turning without removing her hands from the dishwater.

"I've got a poker game."

Mama stared, disbelieving.

"Now don't start in," Papa told her.

"Don't tell me not to start in. How could you do this? And on a bridge night at that?"

"I forgot."

"You didn't forget. Since Lark was a baby, bridge club has been every other Friday."

"I forgot that this Friday was the 'other.' "

"You are a liar, Willie. You enjoy spoiling my good times."

"Well, get on the phone and get a high school kid to stay with her," Papa said.

"I will not. This is *your* fault. You get on the phone."

"I don't know their names. You're the one who knows them." He threw down the paper. "You damned well better get someone before you leave here."

"The hell I will," Mama retorted, shoving the clean skillet at me.

"Then take her with you."

"No. The girls all agreed we wouldn't bring our kids. If everyone brought one, it would be a madhouse. You knew you were supposed to stay with her tonight. You did this on purpose."

"For Christ's sake, Arlene, why would I forget on purpose?"

"Because you don't like the bridge club." She turned to face him, the dishcloth in her hand. "You never liked it."

"A bunch of cackling hens." A smile began to pull at one side of Papa's mouth, and he raised his empty coffee cup to hide it.

Mama burst into tears and hurled the wet dishcloth at him, striking the coffee cup and knocking it to the floor, where it shattered at his feet.

"It's just like our house that doesn't get built," she cried. "You sit there eating pie and smirking. Everything is a joke. All my plans," she choked, "are funny, aren't they?"

Papa was already out the door and heading down the platform to the depot office. Mama fell upon the dishcloth and flung it against the wall above the sink. "Goddamn him," she cried, "I'll show him."

2

A LITTLE before eight, Mama emerged from the bedroom, skittery and bright eyed, nerved up for the competition. Stored away for the evening were her anger and tears. Mama loved bridge club: the sociability, the drink or two, the exotic dessert. But especially the competition, the possibility of carrying home first prize. Not that she cared much for the prize itself, a box of fancy face soap or a china ashtray. It was the winning of it. Mama was a competitive apple pie baker and a competitive bridge player.

Did the bridge club ladies notice this? They were a jolly circle, women who laughed until tears came to their eyes. Their running jokes carried over from meeting to meeting, embroidered and appliquéd with fresh fabric and threads at each gathering until a complex tapestry of humor joined them in a tight sisterhood of group memory.

Papa's "cackling hens" epithet was not without basis. One or two of the women cackled, a couple of them tittered, some honked or snorted or squealed. But it was a satisfying racket. When Mama entertained bridge club in our living room, I would lie in the crib and wrap myself in the female voices, feeling safe in their company, and wondering if I would ever be part of such a group and have so much to laugh about.

Mama was nourished by the cabala and the kinship, but she was exhilarated by the competition. She had learned the self-deprecating ways of the woman who does not want to be thought hard and grasping, but her artifices could not always cover the nakedness of her need to excel.

Now Mama's Tabu perfume preceded her into the living room, where I sat folded up on the couch with the spring/summer Monkey Wards catalog.

"You look beautiful," I told her, thrilled by her bridge night glamour. She wore a simple black dress of an elegant, crinkly fabric. It was one she had made. On one shoulder was pinned a large, round brooch encrusted with different colored stones." It looked old and expensive although she'd bought it for less than a dollar on sale at the Golden Rule department store in St. Paul.

Adjusting an earring, Mama turned her back. "Are my seams straight?"

I said yes, and she came to me and bent to kiss me. I made her kiss me on the mouth so that I would get some of her lipstick on my mouth. She always did that on bridge night. I had to be very careful not to smudge her makeup. We touched lips gingerly, quickly, and immediately I folded my lips inward to savor the thick, fruity taste of the lipstick.

She looked at her watch. "You can stay up till nine, but I want you in your nightgown right away."

I grabbed her hand, which smelled of Jergens lotion. "If anybody talks about Hilly Stillman, remember what they say so you can tell me."

She laughed and hurried out through the kitchen to the door. "Have a good time," I called, closing my eyes until I could no longer smell the Tabu, then returning to the brassieres in the Monkey Wards catalog.

Hilly Stillman stories abounded at Mama's bridge club, and as I turned the brassiere and corset pages, I wondered if Hilly ever looked at such things. Did he think about people's naked bodies?

Hilly, a veteran of the World War, was about forty, though he seemed much younger to me. His mother, who was not much more than sixty-five, seemed remarkably ancient.

Bill McGivern, husband of Mama's friend Bernice, was a World War veteran, too. He remembered Hilly from before. Hilly's father died when Hilly was a baby. Mrs. Stillman taught third grade at the public school to provide for herself and little Hillyard. A cousin, a young farm girl, had come to live with them in town for a few years to help out with Hilly, but she got into trouble and had no husband, and she disappeared, evaporated into thin air.

When Mama heard this story, she said, "I hope she lit out for California. I hope it was a married man, and he gave her money to get to California. Maybe she's in the movies now."

Mama said this at a sodality meeting and word of it got back to Papa who said that if Mama felt that way, she was no better than that pregnant whore. Mama hit him with a rolled up *Liberty* magazine and Papa slapped her across the face so hard that she had a bruise and couldn't go to bridge club or sewing club for a month. After that Mama cooled toward sodality.

I often thought of Hilly Stillman's cousin and her baby in California. Did they have an orange farm or was the cousin in the movies, as Mama had suggested? I hoped they had an orange farm. It would be pleasant for the baby, playing among the trees and having all the oranges she wanted. Oranges were a luxury in Minnesota in the thirties. Grandpa Browning complained that fellows on relief got oranges but folks who had to work for a living couldn't afford them. It didn't occur to me that Hilly's cousin would be in her middle years now, the baby in its thirties. I imagined them in the warm shade of orange trees, a young mother and her toddler.

Mrs. Stillman nearly lost her job after the cousin took off, pregnant. Although this all happened around the turn of the century, people continued to speak of it in 1934 when Mama and Papa came to Harvester.

A committee made up of several German Lutherans, a number of Baptists, and a Methodist approached the school board and demanded that Mrs. Stillman be dismissed. After all, they pointed out, the offending cousin had been living under the Stillman roof when she got pregnant. Where was Mrs. Stillman when this was going on?

It was a narrow decision. Mrs. Stillman's job was saved by one vote. The town was divided by the issue, and the German Lutherans decided to build their own elementary school.

Bill McGivern said that when Hilly was growing up, he took a lot of razzing about all of it, and about being a mama's boy as well. He was always waiting around school for her instead of slipping off and doing daring, forbidden things that would get him into the proper kind of trouble.

When President Wilson declared war on the Central Powers, Hilly was the first boy from the county to volunteer. A big fuss was made over him. His picture appeared in all the weekly and biweekly papers in St. Bridget County. Girls promised to write him, and everyone was proud to have known him, to have been his friend.

Hilly was sent to France, where he brought glory upon himself with his daring in battle and his courage in the rescue of fallen comrades. At home Mrs. Stillman was invited everywhere. When he was decorated by both the French and the American governments, Hilly's picture again appeared in all the papers. Three different Harvester girls were circulating the story of their imminent engagement to Hilly.

Word that Hilly had been wounded and news of the end of the

war arrived at nearly the same time. A great armistice celebration was held in the school gymnasium, and Mrs. Stillman was installed on a throne bedecked with bunting and flags.

When Hilly's wounds had healed as well as they ever would, he was shipped back to Harvester, where news of his return had preceded him. Lurching down the steps of the railway car, accompanied by another soldier, sent to see him home, Hilly was nearly blown sideways by the spirited strains of "It's a Long, Long Way to Tipperary." Assembled before him at the station were the high school band and a throng of a thousand flag-waving citizens. Right down in front, clutching a gilded, three-foot wooden key, was the mayor, with Mrs. Stillman shy and weeping beside him.

The boy with Hilly held tight to his charge and glanced anxiously around. That, at least, is the way Bill McGivern, who was already mustered out, remembers it.

But Hilly broke into an open-mouthed smile and began flailing his arms in time to the music as if he were conducting the band. The young man beside him spoke some words to him, and Mrs. Stillman ran to fling her arms around her son, but Hilly ignored them. The arm flailing seemed to lift him to a higher level of excitement, and Hilly commenced to jig precariously. Neither his mother nor the attendant soldier could restrain him.

Grinning and flailing and jigging, Hilly careened back and forth across the station platform. Helpless, Mrs. Stillman watched, clutching her coat around her.

Suddenly Hilly stopped. His smile slid away, and he cast his eyes down to the front of his trousers. The widening stain of urine there seemed to amaze him.

The band concluded "Tipperary." Hilly raised his eyes and took in the gathered crowd, bewilderment crimping his features. Staring again at the stain, he spread his hands to conceal it and crumpled to the platform on his knees.

The crowd began to crumble and disperse. Finally there were only the three of them on the platform: Hilly on his knees, Mrs. Stillman crouched beside him, and the attendant soldier standing guard.

Hilly's purely physical wounds—shrapnel in the neck and chest, and trench foot severe enough to necessitate amputation of several toes on his right foot—healed, though he would always walk with a rolling limp. But Hilly's mind had carried him back to early childhood. About age five, people speculated. Doctors held out hope that he would recover his sanity spontaneously, but it was only a hope, not a prognosis.

Hilly and his mother lived in a small apartment over Rabel's Meat Market on Main Street, across from the post office. When Mrs. Stillman was home from school, where she still taught third grade, Hilly sat at the window in his room watching people come and go on the street below, particularly the steady flow in and out of the post office. There was no mail delivery in Harvester, so everyone picked up their own. Hilly liked to see people coming out with packages and imagine what was in them.

After Mrs. Stillman left for school in the morning and Hilly had eaten the breakfast laid out on the kitchen table, he dressed himself and descended the outside stairs, drifting out onto Main Street. So proud was he of being able to dress himself that one spring morning, a couple of months after his return, Hilly hobbled naked down the stairs, carrying the garments Mrs. Stillman had left on the chair beside his bed. Hitching his way into Rabel's Meat Market, he threw down the clothes and grinned widely at Mr. Rabel, Mr. Rabel's apprentice, and three ladies come to do marketing, exhorting, "Watch." Then one at a time, Hilly picked up the articles of clothing, held them up to show his audience, and painstakingly pulled them on, taking great care to match buttons to buttonholes. Two of the three ladies ran out of the store without their purchases. The third, Bernice McGivern's sister, Maxine, who was Dr. White's nurse, remained, and when Hilly was done dressing himself, she clapped and told him he was a clever boy.

That was the first of the Hilly Stillman stories. Although his mother persuaded Hilly never again to appear in public without clothing, short of taping his mouth and tying him to a chair, she could not prevent his going out and talking to people on the sidewalk. Most people turned away when they saw him. They crossed the street to avoid him. Boys taunted him, and if no one were around to stop them, they pelted him with stones, chasing him home and up the wooden stairs outside the butcher shop.

Women were frightened by Hilly. He lacked decorum. He would be on you, talking six to the dozen, before you could extricate yourself, and most of what he said made no sense.

Some women feared, or said they did, that Hilly could be dangerous. Violent or . . . the other. After all, everyone knew he'd appeared naked in Rabel's Meat Market in front of three women. Didn't that prove something? And he still wet himself when he was frightened. That was no picnic to be around.

Men weren't afraid of Hilly but they didn't want him hanging around their stores scaring off customers. He was a public nuisance and embarrassment. And they didn't have time to waste, listening to his nonsense. It was too bad the kid had gone through whatever he'd gone through, but it wasn't their lookout. They had a living to make.

After being shooed out of every business on Main Street two or three times, Hilly had claimed the bench in front of the post office. Townspeople were willing to cede him that.

There were a few in Harvester, among them Bernice McGivern, her sister, and Mama, who stood still for Hilly's disjointed greetings and observations. Descending the post office steps, Mama would call, "I hear you've eaten every strawberry in Harvester, Hilly." (Hilly had once told her, "Strawberries I eat better in my cream than coffee.")

Hilly would smile, showing all his teeth, his tongue, and part of his throat. "Nah." He would shake his head vigorously, like a five-year-old. "Some more of strawberries for you will find." Mama would laugh and Hilly would laugh. Then she would hand him the letters or package she held. Hilly liked to carry people's mail. If you didn't have a car, he would carry it all the way home for you. Sometimes Mama bought him an ice cream cone or a soda pop.

The hardest part of being nice to Hilly was his gratitude. He turned himself inside out for anyone who nodded. Sticking out of his back pocket, summer or winter, was an old rag. If you allowed him to carry your mail, he polished your car. And if you were in a hurry, that could be a nuisance. Mama said sometimes you damned near had to run over Hilly to get away.

Occasionally when Mama went to pick up our mail, she drove an old black pickup that Papa used for delivering railroad freight. Hilly was crazy about the pickup and was always begging to ride in the back. If Mama wasn't busy, she'd give him a little ride around town.

One time she brought him to the depot and asked him if he thought he could wash the windows of our living quarters. There were only three, but they were very tall and ladders made Mama dizzy. Hilly became nearly sick with delight at being asked.

It took him an entire day to wash the three windows inside and out. That was because he was so particular. And he kept polishing them long after they were spotless. When it looked as though he would polish his way right through the glass, Mama would tell him it was time to start the next.

At noon Mama carried lunch out to Hilly on a pie tin—roast beef sandwiches, chocolate cake, and coffee with cream—and she told him he could sit in the back of the pickup to eat it. Later, when she went to collect the empty pie tin, Hilly was on his hands and knees with a rag and bucket, scrubbing out the truck.

At close to five, Mama said, "Hilly, the windows are beautiful. It's time for me to take you home." She gave him a dollar, explaining, "You can buy ice cream cones with that." He seemed very pleased by the idea, and folding the bill carefully several times, he slipped it into his shirt pocket. Mama drove him downtown, dropping him in front of Rabel's Meat Market.

She was home again, paring potatoes to fry, when someone knocked at the door. Setting the potato aside and wiping her hands on her apron, she answered it. On the platform stood Hilly, a collapsed cone in each hand, melted ice cream running down his arms and onto his trousers and shoes.

Though he smiled his wide-open-mouth smile, he was anxious. "Ice cream can't walk so far," he told her, nodding his head up and down, willing her to grasp the demonstrable truth of this and pardon it.

Hilly and the ice cream cones was a story for bridge club. At nearly every meeting, someone had a Hilly tale. Like Mama, many of the bridge clubbers were respectful of Hilly, but two or three of them reflected the general feeling in town. "It's wrong to treat him like anybody. It gives him false hopes. The next thing you know, he'll expect to get married . . . or something," I once heard Bessie Anderson say. And Cynthia Eggers added, "He's a grown man who's been in the war. He could be dangerous. Charlie says I'm not to speak to him."

But Bernice McGivern said, "It isn't Christian to ignore him. Think of what he's been through. Also, if he ever gets his brains back, I don't want him looking at *me* and remembering that I crossed the street to avoid him."

"Wouldn't it be nice," Mama mused. "Wouldn't it just be swell if one day Hilly woke up and he was sane."

AFTER MAMA left for bridge, I got into my nightgown and found the Hershey bar in the cupboard. Mama always left a treat when she was out at night. And I always ate it right away, then was sorry I hadn't had any willpower. It would be smart, I told myself, to break the bar into its many little squares. I could eat some now, some at bedtime, and save two or three for tomorrow. That was the sort of wise thing Katherine Albers, who sat behind me in the first grade, would do. It was one of the reasons it was difficult to like her. Another was her blond, Shirley Temple curls.

Chocolate bar in hand, I climbed into my crib and gazed out the bedroom window. Across the tracks, the grain elevators loomed pale silver against the deepening lilac sky. On this side, half a block away, dim, yellow lights seemed miles distant in the ecru rooms of the Harvester Arms Hotel.

Climbing out again, I fetched the house plan booklets Mama had brought home from Rayzeen's Lumberyard that afternoon, turned on the light beside Mama and Papa's bed, and hoisted myself once more over the side of the crib. Devouring my chocolate two and even three squares at a bite, I turned the pages of floor plans and exterior sketches, marveling at how prettily the trees and shrubs were arranged around the houses and how deftly they were trimmed to resemble balls and cones and half-spheres. No one in Harvester had trees and shrubs like those.

I liked houses with shutters. And brick chimneys. I hoped we would have a house with shutters and a brick chimney. Maybe even a brick sidewalk, if it didn't cost an arm and a leg. Houses with shutters and brick chimneys looked as if Katherine Albers lived in them. If I lived in a house like that, I would develop willpower and be a better person.

Mama had shown me how to make sense of floor plans; which little lines were doors, which windows or fireplaces. Fireplaces were grand. The few movies I'd seen had had fireplaces in them. But fireplaces were expensive, Mama said, so we probably would not have one, not at first.

Now, here was a cottage (a cottage was what we were going to

14

build) that had two bathrooms, one up and one down. The luxury of that made me shiver. I ate the last of the chocolate and closed my eyes to imagine being the little girl of the house in a house with two bathrooms.

This particular cottage (#127—The Cape Ann) had a front entryway with a coat closet so people didn't need to step into the living room with snow on their boots. It also boasted a small den, which Mama was set on having for a sewing/guest room. Before I fell asleep, I would put the booklet on Mama and Papa's bed, open to the Cape Ann.

While I sat studying house plans, the early freight pulled in. No cars needed to be switched to a siding, so the train was soon shrieking and grinding its way toward St. Bridget. As it drew away from the station, its great exertion caused the partition next to my crib to tremble, and the towering window in the room to vibrate. I reached my hand out between the bars of the crib and pressed it to the pulsing compoboard.

There were messages for me in the hissings and groanings of the trains as they stood before the depot; and in the deep succussion sent through the earth as they departed. "Hello. Missed you. Throw a kiss," they jangled and snorted, rolling up to my door. Then, beneath the loading and unloading and the cries of train-men, they whispered praise for my report cards and news of friends far away, like William Powell. Leaving me slowly, reluctantly, they called shrilly, "Sweet dreams. Don't cry. I'll be back."

Soon Papa locked up the office and waiting room and came home. It was nearly nine. In the kitchen he washed his hands and face, then appeared at the bedroom doorway, wiping them on a towel.

"We're going out," he said, casting a sly, confidential smile at me.

"Where?"

"Herbie Wendel's."

"Why?"

"To play poker."

"I don't know how to play poker."

"Not you, dummy." He laughed. "I'm going to play poker."

"Why am I going?"

"Because we don't have a girl to stay with you."

"But I've got on my nightie."

"That's okay. You can lie down at Herbie's."

"I don't think Mama would want me to go in my nightie. I better put on some clothes."

"There isn't time. Come on, now. Get up. You don't want me to miss this poker party, do you?"

"Can I put on my shoes?"

"Okay, but hurry up. I'm already late."

"Mama said you should call a girl to stay with me."

"It's too late. By the time she got here, Herbie would think I wasn't coming. You'll have a good time, don't worry."

"You could call Herbie."

"Look, don't you want to go? I thought you'd be tickled. You're always wanting to go places with me. Get your shoes on." Lifting me out of the crib, he set me down on the big bed and handed me my shoes and socks.

"Mama's going to get mad," I told him.

"I'll handle her," he said, buckling my black shoes that had tiny round air holes across their tops in the pattern of a bow.

From the end of the crib, I took down the pink chenille robe that was like Mama's Sunday robe, and was struggling into it as Papa hurriedly steered me out into the night.

"Should we leave Mama a note?"

"I'll call later from Herbie's," Papa explained and swung me up onto the high truck seat.

Even wearing a nightie and robe, I shivered when my legs touched the cold seat. It was May and, while the days were warm and yellow, the nights were chilly.

The engine didn't turn over right away, but complained in low moans, no happier than I to be going across town late on a Friday night. Papa gave it plenty of choke, and it trembled unwillingly to life, shaking just as I shook. We sat waiting for the engine to warm up, Papa rubbing the cold steering wheel, I hugging myself and letting my teeth click like castanets.

Well, maybe Herbie Wendel's boy, Donald, would still be up. Donald, a silly boy with a rooster's comb of hair at the back of his head and a relentless giggle, was in first grade with me. Maybe Donald and I could color in his coloring books or cut pictures out of magazines. Maybe I could learn to play poker.

We rattled through silent streets, disturbing the dignified cold. There were several cars lined up in front of the Wendel house. Papa parked opposite. I was embarrassed to be walking around the streets in my nightclothes, but I hastened along behind Papa, anxious to get inside where it was warm. Papa didn't knock, but just opened the door and walked into the living room. Mrs. Wendel wasn't home or he wouldn't do that.

"Had to bring my kid," he told the four men at the dining room table. "Sorry. The old lady's at bridge."

Standing in the archway between living room and dining room, I asked Herbie Wendel, "Is Donald home?"

"No, honey. He's gone for the weekend with his ma to her folks over at St. Bridget." Mr. Wendel got up from the poker table and disappeared into the kitchen, returning a moment later with a big red bubble gum jawbreaker. "Donald likes these," he said, handing it to me.

I thanked him and slipped it into my mouth, but when it was in my cheek, it stretched the skin so taut it hurt; and when it was between my teeth, it forced my jaws so far apart they ached. Donald Wendel was just the sort to be fond of a ridiculous treat like this. Hadn't anyone told him about Hershey bars?

I hung at the edge of the dining room, shifting the jawbreaker in my mouth and observing the men peeking at their cards, tapping them with their fingertips and grunting, "Hit me," and "See you," and "I'm in." It was a confusing game. Just when I was getting the hang of it, the rules changed.

I had begun making dents in the jawbreaker, when Papa ordered, "Stop that crunching. You're making me nervous."

"Leave her alone, Willie. She's not hurting anybody," Lloyd Grubb told him.

"I can't think with that noise," Papa said. Then to me, "Go on in the living room."

"Can't I watch? I'm trying to learn."

"Poker's no game for a kid," he said. "Get in the living room."

I sidled a couple of steps away and stopped crunching the jawbreaker. The only excitement in that house was at the dining room table. But when Papa started to get up out of his chair, I backed away. I didn't want him getting mad in front of the other men.

There was *one* magazine in the living room, something from the Knights of Columbus. I read as much as I could, which was most of it, but found not one interesting item. And there were no colored pictures. It had very few pictures of any kind.

In the dining room, the men pounded their fists on the table and swore at one another, and laughed loud enough to be heard across the street. Mr. Wendel dropped out for one hand and went to the kitchen to pour fresh drinks. I heard him call to Papa, "You drinking bourbon, Willie?"

"Yeah, that'll do," Papa answered, "if you haven't got something better." Then he laughed the way people do at phrases that are some key part of an old, shared joke.

I closed my eyes and fell asleep, dreaming that Papa left without me, that he forgot I was sleeping on the couch. I was panic-stricken. The four men at the poker table didn't know who I was or where I lived. I knew who I was and where I lived but not how to get there. When I explained that I lived in the depot, they laughed and said I was mistaken, nobody lived in a depot.

"Go back to sleep," they told me. "When you wake up, maybe you'll know where you live."

Well, I thought, I'm not going to stay here all night. Mama will give me a good licking if she makes breakfast and I'm not there. And what about the nuns? They'll be waiting for me at eight o'clock for first communion instruction and I won't be there. And hadn't they said the first day, "You'd better be pretty sick if you're going to miss instruction. Jesus is going to be upset if you don't at least have pneumonia."

Then I dreamed that I sneaked out the front door. It was black and cold outside. Pulling my robe around me, I turned right and headed south. Mama had taught me directions and told me that the depot was on the south side of town. If I kept walking down this street, headed south, I would come to the railroad tracks and then I would know where I was.

After several blocks I began to wonder, shouldn't I see the tracks soon? I thought I knew what the streets in Harvester looked like, but these streets looked like streets in some other town.

Then, behind me but not far behind, I heard a sound which turned my heart to a cold little stone. A black dog, as big as a pony, skulked at my heels, whipping the backs of my legs with his snarling and sending me flying headlong down the street. When I came to a corner, I didn't stop to look both ways but hurtled ahead.

Now the sidewalk disappeared and I was stumbling down a rutted path between deserted, crumbling houses. And what was this—snow? Drifts of it were in my path. The giant black dog would tear me to pieces and eat me. And I would go to hell because I hadn't made my first confession yet.

The dog was at my shoulder. "Oh, my God, I am heartily sorry for having offended thee," I prayed. "And I detest all my sins . . ."

But it was only a hand at my shoulder, shaking me. "Lark, Lark." It was Herbie Wendel. "We're having homemade turtle soup. Would you like some?"

I was filled with such relief, I had to go to the bathroom. When I emerged, Mr. Wendel handed me Donald's cereal bowl filled with steaming turtle soup. Little rabbits danced around the outside of the bowl. I was glad to have it in my hands because I was shivering. The house had grown cold while I slept.

Papa wasn't at the poker table. "Where's my papa?"

"He'll be right back. He had to go out for a few minutes. Sit down here on the couch and have your soup. I'll bring you some crackers."

So Papa *had* left. It was almost like my dream. Where had he gone? It must be very late. Where would you go at this time of night? Mr. Wendel returned with a plate of soda crackers, which he set on the couch beside me.

"Do you like the soup?" he inquired.

I nodded.

"I made it myself."

"Really?" I'd never heard of a man cooking. None of them in our family did.

"Caught this big old snapper out in Sioux Woman Lake. Fishing for bullheads and landed this instead. Donald's ma doesn't like to clean turtle, so I'm in the habit of making the soup."

"It's good," I assured him. "When do you think my papa'll be back?"

"Any minute." He patted my knee and returned to the dining room.

A few minutes later, Papa came through the door carrying a brown paper bag. "Damned old fool charged an arm and a leg," he told the others. Then, noticing me eating soup, "What're you doing up?"

"Mr. Wendel gave me some turtle soup he made himself. Where did you go?"

"Out. You haven't been pestering Herbie, have you?"

"No. What time is it?"

"I don't know."

"What does your watch say?"

"None of your business, Miss Nosy."

"Did you call Mama?"

He didn't answer, but headed toward the kitchen with the bag. I finished my soup, which was as good as Campbell's. Setting the empty bowl and the cracker plate on the floor, I lay down again and once more fell asleep, this time slumbering deeply and not waking till Papa carried me out to the truck. The sky was light. The first gold peeped through the trees and between the houses on our left. The cab smelled of whiskey.

When we were close to the depot, Papa turned off the engine and we coasted into the little parking lot. Before we climbed out of the pickup, Papa whispered, "We've got to be real quiet. We don't want to wake your ma. Do you understand?"

"Yes," I whispered, noticing that Papa's face was red, and his eyes, too. Did they hurt? Suddenly I remembered something. "Who took care of the late freight train?" I asked, worried that he'd forgotten.

"Art took care of it," he rasped impatiently. "Now keep quiet. I'll come around and open the door. Just wait."

He lifted me down to the gravel, and we tiptoed toward the platform, stones crunching softly beneath our feet. As we rounded the corner of the depot, a pair of grackles, loud and angry, flew down, lit on the semaphore, and starting yawking at us.

"Goddamn," Papa whispered under his breath, turning the door knob slowly, stealthily, and pushing the door open just enough for us to slip through.

At the kitchen table, Mama sat waiting.

4

"GO TO BED, Lark," Mama directed in a too-calm voice, never taking her eyes from Papa, who was at the stove checking the coffee pot, feigning innocence, stalling.

When Mama was preparing to fight, she sent me to the crib. There was no way, without solid walls and real doors, that she could prevent me from hearing every word, but whatever small distance the crib could provide, I was to enjoy.

"Wait a minute," Mama said, grabbing my arm as I passed. "What's in your hair?"

"My hair?" Sure enough there was an awful messy feeling lump in my hair. The jawbreaker bubble gum Mr. Wendel had given me.

"For God's sake, Willie," Mama spat.

"It's not *my* fault," Papa told her, foraging in the refrigerator.

Mama shoved me along toward the bedroom.

Removing my chenille robe and hanging it over the end of the crib, I climbed in. The house plans were still scattered on the Three Pigs quilt. Piling them at the foot of the crib with #127—The Cape Ann on top, I lay down, pulling the quilt tightly around me.

In the kitchen, Mama exploded. "Where in hell have you been, Willie?"

"You know where."

"Until five-thirty in the morning?"

Papa didn't answer.

"What kind of man keeps a child out all night while he gets drunk and loses his money?"

"I'm not drunk."

"You're not sober."

"Oh, for God's sake, Arlene, the kid was fine. She had a good time."

"You're the biggest liar in St. Bridget County, Willie."

"Who do you think you're talking to?"

"I'm talking to somebody who takes a six-year-old that's got to be at first communion instruction at eight o'clock this morning out to a stranger's house, keeps her there till five-thirty A.M., and then says she had a good time."

"Herbie Wendel's not a stranger."

"Where was Vera Wendel while this was going on?"

"At her folks."

"Why didn't you leave a note so I'd at least know where you were? I could have come and got Lark after bridge club."

"That's why I didn't. You'd have flounced in there and made a scene. I wanted to have a good time for a change."

"I don't notice you denying yourself. And you're damned right I'd have flounced in and had a word with a husband who's too damned stubborn to call a high school girl to stay with his daughter, but drags her off to poker like she was the same trash he is."

A chair fell over, and Mama screamed, "Keep your hands off

me, Willie." Then there was the cruel "thung" of a fist landing. I climbed out of the crib and ran to the kitchen. Mama was bent over the table and Papa was standing over her, his fist raised to hit her again. Mama grabbed the Heinz Ketchup bottle from the table and swung around, catching Papa in the ribs. He fell back against the stove, and Mama grabbed a butcher knife from the drain board. She was a formidable fighter.

"Come near me and I'll kill you, Willie."

Papa moaned, "You broke my ribs."

"Good," Mama whispered, breathing heavily. "Get out of here."

Holding his ribs, Papa shuffled to the door. When he had left, Mama stood for a long minute with the ketchup bottle in one hand and the butcher knife in the other.

I hurried back to the crib. It was because of me that Mama and Papa had fought. If Papa had wanted me to tell her I had a wonderful time at Herbie Wendel's, he should have explained on the way home. Was I supposed to know without him telling me? Would most first graders? How did other children keep their mama and papa from fighting?

It was harder to be six than to be five or four. Before four nothing was hard except not wetting your pants and not spilling things.

Before I could fall into dreams, Mama was waking me up. Time to get ready for catechism class. I wasn't going to have my first communion for a year. I didn't see why we had to start so far ahead. It was one more thing that made six harder than five.

Most of the children in my instruction class couldn't even read the *Baltimore Catechism* book that prepared us for the sacraments. We were only first graders. But the nuns said our mamas could teach us the words we didn't know. It was their responsibility as Catholic mothers. Mama didn't mind teaching me the words. Not only was she a Catholic mother, but she was also the mother of a future college student; she was concerned that I know every kind of word so that there wouldn't be a lot of surprises when I started reading college books.

Mama had washed her face and changed into a cotton dress, but I didn't think she'd been to bed. She was slow moving and short tempered. Her hair wasn't combed, and she wore no lipstick.

Normally the first thing she did after washing her face was put on lipstick and comb her hair.

Turning my back and pulling on clean underpants, I asked, "Are you afraid Papa won't come back?"

"No," she said. "He'll come back. *You're* not afraid, are you?"

"No," I lied. One more lie to add to the inventory of sins I was keeping on a pad I had hidden away. If I didn't keep track, I'd never remember them all when I got in the confessional next year.

The nuns had suggested that if we were afraid we'd forget something when we knelt in that dim little closet, we should take with us a list of our sins. We were not to write anything on the paper but sins. The rest of the ritual must be memorized. And no forgetting!

That very night, asking Mama for a tablet for catechism class, I'd begun my sorry record, which I hid in the bottom drawer of a doll chest that had been Mama's when she was a child.

"Have you got your lesson memorized?" Mama inquired, heading me toward the kitchen. There was water heating in the tea kettle, and she poured some into an enamel basin in the sink, then added a little cold from the single faucet.

"I think so."

Soaping a cloth, Mama scrubbed my ears, and after that my face and neck, rubbing me half raw. "A bath tonight," she said, slipping a favorite dress over my head. She always let me wear one of my favorites to instruction. "For luck," she said. This was a red one with little white polka dots and a white collar. Mama had starched it within an inch of its life. I liked the skirt to stand out stiff. It made me feel like I might be able to tap dance. Mama tied the sash in a perfect bow at my back, then fetched my shoes and socks and handed them to me.

"Come in the living room." She carried in a chair from the kitchen and, when I had pulled on my shoes and socks, she motioned me to sit on it. Slipping a comb with big teeth from her pocket, she grabbed my *Baltimore Catechism* from the sideboard and handed it to me.

"Look at that while I get the gum out of your hair." From her glum, resigned tone, I knew it wasn't going to be easy.

I'd gotten gum in my hair before but never such a wad. I only hoped she wouldn't have to cut all the hair off that side of my head. She worked for several minutes with the big-toothed comb, then, grunting in disgust, went to the bedroom for the brush and scissors.

I was in tears from the pain and from the anticipated disgrace of arriving at instruction with half a head of hair. It was impossible to concentrate on the catechism book while Mama yanked my head around as though she were pulling weeds.

At length she said, "Look at that," and held out her hand to show a great, nasty straw pile of hair and gum.

I put my hand to the side of my head. There was *some* hair still there. Mama finished brushing what was left, then fastened it back with bobby pins and little red bows. I fled to the bedroom for a look in the mirror. Thank God for a clever mama.

While I downed a bowl of puffed wheat, a dish towel tied around my neck to protect my dress, Mama sat down at the kitchen table. "How many men were at Herbie Wendel's?" she asked coolly, as if she didn't really care.

"Counting Papa, five."

"Who were they?" In front of whose wives would she have to hold up her head, pretending that Papa's losses were unimportant?

"Mr. Wendel, Mr. Grubb, Mr. Navarin, and Mr. Nelson."

"Axel Nelson?" she said with some distaste.

"Yes."

"Did you watch them play poker?"

"Not very long. Papa told me to go in the living room. He said poker wasn't a game for kids."

With her index finger, Mama traced the flower design in the oilcloth. "So you don't know if your papa lost money?"

I shook my head.

The way to St. Boniface Catholic Church was straight and simple. You went out to First Avenue, which ran past the depot, turned right, and kept going. It was also easy to find Main Street, which ran perpendicular to First. You just walked two blocks toward the Catholic church, and there it was.

Outside, on First Avenue, the morning was sunny and warm and intimately buzzing. Inside St. Boniface, it was dark and chilly and echoing. A few stragglers from daily Mass, mostly old ladies in battered black hats and cotton lisle hose, were leaving the pews. They remained after Mass, saying rosaries and lighting candles. Now and then there was one making her way through the Stations of the Cross. Long after instruction class had assembled and begun lessons, the old woman would be tiptoeing from station to station, denying herself the smell of May blowing in off the prairie and the pleasant sensation of a toasty sidewalk beneath the soles of her chunky black shoes. Could I ever hope to be as devout and self-denying as that?

Seven of the nine would-be communicants were already gathered in the back pew, squirming and poking one another, when I genuflected and pushed Delmore Preuss over. He gave me a kick in the calf and resumed picking his nose. Sally Wheeler, my best friend in first grade, was seated toward the middle of the pew. Sally had thick, black hair which her mother braided into two long plaits that fell over her shoulders in front. Next to having short, blond curls like Katherine Albers, having long, black braids was best. Sally dropped the braid on which she had been chewing and waved to me.

Mrs. Wheeler, like Mama, was a convert. This had created a special bond between Sally and me. Sister Mary Clair and Sister Mary Frances saved the most difficult catechism questions for us. They also reprimanded us more often than the other children, although, really, no one got off lightly. Putting our heads together, Sally and I concluded that because our mothers were converts, the sisters had doubts about our ability to be A-plus Catholics. Our only hope, as they likely saw it, was indoctrination of the sternest, most rigorous kind.

At our mamas' urging, Sally and I studied catechism together on Friday afternoons after Miss Hagen dismissed first grade. One week at Sally's house, the next at mine.

Mrs. Wheeler, Sally's mama, was a pretty, fragile-looking woman who spoke softly and regarded everything with great intensity, as if the true meaning and value of things were eluding her or somehow being kept from her, and she must discover it. Sometimes she waylaid Sally and me for half an hour in the kitchen as she set out milk and cookies, inquiring persistently into the character and respective merits of Fig Newtons and Mallomars.

At four-thirty she walked me to Main Street, explaining that I must stay on it until Truska's Grocery and then turn right onto First. I could easily have found my own way, but Mrs. Wheeler needed to do this. She needed to carry everything out thoroughly and properly, no matter how cumbersome or ritualistic it became. It was her burden and duty to dot all the world's undotted *i*'s.

Now and then, when a regular member was sick or out of town and a substitute was required at Mama's bridge club, Mrs. Wheeler was called. The next morning Mama would say to me, "Look how gray I turned waiting for Stella Wheeler to bid one heart," and she would bend over and point to her imaginary gray hair. Mama was a headlong person with instincts as sharp as darts. She couldn't conceive of uncertainty like Mrs. Wheeler's.

Sally and I never asked her mama to help us with catechism, although she invariably volunteered. Instead we went up to Sally's room, closed the door, and played paper dolls until four, then opened the *Baltimore Catechism* and ripped through the week's lesson.

In June, when school let out, class would meet six mornings a week for a month. I didn't look forward to that.

Most Saturday mornings Mama reviewed the lesson with me before I left home. This morning there had been no time. Now I sat, cramped between Delmore Preuss and the end of the pew, eyes closed, reeling off answers in my head. I was like someone preparing for citizenship in another country—terrified I would be found unworthy.

The nuns rose from the front pew, where they had been praying since Mass, and strode briskly back to where their charges waited— picking scabs, elbowing neighbors, kicking the pew in front, and biting hangnails—torn by our great reluctance to be there and our equally great terror of hell.

Sister Mary Frances stood in the center aisle just outside our pew, while Sister Mary Clair took a seat in the pew directly opposite to observe. They taught us as a team, one spelling the other, as by turns they flagged under the burden of our ignorance.

"Sally," Sister Mary Frances began when we had completed an Our Father and a Hail Mary, "can you tell us what happens to babies who die without being baptized?"

What I had begun to ponder as I sat twitching beneath Sister Mary Frances's gaze, so close to her that I could hear her soft, impatient breathing, was the moral ramifications of gambling. While it was presumptuous to question the state of Papa's soul, I knew that Mama was upset by his poker playing. Was poker a mortal sin? If I could find out, maybe I could put Mama's mind at ease.

While our catechism responses droned or faltered, and we acquitted or disgraced ourselves, I formulated queries for the nuns. Is poker a sin? Is it only a sin if you lose?

"Lark." Sister Mary Frances frowned down her long, perpetually sunburned nose at me. It was not a frown of anger, not yet at any rate, but a frown of speculation. What response has this child failed to memorize? For what was the point of asking questions to which the answer was known?

Taking the heavy cross hanging around her neck into her two hands, which were always red and wounded-looking, as if in her world it was eternally winter and she were forever without mittens, Sister demanded, "Without looking anywhere but at this crucifix, name the fourteen Stations of the Cross."

Pushing myself up from the seat, my heart beating in the perversely pleasant way it did when I was called on to answer a difficult question, I lay my furled *Baltimore Catechism* on the pew behind me. I stared fixedly at the silver and onyx cross and at Sister's knuckles, in whose creases were tiny pinpoints of dried blood.

"Pontius Pilate condemns Jesus," I began, turning under the thumb of my right hand. Did Sister use lye soap to wash clothes? Grandma Browning made her own lye soap, and it was strong and harsh. It could make your hands look like that if you weren't careful.

"Jesus takes up the cross." I turned under the index finger of my right hand. Maybe Sister washed her linens on a washboard.

"Jesus falls to the ground for the first time." Had she been working in the vegetable garden behind the nuns' house?

"Jesus meets his mother, Mary." Did Sister have Jergens lotion, like Mama had, to soothe her hands?

"Simon helps Jesus carry the cross." Maybe nuns couldn't afford Jergens lotion.

"Veronica wipes Jesus's face." Mama had said that nuns were poor, that they promised to be poor when they married Jesus.

"Jesus falls down again." Wasn't it funny how Jesus had so many brides?

"Jesus meets women of Jerusalem." Did Sister mind that Jesus had so many other brides?

"Jesus falls down a third time." Maybe Sister refused lotion. Maybe she offered up her pain.

"The soldiers tear Jesus's clothing off of him." She had told us we could offer up our suffering if we ever had any.

"They nail Jesus on the cross." If you offered up your suffering, you got out of purgatory sooner.

"Jesus dies." Mama had added up for me (based on estimates Sister had provided us) the number of years I would suffer in purgatory for various weaknesses of the body and spirit. According to my calculations, I would spend nearly forever in purgatory unless I was lucky enough to die a martyr's death. Then, if I understood correctly, I would go directly to heaven.

"They take Jesus down from the cross." But surely Sister didn't have to worry about spending millions of years in purgatory, so why refuse Jergens lotion?

"They put Jesus in the tomb." I had turned all my fingers under once, and four of them had gone down twice. Fourteen stations in order, none left out.

Without the smallest congratulatory notice, Sister Mary Frances began again at the opposite end of the pew. "Beverly, the Act of Contrition, please." Sister never congratulated us. Why would one make a fuss over a child learning that which was needed in order to be spared the tortures of hell, torments so heinous they could only be devised by a God of infinite ingenuity and love?

The morning crawled forward on the bloodied knees of martyred saints. Sister Mary Clair took over, and Sister Mary Frances opened the lower portion of the windows. These stained-glass panels bore the names of departed members of the parish, departed members whose families could afford a window in their memory. "In Memory of Our Beloved Mother, Edna Ripath," or "Our Beloved Baby Daughter, Evelyn Shelton."

If I were cut down in my childhood, I hoped that Mama and Papa would buy a pretty stained-glass panel for me. "In Memory of Our Beautiful Lark," it would read. Every time someone opened my window, I would smile and blow the perfume of peonies and wet earth through the opening. The nuns had assured us that in heaven we would have no interest in earth's pleasures, so paltry were they beside the delights of God's home, but I was sure that I'd be interested.

At ten o'clock we were herded out the door to sit on the broad front steps for ten minutes, and we fell apart into twos and threes. Although we were admonished to study, the nuns usually disappeared for a few minutes, leaving the boys to argue and shove and sometimes roll on the ground, getting grass stains on their clothes. Bleeding noses and scraped elbows, full of grit, were also not uncommon. We girls sat on the wide, cement balustrades—country girls on one side, town girls on the other—watching with horrified satisfaction.

This morning a grudging quiet hung over the nine of us. I needed to study. Arvin Winetsky, like me, was poring over his *Baltimore Catechism*, a holy and absorbed expression on his face. Beverly Ridza hastily flicked pages as if searching for pretty pictures, of which there were none. Sister Mary Frances had said that one or two of us might not be ready for Communion next year and might have to take the lessons over. She had stared along her sunburned nose at Arvin, who was slow-witted, and at Beverly, who repeatedly missed the Saturday morning classes and when she appeared, wearing her brother's clothes, was half-asleep.

Leroy Mosley and Ronald Oster were looking at a Big Little Book. With three of the four boys bent over books, the break was peaceful.

My thoughts returned to Mama and poker. I would like to be able to go home at noon and assure her that Sister had said gambling wasn't a sin.

The two nuns emerged before ten minutes had elapsed. Pleased to find things peaceful, they showed their pleasure by engaging in bits of conversation with us, an almost unheard of occurrence.

"Do you ever help your mother bake cookies?" Sister Mary Clair inquired of Beverly.

Beverly's mother didn't have a stove. What the Ridzas cooked, they cooked on an old hot plate.

"Sometimes," Beverly lied casually, to save Sister embarrassment.

When the nuns leapt the wall of their own reserve, the exchanges were uncomfortable. They knew so little about us. And how would they? They lived in an austere, white cottage across the street from the church, and seldom went out on Main Street or elsewhere in town. Their groceries were delivered by Truska's and their meat by Rabel's.

The exterior of the nuns' house was painfully barefaced. Everything was white—clapboard, window frames and sills, gutters and downspouts—everything. There was not a shutter or a scrap of trellis to adorn it. Nor was the front yard more showy than the house: green grass, a pair of self-effacing arborvitae on either side of the door. A three-foot, gray statue of the Virgin with clasped hands floated, lonely and cut-off, on the deep green sea, twenty feet from the door.

However, it was said that in the yard behind the cottage, they raised the finest vegetables and the showiest flowers in Harvester. Mama's friend Bernice McGivern had seen the garden. "Rows as neat as knitting," she had said. "And not a weed anywhere. Carrots and radishes and lettuce and tomatoes and whatever else you could think of. And corn. Beautiful corn. And all around the edge, flowers. Zinnias and marigolds and bachelor's buttons and gladiolas and delphiniums and larkspur and roses as big as dinner plates."

Old Father Delias seemed remote from the nuns, perpetually surprised to see them around the church. His life was very different from theirs. He was invited to dinner everywhere that a Catholic priest was welcome. And he went fishing with men from the parish. He liked to laugh and drink beer and tell funny stories about priests he knew and seminarians he had known. As loved by children as the nuns were feared, he was like the jolly father in a family where discipline is left to the mother.

On May Day, when the young children whose parents could afford it delivered May baskets, Father Delias's front porch and steps were littered with colorful baskets, like spring flowers, filled with candy and home-baked treats. Father chased each child who rang the doorbell and, catching him, gave him a hug and a penny.

It didn't occur to anyone to leave a basket at the nuns' house.

As Sister Mary Clair stood on the topmost step wanting to know about cookie baking in the kitchen of the Ridzas, who lived in a shack on the south edge of town where there was no street, only a hard-bitten path among the weeds, Beverly scratched her thigh and looked at her scuffed oxfords, which were her brother's. She was running out of ready lies.

I shoved myself forward, toward Sister Mary Clair. "Sister," I began, but my voice started to fade, like a radio station slipping out of reach.

"What did you say?" Sister asked, bending toward me. "Speak up."

"I just wondered . . . I just wondered—is gambling a sin?"

"Gambling?" Sister asked in a neutral tone of voice, her eyes retreating from me. Later it occurred to me that she was perhaps thinking of the Wheel of Fortune and other innocent forms of gambling at the annual church bazaar. Was there Protestant criticism out there in the town? she likely wondered, feeling suddenly more estranged. "What kind of gambling?"

"Poker?"

"Well, that would depend," Sister said. Had Father Delias and his fishing cronies been criticized? *Did* Father Delias play poker when he went fishing? It was probable. "Gambling isn't necessarily a sin."

"When would it be a sin?" I asked. I had to know, was Papa going to hell?

Leading the conversation away from anything that might have reference to Father Delias, Sister explained, "If a man gambled and lost all his money, and his wife and children suffered, that would be sinful."

"Would he go to hell?"

"Not if he were truly sorry and went to confession and asked God to forgive him." She fished a pocket watch out of the folds of her garment, glanced at it, and announced that it was time to go back in.

As I reached my fingers out to the holy water font, Sister asked in a voice so low I barely heard, "What made you ask?"

"Nothing."

"You asked Sister *what*?" Mama demanded, bent imminently over me, hands on her hips.

"If gambling was a sin," I repeated, though Mama had heard every word I'd said. "I thought you'd want to know. Sister said it wasn't a sin unless a man lost all his money, and his wife and children suffered. Even if Papa loses all our money, he'll still go to heaven if he confesses and is truly sorry and asks God to forgive him. Aren't you happy, Mama?"

"Did you tell her *your* papa gambled?"

"No."

"Well, she's going to figure it out."

"No, Mama. I told her I was just wondering."

Mama laughed an unhappy laugh.

"Really, Mama. Sister didn't think I was talking about Papa."

"She's not a fool, Lark." Mama sat down across from me at the kitchen table. She had baked a spice cake while I was at catechism class. It was on the table waiting to be frosted. Mama was dressed in a cotton housedress, and she looked tired. "Everyone in town is going to know that your papa lost last night. If his pals don't tell them, the nuns will." Mama was always a little suspicious and skeptical about the nuns.

"How much?" I asked.

"Two hundred dollars."

It was such a large sum, for a second I thought Mama was joking. But she got up and went in the bedroom, pulling a handkerchief from the pocket of her dress. Two hundred dollars was more than Papa made in a month. Some people in town didn't make half that much. Mama had said that Miss Hagen, my teacher, made eighty dollars a month. Two hundred dollars was so much, I was frightened by the number itself, as if its size gave it great power over me.

Big numbers carried awesome potential. Mama said our house would cost four thousand dollars. That was even bigger than two hundred. But it stood for something happy. It was worth the fear it conjured. But two hundred dollars *lost?* I was crushed by the number. I felt that I was carrying it around on my back, just as Mama and Papa were.

§ 5 §

ONION AND bologna sandwiches were my favorite, but I didn't feel like eating the one Mama had waiting for me when I came home from catechism class. I sat staring at it, considering the big numbers in our lives. Mama said we needed a down payment to begin the house building. A thousand dollars was what she hoped to save. I didn't know what part of a thousand dollars two hundred was, but it must be quite a bit.

In the bedroom, Mama had fallen asleep, a cotton handkerchief splashed with red roses gripped in her hand. I couldn't get the buttons at the back of my dress undone, so I pulled off my shoes and climbed into the crib, still in my clothes.

There at the foot of the bed was the pile of house plans, with #127—The Cape Ann on top. The sketch of the house showed two dormer windows, one in each of the upstairs rooms. Sally Wheeler had a dormer window in her bedroom, with a vanity table built into it. It was very nice, but in my book *Happy Stories for Bedtime*, there was an illustration showing a dormer with a window seat built into it. A pensive looking boy in short pants sat on the seat, an elbow on the sill, staring out at the sea. In the illustration we couldn't see the water, but in the story we were told that the boy's father had crossed the sea to fight the Hun. The boy sat gazing across the gray waves, waiting for the soldier-father's return.

I was fond of that boy. He had more serious matters on his mind than a dog named Spot and a cat called Puff. And his body had a grace and casual elegance which seemed foreign and which I admired. What would that boy be when he grew up? I wondered. A professor, maybe.

In my dormer window in our new house, I wanted a seat like the boy's. When Mama woke up, I was going to show her the Cape Ann and also the illustration in *Happy Stories for Bedtime* so that she could start planning the window seat.

She might sleep all afternoon. Mama almost never napped, but she'd been up the whole night waiting for Papa and me. I watched her, her chin set even in sleep, hand clutching the bright, rose-strewn handkerchief as if it might be stolen from her.

The westbound passenger train descended upon us, blowing and groaning. Mama didn't stir. We were so used to the sounds of trains, they could not rouse us from sleep unless we were ready to wake up. Out on the platform, I heard Papa calling to a brakeman or conductor or maybe to a baggage handler.

When at length the train pulled out of the station, the wall beside the crib hummed beneath my fingers. A passenger with a grip in one hand and a sample case in the other walked east, toward the Harvester Arms Hotel, sweat darkening his gray suit between his shoulder blades and under his arms. The May afternoon had grown unseasonably warm.

The freight wagon rumbled over the uneven brick platform. Papa pulled it around the end of the depot and off-loaded several heavy cartons onto the back of the pickup. I lay down, shy to have him see me through the window. He had not come home for lunch. Probably he had gone downtown to the Loon Cafe, where he ate when Mama was out of town. No one at the Loon Cafe would be surprised to see him.

Sometimes he took me there in the afternoon for a root beer. Freckled and pink, the two waitresses were unmarried, Irish Catholic women approaching middle age. They teased and pampered Papa, and he laughed at everything they said and left them a big tip no matter what we ordered.

They asked him about his fancy new Oldsmobile, and he said he'd give them a ride whenever they were ready. He never talked that way to Mama, and she never flattered him as they did. Mama and Papa did not like giving in to each other for fear of being defeated.

Would Papa come home for supper? I thought of him staying away through supper and maybe through the night. It made my stomach feel hard and sharp, as though it had corners.

On the wall beside the crib was a banjo clock. In addition to a clock face, it held behind glass an idyllic country scene. Green meadows rolled away to an intensely blue sky. In the foreground, hollyhocks and larkspur and poppies bespoke a pretty cottage just out of sight.

I lay in the crib, willing myself, as I often did, into that landscape, which I had furnished with everything I could desire: a small grape arbor like Grandpa Erhardt's; a big, red tricycle to replace the little one that somebody had run over out in the parking lot; and a tree house perched among the spreading limbs of an old shade tree.

When I visited the clock, my hair curled and returned to the blond color it had known before kindergarten, my bony arms and legs responded to my every command, turning perfect cartwheels and tapping out pulsing, staccato dances like those Sally Wheeler was learning at Martha Beverton's Tap and Toe classes.

Picking some of the larkspur to carry into the cottage with me, I skipped down a flagstone path to a trellised doorway.

At half past three, I woke, sweaty and rumpled, my starched, red dress drooping like sad, old curtains. Mama was not on the big bed. In the kitchen a spoon scraped the inside of a saucepan. Climbing out of the crib with the Cape Ann booklet, I picked up my shoes and carried them to the kitchen.

"What're you making?" I asked, sitting down at the table to put on my shoes.

"Penuche frosting."

"Is there enough for candy?"

"Yes."

Mama usually made extra penuche frosting for candies, which she spooned out on waxed paper, pressing a walnut half into each.

"Can I show you a house plan called the Cape Ann?"

"Not now."

"Can I go outside?"

She looked at me. "Put on an old dress. Why did you wear that one to bed?"

"I couldn't undo the buttons."

She set down the big spoon and unbuttoned the back of my dress.

"Can I walk down the tracks?"

"Not too far."

When I had pulled on an old pink dress whose bodice smocking was coming unsmocked, I asked Mama, "Do we have any money saved for the house?"

"We had five hundred dollars."

"How much do we have now?"

"Your fool papa lost two hundred dollars, so we've got three hundred left." She poured frosting on the cake. "I could kill him," she said, smoothing the frosting with vicious swipes of the back of the big spoon.

"Is he coming home for supper?"

"I don't know, and I don't care." She was almost as mad as she'd been in the morning. I could feel her anger like the summer heat that rose in waves from the brick platform.

"*You* be home for supper," she said as I went out the door.

Tiptoeing past the office windows, I kept my eyes downcast. It was as though in not coming home to lunch, Papa had turned his back on me as well as on Mama. What would I say to him when I saw him? What would he say to me? I squirmed and hurried west, following the sun down the tracks.

Looking both ways first, I ran fast across Fourth Street. Businesses sprawled messily out along Fourth Street, vacant lots and weedy patches between them; businesses that didn't fit on Main Street, due either to their nature or their size. Rayzeen's Lumberyard. Grubb's Junkyard and Body Shop. The Nite Time Saloon, which because of local law served only beer. And Marcella's Permanent Wave, which Mama said was a cover-up for the bootleg, hard liquor business of Marcella's husband, Barney Finney. Beverly Ridza from catechism class lived down there, past Grubb's Junkyard.

On the other side of Fourth Street, I slowed to stare into the hobo jungle on the left. A couple of hundred yards distant from the depot, the hobo jungle was the exposed basement of a ware-house long ago razed or burned to the ground. It was a hole in the ground with concrete and stone walls, but no stairs. In one corner a pair of empty oil drums, one smaller than the other, served as steps. In the center of the space, someone had collected old bricks, lined them up, and laid a metal grill over them. Here the men who stopped over cooked cans of beans or soup, toasted bread, and made coffee.

If the weather was good and Mama had half a dozen magazines to throw away, she'd pack them in a grocery bag with a couple of cans of Campbell's soup and send me with them down to the jungle. If someone was there, I'd leave them at the edge, telling the men, "From Mama." If no one was camped, I'd climb down the oil cans and rummage around. Interesting relics could be found: a key to a door somewhere, a half-full can of snoose, a jewellike piece of melted glass from the ashes of the fire. Once I found a letter, never sealed, addressed, or mailed.

"What does it say?" I asked Mama.

"I don't think we should read it," Mama said. "Maybe he's just gone looking for a meal. He'll come back and find it gone."

"No, he won't. Nobody's been in the jungle for two days."

Mama sat down at the table and looked at the envelope. She was of two minds. At length she slipped the letter out and un-folded it. Written on cheap, lined paper, it was dated October 15, 1938.

Dear Bill,

I'm writing from a little burg called Harvester up here in Minnesota, Land of the Swedes and Home of the Nor-wegians. There are more Johnsons and Olsons than leaves on the trees. But matter of fact, there aren't too many leaves on the trees, it being the middle of October. Nights are getting cold and sometimes, along toward morning, it almost smells like snow! Christ, I've got to head south. No more work here and no work there, but I can't stick around Minnesota, especially since I lost my heavy jacket outside that goddamned Cicero last spring.

I was sure glad to hear from Eddie P. that you found something steady in Florida. Do you have Elda and

the kids with you now? Splitting up the family is the
worst.

I had some work up on Lake Superior on an ore boat
this summer, but those damned things can't run in the
winter so I'm traveling again. I'd hoped to get something
around here to see me through the winter, but nothing's turned up, and I can't stick much longer. Maybe I'll
head for Texas. God, I'm sick of boxcars.

If I get over Florida way, I might stop for a day or two
if that's all right. I haven't seen Sis since the farm was
sold. Six years! If Elda and the kids are in Florida, I'd
like to see them, but I don't mean to sponge, Bill. I think
you know that.

I suppose Ma is still at Aunt Mary's. That's where I write
her. I'd like to get back East next spring to see them. I
was in Oregon in '33 when Pa passed on. There wasn't
any way to reach me. If anything happened to Ma and
I didn't know, I'd just as soon ride the goddamned railroad right into the Gulf of Mexico.

Summer before last I was on a farm east of here, near
a place called New Ulm. That was beautiful country,
along the Minnesota River, but the owner didn't want to
keep me over the winter because the daughter was getting interested. She was a nice girl. If I could have
found something steady around here, I'd have written
to her.

When do you think there'll be work, Bill, and where
do you think it'll be? I'd like to be there when it opens
up. I've bummed so damned long, I'm getting to feel like
a bum. Sometimes I stink till I don't want to lie down
beside myself. I remember Saturday nights on the farm,
and the old galvanized tub that Ma filled. God, she
scrubbed my head so hard, I thought she'd leave scars.
I'd sure like to feel that clean again.

Your brother-in-law,

Earl Samson

"I wish I knew where that Bill lived, and I'd send him this,"
Mama said.
"Why didn't Earl mail the letter, Mama?"

"Maybe he didn't have the price of a stamp." She carried the letter in the bedroom and put it in her bureau drawer.

I found the letter in the hobo jungle last fall, in October. This was May. Had Earl Samson come back to Minnesota with the warm weather, or had he found "something steady" down south? I would like to meet him. Could he be one of these men in the jungle today? The one reading the magazine looked too young, the one sleeping, too old.

I passed by. Leaving the tracks, I crossed the shallow ditch, wading through the high, warm grass. It was cool among the cottonwoods. This was where the tramps lay around during hot summer days when they weren't out looking for work or a hand-out. At night they slept in the basement, where dogs couldn't bother them. There were a couple of wooden crates here, big ones, that gave some protection from the rain.

I picked my way through the silken grass and debris, searching for relics. Maybe evidence of Earl Samson. There wasn't much here today. I crouched to inspect a brown leather shoe, cracked and scuffed till it was nearly white, a hole in the sole the size of a silver dollar. I put my hand inside the shoe and stuck my fingers through the hole. All of them fit. Further on I picked up an empty half-pint whiskey bottle, decided the label wasn't pretty, and threw it aside again. Propped against one of the cotton-woods was a hoe with a broken-off handle. The men used it to bury their bowel movements when they relieved themselves in this grove.

When I had sifted through everything that was new and found no treasures, I returned to the tracks and continued west out of town, tightrope walking, putting one foot directly in front of the other, along the rail, my arms outstretched, like someone trying to fly.

As Harvester fell behind me, tall shrubs and pussy willows sprang up along the ditches on either side of the rail bed. They were forests for short people like me. I had come earlier in the spring with Mama to pick pussy willows for the living room, for Mama's friends, and for Father Delias. Mama took special care for old Father Delias. She asked at the Loon Cafe for an empty lard can, and they gave her one the size of a slop pail. She scrubbed it out, covered it with a scrap of maroon-and-cream-striped satin upholstery fabric, weighted it with small rocks, and arranged tall pussy willows in it for his office in the rectory.

When Father saw it, he exclaimed, "Why, that's fit for a castle, Arlene." He always called Mama by her first name, as if she were a little sister or a favored niece. "You must have remembered the dark red chairs in the office!"

Cinders were one of the few bad things about trains. I sat down on one of the rails, pulled off a shoe, and dumped out a cinder. Ahead about a hundred yards was a trestle over a dry gulch. It wasn't very high, but "high enough to break your neck," Mama told me. She didn't know that I sometimes crossed it when she wasn't with me. I was careful, though. I didn't want to break my neck. Otto Monke, one of the custodians at school, broke his back when he was young. Now he was bent over and looked like he had a box in his back.

When I came to the trestle, I walked between the rails, stepping carefully from tie to tie, looking down at the scrubby gulch. Leroy Mosely from catechism class had told me he'd seen a rattlesnake down there. But he was a liar who spent his spare time scaring girls. The only good thing about him was that he would be in the confessional longer than I was, when we had our first confession next spring.

Mama said there weren't any poisonous snakes in south central Minnesota. Up in the North Woods there were a few timber snakes that were poisonous, she said, but she'd never seen one. If Leroy Mosely had seen a snake in the gulch, Mama explained, it was a garter snake or a gopher snake, and they weren't poisonous.

A jackrabbit jumped up like a jack-in-the-box and shot across the gulch. It startled me and I lurched, nearly losing my balance. My heart raced. I sat down on the trestle. For several minutes I rested, but my heart went on pounding. I was afraid. Yet a jackrabbit was nothing to fear. Snakes must be making me feel this way. Thinking about snakes could make you sweaty and shaky.

At the other end of the trestle, on the embankment, was a big patch of mustard, looking like butter spread across the ground. I thought I spied wild onion not far from some box elders at the top of the embankment, maybe fifty yards down the gulch.

Rising slowly, gingerly, I stood up, not moving, like someone who has had a dizzy spell. At length I set out, but hesitantly, not as jaunty as I'd been. When I reached the far side of the railroad bridge, I turned right, toward the wildflowers. The dry earth of the embankment crumbled beneath my feet. My shoes filled with it, and my socks turned dusty gray.

I was snapping off a good bundle of mustard and at the same time working toward the wild onion, which lay between me and the stand of box elders. The white onion flowers were going to be pretty mixed into the vibrant yellow of the mustard. Mama would arrange them in the cut-glass vase that had been a wedding gift from her Aunt Essie who lived in Fargo.

I didn't see any snakes. A gopher scurried down his hole as I came near, and several squirrels ran up the box elder trunks and began jumping from tree to tree, like children pretending to be frightened. Across the gulch, a meadowlark sang prettily.

It was warm and dusty among the scrub and flowers. I was beginning to feel itchy and drowsy. It would be pleasant to put the flowers down, sit on the ground, and scratch my legs, but the sun was falling behind the box elders and the buzz of insects was dying. I should start home if I didn't want to be late for supper. I had come a little further than I ought.

In the shadows among the trees at the top of the embankment, the figure of a man appeared. Who could that be? A tramp, maybe. I stood frozen, staring up at him, feeling small and very short legged. Maybe it was someone who had come to arrest me for picking flowers that didn't belong to me.

I threw the flowers down and took off as fast as my legs would carry me, directly through the mustard, toward the trestle. If I had thought, I would have run across the gulch and up the other side. It wasn't necessary to take the trestle. But I wasn't thinking. I fled as I had come, across the railroad bridge.

Back by the onion flowers a voice squawked and screamed. Was this the bogeyman Grandpa Erhardt had told me about? The one who waited at the top of the stairs? The one Mama had assured me was only a joke? This bogeyman had waited at the top of the embankment, among the trees.

Running on the rough ties was awkward. I stumbled, caught myself, and stumbled again. If I fell over the edge, I would break my neck, and the bogeyman would get me for sure, down there in the wash. I didn't know what a bogeyman did when he caught you.

A sharp pain pierced my right side, below the ribs. I pressed my fist against it. Behind me now, heavy shoes thudded on the bridge. The voice howled unintelligible words.

Even if I made it across the trestle, it was a long way back to town. The water tower and the grain elevators looked like gray giants lined up on the horizon, distant friends I would never reach.

If I gained the far side of the bridge, should I dash into the brush? Could I hide there? The heavy shoes were close. They would catch me before I could escape. Only a few feet now. His grunting breath touched my hair.

"Oh, My God, I am heartily sorry for having offended Thee, and I detest all my sins because I dread the loss of heaven and the pains of hell, but most of all . . ."

Fingers brushed my dress. Propelled by horror, I flew through the air, landing hard on cinders and gravel and solid earth, twisting and kicking, rolling through the grass and screaming, ". . . because they offend Thee, My Lord, Who art all good and deserving of all my love . . ."

There was nowhere to go. I curled into a ball, wrapped my arms around my head, closed my eyes, and sobbed, "I firmly resolve, with the help of Thy grace—" Nothing happened. I stopped praying. There was absolute stillness except for the sound of my thick breathing. Turning my head slightly, I opened one eye.

Sitting on the grass beside the rail bed, wildflowers cradled in one arm, was Hilly Stillman.

6

I SAT UP. "What are you doing out here?"

Hilly held up the yellow and white flowers. Tears stood in his eyes, and his nose was running. He misunderstood my question, and I didn't ask him again.

Getting to my feet, I surveyed the damage. Both my knees were scraped and dirty, likewise one of my elbows. There were long scratches on my thighs where I'd dived into the cinders and gravel, and my chin was hot and tender.

In the west, the sun was lying flat on the tracks. A pinkish yellow shaft of it lit Hilly, washing his profile and his white shirt in a dramatic glow. His unhappiness began to smooth away. In repose, Hilly's face retained the curved, unformed look of an eighteen-year-old boy's. The skin was still soft despite years in the sun and cold of Main Street. If Hilly got his sanity back, would his face become old? He held the flowers out to me. They felt cool in my hands.

"Pretty," Hilly said.

I nodded. "I have to get home," I told him. "It's late. Mama's going to be mad."

We walked along the verge of the rail bed, saying little. You didn't have to talk a lot to Hilly. Sometimes words confused him, as when Mama had told him he could buy ice cream with his earnings. But he liked to listen to others talk. Mama said Hilly listened to other people's conversations with sweet rapture, as though he were at a concert. This made some people nervous, but not Mama. When Hilly was around, she talked to me about anything that came into her head because it entertained him.

When he was excited, Hilly lost what little control of his words he had. No one wanted to sit by him at a softball game because he screamed like a banshee when the ball was hit. Bill McGivern said that when Hilly first started going to softball games after the war, he'd jump down from the stands and run after the ball. The players on the Harvester Blue Sox would just tell him to get the hell back up in the stands, but a first baseman from Red Berry once got so riled, he hit Hilly with his fist and knocked him down.

Hilly never hit back. Not the softball player, and not the eleven- and twelve-year-old boys who taunted him and threw things at him. I thought it was strange that someone who'd been a hero in the war never hit back. When I told this to Mama, she said thank God he didn't, or people around here would throw him in the state hospital for the insane and retarded faster than you could salute the flag.

The six o'clock whistle blew. We could hear it plainly. Supper was always on the table at five-thirty. Hilly looked at me.

"Don't worry," I told him. But *I* was worried. I didn't want to get the back of the brush.

As we reached the hobo jungle, I scanned the open cellar for anyone new, any latecomer. There was a third man now, one who was clean shaven and looked recently bathed. He'd probably been out scratching for work when I'd come by earlier. He was sitting by the fire, heating a can of Campbell's Pork and Beans.

In a sudden flush of temerity, I went to the edge of the basement and called, "Do you know Earl Samson?" Then I was shy and couldn't believe I had called to them that way.

The oldest of the three, the one who'd been napping before, glanced at the others. "I guess not, little lady," he said. "Is there a message if I meet him?"

But my courage was gone. I shook my head and turned away, hurrying toward home with Hilly. And whom should we sight striding down the track, anger in every step, but Mama.

"Where in *hell* have you been, Lark?" When Mama was mad, she didn't mince words, and it didn't matter who was around. "I've been worried sick." Reaching us, she grabbed my upper arm, giving me a good pinch. "I sat down to read," she explained, relief and worry and impatience mixed in her voice, "and fell asleep with the book in my hand, or else I'd have been out here with the brush an hour ago." She didn't have the brush with her. If she was feeling guilty for falling asleep and not keeping a check on me, she might not use the brush at all. "I told you to be home for supper," she continued, grasping my hand and pulling me roughly along at a trot.

"I brought you a bouquet," I told her, holding up the mustard and onions, which she ignored. "I met Hilly while I was picking flowers." Hilly loped along beside us in his tipsy fashion. Mama's lips were pressed tightly together, so I stopped trying to make conversation.

It was embarrassing to be dragged along like this. I hoped not too many people were watching, especially not too many first graders. Some mothers covered up their anger until they got home, but Mama would swat me on the backside right in the middle of Main Street if I were being "incorrigible." Incorrigible was a favorite word of Mama's. I was an incorrigible nail biter. Papa had been trying to get me to stop biting my nails for as long as I could remember. He'd recently begun weekly inspections. Every Monday at supper, he ordered me to lay my hands on the table while he examined my nails. Last Monday he was so upset, he said if there wasn't improvement by next Monday, I'd get the back of the brush.

Papa believed that ladies, big and little, should be as pretty and perfect in every detail as was possible. He had limited control over my too-fine, straight-as-a-stick hair and my scrawny arms and legs (though sometimes he kept me at the table until nearly bedtime to see that I cleaned my plate), but over my fingernails he was determined to prevail.

The fact was, Mama bit her nails, too, but Papa had long ago despaired of breaking her of the habit. For that reason it was twice as important to him that I be made to quit the filthy practice.

Mama had painted my nails with pink polish, and when that didn't discourage me from biting them, she'd dipped them in some foul-tasting stuff, just as she had done to her own. It was no more successful with me than it had been with her.

I did try to stop. I was still trying. Every night when I went to bed, I asked God to help me, but so far He'd kept out of it. Each night I swore that I would not put my fingers near my mouth the next day. It was a mystery to me how I kept doing it after all my praying and swearing. I must truly be incorrigible.

I was also an incorrigible dawdler, and as Mama dragged me into the kitchen, she remarked to Hilly, "This child is an incorrigible dawdler. I'm always thinking she's been kidnapped, like the Lindbergh baby, although I don't know who would want a dawdler who takes an hour to walk five short blocks home from school. Sometimes longer." She let go of my hand and held the screen door for Hilly. "Your mother's going to worry, too, Hilly. I'll give her a ring." She started for the living room. "Would you like to stay for supper?"

Hilly nodded vigorously. "Supper."

It was seven-thirty when we sat down to hamburger patties, skillet fried potatoes, canned peas, bread and butter, and the spice cake with penuche frosting. Papa had not come home. If Papa had been home, Mama would not have invited Hilly to stay. Papa thought Hilly was a "damned nuisance," always getting under foot when you were coming out of the post office and holding you up, hanging around the Oldsmobile or the pickup with his damned old rag, wiping the fenders and hood. Papa didn't like it when Hilly came to wash our windows. How did it look to passengers getting off at Harvester to be greeted by an idiot? Someone might complain to the railroad, and then Papa would get the blame. "Magdalen Haggerty says they put a stop to him coming in the Loon Cafe." Magdalen was one of the two waitresses there and had probably served Papa his supper tonight. Magdalen Haggerty or Dora Noonan. "Shanty Irish," Mama called them to irritate Papa.

"They're good Catholic women who're at the communion rail

every Sunday." Mama only took communion at Christmas and Easter, one time more than the law demanded, as she pointed out. Papa only took communion at Christmas, Easter, and when we went to visit Grandma and Grandpa Erhardt.

"Another piece of cake, Hilly?" Mama cut a big square and lifted it onto Hilly's plate, then she refilled their coffee cups. Seated again, holding her cup in both hands, Mama told Hilly, "Lark has First Communion classes every Saturday morning at the Catholic church. Eight o'clock in the morning she has to be there. That's pretty early for a six-year-old. Next year she'll take her first communion. This year she was an angel." Mama touched me lightly with the offhand, proprietary glance mothers use when discussing a child who is present, the same glance they use while sitting on the davenport and observing that the thing has held up well, but probably needs a new slipcover.

"The angels," she went on, "are the ones who escort the First Communion children up to the altar and back to their pews again. They wear white organdy dresses and white organdy wings and silver halos. The wings are separate from the dress. They tie on with white satin ribbon. Well, you can't send away to Monkey Ward for an outfit like that, the way you can for a party dress. The mothers of the angels had to sew the dresses and the wings, and make the halos. I ended up making two, because Stella Wheeler doesn't sew, and Sally needed an angel dress. You know the Wheelers, they live a block east of the school in the new cottage. He travels for an office supply company. Stella has bad nerves, but she's a good soul, always nice to Lark."

This was Mama entertaining Hilly. He sat there eating the last crumbs of his cake, mashing them with the back of his spoon and sucking them off, happily enthralled. "Lark, get the picture from the sideboard," Mama said.

I went to fetch the studio picture Mama had had taken of me in my white dress, wings, and halo. In order to show the wings, the photographer had taken a side shot. I was kneeling, hands folded in prayer, looking very Catholic and uncharacteristic.

"Doesn't she look pretty?" Mama said, handing it to Hilly. "Those wings were hell to make. But you haven't heard the best. A week before Lark and Sally were going to wear the angel dresses, Sister Mary Clair sent home a note with Lark. 'Dear Mrs. Erhardt,' it said, 'Lark and Sally's dresses should be long enough to cover the kneecap. Sister Mary Frances and I feel that Lark normally wears her dresses shorter than angels do. Thank you. Sister Mary Clair.' Tell me, what angel flew down to tell Sister Mary Clair the style they're wearing in heaven this year?" Mama rose and refilled the cups.

"Lark likes her dresses short and starched, like Shirley Temple. In my opinion, that's a lot cuter than below the kneecap, which makes you look like a refugee from a poor Catholic country."

Eventually we cleared the table. Mama washed, Hilly dried, and I put away. Hilly was careful and very slow. Mama was finished long before Hilly, so she cut a big hunk of cake and wrapped it in paper napkins for Hilly to take home.

"You and your mama can have this before you go to bed," she told Hilly.

We drove him home in the pickup. Hilly wanted to ride in the back. "Wind," he said, brushing his hands back over his face and hair.

Main Street was lighted up and full of the noisy self-importance of a small town Saturday night: cars driving up and down, people hollering across the broad street to each other. All the farmers and half the townspeople were on the streets and in the stores, seeing to Saturday night duties and pleasures.

When Mama stopped in front of Rabel's Meat Market, Hilly jumped off the back of the truck and came around to say good-bye. I handed him the cake.

"Good . . . bye," he said. "Thank . . . you."

We waited for him to climb the stairs and open the screen door, then we drove off. "Is Hilly getting his sanity back?" I asked Mama.

"I don't know. Sometimes it seems that way." She didn't sound as excited as I thought she should. I wanted to ask her why, but I kept quiet. When it came to pressing for answers, I was often shy, as if it were not yet the time for me to know.

Instead of going right home, Mama drove around town with the windows rolled down. The evening was warm, and there was a Saturday night edge to it, as though something exciting ought to happen. We passed Bernice and Bill McGivern's. Mama gave the horn a tap. Mama couldn't carry a tune in a bushel basket, but we sang "Put on Your Old Gray Bonnet." If they hadn't known us, people would have thought we were coming home from The Nite Time Saloon.

Mama pulled the big, galvanized tub out from under the crib

when we got home. "Bath time," she announced, dragging it to the kitchen. While I got undressed and into my pink chenille robe, Mama put kettles of water on the stove to heat. I sat down on the davenport to look at the new *Life* magazine.

After my bath, Mama dried me, sprinkled me with Sweet Memory talcum powder, and helped me into a clean nightie. We carried the tub out to the tracks and dumped the water. "It's almost time for the last freight," she said. "We'd better use the toilet now."

Quietly we crossed the dimly lit waiting room to the rest room. The lights in the office were burning, but we didn't stop to see if Papa or Art Bigelow was working. Sometimes they both stuck around in the evening until after the second freight.

As quietly as we had come, we left, scurrying back to our house before the train pulled in and surprised me out and about in my nightie.

"Do you want a bedtime read?" Mama asked, helping me into the crib.

I remembered the house plans. They were lying on Mama's bed. "There's a pretty house I want to show you." I pointed to the booklets, and Mama handed them to me. Riffling through the pages until I found #127—The Cape Ann, I held it up. "This one."

Mama sat down on the edge of the big bed to study the floor plans and the exterior sketch. "Mmmmm," she murmured, not at once dismissing it.

"It has two bedrooms upstairs and one downstairs for your sewing room. And it has shutters. And a big living room, I think, and two dormer windows." I opened *Happy Stories for Bedtime*. There was the boy, still sitting in the window. "Look at this, Mama. They made a window seat in the dormer. Can we do that?"

"This Cape Ann has possibilities," Mama said, looking up from the plans. "A window seat. Yes. You could keep your toys in there."

I hadn't thought of that. "Oh, yes," I squealed, bouncing up and down. Did the boy waiting by the sea for his father have toys in his window seat? I bet he did.

"I like this plan," Mama said, "because it has a breakfast nook at the end of the kitchen, and the back door's right here by the cellarway." She showed me where the back door was. "We could plant flowers along here," she added, indicating an area beyond the breakfast nook windows. "Nasturtiums and zinnias and marigolds and poppies. I like flowers that have a lot of color." So did Sisters Mary Clair and Mary Frances.

"And hollyhocks?" I begged. "I like hollyhocks."

"We'll grow hollyhocks along the fence." Mama ran to the kitchen for a pair of shears. "I'm going to cut this out and tack it up on the wall," she explained, "so we can look at it every day."

"Put it up here by the clock." I stood up to show her where it should go.

"Yes, that's good."

"Mama, how can we get some money for the house?"

She finished cutting the two pages from the booklet, then set the scissors aside. "I don't know," she said, "but I'll think of something."

7

SOMETIME IN the night, Papa came home and slept in the big bed. But in the morning, and for weeks afterward, Mama was only civil to him and nothing more.

After church Mama and Papa read the Sunday paper. Papa pored over the sports section, keeping track of the Chicago Cubs, his favorite team and winner of the 1938 World Series. Mama studied the classified ads for money-making schemes. Armed with a grease pencil, she circled anything not requiring the applicant to relocate.

There were opportunities for refined women to sell Lady Sylvia corsets and undergarments in the privacy of their homes. There were openings for ambitious salespeople to call on friends and neighbors, introducing them to the comfort, durability, and beauty of Ayler's A-One shoes ("Hard-to-fit Sizes Our Specialty"). And there were once-in-a-lifetime chances for folks with get-up-and-go to make big money as dealers for Bismark brushes ("Brushes for Farm and Home").

None of these held much appeal or promise. No work was to be had locally, either, except for sewing or house cleaning or selling magazine subscriptions. But a glut of seamstresses and cleaning ladies and subscription salespeople existed already, so the employment picture was bleak. Bleak was not the same as hopeless, however. "I'll think of something," Mama had told me.

But would she? If there were jobs to be had, the young men down in the hobo jungle would be working. They were always out looking, knocking on doors, scouting the filling stations and junkyards, anyplace there might be something temporary that could lead to something permanent. They would mow your lawn, burn your trash, and wash your windows for a meal and half a dollar. Where, then, would Mama find work?

Late in the afternoon, Papa fell asleep stretched out on the davenport, the funny papers lying across his chest. Mama pared potatoes and cut up the chicken for supper. At times like this, Mama and I played "Lady Caller."

In the bedroom I combed as much of my hair as I could see, pulled on an old navy blue cloche Mama had donated to me, and tiptoed past her as she melted Crisco in the iron skillet. Outside, I adjusted the hat, smoothed my dress, and examined the contents of my red patent leather purse: one powder puff, stiff and lumpy; a pencil stub; a cracked and badly tattered St. Joseph's missal Grandma Erhardt had passed along when she'd received a new one; a dainty black rosary from the same source; and in the very bottom, jingling as I shook the purse, two pennies.

Snapping the bag shut, I tucked it under my arm, patted my hair, stepped up to the door, and knocked. Mrs. Erhardt answered, opening the screen.

"Why, Mrs . . ."

"Brown."

"Mrs. Brown, it's nice to see you. Can you come in and visit? I was just putting chicken in the pan to fry."

"Thank you. I can only stay a few minutes. I have to get home and make supper for my husband and my little girl."

"Well, sit down here at the table. Can I get you anything?"

"Do you have any penuche candy?"

Mrs. Erhardt appeared a little surprised by this request. "Yes . . . let me see." She went to the cupboard and from the top shelf brought me a candy. "I'm sure you'll want to save it to share with your little girl after supper," she suggested, handing over the piece of penuche on a circle of wax paper. "I seem to have forgotten her name."

"Myrna Loy."

"Myrna Loy?"

"Yes. Myrna Loy Brown. Don't you think it's pretty?"

"Very. How is Myrna Loy?"

"She's fine. She had tonsilitis a while back though."

"Was she very sick?" Mrs. Erhardt asked, dropping pieces of chicken into a brown bag of flour and seasonings, shaking them, then placing them one at a time in the hot skillet, where they squirmed and sizzled and spattered.

"I'm afraid she was. She ran a fever of a hundred and four, and she had to have her throat painted every day. The poor thing missed a lot of school."

"I'm sorry to hear that. Will she pass to second grade?"

"Oh, yes. She's very smart and she works hard. Her papa is strict though. He doesn't like A-minuses."

"A-minuses don't seem so bad to me," Mrs. Erhardt said sympathetically.

"I know, but Mr. Brown wants her to be the best. The same at catechism class." I crossed my right leg and swung it importantly. "Myrna Loy has a whole cigar box full of holy medals and those little cards with pictures of Jesus and saints on them. She wins something every week at catechism."

"You must be proud of her."

"Yes, I am. But Myrna Loy worries about confession."

"Why is that?"

"She has so many sins," I explained.

"She's only six years old!"

"Six-year-old children can be very bad, even when they're not trying."

"Well, six-year-old children should remember that their mama and papa love them no matter what they do."

"Yes, I tell Myrna Loy that, but she worries anyway. Sometimes I think she'll worry herself to death. Did you ever know anyone who worried themselves to death?"

"No. I don't think that happens but once in a blue moon."

"I'm glad to hear that. I make Myrna Loy penuche candy, like you do for your little girl, and nice dresses like the ones in the catalog. She has a lot of nice dresses. I sewed her an angel dress for church. *That* was a lot of work. We had her picture taken, and I sent one to my friend Earl."

Mrs. Erhardt turned the pieces of chicken as they browned. When they were all turned, she put the lid on the skillet, lowered the heat, and flicked on the burner under the potatoes. After this she opened a large can of green beans and emptied them into a saucepan. "I don't think I know about your friend Earl," she said, pulling out a chair and sitting down opposite me. "Is he from around here?"

"No, Earl's from back East. He and his sister, Elda, lived on a farm when he was a boy. Then the family had to sell the farm. Elda is married to Bill, and Bill just got a job. He was out of work a long time, and they couldn't be together. Earl hasn't seen Elda for six years. He's out of work, too."

"That's a pity."

"Earl's smart and good looking, like William Powell, so I think he'll find something soon. There's a girl near New Ulm he might marry if he gets work. Her name is Angela."

"I think it's all going to turn out hunky-dory."

"I would like Earl and Angela to live near Mr. Brown and me. Earl could build a house like ours."

Mrs. Erhardt poured herself a cup of tea from a pot on the stove. For me she poured a second cup, half-full, filling it the rest of the way with milk. "What kind of house do you have?" she inquired.

"You'd like my house. It's white with blue shutters and a brick sidewalk. It has a white picket fence and hollyhocks. Upstairs in Myrna Loy's room, there's a window seat. Across the street there's a house just like ours, and a boy named Phillip lives there. Phillip's father is away at the war a lot, so Phillip's mother, Helen, comes over and visits almost every day. I think Myrna Loy will grow up and get married to Phillip." I sipped my tepid tea. "I forgot to tell you, Phillip's mother is a tap dancer. She's won hundreds of prizes for tap dancing. She says one day when she was about six or seven, she woke up and put on her black patent leather shoes and a dress that had a lot of starch in it, and just like that, she started to dance, without any lessons." I blotted my imaginary lipstick with a paper napkin. "They moved here from England. Helen's sister, Cynthia, moved here, too, but she's living at the Harvester Arms because she and her husband can't afford a house."

"That's a shame," Mrs. Erhardt said, carrying her cup to the sink.

"Cynthia's husband plays poker," I told her confidentially.

"I see."

"He lost a thousand dollars."

"Oh, dear."

"Cynthia says she doesn't want to live at the Harvester Arms all her life because she has to go down the hall to the bathroom, and her little girl, Sonja, doesn't have her own room. Cynthia's going to get a job."

"Jobs are hard to find."

"Not for Cynthia. She can do anything."

It was nearly time for Mrs. Erhardt to put supper on the table for her husband and her little girl, Lark, so I said, "I've got to get home now. Myrna Loy and her papa will be hungry."

"Next time you come, bring Myrna Loy with you. I'd like to meet her."

"Thank you for the tea and penuche. I'll save the candy and share it with Myrna Loy."

Mrs. Erhardt let me out, and I strolled twice around the depot and once past the Harvester Arms. Returning, I pulled off the cloche, stuffed the red purse inside it, inched open the screen door, and sneaked past Mama who was looking into the refrigerator.

A few minutes later she called Papa and me to dinner. Mama had made milk gravy in the chicken pan. No one has ever tasted better gravy than Mama's milk gravy. I quickly made a big well in my potatoes and watched as she poured the creamy, freckled liquid, so dear to my stomach, into the depression.

"Papa, don't wreck my well," I implored.

He laughed heartily and reached for a drumstick. "Who? Me?" he asked and, as he spoke, the drumstick fell from his hand into the potato well, spilling the gravy over the plate. Papa laughed until he nearly choked on his green beans.

After Mama and I had washed and dried the dishes, Papa asked me, "Want to tag along while I check the boxcars?"

"Take the pails with you," Mama said, so Papa and I each carried a slop pail out to the tracks and dumped it. Then, leaving the pails on the platform, we walked across the tracks to the furthermost one, alongside the grain elevators. Papa carried a clipboard and papers, and he checked the information on these against information on the boxcars. He slid open the doors of the empty cars to see that no one was sleeping in them. He never made a fuss about men *riding* in the empty cars, but he wouldn't let them *sleep* there. Papa told me that in some places, men were hired to beat up tramps found coming into town on the train. Papa didn't approve of that. He'd gone to school with fellows who'd had to take to the rails. A man who voted a straight Democratic ticket wouldn't beat up on tramps, he'd told me. "I hope you'll always vote a straight Democratic ticket," he'd added. I promised him I would.

When Papa had checked every car, we walked back again to the depot, our shoes crunching and munching the cinders and gravel. I followed him into the office and waited while he typed up some forms. I sat in Art Bigelow's chair, swiveling around and around until Papa told me for God's sake to stop. From one of the tall, green, ribbed-metal wastebaskets I retrieved a sheet of paper, and pulling the cover from Art's typewriter, I inserted the paper, clean side out, and began to type.

"Be careful of Art's typewriter," Papa warned.

"I will. I'll just type one key at a time." I'd gotten into trouble when I was little, trying to play the typewriter like a piano.

"Dear Phillip," I typed. "How are you. I am fine. I wish you were here. I am going to get a window seet. Love, Lark Ann Browning Erhardt." Pulling the paper out of the roller, I folded it several times and put it in my pocket.

Papa fitted the dust cover over his typewriter, switched off the gooseneck lamp, and inquired, "If you were getting an ice cream cone, what flavor would you order?"

"I always order chocolate."

Leaving the light burning on Art's desk as was depot practice, we left, locking the outside door behind us. We took the new Oldsmobile, and Papa drove slowly all the way down Main Street to the end, U-turning and driving back to park in front of Anderson's Candy and Ice Cream, next to the Majestic Theater where Bette Davis was playing in *Jezebel*. Anderson's stayed open until seven-thirty to accommodate moviegoers.

"We'll have a chocolate cone here," Papa told Mr. Anderson, pointing to me, "and I'll have a strawberry." While Mr. Anderson scooped the ice cream, Papa studied the candy case. "Want some gumdrops?" he asked.

I clapped my hands.

"Give us a dime's worth of gumdrops, too, while you're at it." A dime's worth was a lot, much more than I usually got.

Headed home again, Papa asked, "Do you think your ma is really going to look for work?"

"Yes."

"Why would she do that?"

"To make money for the new house."

"I don't like to see women going out to work unless the man passes away. Or loses his job."

"Why?"

"It doesn't look womanly. My ma never thought of foolishness like that. She had plenty of work at home. Your ma has some fast ideas. I don't know where she gets 'em. When you're grown up, don't try to make a fool of your husband by going out to work," he advised, chucking my chin. "Be pretty and womanly."

I didn't point out that Mama wouldn't feel compelled to work if Papa hadn't lost two hundred dollars at poker. Nor did I bring up my plans to find work as a tap dancer. The Fourth Commandment admonished, "Honor thy Father and thy Mother." Sister Mary Clair had said that we honored our father and mother by loving and *obeying* them. When it came time to make my first confession, what could I say about the Fourth Commandment?

While my mind examined these distressing concerns, like a curious tongue traveling back and forth amongst half a dozen rotten teeth, it entered my head that Mama, too, was committing a mortal sin by disobeying Papa. If he did not want her to work, and her marriage vows said she must love, honor, and *obey* him, Mama's soul would turn black as the piece of coal Sister Mary Clair had brought to catechism to illustrate the condition of a sinful soul. She had explained that a sinful soul dropped into the fire of hell burned like coal, but never turned to ash. It burned forever.

It was difficult to imagine that there were thousands of people in the world without the blackness of mortal sin on their souls. There were only three people in my family, and we were all headed for hell as things stood. Sometimes I thought that if I were born again, I'd like to be a Methodist, like Katherine Albers.

When we pulled up beside the depot, Papa said, "You'd better hide those gumdrops or your ma'll throw a fit."

I pushed them into my pocket with the letter to Phillip and wondered whether it was a sin of omission not to tell Mama about the candy. Later, sitting cross-legged in the crib with my confession notebook, printing by the light escaping from the living room, I entered: "lied to Mama—gumdrops" and "disobeyed Papa—tap dancing."

The WCCO ten o'clock news came on the radio in the next room. Papa always came to bed right after the news. I closed the notebook, climbed out of the crib, and stashed the record in the bottom drawer of the doll chest.

"Are you awake in there?" Papa called.

Climbing back into the crib, I lay turned to the wall, guilt compressing my chest until I could barely breathe.

I studied the picture in the clock, easing myself into the garden where everyone was in a state of grace. The bluebird that was perpetually on the wing flew down, lighting at my feet, and began pick-pick-picking up the birdseed I had scattered for him.

8

LEAVING SCHOOL at two thirty-five as usual, Sally and I found the afternoon sharply bright after the cool dimness of the main hall. We drifted out to Main Street, past the park where we skated in winter and the band shell where we watched penny movies on summer Saturday nights. Old, grainy, and harsh-sounding, the movies were an intense treat. I had seen *Broadway Melody*, with Bessie Love, at the penny movies, as well as *Applause*, with Helen Morgan.

We paused in front of the Majestic Theater to study the pictures of Bette Davis in *Jezebel* before poking along to the window of Eggers's Drug Store, where we argued desultorily over our first purchase should we fall heir to a fortune.

Sally opened the screen door and held it for me. Brushing the backs of the stools with our fingertips, we passed the mahogany-and-marble soda fountain. Ignoring Mr. Eggers at the prescription counter, we lingered among the perfume and makeup displays.

Down aisles of foot pads and tooth powders, heating pads and pipe tobacco we dallied.

"The Eggerses own all this," Sally murmured, eyeing shelves of Kreml shampoo, Pebeco and Dr. Lyons tooth powders, Eversharp pens, Whitmans Chocolates and Dr. Graybow's Pre-Smoked Pipes. "They must be rich."

The great paddle blades of the overhead fan stirred together essences of pine tar soap and Coca-Cola syrup and bath salts and oiled wooden floors. It was a rich, thick soup of smell.

What did you do with a truss? we wondered. Or with sanitary napkins, which were wrapped in brown paper? I knew what you did with an enema bag. With trills of giggles and explosions of whispers, I explained to Sally while she made disgusted faces and stamped her foot. "No, no," she cried in a tiny voice, not moving her ear from my mouth.

Before Mr. Eggers suggested that our mothers might be pacing the floor with worry, we dragged ourselves from the drugstore, slouching out to the dusty street.

On such a golden, spring afternoon it was hard to think of going home, so we sat down on the curb at the corner and took turns saying hello to everyone who came by, those in cars and those on foot, testing our memories of people's names.

"Hello, Mrs. Soule."

"Hello, Mrs. Mosely."

"Hello, Mr. Monke."

If you missed a name, you picked up a little pebble from the gutter and held it in your hand. If the other person missed a name and *you* remembered, you discarded one of the pebbles in your hand. Whoever had the fewest pebbles won. A blue Oldsmobile bore down on us.

"Get in girls." It was Mama. "Do you know what time it is? It's a quarter to four."

Sally and I looked at each other in disbelief as Mama continued, "I've just come from a meeting at church, and I've got picnic tickets for you to sell, Lark. And I'm sure Sally's mama has tickets for her, too. You should have been home an hour ago," she said in her patient-Catholic-mother tone.

"What picnic?"

"The Knights of Columbus Memorial Day Picnic."

"Why don't the Knights of Columbus sell the tickets?" I asked.

"Because they've got better things to do," Mama explained, pulling up in front of the Wheelers' house. "Good-bye, Sally. Can you get the door?"

"I'll see you tomorrow, Sally," I called. And off we shot.

At home I told Mama, "I don't like to sell tickets."

"Nonsense," she scoffed, handing me an envelope full of them. "Everyone says you're wonderful."

"I still don't like to." I did not believe that everyone said I was wonderful.

"Well, you don't have a choice."

"Couldn't you sell them?"

"I'd have them sold in half an hour," she said, "but you know it's the children who sell the picnic tickets. People would say, 'Arlene, where's your little girl? Is she sick?' And then what would I say?"

"Say I don't like to sell tickets."

"Don't be sassy, young lady."

Away I plodded, Mama's voice in my ears. "They're twenty-five cents apiece. A bargain. There'll be games and prizes. If they don't have change, you'll come back later. Everyone will be there. It's for a good cause. Be polite no matter what, and don't forget to smile and say thank you."

I was not new to selling tickets. I'd started when I was four, twice a year, spring and fall, the Memorial Day picnic and the October bazaar. It never got any easier. I was embarrassed to ask people for money and fearful they might turn me down. If twenty people bought tickets and one turned me down, the one who turned me down hung around in my mind, haunting me. Had I forgotten to mention the games and prizes? Would they have said yes if I'd had blond curls, if I'd worn my pink dress with the tulip on the pocket, if I'd smiled more?

Now here I was again, trudging down the street with an envelope full of tickets and a heart full of misgivings. Start with a sure sale, Mama said. Mr. Navarin at the Sinclair station was a sure sale.

I waited until he had serviced the Model A at the pump and it had snorted and pranced away, as Model A's seemed to do. For a minute Mr. Navarin stood with one arm outstretched, leaning against the pump, watching the car disappear down the street. Then he removed his cap, which said Sinclair, and mopped his forehead and neck with a blue handkerchief from the hip pocket of his uniform. Beneath the cap his sand-colored hair had grown quite thin, so that he appeared ten years older with the cap off. I wished him to put it right back on and leave it on. I didn't like the idea of him changing.

He turned and caught sight of me. Slipping the cap back on his head, he smiled. He was one of the men at the poker party at Herbie Wendel's on Friday night. Though I doubted that he had lost two hundred dollars, or even twenty. Mr. Navarin was shrewd and contented. He was not a man to gamble what he didn't want to lose.

"Mr. Navarin, I'm selling tickets for the Knights of Columbus Memorial Day Picnic at Sioux Woman Lake. They're twenty-five cents apiece. There'll be prizes and games. And food. Mama's baking pies and cakes." I thought that last one would interest Mr. Navarin.

"Come in the office," he said, leading the way. "Memorial Day?"

"Yes."

He opened the cash register and took out a dollar bill. "I guess I'll need four," he said. "For me and the missus and Danny and his wife." Danny was Mr. Navarin's son, who drove a Sinclair truck.

Four, right off the bat. Mama was right about starting with a sure sale. I pulled four tickets out of the envelope and handed them to Mr. Navarin, then carefully slipped the dollar bill in beside the unsold tickets.

Mr. Navarin closed the cash register and motioned for me to follow him into the garage, where he and Sonny Steen worked on cars. Axel Nelson's Studebaker was on the hoist, where Sonny was doing something serious to its underside with a wrench while Mr. Nelson leaned on a workbench chatting with Barney Finney, the bootlegger. Axel Nelson and his wife, Minerva, owned the Harvester Arms Hotel. He, too, had been one of the men sitting around the poker table at Herbie Wendel's house.

"Well, boys," Mr. Navarin called to them, "the little Erhardt girl is selling tickets to the Knights of Columbus picnic. I told her you'd be happy to take some off her hands." He hadn't told me any such thing, but I didn't mind his pretending.

Axel Nelson looked askance at Mr. Navarin, grinned, then winked at Barney Finney. "I guess I could use a few of those, little lady," he said, reaching for his billfold. "Let's see: one for me, one for Min, and maybe six to pass out to guests stuck in town over the holiday. How much does that come to?"

I had no idea. It was eight tickets, but how much money I wouldn't be able to figure until second grade, when we had real arithmetic. Mr. Nelson studied me through narrowed lids, a smirk twitching the muscles around his lips. He didn't like children, I could see, but he didn't know it.

"It's eight quarters, Mr. Nelson."

"Heh, that's pretty good." Sonny Steen laughed.

Mr. Nelson put a hand in his pocket and brought out his pocket change. He looked it over. "I'm really sorry," he said, "but I don't have eight quarters on me."

In my head I was counting my fingers. From the envelope, I removed four tickets. Mr. Navarin had given me a dollar for four tickets. Handing four tickets to Mr. Nelson, I said, "That costs a dollar." I reached for another four and gave those to him. "And that costs a dollar." Two dollars. I doubted I would have any more customers buying eight tickets, but if I did, I was going to remember.

Mr. Nelson opened his billfold. "Well, for crying out loud, I've only got a five-dollar bill. Can you make change?"

"I've just got one dollar."

"Gee, that's too bad," he said, lifting his shoulders in a gesture of helplessness and innocence.

"That's okay, Mr. Nelson. I'll go get the money from Mrs. Nelson."

All the men laughed. "Give the kid the money, Axel," Mr. Navarin said, and Mr. Nelson pulled two one-dollar bills from the wallet. He held them close and made me reach for them. Under the grin and the teasing, there was something unpleasant between me and Mr. Nelson. I was relieved when the two dollars were in the envelope. I didn't like the feel of them.

Barney Finney had a half dollar out. "I'll take a couple," he said, "and that good-looker under the Studebaker'll have a couple." Sonny put down the wrench, wiped his hands on a rag, and pulled two quarters out of his trousers pocket.

I thanked everyone and smiled at everyone and drank deeply of the rich, dark primeval smell of the place. Feeling that I had not quite given them all they deserved, I assured them, "There'll be food and games and prizes and everyone will be there." Waving good-bye, I saw myself out, skipping to the corner and across the

street. Sixteen tickets. I had sold sixteen tickets. I felt as though I
could fly, or at least jump very high.

Where next? Mr. and Mrs. Grubb lived at the end of this
block. I'd try Mrs. Grubb. She was young and pretty, and had a
Pekingese named Baby. Mama called it a "yappy little devil," but I
thought it looked like a crabby little old man.

Baby danced around Sheila Grubb's ankles, complaining and
offering advice, as Mrs. Grubb opened the door to me. "Baby
won't bite," Mrs. Grubb assured me, stooping to pick the dog up
in her arms.

If I could look like anybody when I grew up, I might have
chosen Sheila Grubb. She had short, blond hair that fell in a
disarray of curls, wide-set gray eyes, and a mouth like a child's:
trustful and vulnerable. She always wore pink rouge and deep pink
lipstick to set off her natural coloring, although Bessie Anderson in
Mama's bridge club insisted that Mrs. Grubb's hair color wasn't
actually natural. Very few women in Harvester colored their hair.
It was thought to be fast. But Mama said someday when she was
feeling reckless, she was going to have *her* hair hennaed. Bessie
Anderson had laughed at that as though it were the funniest and
least likely thing she could imagine.

Baby alternated between licking Sheila Grubb's chin and scowl-
ing at me. When I put a hand out to pet him, he yapped and
nipped the air.

"He wouldn't really bite," Mrs. Grubb told me. "Would you
like to come in?"

I followed her into the living room. "I'm selling tickets to the
Knights of Columbus Memorial Day Picnic," I said, and went
through my entire speech.

"Twenty-five cents? I'll get my purse."

She put Baby down and left the room, and the minute Mrs.
Grubb was out of sight, Baby was after my shoes, gnawing viciously on the toes. With his little mouth, it would have been
tricky for him to get a good hold, but the tops of the shoes were
decorated with tiny air holes in the shape of a bow, and Baby's
teeth punched down through these and into my feet. I didn't just
stand there and let him ruin my shoes without a struggle. I was
doing a regular tap dance, trying to stay out of his jaws, but when I
moved, he nipped my ankles. I didn't dare kick him. It went
against my upbringing and, besides, if Mrs. Grubb came back and
saw me giving him a boot, she would not buy tickets from me.

The minute Baby heard her mistress's footsteps, she dashed to the davenport, jumped up on it, cocked her head, and proceeded to go through her tail-wagging, innocent dog routine. I had known children who did the very same thing.

"Naughty Baby," Mrs. Grubb admonished sweetly. "Get down off Mama's brand new living room suite." She had opened her purse and was sorting through it. Of me she asked, "Do you like my new living room suite? Isn't it pretty?" She pronounced it "living room suit."

"Yes, very." The blue was too bright, and against the yellow walls, it turned the room green.

"I just got it Saturday over at Knoppler's in St. Bridget." She sat down on the over-stuffed blue chair and began emptying the contents of the purse onto her lap. "My coin purse is here *somewhere*. I had it this morning at Eggers's." She went on, "Mr. Grubb won a whole lot of money at poker Friday night, and I told him, 'That's like *found* money, and we're going to go out and splurge.' So we drove over to St. Bridget with the truck and threw our money away on this. But it is pretty, I think." She was turning her purse upside down and shaking it. "I'll bet I left my coin purse at Eggers's. I'm real sorry." Her child's mouth was pouting. "I'd've been happy to buy a ticket from you, honey." With her lap full of pocketbook trash, she couldn't get up. "Can you open the door? Don't let Baby out."

As if on cue, Baby hopped down from the davenport and headed for my heels, leaping against my calves, scratching them with his sharp little claws, nipping at my ankles and shoes. I opened the screen door a crack and squeezed out. Baby still had hold of one of my shoes, and I had to jerk my foot out of his mouth.

"Oh, be careful," Sheila Grubb called to me, "you might pull his little teeth out."

Outside, I sat on the curb and examined my shoes. They were covered with scars now and torn in a couple of places where Baby had gotten his teeth into the holes. I'd had these shoes a month or so, and they were supposed to last through the summer until I got my new school shoes.

I started to cry. That blue living room suite of Mrs. Grubb's was the ugliest living room suite I'd ever seen, and I hoped I never had to look at it again.

☆   ☆   ☆

"What's wrong?" Mama asked when I got home. "You've been crying."

"Nothing. I slammed my finger in Mrs. Grubb's screen door."

As Mama cleared the supper dishes, Papa took my hands and laid them, palms down, on the kitchen table. "These nails are freshly chewed," he said.

"But, Papa—"

"No 'but Papas.' You don't seem to understand that when you promise not to do something, and then you do it anyway, it's a sin. Biting your nails is a sin."

"But, Papa . . ."

"Get the brush," he told me.

"Please, Papa."

"Get the brush." His face was starting to flush. "How can you go to confession next year?" Papa asked, leaning close.

"What?"

"Doesn't it bother you, having so many sins? What is Father Delias going to think of *me* when he hears your confession?"

I was trying not to cry. "Father Delias won't know it's me, Papa. There's a little screen between us. He won't know it's me!"

"Are you stupid? He's known you all your life, and he won't know your voice?" he asked scornfully.

"No!" I screamed. That was my worst fear—that Father Delias would know it was me, would know that all those sins on the tablet were mine. I loved Father Delias, but how could he love *me* after he knew?

"Don't scream at me, young lady," Papa warned, rising and heading purposefully into the bedroom.

"Willie," Mama said, "that's enough."

"You stay out of this. This kid is going to hell from being spoiled," he shouted at her, accusing her of ruining me.

"Willie, she only bit her nails!"

But Papa was resolved. I ran into the living room and wedged myself into the corner of the davenport. A moment later he stood in the doorway, the brush with the wide, flat wooden back in his hand.

As he crossed the room and grabbed my arm, I screamed, "No! No! No!"

"For God's sake, Willie," Mama yelled, "everyone will think she's being murdered. Stop it!"

"They will, will they?" he grunted, trying to hold me. I was kicking and thrashing and screaming. It was as though another child fought while I watched, unable to quiet her.

Shouting over my screams, Papa said, "If she thinks I'll stop because someone's going to hear, she's wrong." He shoved the brush at Mama, snatched me up with both hands, and threw me over his shoulder like a sack of potatoes. Off he marched, through the kitchen, out the screen door, and around to the parking lot. "Open the back door," he told Mama when we reached the Oldsmobile.

Into the backseat he tossed me, still screaming, unable to stop. "If she wants to scream," he said to Mama as he climbed into the driver's seat, "we'll take her someplace where she can scream and no one can hear. Get in." Mama got into the front seat.

Papa drove out of town with the windows rolled up. He didn't drive far into the country, only to the gates of the Catholic cemetery. He pulled the car up to the gates, cut the engine, grabbed the brush from Mama, and got out. Opening the door, he pulled me from the backseat and began to spank me with the brush across my bottom and the backs of my thighs.

My screams continued, though they had nothing to do with the spanking. By now I felt nothing.

Papa paused, breathing hard, and asked, "Have you had enough?" I couldn't stop, so he began again.

Again he halted. "You like it out here? Maybe you'd like to stay." The only response was screams, and he took up his duty again.

The third time he held off, Mama shrieked, "That's enough! She's never going to stop. You'll make her sick."

"I can stay all night," he panted. "She might change her mind when it gets dark. A night out here might do her some good."

Mama slid into the driver's seat, rolled down the window, and started the engine. "I'm leaving, Willie. You can walk back if you don't get in now." Papa stood very still for a long time. My screams had subsided. His grip on my arm tightened. The engine hummed, and mourning doves cooed in their nests along the cemetery fence. He released me and tramped away to the car, opening the door on the passenger side and dropping angrily into the seat.

"How will she ever respect me if you do this?" he hissed.

Mama reached back and opened the door for me. I climbed in and pulled the door closed as she put the car in reverse and backed onto the main road. At home, Papa left to prepare for the early freight. Mama helped me out of my dress and washed my face a little. She lowered my nightie down over my head and went to find an aspirin. I felt cold, except for my bottom, and I shivered a little. When I had taken the aspirin, she boosted me into the crib.

"Lie on your stomach," she told me. Then I heard her in the kitchen, emptying ice cubes from a tray, dumping them into a basin. She ran water into the basin and carried it into the bedroom, setting it on the table beside the big bed. Dipping a washcloth into the basin and wringing it out, she laid it on my bottom for a few minutes, drawing the heat from my skin. She dipped the cloth again and again, laying it on my throbbing back. At length she sprinkled fragrant talcum on me, pulled my nightie down, and covered me lightly with the quilt.

"Try to sleep." Skinning off her own clothes, she got into a nightgown and slipped into the other bed. In a minute she was up again, turning off all the lights in the house. It was still twilight outside, and pale light crept in around the venetian blinds. Mama settled back into bed for the night and, although she said nothing more, she did not fall asleep immediately. I could tell from her breathing that she was lying awake thinking. It seemed that if I held my breath and strained to listen, I would overhear her thoughts.

But I had thoughts of my own: sad, not wholly formed thoughts about fairness and justice and punishment. I dreamed of running away and knew I never would.

In the dark, I couldn't see the banjo clock, but I knew its picture by heart, every flower and shadow. In that place, sunbeams danced on the kitchen floor as I sat sipping tea and milk.

Later I woke as Papa came home, put on his pajamas in the dark, and stood beside the crib. I pretended to be asleep.

He put a hand on my shoulder. "Lark," he said, giving me a little shake, "I'm sorry. We'll go fishing next weekend, just you and me. Would you like that? Do you forgive me?"

But I kept on pretending to be asleep.

9

THE FOLLOWING night at supper, Papa warned me, "Those nails had better look prettier next Monday, or it'll be the brush again. And the cemetery." To Mama he said, "I don't know why I never thought of the cemetery before. It gives Lark a real good chance to exercise her lungs without an audience, at least not an audience that'll complain about the noise." He smiled at his little joke, and at me, in a genuinely jolly way, as if to share the humor with me.

I didn't want to cry in front of Papa. Slipping from my chair, I ran into the bedroom and climbed into the crib. I covered my head with the quilt to keep Papa from hearing me.

"You get yourself right back to this table," he called to me, "and finish your supper."

"Let her go, Willie," Mama told him, speaking in a low, distinct voice that meant business.

With the memory fresh in his mind of Mama with a ketchup bottle in her hand, maybe Papa didn't want to cross her again so soon. In any case, he let her change the subject.

"I had a letter from Betty today," she told him. "She's sick most of the time, she says. The doctor wants her to stay in bed until after the baby comes."

"When's that?"

"Around the first of July. I worry about her in that little burg, with the doctor twenty miles away. She's not a kid."

Aunt Betty was Mama's older sister. She lived a hundred miles away in Morgan Lake with her husband, Stan Weller, who traveled for a farm implement company. Last Christmas at Grandma Browning's in Blue Lake, Aunt Betty and Uncle Stan had told everybody that they were expecting a baby.

"It's about time," Grandma Browning had declared happily. Aunt Betty and Uncle Stan had been married eight years, and Grandma thought they should have had a baby by now.

"It isn't as if we haven't tried," Aunt Betty had told Grandma, smiling and acting embarrassed. Everyone laughed. I laughed, too, but I didn't know why.

There was a lot about having babies that I didn't know. For instance, if the stork brought the baby from heaven, why did the woman get fat and sick? Cynthia Eggers in Mama's bridge club had had a baby a couple of years ago. Although I'd only been four, I remembered it very well because it left so many questions unanswered, questions I pondered again and again at nap time, lying in the crib listening to the sparrows in the parking lot, or at bedtime after my prayers.

I had asked Mama questions at the time, but the answers led me into wider circles of mystification. "How come Mrs. Eggers is fat?" She's going to have a baby. "Where does the baby come from?" God. "But how does God get the baby to Mrs. Eggers?" The stork flies down from heaven with the baby. "What's a stork?" A big bird. "How does he carry the baby?" The baby is wrapped in a blanket, and the stork holds the blanket in his bill. "Don't a lot of babies fall and get killed?" No, I never heard of one falling. "How come you have to go to the hospital to get the baby?" Because the baby is tiny and helpless, and the hospital is a safe place to keep it for a few days until it's stronger and used to being on earth. "Why doesn't God keep the baby in heaven until it's stronger?" I don't know.

I thought that God didn't always use good judgment in the way He ran things. If Mama or Grandma Browning or Grandma Erhardt were running the world, they would never entrust a baby to a big bird.

"After school is out, I think I'll take Lark and go stay with Betty until the baby comes," Mama said.

"Can't your mother go?" Papa wanted to know.

"With her broken ankle?"

"I forgot."

I was excited at the prospect of going with Mama to Aunt Betty's. For one thing, I would not have to worry about my fingernails and the cemetery while I was away. How many Mondays would we be gone? I wondered. Already I feared next Monday. I had been sore on my bottom all day at school. At recess I stayed away from the slide and even the swings.

Biting my nails was "a nasty, unattractive habit." I was willing to admit that. And it ruined the appearance of my hands. I could see that that was true. I yearned for long, shapely nails like the ladies in magazines had. Mama had said she would paint them with pale pink polish if I let them grow. I dreamed of resting my chin on the palm of a hand with long pink nails and having strangers remark to Mama, "Your little girl has beautiful hands, such long nails. She should be in a magazine."

I couldn't figure out why I bit my nails. I did it without thinking. Suddenly I would find my fingers in my mouth and not know how they came to be there. Papa found this hard to believe.

Papa wanted girls and ladies to be pretty and obedient and holy. That didn't sound unreasonable, even if it was impossible. I got down from the crib and tiptoed to Mama's bureau for a handkerchief. In the mirror I caught sight of my face, puffy and red from crying. My mousy hair hung in defeated remnants of what had early in the day been curls. I looked like one of Cinderella's stepsisters.

But I was going to Aunt Betty's, and while I was there, I might turn pretty. I ardently believed in such miracles. One time I asked Mama if she believed in miracles, and she said, "Oh, yes. That's how God holds our attention." Then she'd added, "It's just the kind of cheap trick I'd pull if I were God."

"What does that mean?" I'd asked.

"Never mind. It doesn't matter. Forget I said that."

But I didn't forget. I memorized her words. When someone said something that I didn't understand, something that I wanted to remember until I was old enough to understand, I memorized the words or I *used* to memorize the words. Now I printed them in the back of my first confession notebook. Once in a while I read them, just to see if I understood yet.

When she had washed the supper dishes and emptied the slop pails, Mama took me to the toilet before getting me ready for bed. Crossing the waiting room, I kept my eyes on the floor. I didn't want to look at Papa or have him look at me.

"How long before we go to Aunt Betty's?" I asked as Mama helped me into my nightie.

"About a month."

"That long?"

"Time will go by fast. Remember, the Knights of Columbus picnic is coming. If it's hot, you can go swimming."

"My old bathing suit is too small."

"Then we'll get a new one."

I hugged her so hard, she said I was squeezing the pudding out of her.

"Will you read a story?"

"What do you want to hear?" she asked.

"The Man of the House." That was the story about Phillip, who wore brown corduroy knickers and a brown Eton jacket, and sat on the window seat waiting for his father, who was fighting the Hun.

"That one again? Wouldn't you like a new one?"

"No." I closed my eyes and saw Phillip's house by the sea, a stone bench in the garden. And there was Phillip in the nursery, sitting in the window seat. "Doesn't that sound like our house, Mama?" I asked, but fell asleep before she could answer.

In the deepest part of the night, Papa shook my shoulder and said, "You're still biting your fingernails. We're going to the cemetery." I had on a new bathing suit, and I shivered as we stepped out into the night. No one was stirring in Harvester except me and Papa, bouncing along in the pickup.

Papa turned off the main road and drove up to the gate of the cemetery as he had done before. But this time when he dragged me out, he hauled me up to the gate, lifted the latch, and marched me in.

Straight through the cemetery we hiked, between tall headstones and pious trees, grown sinister in the dark. I howled like a banshee and tugged to free myself, but Papa stepped along without hesitation, paying no attention. At the far end of the cemetery, where a fence separated the graves from cornfields, he let go of my hand.

"Stay here till your nails are long," he said, and turned away.

I screamed and ran after him, but he was gone. In a minute, I heard the pickup's engine.

I tried to find the gate, but among hundreds of headstones and monuments, trees and peony bushes, I lost my way, finally sinking down on a cold bench and burying my face in my hands. In the inky shadows around me, animals glided through the grass, soundless but for the whisper of their feet. Something cool and smooth slid across my instep.

As I bolted, the earth fell away, and I tumbled down and down, into an open grave with water standing in the bottom. Bathed in slime, I heard from above a laugh much like Papa's, but when I turned to look, a leering face hovered at the rim of the grave, shrieking, "Everyone knows!"

After a long time, I peered between my fingers. The face had disappeared. Scrabbling up the side of the grave, I pulled myself out onto the grass.

A dawn breeze from the west churned the trees and coaxed the lilac bushes to dance. A great whispering passed among the willows and even the stone angels took it up: "Everyone knows."

Less than fifty yards distant was the gate, and beyond, the outline of Harvester beckoned. In the east, flames were creeping over the horizon. Above, the sky was clear and a most remarkable cornflower blue.

In the distant sky to the southeast, a lone bird appeared, enormous, bigger than a swan or goose. The corners of a sheet or blanket were gathered into its beak!

Hadn't Mama said that the stork carried babies that way? I was seeing a baby delivered to someone. Probably to Aunt Betty. She was the only person I knew who was expecting one.

I stopped in the road to watch it pass. But something was wrong. One corner of the blanket had slipped from the bird's beak. A second appeared to be giving way. If I ran hard, out into the field alongside the road, I could be there to catch Aunt Betty's baby.

Scaling a rickety wooden fence, I started across the unplowed field. Then something happened to my feet. They grew to the size of watermelons.

The bird was close. I could hear the baby cry. The fabric was slipping. A small hand waved, appealing to me. But my feet would not budge. Stretching out my hands helplessly, I watched in horror as the baby fell through the cornflower sky.

I didn't tell Mama about the dream. All day I was heavy with it. At recess I couldn't pump up properly on the swing. Jumping rope, I tripped time and again.

After school I went out selling tickets to the Knights of Columbus picnic. Plodding from house to house, knocking on doors, reciting the same old tale of games and prizes, I found it hard to smile and show the enthusiasm Mama expected. The baby, its little hand waving to me, filled all the space behind my eyes and in my heart. It was fortunate that the customers were more enthusiastic about buying than I was about selling. Returning home, I had only three tickets remaining in the envelope, and Mama was pleased.

"Didn't I say you'd be a wonderful salesman?" Mama asked, putting the envelope in the cupboard for tomorrow. "Set the table. It's almost supper time." Mama was in a happy mood, humming in her random, no-tune way as she checked the baked potatoes.

"What's that?" I asked, laying out the silverware beside the plates, fork on the left, spoon and knife on the right. Tacked to the wall above the kitchen table was a chart with the alphabet set out in rows. But the letters were all mixed up.

"That's a typing chart. I sent away for it. There's a book that goes with it. I'm going to learn to type."

"You're going to teach yourself?"

"The book says it's easy."

I folded paper napkins and put them under the forks. "Why do you need a chart? The letters are on the typewriter keys."

"Because you're supposed to learn to type without looking at the keys, the way Papa does. Haven't you noticed how he never looks at the keys?"

"How long will it take?"

"That depends on how much I practice."

"What're you going to type on?"

"Art Bigelow gave me that old typewriter that was in the office. He said they were going to get rid of it anyway."

"Why do you need to know how to type?"

"You never know when it might come in handy."

Secretaries knew how to type. Knowing how to type was a glamorous and exclusive thing, like owning a set of encyclopedias or suitcases that matched. The image of Mama typing, knowing where the keys were without looking, sent a thrill through me. This was a person I didn't thoroughly know, a person who had ideas I would never have guessed at. It was a little frightening.

Handing me a bowl of carrots, Mama gave me a sort of sideways glance and smiled, all the while humming something which only accidentally sounded like "Jeepers Creepers."

⚘ 10 ⚘

LATE THURSDAY afternoon, as I was selling the last of my tickets to Dr. White and his nurse, the sky began to lower and by the time I reached home, the first drops of rain were wetting the brick platform in front of our door.

When Papa came home to supper, he announced, "I called Joe Navarin and he said I can come over and hunt night crawlers."

"Can I come?" I asked quickly.

Papa looked at me speculatively. "Do you promise not to start whining to come home the minute we get there?"

"I promise."

"If you start whining, I won't take you again."

Joe Navarin, who owned the Sinclair gas station and bought four tickets for the Memorial Day picnic, lived at the edge of town in a house that sat on a half-acre lot. When it rained Papa sometimes went to gather night crawlers from Mr. Navarin's yard, which teemed with them during a good downpour. Papa had never taken me. He was afraid I'd get cold or start to fuss before he had enough worms.

I didn't have a real raincoat, but Mama had a jacket that kept off the rain. After dinner she got it out, buttoned it on me, and rolled up the sleeves until my hands stuck out. From a box under her bed, she retrieved my buckle-up galoshes and put those on me.

As she did, she inquired, "What happened to your shoes? They're torn here on top."

"Mrs. Grubb's dog."

"That yappy little devil?" She fastened the buckles. "What about an umbrella, Willie?"

"No umbrellas. You can't hunt night crawlers with a flashlight in one hand and an umbrella in the other, for God's sake."

From the freight room at the other end of the depot, Papa fetched a couple of minnow pails and a shovel. His fishing and hunting gear were kept stored in the freight room. "We'll drive out Cemetery Road and dig up dirt for these," he said, handing me the pails.

Cemetery Road. I looked at Mama. Her face did not reveal any awful knowledge. She was calm and smiling. But Cemetery Road? Why there? Why not Red Berry Road or Sioux Woman Lake Road?

I was silent climbing into the pickup. Of course Papa wasn't going to leave me in the cemetery, especially not in the rain. The darkness and confusion, the listening, waiting animals gathered silently around, all the dream images fluttered in my brain like frantic moth wings. I huddled deeper inside Mama's jacket.

On the left was the unplowed field where I had tried to catch Aunt Betty's baby. I looked quickly, then turned away. It was wrong to tempt whatever dark forces created bad dreams. What if I were to look up now and see a baby falling through the sky? I closed my eyes tight. Could a person try to run and find that their legs wouldn't move, that their feet were nailed to the ground? What if the stork dropped the baby in the field behind Aunt Betty's house? It was an unplowed field much like this one. What if I were there, and I couldn't run?

Papa pulled the truck over onto the shoulder and killed the engine. "We can get our dirt here," he said, jumping down from the cab and removing the shovel and pails from the back. We were a good hundred yards from the cemetery drive. Thank God for that. Papa helped me down and handed me the flashlight. "Hold this where I dig," he told me.

There were worms here, too, in the grass and crawling across the road. "Should I get those worms for us, Papa?"

"No. Leave them be. We'll get bigger ones at Joe's."

I stood with my back to the plowed field, holding the light, the rain falling, steady and gentle, on my shoulders and on the old fishing cap of Papa's, which Mama had clapped on my head as I was going out the door. When the pails were half-full, Papa lifted them into the back of the truck and we headed for town, the windshield wipers slap-slapping the rain from our view.

Papa pulled into Mr. Navarin's long driveway. We didn't stop at the house. We'd come for the worms, and we set to work hunting them. Papa walked, carrying his pail. He was right about the worms. They were everywhere and they were huge, a foot or so long many of them, and as big around as my fingers. I held the flashlight in my left hand and snatched up the struggling worms with my right, tossing them into the pail.

I was reminded of dreams in which, gazing casually at the ground, I'd spy money in the grass. Falling to my hands and knees with great excitement, I'd gather up the coins and stuff them into my pocket. The more I found, the more appeared. I began to plan all the things I would buy: a big, red tricycle for me, a fur coat for Mama, and a fishing boat for Papa. I put the money in the cut-glass vase from Aunt Essie on top of the sideboard in the living room and told myself that when I woke in the morning, I'd get it and show Mama. How thrilled she would be. Several times it had happened that the dream was so real that when I woke, I ran to the vase and couldn't believe there was no money in it. But this was no dream, I was pretty sure.

I picked up my pail and moved along. The wealth of worms was beyond anything I could have imagined. I tried not to step on them with my galoshes, but it wasn't easy. The worms felt different than they looked. They looked smooth and slimy, but they were rough to the touch and not at all disgusting. I had handled worms before when we went fishing, handing them to Papa to put on my hook. This year I was going to learn to bait my own hook.

"Papa, when we go fishing this weekend, will you teach me to put the worm on my hook?"

Papa was all the way across the yard and didn't hear me. I don't know how long we gathered worms. The time flew. Very soon Papa said, "My pail's full. What about you?"

"Mine, too."

He slapped the lid down on his pail. The lid resembled a colander, full of holes so that the minnows or worms wouldn't die. Night crawlers were too fat to slip through the holes. I slapped the lid on mine and followed him to the truck. When he lifted my pail to the back of the pickup, he opened the lid and looked inside. "Pretty good," he said.

I savored the "pretty good," sucking out every bit of flavor as if it were Christmas candy. I was turning it over pleasantly in my mind the next afternoon, which was Friday, as Sally Wheeler and I walked to her house from school.

"Papa and I went hunting for night crawlers last night."

Sally made a face. "You *picked them up?*"

"It's easy. They can't bite."

"They're so icky."

"No, they're not. They're nice. I got a whole pail of them. There must have been a million at Mr. Navarin's. We had a real good time, Papa and me, and he said I was a very good night crawler catcher."

Sally shuddered and made an awful face. "Don't tell Mama."

"Why not?"

"She doesn't like to hear about killing things."

"I didn't kill them."

"You will when you go fishing."

That was true. It was something to think about.

"Did you ever see the Rabel's dog?" Sally asked.

"A black one?"

She nodded. "Mama hit it with the car. She didn't mean to, but it chased cars all the time, and it ran right out in front of her."

"Did she kill it?"

"Sure." Sally shifted her reader, her speller, and her lunch pail. "I was with her. We had to walk home. Mama couldn't drive. She left the car in front of the Rabels' after she told them about the dog. She never went back for the car. When Daddy came home on Friday, he went and got it. I had to hold Mama's hand walking home. She kept telling me she wouldn't ever drive the car again."

"When did it happen?"

"Before Easter."

"Does she drive the car now?"

"Once in a while, but I don't like to ride with her because she slams on the brakes all the time. It's scary." As we crossed the Wheelers' backyard, Sally said, "She still cries about the dog sometimes. I wish she wouldn't do that. What if she cried in Truska's store? People would think she was crazy." Sally lowered her voice and added, "Sometimes she cries and there's not even a reason. She says, 'I'm sorry I'm crying. I can't stop.' I don't see why she can't stop. She's a grown-up."

"Lark, it's so nice that you could come study with Sally," Mrs. Wheeler told me, as if this were the first instead of the eighth or tenth time Sally and I had studied catechism together on a Friday afternoon. Mrs. Wheeler's eyelids were puffy and red along the edge.

"Sit down at the table now," she insisted, "and have some cookies and milk." She brought two plates and two glasses, and set them before us. From a big jar she removed handfuls of Fig Newtons and stacked them on our plates, six or eight on each plate. "Do you like Fig Newtons, Lark?"

"Oh, yes. Thank you." I didn't like Fig Newtons. They tasted like dried prunes. Also, the seeds made it seem like I was eating sand. But I didn't want to make Mrs. Wheeler sad so I ate them and smiled.

Mrs. Wheeler poured herself a cup of tea. I wished she'd put some in my milk. I wasn't fond of milk without something to kill the taste. Mama usually put in a little tea or coffee. Mrs. Wheeler's back was to us, but I saw that her shoulders were shaking. Not another dog, I hoped.

Without turning around, she said, "I'm sorry to be upset, but a terrible thing happened today."

Oh, dear, had she killed something?

"It was Hilly Stillman," she began, her voice wavering but not breaking. "I drove out to the Catholic cemetery to set out plants on Wheeler graves. I wanted them to look nice for Memorial Day. I don't drive much, but sometimes you have to—to do things.

"I was leaving the cemetery. I'd gotten out of the car to close the gate when I saw another car, coming down the main road, heading into the country. There were three young men in the car— no, two young men in the front seat and an older man in the back. It looked like . . . I'm not sure who it was. I'd never seen the young men before. They must be from St. Bridget or Red Berry, or maybe they're staying at the hotel.

"I closed the gate. There was someone running ahead of the car. I thought maybe it was a high school boy training for a race, but he was wearing a regular shirt and . . . they didn't see me right away because of those big spirea bushes on either side of the drive." She paused. She was trembling, and I wondered if we should go to her. I thought maybe Sally would, but Sally didn't move. I could feel her discomfort across the table. I wished that I could tell her not to be embarrassed, *most* people were strange when you got to know them. Anyway, I didn't think it was strange to cry about a dead dog. And the story Mrs. Wheeler was telling sounded exciting and mysterious. I was anxious to hear the rest.

"The car got closer," Mrs. Wheeler resumed. "It was going slow, and the two young men in the front seat were honking the horn and yelling at the one who was running. They were saying . . . awful things to him. They were chasing him with the car, chasing him like he was an animal, honking and yelling. They were telling him what . . . what they would do to him when they caught him." Mrs. Wheeler spoke haltingly, like someone editing as they go. What had those men said, and why were they chasing someone?

"Then I saw it was Hilly Stillman they were tormenting. He was frightened half to death. He can't run very well because of his game foot, but he was going as fast as he could. He was about to drop." She was sobbing. "I couldn't believe my eyes. It was like a nightmare. I ran to the end of the cemetery drive and screamed at them. I waved my arms and screamed. They pulled out and drove around Hilly. Then they took off. Hilly fell down in the grass and curled up and cried like a little child. It was a terrible thing." She grabbed a towel and covered her face.

I looked at Sally, who sat with her hands clasped on the table before her, her eyes cast down, as if she were praying. I think she was praying for her mother to stop crying. She was ashamed to have her mother cry in front of me.

A minute or two passed. Then, in her phlegmy, tear-filled voice, Mrs. Wheeler continued, "I got him into the car. He was frightened to get into the car. He cried all the way into town. . . ."

"Mrs. Wheeler?"

Sally's mother still stood with her back to us. Groping in the pocket of her dress, she found a handkerchief and began blowing her nose. At length she turned around, her face red but dry. She smiled guiltily. Hilly couldn't have looked any sadder than Mrs. Wheeler just then. "I'm sorry, children," she said. "I shouldn't have cried, and I shouldn't have told you about Hilly. I've upset you. Try to forget."

"Mrs. Wheeler? One time Mama came home from downtown, and she was crying because some sixth grade boys were throwing snowballs at Hilly. She said he gave his sanity for his country." I hadn't understood what that meant, and Mama had explained.

But Mrs. Wheeler, having regained her grip, was too embarrassed and upset by her own behavior to hear anyone's support of her. She looked panicked, as if she'd just woke up in a strange place and didn't know how she got there. Without a word, she flitted out of the room.

I began wolfing the gritty Fig Newtons as though what we had just witnessed were the most ordinary thing I'd ever seen. "Do you know where babies come from?" I asked Sally.

Sally wasn't in the mood to talk about where babies come from, nor was she in the mood to study catechism. In her room with the dormer window, we picked halfheartedly through the next day's lesson, and then she said she was too tired to do anything. Taking off her shoes, she got into bed and said good-bye.

Mrs. Wheeler was nowhere to be seen, so I let myself out and, for once, hurried home. I wanted to watch Mama practice the typewriter. And there she was, hunched in a knot of concentration at the kitchen table, her fingers spread out across the keyboard of the old office-model Royal, leaning slightly forward and peering intently at the diagram on the wall. Click. Pause. Clack. Pause. Click. Pause. It wasn't going very fast yet. Now and then Mama glanced down at the keyboard.

"Hello," she said, not looking up.

"You aren't supposed to look at the keys."

"I *know*," she told me impatiently.

The clock over the stove said five. "Are you going to make supper pretty soon?" Usually she had something in the oven or in the skillet by now.

"Papa went fishing with Joe Navarin. They just left. I'll make us bologna sandwiches."

"Did they take *my* worms?"

"I'm not sure." Click. Pause. Clack. Pause. "Now let me practice for half an hour more."

"I'll make the sandwiches."

"Fine." Click. Pause. Clack. Pause.

I cleaned out my lunch pail and set it to dry on the drain board. Then I checked the slop pails and found that one of them was nearly full, so I carried that across the tracks and emptied it. While I was there, I picked some mustard flowers and brought them back to put in a ketchup-bottle vase on the table. I was Mrs. Brown. Soon I would make bologna sandwiches for my little girl, Myrna Loy, and for Mrs. Erhardt, who was practicing the typewriter at our house.

After I put the slop pail back under the sink, I washed my hands and found an apron. By five-thirty the bologna sandwiches were ready, except for the sliced onion. I peeled an onion and took a sharp knife from the drawer.

"Mrs. Erhardt, would you please slice this onion while I set the table?"

Mrs. Erhardt looked at the clock, gathered up her typing manual and heavy typewriter, and carried them into the living room. While she sliced the onion, I set the table.

"Mrs. Erhardt, Mrs. Wheeler told me a sad story today about Hilly Stillman. You know Hilly Stillman?"

"Yes," she said, sitting down at the table without yet having been asked. "What did she tell you?"

I recited to Mrs. Erhardt everything Mrs. Wheeler had said, and I told her, "The poor lady was crying. Her little girl says she cries a lot."

"Mrs. Wheeler isn't strong," my guest observed. Then she said, "Mrs. Wheeler didn't know the man in the backseat of the car?"

"She said she wasn't sure, but I think she knew."

"Did she see the license number of the car?"

"I don't think so. She didn't say."

"She should have gotten the license number," Mrs. Erhardt fretted. "She definitely didn't know the young men in the front seat?"

"She said maybe they were from St. Bridget or Red Berry, or maybe they were staying at the hotel."

Mrs. Erhardt chewed her bologna sandwich, two lines appearing between her brows.

⚜ 11 ⚜

"ARE YOU going to practice the typewriter tonight?" I asked when we had washed and dried our few dishes.

"No. I'd like to call on Mrs. Stillman. Would you like to come along, Mrs. Brown?"

We washed our faces, and Mrs. Erhardt put on fresh lipstick and changed her dress. "Maybe you'd like to bring along a book, Mrs. Brown."

I fetched *Happy Stories for Bedtime*, my red patent leather purse, and the old blue cloche. Heading downtown in the Oldsmobile, we stopped at Anderson's Candy and Ice Cream to pick up a quart of chocolate ice cream before calling on Mrs. Stillman.

Rabel's Meat Market was at the corner of Main Street and Second Avenue, and the stairs to the Stillman apartment above were outside on Second Avenue. The steps were wooden. They creaked pleasantly as we mounted, Mrs. Erhardt first, with the ice cream, me following with *Happy Stories for Bedtime* tucked under my arm. Mrs. Erhardt knocked at the screen door.

"Yes?" Mrs. Stillman inquired, pushing the door open.

"I only stopped to say hello and see how you're getting on, Mrs. Stillman."

"Oh, it's *you*, Mrs. Erhardt. Come in. And you've got Lark with you. Isn't that nice." She held the door for us.

"I brought some ice cream," Mrs. Erhardt explained, holding out the quart carton. "I hope you and Hilly like chocolate."

"Isn't that nice. We'll all have some. I'll call Hillyard. He's so fond of ice cream. We don't have an electric Frigidaire, just the icebox, so we'll eat to our hearts' content." She allowed herself a dainty, old-fashioned giggle. Mrs. Stillman's life was so sparing of meed, she took utmost delight in what was proffered.

"Why don't you sit down on the davenport with your book?" Mrs. Erhardt suggested. I climbed on the davenport, taking care not to put my feet on it. Mrs. Stillman had covered it with a flowered throw, and on top of this were lace antimacassars. The room had a strange, not unpleasant odor of old things and Murphy's oil soap and meat market. On the table beside the davenport was a studio photograph of Hilly in his uniform. He was darkly handsome, with an unsullied sweetness to his features, like Mama's face in her high school yearbook, looking happily off, far into the distance. Hilly must have been looking far off to France.

"Wasn't Hilly handsome?" I commented to Mrs. Erhardt as she sank down in a green wicker armchair at the other side of the table.

"He still is," she replied, and I realized that this was true.

Mrs. Stillman came in from the kitchen with a tray of ice-cream-heaped sauce dishes. "Hillyard," she called, "come have ice cream." She added, "Put on your robe."

When Hilly appeared in house slippers and an old, plaid flannel robe, his eyelids were puffy, the rims red, just like Mrs. Wheeler's.

"Come sit here on the davenport by Lark," his mother told him. She tucked a napkin into the vee of his robe and handed him a sauce dish and spoon. "Mrs. Erhardt brought a whole quart of ice cream. Think of it," she exclaimed.

We ate in silence, the only sounds the clicking of utensils against crockery and Hilly's sucking of his spoon. Hilly finished first. Mrs. Stillman carried his bowl and napkin to the kitchen and returned with a cloth for him to wipe his hands and face.

Hilly was quiet. He sat there, playing with the sash of his robe and staring across the room. Mrs. Erhardt carried my empty bowl and her own to the kitchen. I could hear her talking with Mrs. Stillman about "this and that," as she would say. Mrs. Stillman spoke of someone in Germany named Hitler. She had been reading about him, and she was worried.

"If there's a war, I thank God that Hillyard is too old to go," she said, as though the army would take him if he were younger.

Hilly picked up *Happy Stories for Bedtime.*

"Would you like me to read to you, Hilly?"

He nodded. Never had I seen Hilly so woebegone. His eyes were kept downcast, his hands folded between his thighs. He would rather be alone in his room, I thought. He had joined us only for courtesy's sake.

In the kitchen Mama said, "Willie's got a stiff leg from falling out of a tree when he was a boy, and the leg's not being set properly. It's not much, but the Army probably wouldn't want him."

I riffled the pages of my book. I'd read every story at least twenty times, but they were all new to Hilly. Finally, I chose "Peggy Among the Pansies," about a little girl who took over caring for her mother's flower garden while her mother was ill. The main illustration, in color, showed Peggy on her knees among the many colorful flowers, digging with a trowel. But, not only could Peggy garden, she could also cook and mend and look after her mother.

Mrs. Stillman's delicate voice, which reminded me of little twigs snapping, piped, "Italy going into Albania, that doesn't sound good. I never thought the Italians were like that."

" 'In the town of Pemberly,' " I read, " 'on a quaint, winding street called Rose Lane, lived a girl named Peggy who was, as we shall see, both wise and clever.' " Besides becoming pretty, I wanted to become wise and clever like Peggy. Mama said that being wise was knowing what to do with being clever. I had written that down because I wasn't certain I understood.

How glad I was, reading to Hilly, that Mama had made flash cards for the words in my books I didn't know. Now, instead of inserting any old thing where the hard words were, I could *read* them, barely stumbling at all over "Pemberly" and "quaint." I felt grown-up and powerful entertaining Hilly.

With his index finger, Hilly traced the tall hollyhocks in the beautiful illustration, then abruptly withdrew his hand, sliding it back between his knees.

"We'll get to that part of the story in just a minute," I told him, as Miss Lamb, the kindergarten teacher, had several times patiently explained to me.

As I concluded "Peggy Among the Pansies," Hilly nodded slowly, thoughtfully, pleased by the outcome. Mama and Mrs. Stillman were standing in the doorway to the kitchen. Mama had waited for me to finish before announcing that it was time to go home.

"I'll come back and read to you again, Hilly."

"He loves to be read to," Mrs. Stillman said. "I used to read to him for hours, but my eyes tire so quickly now."

Mrs. Stillman followed us to the door, thanking us for coming and for bringing ice cream. In the car I asked Mama, "Did Mrs. Stillman say anything about what happened to Hilly?"

"No. Maybe Hilly didn't tell her. Or maybe she doesn't want to talk about it."

Here was another mystery. Sometimes life was thick and dark with mysteries. Patches of mystery, like patches of fog, obscured what I ought to know if I were to be ready for seven years old.

🌿 12 🌿

"LET ME SEE those hands," Papa demanded Monday evening when we sat down to supper.

"No," Mama said. "Not till after we eat. Leave her alone now."

My nails were no longer than they had been the previous Monday. I didn't know why I couldn't stop biting them, especially when I'd promised. We were having meat loaf and fried potatoes, two of my favorite foods, but I wasn't hungry. All I could think of was the upcoming trip to the cemetery.

Mama and Papa finished eating. "Get going on that food," Papa told me.

"I'm not hungry."

"I don't care if you're not hungry. In this family everyone cleans their plate. What did you do, eat cookies before supper?"

"No." I started to cry. I didn't want to, but I was filled with so much self-pity, it spilled out of my eyes and rolled down my face. "I don't want to go to the cemetery."

"You should have thought of that when you were biting your nails."

"Please don't make me, Papa."

"Eat your supper. I've got all night. We'll sit here until you've finished. If you waste enough time, it'll be dark when we get to the cemetery."

I began stuffing food into my mouth—sobbing and swallowing, wiping my nose with my napkin, and shoveling in more. When I was nearly finished, Mama grabbed the plate away.

"You'll spoil her until she's worthless," Papa told her.

Mama said nothing, but went on clearing away while Papa put my hands on the table, palms down. "They're worse than they were last week," he said.

I pulled my hands away and shoved them between my thighs. They were *my* hands, weren't they?

"I'd hide my hands, too, if they were as ugly as those," he told me.

"I'm not hiding them because they're ugly," I explained. "I'm hiding them because they're *mine*."

"What's that supposed to mean?"

"Nothing."

"If you sass me, you'll *stay* at the cemetery."

"Willie," Mama said, "skip this week. Forgive her this time."

"You stay out of this. This is between Lark and me. I don't want to punish her, but she has to learn to mind." He got up from the table and fetched the brush from the bedroom. Heading toward the outside door, he turned. "Come on."

"No, Papa, please." I ran into the bedroom and crawled under the bed. The linoleum was cool and smooth.

"Come out of there," Papa yelled, dropping to his knees and looking under the bed. "You come out of there or we'll drive to the cemetery every night this week, do you hear me?" He reached under the bed, but I scooted away.

"If you know what's good for you, you won't make me mad."

I huddled against the wall under the head end of the bed, not making a sound. Mama kept a couple of boxes under the bed with our galoshes and winter things in them. I hid myself behind them.

"Arlene, get in here," Papa called.

Mama came in and knelt beside the bed. "Go in the other room," she told Papa. "Lark, I'll go with you to the cemetery." She reached her hand under the bed. "Take hold of my hand."

I touched the end of her fingers, but didn't grasp them.

"Lark, please don't make him madder," she whispered. She wiggled her fingers, and I took hold of them. "That's a good girl. Come out now."

I crawled out. I was still crying. Mama took the embroidered hanky from her pocket and handed it to me. With her hand she brushed the hair back from my face. "You'll make yourself sick," she said.

"I don't care. I want to die."

"Don't ever say that. Things will get better."

"No, they won't. I try not to bite my nails, but I can't stop. How can I go to first confession if I can't stop biting my nails?" I started to cry again. "I'll go to hell, Mama."

"No, you won't."

"Papa said." I explained, "Biting my nails is a sin of disobedience."

Papa's impatient voice came to us through the thin partition. "Are you two coming?"

Mama took my hand, and we walked out of the bedroom. All I remember of the trip to the cemetery is how lavender the sky was growing, how fiery the clouds were above the disappearing sun, how still and quiet the air, not a leaf disturbed, and then, how I spoiled it with my crying.

Everything was the same as on the first trip except that I threw up my meat loaf and potatoes at the edge of the lane. When we were home again, Mama put me to bed. I hated Papa and didn't ever want to see him again. That he was going to be sleeping in the same room made me sick with revulsion. After a while I thought how sinful my feelings were. I felt like two people, one angry and loathing, the other guilty and loving.

At breakfast Papa was jolly, admonishing me to eat my Wheaties if I wanted to be like Jack Armstrong, the all-American Boy.

"I don't want to be like Jack Armstrong."

"Well, like what's-her-name, Betty."

"I don't want to be like Betty, either."

"It makes me sad when you're sullen," he told me. "Because I know that God hates sullen people."

"How do you know that?"

"Everybody knows that. Ask Father Delias."

Did everyone know it? Was I the only one who didn't know all these things? When did they learn them?

It was my good fortune that the following Monday was the day before Memorial Day, and Mama and I worked without coming home, all afternoon and evening, at Sioux Woman Lake, setting up booths for the Knights of Columbus Memorial Day Picnic. Actually, Mama worked and I tried to keep out of the way. It was

the first day of summer vacation, and many of the women had
brought their children.

The public park lay on the east side of the lake, and that was
where the picnic was held. There were normally picnic tables
dotting the park. These were supplemented now by big tables
hauled from the church basement and the American Legion hall,
in the back of a Mosely's Dray truck. The KC men who loaded
and unloaded the tables were cheerful and self-congratulatory.
Because this was work they did only once a year (except for Harry
Mosely), they laughed a good deal and shouted excessive instructions ("Watch that end there, Bob" or "Careful lettin' 'er down
now, Pete"), like boys playing at being draymen.

Papa didn't belong to the Knights of Columbus. He thought it
was for people who liked to put on airs. But I thought he was
missing some fun, at least at times like these.

Eight or ten members of the KCs who were handy with tools
built the booths from which food, handiwork, and rummage and
white elephant objects would be sold, and where games of chance
or skill would be played. Somewhat apart, at the edge of the park,
a bingo tent was raised.

Next to the parking lot, an outfit from Iowa was setting up a
merry-go-round and tilt-a-whirl. Tomorrow the park would ring
with the drunken clangor and wheeze of carnival music.

"Don't get in the men's way," Mama warned as I trailed off with
Sally Wheeler and several others, to watch the merry-go-round
taking form. We sat on the grass, shielding our eyes from the sun
and marveling as, magically, the parts fit together into a toy
overwhelmingly grand. Its prancing horses and bounding lions,
were mythic; its flashing mirrors and portraits of Arthurian beau-
ties, crushingly splendid. I was deliciously oppressed as the fore-
shadowing limits of time and money clashed with my inexhaustible
desire to ride, to be a part of the machine.

Simply witnessing its assembly, I was overcome. The merry-go-
round was part of the land beyond the larkspur and hollyhocks, in
the banjo clock. But it was a part capable of passing from that
Elysian field to this world of heat and dust. And while I rode, it
carried me with it into the valley of dreams.

With the idea of splashing in the water around the dock, Sally
and I trotted off to the bathhouse after lunch to change into our
bathing suits. The lake was still very cold, so we played in the
shallows, collecting pretty stones and trying to catch minnows in

our hands. Two or three times we found tiny leeches clinging to our feet, and we ran to Mama, who sprinkled them with salt and brushed them off.

Mama had spread an old blanket on the grass for Sally and me, and when we tired of playing in the water, we collapsed on the blanket to watch the grown-ups work. How satisfying to be a grown-up, allowed to work morning till night at *real* work instead of pretending. Of course, Mama let me do simple chores like dusting and carrying the slop pails, but I still couldn't bake a pie or sew a dress. Or decorate a baked goods booth with crepe-paper flowers, as Mama was doing. How powerful a person who could do that sort of job must feel.

Mama, Bernice McGivern, Stella Wheeler, and Maxine, Bernice's sister, were going to run the baked goods booth. Stella Wheeler had asked to be on the baked goods committee, although she was "the worst baker in town," according to Mama. "The woman can't boil water without burning it," she said. Still, Mama was not disposed to say no. "Stella Wheeler *needs* to work in the baked goods booth," Mama explained, "for her nerves."

"Nerves" must be what caused Mrs. Wheeler to cry so often, and to sometimes talk too much and other times not talk at all. What *were* nerves? Mama said they were not catching. On the telephone to Bernice McGivern, Mama said of Stella Wheeler, "She's not more than thirty-five, but I think she's having her change already." Mama had been in a hurry when I asked her what Mrs. Wheeler's change was. "Oh, honey," she'd said, "it's when ladies stop having babies."

I wrote it down in the notebook. Did a lady decide one day that she wouldn't have any more babies, or did the stork decide not to deliver them, or did God decide not to send them? And why would that give a lady nerves unless, maybe, she grew sad thinking of the cute little babies who would go to live at someone else's house. If Mama had already had her change, would I have gone to live with someone else? With Cynthia Eggers? And when Mama saw me, would she have recognized me or known that I could have been her little girl if she hadn't changed? I saw how it was possible that such a change could make a lady nervous.

I hoped that Mrs. Wheeler didn't run across a baby at the picnic who looked too familiar. That would start her crying.

I was fond of Sally's mama, and I thought she was pretty, although she never wore makeup. She'd look like a movie star if

she wore some. I didn't think it was a practice to which she was
morally opposed. It was something that didn't occur to her. Just as
paying a lot of attention to clothes didn't occur to her. She had
other things on her mind. Many things, painful things, it seemed.

Mrs. Wheeler had crisp black hair that fell in waves to her
shoulders, though she usually kept it pulled back and tied at the
nape of her neck with a narrow black ribbon. Her eyes were large
and shining and slightly hooded. The irises were a deep, periwin-
kle blue. She was too thin for her own good, Mama said, but I
liked the way her clothes fell along the sharp planes of her body,
like heavy rain sheeting down a windowpane.

"Your mama's pretty," I told Sally.

She shrugged.

"Don't you think she's pretty?"

"I just wish she wouldn't cry so much."

"Is your papa coming to the picnic?"

"Yes," she answered excitedly, sitting up. "He promised to take
me on the tilt-a-whirl." Sally's papa traveled, selling office sup-
plies. He was gone all week. That was sad. It was also true,
however, that he never spanked her, and I think that was because
he was away so much.

When we grew tired of watching the women, Sally and I took
our old coffee cans and tablespoons, and meandered back down to
the water's edge to dig in the sand. Some children were playing tag
among the picnic tables. Ronald Oster and Leroy Mosely were
playing cops and robbers among the trees beyond the bathhouse.

"Are you going to watch the parade tomorrow?" Sally asked.

"I think so. We always do." It wasn't a very big parade. The
local American Legion unit and auxiliary led the procession. They
were followed by a handful of non-Legion veterans, who enjoyed
showing off their uniforms once or twice a year. Hilly Stillman
was one of these. Then came the high school band, three or four
majorettes in front, twirling their batons and strutting smartly, like
circus ponies. After the band, last year's homecoming queen and
her attendants rode by in an open car, borrowed from somebody in
St. Bridget. The girls wore formal dresses overlaid with pink or
blue or yellow tulle, and corsages of red roses. A gaggle of kids
wheeling along in broken ranks on crepe-paper-decorated bicycles
were next, and behind them others pulled crying baby brothers or
sisters in similarly decked-out wagons. Finally, the hearse, sporting
American flags and bunting, crept along in the rear, maybe to pick

up anyone who dropped dead in the parade. Once around the schoolhouse block, and then down Main Street as far as the railroad tracks, that was the route.

I liked the majorettes best. Their white boots with tassels on them made my pulse quicken. If I had white boots with tassels, I would wear them all the time. For Christmas I was going to ask Santa to bring me a baton. Maybe someone would teach me how to twirl it. It didn't look so hard. If I twirled it very well, I might be asked to be in the parade, and if I were in the parade, maybe Mama would buy me white boots with tassels.

It was not only Sally and I who were thinking about the parade. I found a leech between my toes, and when we skipped back to the baked goods stall to have Mama put salt on it, Cynthia Eggers was chatting with Mama about the parade.

"Marilyn wanted a new formal, so we had to make a trip to Minneapolis this week." Marilyn was Mrs. Eggers's daughter. She was last fall's homecoming queen and would be riding in the open car tomorrow. "At first I said no, but Marilyn said she'd be needing a new formal for college anyway. Well, that's true. She's going off to the university. So, we got her a beautiful rose satin that's really too sophisticated for Harvester, but it was what she wanted." Mrs. Eggers sighed. She enjoyed being Marilyn Eggers's mother. She enjoyed the small discomforts and inconveniences, the imagined embarrassments. She could stand all day without boredom or weariness in front of the mirror that was Marilyn.

"I only wish," Cynthia Eggers continued, "that Helen Stillman had the sense to keep Hillyard at home."

"What?" Mrs. Wheeler looked up from the green crepe paper she was twisting into flower stems.

"He ruins the parade every year. We have company coming from Mankato, and I'm going to be humiliated."

"But he's a war hero," Mrs. Wheeler observed, "a genuine war hero."

"That was a long time ago," Mrs. Eggers pointed out. "Now he's a nuisance. Poor Marilyn will just die if he does some awful thing this year. And you know he will, he always does."

"What does Marilyn care?" Sally's mama asked, looking increasingly distracted. The question was notably out of character for Mrs. Wheeler, who was not confrontational.

"What does she care?" Cynthia Eggers repeated, beginning to show irritation.

"Yes," Mrs. Wheeler pressed. "The parade isn't about Marilyn. It's about soldiers who have fought for their country. Think of how insignificant Marilyn's embarrassment is compared to what Hilly and his mother have suffered."

Cynthia Eggers turned on her heel and marched away, her back as straight and stiff as any soldier's. Mrs. Wheeler looked blankly after her and started to cry.

"Jesus Christ," said Sally.

≥ 13 ⍨

MRS. WHEELER couldn't stop crying.

"I'll take her home," Mama told Bernice McGivern, "and then I'll be back."

"Stay as long as you need. I can take care of things here."

We headed for the Oldsmobile. People either stared at us or conspicuously didn't. Sally and her mama had ridden out with us, and now we were taking them home. Stella sat in the front seat beside Mama and wept quietly. Her shoulders didn't heave, her face did not contort. She stared ahead of her in a state of mild perplexity, the source of her sorrow lying too deep for examination.

In the backseat, Sally sat on the floor, her knees drawn up in a tight, angry package. She wanted no one to see her in the car with her mother. How could her mother do this, humiliate her in front of half the parish? What was wrong with her mother that she could make such a spectacle of herself? I heard what Sally was thinking as clearly as if she'd shouted it.

The drive to town was unending. To fill the silence, Mama spoke casually to Mrs. Wheeler of unimportant matters. "I think I'll get up early tomorrow to bake my pies. I've got twelve dozen cookies made up and packed. I made some double chocolate cookies and some molasses and ginger. The molasses and ginger cookies are from a recipe of my Aunt Geraldine's.

"It's turned so hot, I'm going to get out my summer clothes. I've got a pink cotton with a white sailor collar that's kind of dressy, but not *too* dressy. I think I'll wear that. And my white pumps. Now that it's Memorial Day, we can wear our white pumps."

Mama glanced at Mrs. Wheeler. From where I sat, behind Mama, I could see the tears still falling from Mrs. Wheeler's chin.

"My sister Betty's expecting a baby around the first of July. Lark and I are going to take the train in a couple of weeks and go stay with her till after the baby comes. I wonder what they'll name it. This is their first." And so on.

Before we reached the Wheelers' house, Mama asked, "Is your papa home, Sally?"

"She's nodding her head yes," I told Mama.

As the car pulled up in front of the house, Mama said to Mrs. Wheeler, "I wish you wouldn't take it so hard. You were absolutely right to call Cynthia Eggers on what she said."

But the perplexity on Mrs. Wheeler's face deepened. She wasn't crying about Cynthia Eggers, it said. Mama patted Mrs. Wheeler's hand, then opened the door and got out to escort Stella Wheeler and Sally to the house. From the backseat, Sally grabbed her doll and the dress she had worn to the lake over her bathing suit. Mama opened the back door and Sally left without a word.

How cheerless and solitary Sally and her mother each looked, drifting up the walk to the front door, Mama behind them, carrying Mrs. Wheeler's purse.

On the floor of the car was a coffee can full of stones Sally had collected at the lake. "Wait," I called and ran after her with the can. "Here are your pretty stones." Sally took the can and looked at the stones, now dry and dull, their greens and pinks and blues faded to powdery gray.

"I don't want them," she said. "You keep them."

Mr. Wheeler appeared at the door. Mama told him, "Stella's not feeling well so we brought her home."

Mr. Wheeler didn't look surprised. He looked tired and weighed down. When we had turned Mrs. Wheeler and Sally over to his care, and the three of them had disappeared into the house, I set the can of stones on the bottom step. Tomorrow Sally might want to pour water over them and bring back their colors.

We stood on Main Street in front of Johnson's Chevrolet and Buick, the noon sun beating hard and hot on our shoulders and on our scalps where our hair was parted.

Bill McGivern marched by with the American Legion, and Bernice McGivern stepped smartly along in the auxiliary. Bill smiled and Bernice waved. The majorettes twirled and glittered, exotic butterflies amidst a flock of plain moths. The tassels on their freshly whitened boots danced and spun. Was there *any* chance that Santa would bring boots as well as a baton?

Here was Hilly, uniform fresh and neat. My, but he looked handsome in his tunic, marching along with the other soldiers who weren't legionnaires. He had difficulty keeping in step, and of course his gait was lurching due to his bad foot, but he made a great effort to conform. He didn't break rank, dashing ahead of the band and waving his arms, as he had the year before last. Nor did he jog alongside the Homecoming Queen's open car, polishing the fenders, as he had last year.

"Mama, Hilly's doing real good, isn't he? Do you think he's getting sane?"

Mama waved to Hilly. "I don't know," she murmured. "He looks scared and sick to me. I don't think he should have marched today."

Hilly had performed quite respectably, though. Even Cynthia Eggers couldn't complain.

Mrs. Stillman didn't allow Hilly to attend the Knights of Columbus picnic. He couldn't be trusted not to hurt himself on the merry-go-round or tilt-a-whirl. Mama and Papa and I had to dash away from the parade to reach Sioux Woman Lake with our pies and cookies before the picnic began at one o'clock. We would tell Hilly later how well he had marched.

"I feel sorry for Hilly," I told Mama as I clambered into the back of the pickup to mind the baked goods during the ride. "He's got no place to go but home."

"Maybe we'll bring him a little present from the picnic," Mama said. "Be on the lookout for something he'd like."

Jumping down from the back of the truck in the dusty parking lot, I heard Papa warn Mama, "I'd be careful if I were you. You treat him like he was anybody, but he's crazy."

"Shut up, Willie. You don't know what you're talking about."

"Don't come crying to me if something happens."

"You're the last person I'd come crying to," Mama declared, reaching into the rear of the truck for pies. "Lark, can you carry this big box of cookies without falling down? Don't dawdle. Willie, grab that second box of pies."

Laughing, Bernice McGivern and her sister, Maxine, were

setting out trays of cookies, cakes, bread, and pies. Some were under wax paper to keep off flies, some still in boxes, to be brought out as needed. Bernice and Maxine were wonderful laughers, and I liked to be near them to listen. But Mama didn't want me hanging around during the first rush of customers buying dessert for their midday meal. She gave me some change and told me to buy a hot dog and something to drink. "Come back later and I'll give you a piece of pie."

"A grown-up piece?"

"Yes. If you're good and don't bother me."

"Blueberry?"

"I'll cut it and set it aside right now. Run along."

"Do you think Mrs. Wheeler is going to come?"

"I . . . don't know."

There would be other first graders at the picnic, but none of them as close a friend as Sally. I bought a hot dog and a bottle of root beer, and sat on the grass where I could watch the merry-go-round. When I finished eating, I would find Papa and ask for money for a ride. Better get it now before he lost it at bingo. He'd headed in that direction. Last year he and Herbie Wendel and Lloyd Grubb and a couple of his other pals spent most of the day in the bingo tent.

The park was filling. Nearly everybody in Harvester showed up at the picnic. Even if they had to bum a ride with the neighbors and pack a lunch from home, they came to sit on an old quilt and visit, or take a swim, or play horseshoes. Half of St. Bridget and Red Berry usually turned out, too. The parking lot was full, and cars were parking along the road leading back to town. I kept an eye out for Sally, but it didn't look as though she was going to show up.

Beverly Ridza who was in my First Communion class collapsed beside me. She was wearing an old pair of overalls and nothing else but a little red barrette in her uncombed hair. "What you doing?" she asked.

"Eating."

"Can I have some?"

I handed her the hot dog, and she took a healthy bite, washing it down with half the bottle of pop. Beverly had no manners, but Mama said it wasn't Beverly's fault. Beverly's drunken, good-for-nothing papa had done a disappearing act, leaving Mrs. Ridza with three young ones to feed. Mama said Mrs. Ridza was short of cash and brains, and she did the best she could, cleaning people's houses and taking handouts. Mama always sent the Ridzas an anonymous basket at Christmas, and she said she would take a brush to me if I told Beverly where it came from.

"You got any money?" Beverly asked.

"Not yet."

"You gonna get any?"

"I guess." I could see what was going to happen. Beverly was going to stick with me and ask for half my money. Maybe she'd get tired of following me around. "I'm going swimming now," I told her getting to my feet.

"Where's your suit?"

"In the truck. Where's yours?"

"Don't have none."

There was the answer. She wouldn't want to hang around and watch me having a good time, would she? But she followed me to the truck to fetch my new red-and-white polka dot bathing suit, bought at Lundeen's Dry Goods.

Then she trailed me into the bathhouse and would have come right into the changing stall with me. "Don't come in with me," I told her. "I don't like to undress in front of people."

"Really?" She sounded disbelieving, but she stood outside the canvas curtain.

When I emerged, carrying my bundle of clothes which Mama would keep for me, Beverly said, "That's a nice suit. Can I wear your underpants?"

"My underpants?"

"If you let me wear your underpants, I can go swimming with you."

It was perfectly true that children our age sometimes went swimming in their underpants, but I wasn't really sure I wanted to lend mine.

"I'd let *you* wear *mine*," she said. I must have looked unimpressed, because she added, "Please."

Beverly wasn't a child easily moved to say "please." In her need, she had stretched to the furthest boundary of her social grace. I pulled my cotton underpants from the bundle.

"You can come in while I take off my overalls," she told me. "I don't mind."

"I'll wait out here."

We left our clothes with Mama, who noted my white underpants with pink rosebuds on Beverly's tight, meager behind but said nothing. Except for her size, Beverly seemed very unchildlike to me. She had none of the shyness I associated with little girls. The niceties of social behavior were of no interest to her. What was important was to manage—to manage to get underpants, to manage to get money for a ride on the merry-go-round, to manage to get food. Beverly managed pretty well, though I felt a trifle buffeted in her wake, a bit resentful at her lack of conspicuous gratitude. Now I lagged peevishly as she marched like a quick shore bird on twiggy legs, head up, hurrying toward the water. Reaching the dock, she sprinted its length, hurling herself into the cold, glittering lake.

I plunked down at the edge of the dock and tested the water, scooping in and out with my feet. Beverly was swimming, really *swimming*, beating the water viciously with long, skinny arms, kicking—shlupp, shlupp, shlupp—with bony feet. I didn't know how to swim yet. I could only do the dead man's float, a sport about as exciting as its unfortunate name, and one marking me as a member of the Pollywog swim class. I'd never seen Beverly at swim class, but she was surely a Sunfish at least.

This was the summer, my instructor had assured me, when I would learn the crawl. The crawl was *power*. It was self-propulsion. It got you from here to *there*. Not from here to *here*, like the dead man's float. If I could do the crawl from the dock to the diving raft and back, I'd be allowed to use the raft. Then I could learn to dive. The mere thought of diving made my head light. Diving was like singing harmony or typing without looking at the keys. It seemed like magic, but was something which could be learned. I marveled at that.

There was Beverly, hacking her way through the water as if she were cutting a path, clearing the way to the raft. Here was I, dabbling with my toes. There was she, *diving*. Well, belly flopping, but it was advanced belly flopping, with a purposeful, unabashed flair to it. Each time she hoisted herself onto the raft with her chow-mein-noodle arms, she'd hitch up my cotton underpants with the pink rosebuds on them, and then fling herself fearlessly back into the deep, dark ice water.

I poked along back to the shore and stood on the sand, where a delicate, brackish foam, like a lace frill, gathered at the water's edge. Slowly, pulling my courage together, I inched forward, encouraging myself by reporting silently, "Now it's covering your feet. Now it's over the little white scar where you got cut on a nail in Aunt Betty's garage. Now it's at the bottom of your knees." After a long time it reached my waist, and I ducked under to let the water cover my shoulders. It was colder than the inside of our refrigerator.

A hundred or more children and grown-ups were splashing and swimming and playing games. I tried to find an empty space to practice the dead man's float. Now and then a vacant five feet or so would appear, and I'd lay myself out on it, bobbing like a cork until I ran out of breath or someone knocked into me. I loved the quality of sound when my ears were covered by water, the shouts and jokes and merry-go-round music muffled to murmurs, like those coaxing voices that drift into your ears from far away when you are falling asleep.

Then Beverly was there, pushing my head down further. I came up spluttering and coughing. "Don't do that!"

Hands on her hips, bony chicken breast thrust out, she laughed and promised, "I'll teach you how to swim."

"Really?"

"Sure. You know how to float. I seen you floating."

I nodded.

"Well, watch me." She lay down on the water, arms extended ahead of her, floating as I had. Then she began to kick. Shlupp, shlupp, shlupp. And she was moving forward a little. I was amazed and delighted. That was something *I* could do. When Beverly stood up, I lay out and kicked my feet. Sure enough, I moved a little, too.

When I planted my feet to rest and breathe, Beverly ordered, "Now watch this." Again she lay down in the dead man's float. After a moment she began to kick. When she had propelled herself a short distance, her arms, one after the other, rose out of the water and flailed down through it, to reemerge a second later and repeat the arc. It was hardly graceful, but there was no denying that Beverly advanced through the little jostling waves.

"You see," she said, returning to where I stood, "swimming is just the dead man's float with kicking and hitting."

She was absolutely right. Why hadn't I seen that? I lay down as she had, began to kick as before, and when I'd got that rhythm going, I started slapping away at the water as if I had carpet beaters attached to my shoulders. It took so long to coordinate all of this that I was nearly out of breath before I got organized, but I was going forward, even against the waves, and excitement overtook me so strongly I forgot to hold my breath. Choking, I waded back to shallower water, for I had plowed out into depths nearly over my head. I threw my arms around Beverly. "Thank you."

"Godsakes," she muttered, backing away.

"I can swim."

"There's more to it," she pointed out practically. "You don't know how to breathe." Once more she admonished me to watch, though she needn't have bothered. Nothing could have induced me to look away. Beverly was sharing her *power*, and I was deeply impressed by her generosity.

As I watched, she repeated the previous lessons, but this time when she'd whipped along for several feet, she lifted her head straight out of the water and gulped air. Then she resumed whipping and kicking. This was the tricky part, keeping yourself afloat while you raised your head to breathe.

I gave it a try, raising my head, glimpsing a rushing world of water and light, drinking half a glass of lake water as the swells from my own efforts sloshed into my open mouth. Sputtering and spitting, I waded sheepishly back to Beverly.

"I did that when I was learning," she said. "So did Charlie."

Charlie? Charlie was her little brother, a year younger than Beverly and me. Charlie was only in kindergarten. "Charlie can swim?"

"Sure." She waited for me to get my breath. "Try again," she exhorted.

Again and again I tried, each time taking on water until I began to feel half-drowned. Still I was buoyed by accomplishment. I was swimming, sometimes only a couple of yards, but *swimming*. This was one of the best days of my life. Life could go by, weeks and months of it, and you didn't feel that you were growing any older or any bigger. Then unexpectedly a day would come along when you learned something valuable, something powerful, and afterward you were bigger and older, and you knew it. And forever you loved the person who had taught you.

When I was exhausted, Beverly and I lay down on the dock. From the corner of my eye, I studied her. Her skin was slightly blue and transparent, like skim milk. Just under the skin of her narrow breast, her temples, the insides of her arms and thighs, lay intricate patterns of blue veins. Her shoulders and ribs and hip bones stood out in sharp relief beneath the sheer covering of skin. There wasn't much to her. Where did she get her strength?

Beverly's face was a pointy, mouse face. Her eyes were hazel, the surrounding lashes pale, thin, and stubby. She looked like she'd been lacking a little bit of everything when she was born, and had never caught up. But she could swim and she could dive. And she'd taught me to swim.

Beverly lived in a one-room shack, out past the lumberyard, without a refrigerator or running water, but there was something inside Beverly that was as staunch and sturdy as a telephone pole. My beloved Sally lived in a new cottage with dormer windows and a spare room, but she was hidden away at home on Memorial Day because her mama cried too much. Both were my friends now.

"I'm going to go tell Mama I can swim."

"I'll come with," Beverly told me, jumping to her feet.

Halfway up the path, I started to run. "Mama, Mama, guess what! I can swim. Beverly taught me." As I called out the news, a thrill ran through me; it was so strong it shook me like a chill. "Can you come watch?" My teeth were chattering, not from cold but from excitement.

"That's wonderful. I'll come down a little later. Put the towel around your shoulders. You're shivering." She set out my wedge of blueberry pie on an old piece of church crockery. "Here's a fork," she said. "Bring them back when you're finished. Beverly, what kind of pie would you like?"

"I ain't got no money."

"This would be for teaching Lark to swim."

"What kind you got?" Beverly asked, pressing herself up against the counter.

"Apple, blueberry, and raisin."

"Raisin. I never had that."

Mama cut into a fresh pie and lifted out an extra large slice. Handing it to Beverly on another church plate, she said, "Thank you for teaching Lark to swim. I'm proud of both you girls."

When Beverly and I returned our plates and forks to the baked goods booth, Mama warned, "Now don't go swimming for half an hour. You don't want to get cramps." Bending down to me, she placed a quarter in my hand. "That's for you and Beverly."

If this day got any better, I'd have to sit down because I'd be too excited to move. Passing the quarter to the merry-go-round man, I asked, "How many tickets for that?"

"Three for you, three for your friend, and a nickel left for an ice cream cone."

Beverly and I grinned at each other in disbelief. "Godsakes,"

Beverly breathed. Climbing onto the merry-go-round, we each scurried to claim our favorite animal before someone else got to it. I mounted a wildly galloping black horse with bright, colored-glass stones in his harness, while Beverly, still wearing only my cotton underpants, scrambled onto the back of a vaulting lion.

How we flew! With each rise and forward leap of my horse, my happiness rose and leapt similarly until it seemed the great black steed would spring into the musical air. I gripped the pole with both hands, but Beverly, some distance away, held on casually with one bony blue hand and waved to me. I smiled and nodded. She waved to people waiting to get on the merry-go-round, and she waved to the man who ran it. Then she waved to picnickers far afield. When bootlegger Barney Finney, who'd given Beverly a lift to the picnic, strolled by on his way to the bingo tent, she waved and called out, "Hey, Barney, look at me on the merry-go-round!"

Beverly wanted to ride three times in a row. "I'm going to ride two times and come back later," I told her.

She looked dubious. "What if we lose our last tickets?"

We left our tickets and nickel with Mama and made our way over to the tilt-a-whirl to watch it swinging round and round, up and down, the cars spinning in violent circles. "I'd like to ride *that*," Beverly declared warmly.

"Not me."

"Why not?"

"I'd be so scared, I'd cry."

Beverly gave me a scornful glance. "Godsakes," she muttered disgustedly.

"Let's look at the booths."

Wandering from stall to stall, we inspected ratty-looking fox-tail collars and imitation Dresden vases in the white elephant booth; gaped admiringly as high school boys hurled balls into the open mouth of a plywood clown; fingered crocheted antimacassars in the handiwork stall until Cynthia Eggers told us our hands were filthy and we shouldn't touch. Taking in Beverly, Cynthia queried pointedly, "Where are your clothes?"

"Mrs. Erhardt's got 'em."

"You shouldn't run around in just your panties."

"They're not *my* underpants," Beverly explained.

"That's even worse."

Ambling back past the white elephant booth, my eye was struck by an item I'd missed before. "What's that?" I asked Mrs. Navarin.

"An ocarina," she said, laying it on the counter in front of me. "Sometimes it's called a sweet potato."

"What do you do with it?" I wanted to know.

"You play it," she said, putting it to her mouth and blowing into it. It was apparent that Mrs. Navarin did not know the first thing about playing the ocarina, but it was also clear that the strange instrument was capable of producing sweet, round notes.

"How much is it?" I pursued.

"Ten cents." She put it back on the table. "Would you like me to save it a few minutes?"

"I'll run get Mama," I promised, hurrying off, Beverly behind me.

"Mama, come quick. There's a present for Hilly at the white elephant booth. Mrs. Navarin's saving it."

"Go on, Arlene," Maxine told her, and Mama came away, wearing her frilly white-organdy bake-sale apron, her purse under her arm.

"Isn't it perfect?" I exclaimed as Mrs. Navarin blew into it again.

"Well . . . I guess," Mama agreed hesitantly. "I'm tone deaf, but if you think he'd like it, we'll take it."

Mama carried the ocarina (it even had a pretty name) back to the baked goods booth, and Beverly and I headed for the bingo tent to "have a look."

"There's Papa!" He was approaching from the parking lot, a paper cup in his hand from which he drank, Barney Finney in step beside him. Barney said something which caused Papa to laugh hard.

"Papa," I called, running toward him, "guess what I can do! I can swim! Beverly taught me. Isn't that something? I'm getting to be really big now, aren't I?"

Papa laughed and reached into his pocket. Drawing out a handful of coins, he gave me a quarter. "Run along now and play," he said, laughing again.

"Can I go on the tilt-a-whirl now?" Beverly asked.

We bought three tickets for her, and she climbed the stairs to the tilted platform and slid into the capacious semicircular seat. The man who ran the ride lowered the bar in front of Beverly to prevent her flying out when the platform spun dizzily around. Eight or ten others climbed the stairs in twos and threes, and filled other seats in the circle. Beverly was the only person riding alone.

"Hang on tight," I yelled as the man threw the switch and the machine started up, slowly at first, then gaining speed until Beverly was whirling past like a wild creature, hair flying, thin body flinging itself one way, then another, goading the seat to spin more recklessly.

I felt dizzy, and after a bit I retreated, sitting under a cottonwood and looking away, afraid Beverly would propel herself right out of the seat and into a tree. Beverly stayed on for three rides. Maybe from her I could learn to be daring and unafraid.

Close by me, in the shade of the same cottonwood, three men were talking in low voices, punctuating their conversation with dry, humorless laughter. One was Axel Nelson who, with his wife Min, owned and operated the Harvester Arms Hotel. The other two were much younger, maybe eighteen or twenty, and unknown to me. All wore second-best trousers and white shirts, open at the neck, sleeves rolled up to the elbows.

The day I'd sold tickets at Mr. Navarin's Sinclair station, Axel Nelson had bought eight, saying that he'd pass some out to hotel guests stuck in town over the holiday. Maybe the two men with him were such guests.

I would have paid little attention to them except that one of the younger men was smoking, and instead of dropping the cigarette and crushing it with his shoe when he was finished, he tossed the butt carelessly away, hitting my arm. I cried out, not much hurt, but startled. Sparks from the cigarette, like little needles, burned on my forearm, and I put the injured part to my mouth.

"Are you all right?" Axel Nelson called, without bothering to come see for himself.

"Yes."

"Damned fool," he swore softly to the fellow who'd been smoking. "Watch what you're doing."

I was surprised to hear Mr. Nelson talk that way to a guest. The Harvester Arms didn't do a land-office business. The young man must be a regular.

At last descending the stairs of the tilt-a-whirl, Beverly called, "What you want to do now?"

"Swim."

Off we ran. "I wish I knew how to dive," I said.

"You have to be able to swim to the raft if you're going to dive," Beverly pointed out.

For a long time we swam in the waist-high water around the dock. Mama came down to the water to watch. "My goodness," she said, surprised, "you really *can* swim."

After Mama had admired and fussed over us, and legged it back up the path to the baked goods booth, cautioning me to be careful and not drift out too far, Beverly grew bored with swimming in shallow water.

"I'm going to do some belly flops," she informed me and churned away to the raft.

I practiced swimming and lifting my head out of the water to breathe. It was easier now that the sun was falling low and the lake had grown calm. The only waves were the ones I was making. The surface of the water was so placid, it looked as though you ought to be able to sit right down on it. For a long while I stood beside the dock, watching Beverly and the older children on the raft, cavorting like monkeys.

Sometimes they jumped pell-mell into the water, creating a big splash that got the others wet, wetter than they already were, at least. Then the ones who got splashed made a big to-do about it and tossed the splasher into the water when he tried to climb out onto the raft. It looked like more fun than anything I'd ever seen. I wanted to be one of the children who got tossed into the water, who squealed and giggled and pulled themselves out, flinging themselves right in again, splattering water in all directions, like a diving elephant. I wanted to be part of that silliness of flying arms and legs.

If I could get out there, I'd be able to belly flop and splash. I knew I could. Hadn't I already learned how to swim today? The serene stretch of intervening lake beckoned. "You can do it. I'll help. I'm like a table now, that you can crawl across."

Goose pimples covered my arms. I was growing cold, standing still. If I swam, I'd get warm again. I could just *start* to swim toward the raft. If I felt tired, I could turn around and swim back. Beverly would do it. Beverly wouldn't stand around all night like a scared baby, hugging herself and growing cold.

I began inching forward, advancing almost imperceptibly, the water rising on my body until it was beneath my arms. Then, giving a hop to launch myself, I started to swim toward the raft. Right away I knew I had made a mistake. I had waited too late in the day. I was tired all over, especially my arms. And I was cold. Numbed and leaden, my limbs were less and less willing. No matter how hard I drove them, they barely moved. But without a solid place to put my foot down, I couldn't turn around. I didn't know how.

Would anyone notice? There was a Knight, Mr. Beverton, who had spent the day watching out for swimmers in trouble. Would he see me? Would he know I was in trouble? Although it was late and the sun's red rays lay slantwise across the darkening lake, there were still many picnickers in the water.

I wasn't sure I could call out. I had almost no wind left, and I couldn't keep my head out of the water for more than a moment. That moment was needed for gulping air. As my arms and legs grew weaker and my body sank lower into the water, it was more difficult to raise my head high enough to breathe.

If Mr. Beverton noticed me at all, how did I look? Did I look like someone who knew how to swim and was making her way to the raft? Or did I look like a beginner: tired, in trouble, and about to drown?

Wouldn't it be nice if Mr. Beverton got into his rowboat and, without making a fuss, rowed out to me and said, "I know you don't need help, but would you like a ride in my rowboat?"

If a fuss were made, Papa would find out and I'd be in trouble. He'd never let me forget. If it were known that Mr. Beverton had had to save me, Papa would be embarrassed and angry. His embarrassment and anger would be multiplied by the number of people who had seen, who knew that I had nearly drowned. It would be a reflection on him. Some people might even blame him. If I could find the strength to call, I still wouldn't.

But if I drowned, what about my soul? I remembered the long list of sins, mortal and venial, neatly entered in my notebook. My soul was bound for hell. And Papa would inevitably find the notebook. He would discover the sort of child I had been. Even dead, I didn't think I could face that disgrace and humiliation, that betrayal of him.

In the watery blur of my visions, outer and inner, a hand appeared, reaching for me, grasping hold of my hand and tugging mercilessly. Something hard edged slammed into my chest and a raspy, boyish voice exclaimed, "Godsakes."

Eventually, between us, we hauled me onto the raft. I lay there for a long time, only vaguely aware of children squealing, gently rocking the raft with the vigor of their play. A pleasant, drunken inertia overcame me. It wasn't only that I couldn't move, I couldn't think. Over me Beverly's voice declared, scolded, advised, but she might as well have been in Red Berry for all that I could hear.

As I lay nearly passed out on the wet raft, twilight fell. One by one the children swam back to shore. Parents called, loons cried, dim lights winked on in the park. The merry-go-round lights blazed, and its music pounded across the water and seemed to shake the very earth beneath the lake.

"It's getting dark," Beverly pointed out. "Mr. Beverton's gonna call us to come in. We gotta go back."

"I can't."

"Godsakes. You shouldn't've swimmed out here. You just learned today. That was stupid."

"You go," I told her. I was shivering and my teeth chattered so that I could hardly get the words out.

"You want me to send Mr. Beverton out?"

"No! Don't tell Mr. Beverton."

"Why not?"

"Because."

"Godsakes."

"Tell Mama to get me."

"What about your pa?"

"No!"

Beverly belly flopped into the water and was gone. I was too sleepy to watch her. Willingly I slipped down into a profound unconsciousness. I didn't hear Mama's voice or Beverly's. Then Beverly was shaking me hard, impatiently. "Get up. Your ma's here."

With great effort I moved my head, laying my face down on the other cheek. In the purple gloom Mama sat in a rowboat, Mr. Beverton's, her hands at the oars, keeping the boat tightly alongside the raft.

"Get up, Lark," she said in a serious, subdued voice.

Beverly pulled my arm hard enough to loosen it from the socket. As I struggled to my knees, she held onto me. "Sit on the edge of the raft," she told me, "and put your feet in the boat."

I did exactly as I was told because I was not able to form an independent thought. It was all I could do to hang on to Beverly's simple words and interpret them. With Beverly and Mama both helping, I finally lumbered into the rowboat, falling in a heap between two seats.

"Here's your towel," Beverly said, putting it around my shoulders.

Later, I found myself lying in the back of the truck, Beverly in her overalls sitting beside me, bouncing down the road to town. I was feeling very bad. My face was burning and my head throbbed. The rest of me, despite an old blanket, was freezing. My stomach began to rise ominously. I pounded on the cab. The pickup ground to a halt. Hanging my head over the side, I threw up. Mama climbed down out of the cab and came around to the back. She held my head, then wiped my face with the towel. "Done?"

I nodded and lay down. Beverly moved to make room for Mama, and we were on our way again, the truck jouncing and swaying, the night air rushing past.

"Where's Beverly?" I demanded, waking in my crib, dressed in my nightie.

"Papa took her home."

There was a knock at the kitchen door. Mama hurried to answer.

"Well, now, where's the patient?" an avuncular voice inquired. As if Dr. White didn't know. As if he hadn't been here dozens of times. Between October and May, I never had fewer than four bouts of tonsillitis or bronchial pneumonia. "You took her temperature?"

"It's a hundred and four on our thermometer," Mama said. They were in the kitchen. "I can't help thinking about . . . President Roosevelt," Mama stammered. Though I was drifting in and out of sleep, I was sure I'd heard right. President Roosevelt?

"I wouldn't worry," the doctor assured her, seeming to know what Mama meant.

His dry, cool hand was on my brow, my cheek. His fingers were lifting my eyelids. "Open," he said, sticking a thermometer in my mouth. "Keep it under your tongue. Don't talk."

My eyelids were heavy and swollen feeling, so I kept them closed. The bed springs whined as Mama sat on the edge of the bed, waiting.

"She was in the water a long time today," she told the doctor. "Too long. I was busy and not paying enough attention."

"Whatever it is, today didn't cause it," he said.

"I don't know. Hadn't Roosevelt been swimming? So many people seem to get . . . sick after they've been swimming. She got overtired, I know that. She couldn't even sit up on the way home."

After the thermometer came out, Dr. White grasped me under the arms. "Sit up now, Lark, so I can have a look at that throat."

Mama carried the bedside lamp and held it high. Dr. White

took out his little flashlight and his tongue depressor. "How does your throat feel?" he asked.

"Hurts."

"Hmmmm," he murmured, studying my throat, this way and that, asking me to say "ahhhh," directing the light from Mama's lamp more to the left. Then he snapped off his flashlight and felt my glands. Straightening at last, he said, "Looks like the same old problem to me. I'm not going to paint her throat tonight. I'll stop in tomorrow and have another look. Give her an aspirin now and take her temperature again in an hour. If it goes higher, call me."

Mama followed him into the kitchen and saw him to the door, thanking him for coming, relief melting her voice almost to tearfulness. It was as though she credited the doctor with warding off the dreadful contingency having to do with President Roosevelt.

"I was planning to go to my sister's in a couple of weeks," Mama told the doctor. "She's expecting around the first of July, and she's had a hard time. Do you think Lark will be able to go?"

"Hard to say. I'll be able to tell more in a day or two."

But I have to be there when the stork comes. I've got to catch the baby.

14

FOR THE NEXT four or five days, I was flat in my crib. Dr. White returned to paint my throat four days running. I made a scene every time, crying and begging, but I might as well have saved my energy.

For the first week, it was soup and tea and tea and soup, and late in the afternoon, for a treat, a tall glass of Coca-Cola with ice and a straw. The day after the picnic, Beverly came calling. I heard Mama at the door.

"She okay?" Beverly asked.

"She has a bad case of tonsillitis," Mama told her, "but she'll be well in a couple of weeks."

"Godsakes."

"I don't want you to catch Lark's germs," Mama explained, "but maybe you could put your head in and say hello. Don't go near the crib," she warned.

Beverly poked her head in the doorway. "You still sick?"

I nodded. It hurt to talk.

"You know that money you had after you paid for the tilt-a-whirl?"

I couldn't remember.

"It was with your towel. I went down to Lundeen's." From behind her overalls she pulled a big, thick coloring book with a mama and baby giraffe on the cover. "I think it's about California or someplace where there's lions and elephants and alligators." She heaved the book across the room and into the crib.

"It's real nice," I whispered.

"You got Crayolas?"

Again I nodded.

"Then I'll come back and color with you. Don't color all the pages." She turned and was gone.

In the kitchen Mama said, "It was nice of you to bring Lark a present. Would you like some cookies before you leave?"

"Yes."

I heard Mama getting milk from the refrigerator and cookies from the cupboard.

"What's this thing called again?" Beverly asked.

"A typewriter," Mama told her.

"What're you doing with it?"

"Teaching myself to type."

"Why?"

"So I'll be ready for a job when one comes along."

"You any good at it?"

"Not yet. I want to type fifty words a minute. I type about ten right now."

"Think you'll make it?"

"Yes, I will," Mama told her.

Friday morning Mama drove to school to pick up my report card. "Mrs. Rath was sorry to hear that you were sick." Mrs. Rath worked in the office.

"Is my report card good?" I asked from the crib, where I was coloring in the new coloring book.

"It's fine."

I put down the yellow crayon with which I'd been filling in the basking lion on page thirteen. Something must be wrong if the report card was only fine. Was it printing again? That was my bad subject. "Can I see it?" I had to absorb my failure through my own eyes, surrounding it wholly with my senses. If I imprinted it seriously on myself, like a tattoo, next year it would be a reminder to do better.

Mama handed me the card. Everything was A or Excellent, except for printing. The damned printing was A-minus. "Do we have to show Papa?"

"I'll put it away. If he asks, I'll show it to him. If he doesn't, I won't." She slipped it into her top bureau drawer, under the hankies.

Papa thought I was fooling around if my marks weren't straight A's. "If you were doing what you're supposed to, you'd have an A in printing," he'd told me when I brought home my last report card with a B-plus in printing. "I'm going to tell your teacher to phone me up when you're not doing what you're supposed to." I never knew if he told her or not. "I have ways of finding out when you're bad," Papa had told me more than once. "People tell me."

"What people?"

"That's for *me* to know."

Maybe one of Papa's spies would tell him that Mama had picked up my report card. I didn't feel like coloring any more, so I slipped into the garden in the clock and discovered a pair of roller skates beside the dutch door to the cottage. Strapping them on and tightening the clamps with the key, I flew down the tree-shaded street, breezes lifting my hair and whipping my skirt as I clicked along.

Mama brought me supper on a tray again. Vegetable soup and oyster crackers, and tea with honey. I listened carefully to the conversation in the kitchen, but Papa didn't mention my report card. On Sunday, he said, he was going fishing with Mr. Navarin and Mr. Navarin's son, Danny, who drove a truck for Sinclair. He talked about Mr. Navarin's new outboard motor and how he wished he had one like it.

There had been a letter that day from Grandma Erhardt. Grandpa was laid up with a bad cold, she said. She hoped to see us all in

July, if not before. This year's garden was the best they'd ever put in, and she would have plenty of fresh vegetables by the time we came, including "the little yellow tomatoes Lark likes so much."

Mama and Papa discussed a trip to New Frankfurt to visit Grandma and Grandpa. "After I get back from Betty's," Mama said. "With Lark sick now, that's the soonest I can go."

As Papa was preparing to return to the depot office, Mama told him that she was going to call on Mrs. Stillman to give Hilly our present. "Lark will be all right. If she needs anything, she'll knock on the wall."

"What present is that?" Papa wanted to know.

"Lark bought Hilly an ocarina at the white elephant booth."

"What for?"

"Because he marched so well in the parade. Didn't you notice?"

"He didn't pee in his pants or fall down and foam at the mouth," Papa said, laughing.

Before she left, Mama told me, "The potty and toilet paper are under the crib if you need to go before I'm back."

"Can I write a note to Hilly?"

Mama got paper and pencil, and I wrote a letter, with some help in spelling.

Dear Hilly,

How are you? I am fine except I have tonsillitis. You marched very well, and I am proud to know you.

Love,

Lark Ann Browning Erhardt

It was A-plus printing, Mama said.

While Mama was out, I pored over the house plans, comparing each plan with the charming and suitable #127—The Cape Ann. There were always fresh details to be noted in the various designs—a particularly well-placed back hall closet or the clever way in which foundation plantings were used.

I'd got through only one of the booklets when Mama returned. "Hilly missed you," she said, coming into the bedroom to give me a report. "He was hoping you'd come with your book. Mrs. Stillman says he talks about—what was it, something to do with pansies and a garden."

" 'Peggy Among the Pansies.' That's the story I read him."

"Well, evidently it pleased him. And you told him we were going to build a house, and he could come and pick flowers." Mama handed me a picture torn roughly from a magazine. It was an advertisement for face soap. A woman was holding a bouquet of flowers to her face. "Hilly sent that to you."

"Did he like the ocarina?"

"He started playing it right away. Mrs. Stillman had to send him into the bedroom so we could talk."

"I wish we had our house so Hilly could come visit us and pick flowers. When do you think we'll get the house?"

"As soon as I make some money. Then you and I are going to march over to Rayzeen's Lumberyard and order our house."

I pictured Mama and me, hand in hand, marching down dusty Fourth Street, our house plan in Mama's purse.

"We'll step right up to Mr. Rayzeen's desk," she continued, "and drop that house plan in front of him and say, 'We want one of those, as soon as you're able. And it had better be ready before the snow flies.' "

Mama shook down the thermometer. "Open," she said, and put it under my tongue. "A hundred and two," she read, removing it minutes later. "That's too much."

She brought aspirin, a jar of Vicks, and a piece of old, soft flannel. Next she carried in a bowl of cold water with ice cubes in it and set it on her bedside table.

"Do I have to have the cold rag, Mama?" My voice sounded awful, even to me.

This was one of Grandma Browning's cures. First, you slathered a lot of Vicks on the sick person's neck. Then you put an old cloth or towel in the ice water, wringing it out and wrapping it around the patient's neck, over the Vicks. On top of the wet cloth you wound a dry towel and left it on over night. Although I hated it, I had to admit that it did seem to help.

When Mama had me all ready for the night, she began unloading the crib. There were house plan booklets, *Happy Stories for Bedtime*, Crayolas, and the coloring book Beverly had given me. A nagging little thought surfaced.

"How much did that coloring book cost, Mama?"

The price was printed on the upper, right-hand corner of the cover. "Twenty-five cents," she told me.

"Is twenty-five cents a quarter?"

"Yes."

Papa had given me a quarter, and I had bought three rides on the tilt-a-whirl for Beverly, so there hadn't been twenty-five cents with my towel when she found it. Beverly never had any money of her own, so where had she got the extra? She had gone to some trouble to get me that present.

"When we have our house, can Beverly come and stay sometimes?"

"Yes." Mama turned out the light. "No more talking."

After our new house was built, Beverly and Sally could stay over whenever they wanted. The new house would be a place where Sally wouldn't worry and Beverly could have a bath in a real tub. For that matter, *I* could have a bath in a real tub.

≈ 15 ≈

EXCEPT FOR a cough that hung on, as it always did after tonsillitis, I was well by the time Mama and I left for Aunt Betty and Uncle Stan's house on Monday, June 19. Dr. White said I could travel to Morgan Lake, but I couldn't go swimming until the cough was gone.

Now that I knew how to swim, I wanted to be in the water, but there wouldn't be time for swimming in Morgan Lake, even if the cough went away. I would be watching for the stork.

Papa wasn't pleased that Mama and I were going to Aunt Betty's. He hated baching. Seeing us off, he advised Mama, "If Betty's putting on an act, you turn around and come home."

Mama bridled. "Betty doesn't put on acts," she told Papa, and briskly climbed the stairs into the railway car.

We traveled by the eastbound passenger train, leaving Harvester at ten in the morning. Mama stayed up the night before until after two, baking for Papa and hand washing clothes she decided at the last minute she needed. I didn't see how she could find excuses to wear so many outfits in a place like Morgan Lake, but Mama was clothes proud. At home she wore cotton housedresses with frilly collars and pockets and pretty buttons down the front, but when she went out, Mama wore the appropriate costume or what she had decided *ought* to be the appropriate costume. In the entire town of Harvester, maybe in the entire county of St. Bridget, Mama was the only woman who owned jodhpurs and English riding boots. Mama didn't ride, but she liked to wear the pants and boots pheasant hunting. She was an excellent shot, and smart as money in her habit.

Occasionally Papa turned on Mama, ridiculing her for her wardrobe, but he liked to show her off. And Mama was a superior seamstress who stitched up many of her most unusual costumes herself. You couldn't always count on Lundeen's Dry Goods or even the Golden Rule in St. Paul. If you wanted trousers like Marlene Dietrich's, you'd better be clever with a needle.

Mama also sewed for me. She'd made the dress I was wearing, a summery, poppy-sprigged dimity with smocking across the bodice. It was every bit as nice as what you could buy at Dayton's in Minneapolis.

I did not want to muss my dress before Aunt Betty saw it, but I was drowsy. The smell of old, innocent dust in the red, plush upholstery; the strong-soap smell of the white linen antimacassar arranged over the tall seat back; the tipsy sway of the murmuring railway car; and the click-clack-clack, click-clack-clack of iron wheels on iron rails led me through the fuzzy curtains of sleep.

When I woke, my cheek against the upholstery was prickly. I had drooled a little from the corner of my mouth, a circumstance always embarrassing to me as I associated it with old, musty-smelling people like Grandma Browning's Aunt Carrie from Marshalltown, Iowa. I wiped my moist cheek on the inside hem of my dress and picked the tiny grains of sleep from the corners of my eyes.

Mama, sitting opposite, was asleep, her head fallen against the closed window beside her. As with everything she did, Mama slept totally, without qualification or reserve. And sleep took her elsewhere, someplace far away, so that her body was uninhabited. When you shook her, she returned to you from a distant and unfamiliar place—California or Texas, maybe.

My own window was open. Hot, gritty air, laden with the perfume of coal smoke, bathed me—the happy, satisfying smell of going away. Down the aisle came the conductor. "Weed Lake," he called, his voice drawing out the vowels and rising on "Lake." He announced each stop as if it were an important place. I wondered, gazing out at the half dozen dusty, unpaved streets crisscrossing each other, the handful of barefaced little houses gathered indifferently around a general store–post office, what secrets, known to the conductor, colored his cry: "Weeeeed Laaaaake!"

The brakeman and conductor let the door close behind them as they stood in that noisy, shifting bridge between two cars, waiting for the train to grind to a halt.

I had to go to the toilet, but it was too late. We were nearly stopped, and it was forbidden to go to the toilet while the train was in the station. I crossed my legs. Weed Lake was always a long stop because our train, the eastbound train, was put onto a siding to await the arrival of the westbound train.

Two passengers alighted separately, the first a sturdy young man of twenty or so, wearing patched and much-mended gray gabardine trousers and a clean, white shirt, sleeves rolled to the elbow. On his feet were heavy, brown work shoes, rough and cracked across the instep, but cleaned and polished. He was bareheaded, and the tops of his ears were burned the color of leather. His hair was cut very short, so that it would not soon again require barbering, and it was slicked down from a high, side part. Carrying an ancient and darkened crocodile valise as lightly as if it were a lunch pail, he swung down the aisle, ducking his head again and again to dart a glance out the windows, searching out a face expected or hoped for.

Heart skipping, I asked myself, could this be Earl Samson, come to marry the farm girl he'd left behind? But no, I reasoned, Earl would be older.

The second departing passenger was a stocky, heavy-moving woman about Mama's age. Her body seemed unwilling to leave the train. She dragged her feet, forcing them toward the door. Above white anklets and oxfords, her featureless body was clothed in a starched, percale housedress whose once-bright flowers were faded to ghostly memories. Below the sleeves, her arms were muscled and red, and on the wrist of her right hand was a huge knot of flesh, hard as an enormous marble. Women developed these cysts during canning season. Grandma Browning always did. Usually they went away during the winter, when the paring and cutting of fruits and vegetables and the tightening of jar lids abated. Sometimes they didn't.

The woman didn't look out the train windows. She stared ahead, as though what awaited her were fatally familiar.

Would the once-pretty farm girl who had loved Earl Samson have grown old and colorless like this woman? Could this *be* that girl? I wouldn't let myself consider it. I turned my gaze to the brick platform of the approaching depot. The depot agent waited, loose and sweaty, but with a flicker of excitement in his eyes at the oncoming engine. No matter that ten thousand engines had snorted and screeched and groaned to his door. A great steam engine, bearing down, was every time an experience that trembled through you, through your physical parts and through the other parts as well, shaking things up and rearranging them in unforeseeable ways.

Beside the agent a woman waited, a small piece of handsome luggage at her feet. Like the alighting woman, she was about Mama's age, perhaps a little older. But age was surely the only thing about her that was like the weary passenger in the faded housedress.

The woman on the platform wore a lightweight bisque-colored skirt and an ivory shirt of soft, supple fabric, a cameo at her throat. Over her arm was draped a jacket to match the skirt, and on her feet were pale kid pumps.

Her face, classically oval and with that straightforward plainness that is beauty, was lightly made up. Her dark blond hair, collar length, was straight, but turned under at the last minute (like Jean Arthur's in *You Can't Take It With You*, Mama later said). The woman was not attempting to impress anyone, but she succeeded in impressing everyone.

The tired woman in the percale housedress was handed down by the conductor onto the portable step placed on the platform. Blinded by midday brilliance, she raised an arm and held it across her brow, shielding her eyes and acknowledging a dull pain.

The other woman waited for the first to get her bearings, to emerge into the atmosphere of Weed Lake. At length the unwilling one gazed about, and seeing no one there who was hers, headed in the direction of the general store–post office.

The women weren't acquainted. The boarding passenger put her hand in the conductor's and placed a slender foot on the portable step. The agent passed her small bag to the conductor and studied the woman's retreating figure.

Along the dusty street, down which the first woman had disappeared toward the town's meager life, came a hurrying figure, a leggy collection of acute angles and bony corners, wearing a white apron over regular clothes and carrying a carton held out before him—the lunch man.

Back along our route the conductor had taken orders. These were telegraphed ahead to the Weed Lake agent, who carried them downtown to the Depot Diner, where twin tapes of flypaper hung inside the screen door and swayed gently in the breeze. There the agent sat at the counter to enjoy a cup of coffee and doughnut, tiding himself over until after the eastbound and westbound trains met and were sent on their ways. The meeting of the two trains down at the depot was the centerpiece of the town's day, dividing it into halves: before and after.

The conductor was back on the train, distributing box lunches and punching the new passenger's ticket.

"Chicago," he observed, slipping a stub into the clip above her seat. "Live there?"

"Yes." Her voice was soft without being wispy. An Evening in Paris voice.

The conductor had lost his easy palaver. "A big place," he offered.

She said nothing, but laid her suit jacket across the seat facing her.

"Like me to put your bag on the rack?" he asked.

"Please," she answered, again in that peaches-and-cream voice.

The conductor was not at ease, a circumstance I had never witnessed in my hundreds of rides on the train. He couldn't bear to part himself from this beautiful woman. "From around here . . . originally?"

"A farm west of town, originally." There was something odd and disconcerting in her answer. I thought maybe her papa had lost his farm. Where were her papa and mama now? On the county poor farm? The phrase sent waves of cold dread through me. More than once when Papa had gambled, Mama had cried, "You'll put us on the poor farm, Willie." The poor farm was much worse then dismemberment or even death.

Maybe the conductor, too, sensed that he'd struck an unhappy nerve. He changed the subject. "You didn't want a box lunch?"

"No."

"If you need anything, let me know." He moved along the aisle, his hand now and then brushing the top of a seat for balance as the train began stopping and starting in screeching fits, transferring us to a siding to wait for the westbound.

I was absorbed by the woman in the suit. She was sitting kitty-corner across the aisle, facing me. For several minutes she stared out the window. A cluster of scruffy-looking town children, reverential in the presence of the train, on which they had never ridden, had gathered on the platform. The agent shooed them back against the depot lest they fall onto the tracks and get him in trouble with the railroad.

After several minutes of being yanked backward and forward, we were on the siding, up against a grain elevator. If I reached my arm out the window, I thought I could touch the hot, sunbaked wood, but Mama warned, "Keep your arms and head inside if you don't want to lose them."

Leaning toward her confidentially, I whispered, "Mama, there's a beautiful lady sitting over there." I nodded in the direction of the newcomer. "Really, truly beautiful," I emphasized.

Mama didn't trust my assessments of beauty, as I was particularly susceptible to women who wore dramatic makeup in substantial amounts, had their hair dyed unusual hues, and adorned themselves with quantities of large, bright jewelry.

"She lives in Chicago," I went on, "but she used to live here, on a farm west of town. I think her papa lost the farm." I leaned closer. "Do you think she could be the one Earl Samson wanted to marry? I wish I could ask her."

"Well, don't," Mama warned, rising and taking up her purse.

"Where are you going?"

"To comb my hair and freshen my lipstick. I always feel mussed when I've fallen asleep."

"Can I come?"

"No. You can open our lunch. Do you want me to bring you a cup of water?"

"No. I have to go to the bathroom."

She looked at her watch. "We'll only be here a few more minutes."

Mama smoothed the skirt of her dress and took some pains checking in her purse before starting up the aisle toward the rest room. She caught a glimpse of the new passenger out of the corner of her eye as she went through this small ceremony of preparation.

Mama smiled at the woman as she headed toward the rest room. I knew this although her back was to me. Mama's head dipped slightly as she passed the woman's seat, and when Mama had passed, the woman's face was softened and opened up a little.

Mama was not long in the rest room, but she was freshened up and full of life when she came out again. On her return she paused at the woman's seat, laughing a bit and saying something which I didn't catch. The woman smiled and shook her head. Her teeth were small and perfect, like Katherine Albers's.

Teeth were all Katherine and the woman in the pale suit had in common, however. The set of the woman's shoulders, straight and uncompromising, and the almost imperceptible cast of her head, as though she were tuned to an engrossing radio program, spoke more of St. Catherine of Alexandria than Katherine Albers of Harvester.

For knowing all the answers at catechism class one Saturday, Sister Mary Frances had given me a little picture of the martyr, St. Catherine. It was a pretty, colored picture with a gilded deckle edge, and on the back, a list of indulgences I might gain if I prayed to or otherwise observed St. Catherine. I did pray to her a couple of times because I liked her looks as she stood, pleasant and determined, beside the windows in the tower her father had had built for her while he was away. Returning from his trip, he had been furious to discover that Catherine had ordered three windows constructed in the tower, in honor of the Trinity, rather than the two her father had specified. My own feeling was that St. Catherine had ordered three windows because, if you were going to be kept in a tower (as she knew she *was*), the third window's view would be a godsend you would never regret having. I didn't think this interpretation took anything away from Catherine's later martyrdom. I had a special affinity for St. Catherine because of the wheel on which she was to have been broken, and which shattered at her touch, causing her to be the patron saint of wheelwrights and mechanics and, in my opinion, railroads.

"You *talked* to her?" I exclaimed sotto voce when Mama sat down. How did Mama have the courage to go up to a perfect stranger and, just like that, start talking to them? No wonder Mama didn't understand why I hated to sell Knights of Columbus picnic tickets. She wasn't afraid of anything. Maybe Mama should have been a man. Men weren't afraid of anything, either. Except Hilly. Hilly had been afraid the day Mrs. Wheeler saw him running down the cemetery road. But Hilly was a boy, really.

"Of course I talked to her," Mama said quietly, opening our lunch box, which lay on the seat beside her. "I asked if she'd like some of our lunch since we've got so much. It's not hard talking to people if you're thinking about *them*. If you're thinking they might

be hungry, you're not worrying about how embarrassing it is
talking to them. You ought to remember that."

I would try. What Mama said was Common Sense. Mama
placed great value on Common Sense, and I could see for myself
that it made life easier.

"Is she going to have some of our lunch?" I asked. What did a
woman like that eat? Maybe she would think meat loaf sandwiches
were low-class. Would I be afraid to carry her a meat loaf sandwich? If I told myself that she was hungry, and I was doing her a
favor? . . .

"No," Mama answered, "she said she wasn't hungry." The
other train pulled into the station. Pretty soon I'd be able to go to
the bathroom.

Mama went on, "I suggested maybe she'd like a cup of coffee
from the Thermos later. She said that would be nice."

Besides the few words I'd heard her speak to the conductor,
what did a beautiful, high-class woman talk about? Did she talk
about big houses with fancy furniture? Parties where you wore
long dresses? If she talked about things like that, what could Mama
say? Would Mama tell her about our house in the depot with slop
pails under the sink and no toilet? Would she tell her that I still
slept in a crib?

Our train was moving again. We'd switched back to the main
track and were picking up speed on our way out of Weed Lake.
The engine hooted and I stood up.

"I'm going to the bathroom."

Passing the woman's seat, I kept my eyes on the floor. The
heavy rest room door slammed behind me as the train slewed
around a curve. I turned the lock. Carefully smoothing out little
folded pieces of toilet paper from the dispenser and meticulously
laying them all around the toilet seat—and picking up one or two
that fell on the floor—I sat down, greatly relieved, on the noisy
toilet.

The soap powder in the dispenser was strong enough to melt
diamonds, Mama said. I put some in my wet palm and rubbed it
on my hands. It remained gritty and didn't lather, and in a few
seconds my hands felt hot and itchy. Quickly I rinsed them and
dried them on the linen roller towel.

Because I was short, I could only see my face in the mirror, and
I could only see that by standing on tiptoes. My hair was a mess
from sleep. I climbed on the toilet seat. I looked like something

the cat had dragged in. My dress was wrinkled and limp. That was the problem with liking a lot of starch in your dresses: when they got mussed, they were pitiful looking. The woman in the pretty suit probably thought I was an Okie.

I wanted to ask the woman about Earl Samson. I had to know if she was the one, and if she'd heard from him. But she was like a queen, and I was just an almost-low-class child.

I smiled at myself in the mirror, straightened my dress, and smoothed my hair with my hands. How ugly I was when I smiled, all gaping gum where baby teeth had been. I smiled with my mouth closed, and looked like a simpering nincompoop. I didn't have the stuff in me ever to look like that high-class woman.

How on earth had she gotten to be high-class if her papa had lost his farm to debts? What a mystery. Maybe in Chicago she had helped a poor old tramp in the street, who turned out to be a rich millionaire. Father Delias said that every time you helped a stranger, you were entertaining Jesus. Well, maybe Jesus had recognized her goodness and given her a lot of money. Did Jesus ever do that? Did you come home one day and there was a big box of money on the kitchen table? If I watched for the stork and saved Aunt Betty's baby, would Jesus give me money for #127—The Cape Ann?

Mama handed me a meat loaf sandwich and a napkin. "Try not to get that all over."

It was difficult to prevent my eyes from wandering toward the woman across the aisle. Everything about her, from her pale kid pumps and delicate silk stockings to her lips, which looked sculpted, drew my interest and admiration.

Her fingernails were perfectly shaped ovals, the moons left bare, the remainder wearing a nearly clear polish with a slight pinkish cast. The tips of the nails had been whitened underneath with white pencil. The overall effect was elegant understatement.

I wanted to hide my own ragged, torn, unhealthy-looking fingers. I studied them, holding tightly to the white bread.

"Mama, if I don't bite my nails at Aunt Betty's, will you put white pencil under the tips?"

"Sure. And pink polish on top."

"And will you leave the moons white?"

She nodded, pouring coffee from the Thermos, then leaning around the edge of the seat and holding up the cup. The woman smiled without opening her lips. The smile raised the corners of her mouth and the corners of her eyes but, in between, there was a cloud of old sadness which had become a feature of her face, like her nose or cheeks. Was it sadness for Earl Samson?

"Move over, Lark. Next to the window, so the lady can sit down."

She was going to sit next to me. That possibility had not occurred to me. Shyness clamped down on me, sealing my mouth and almost stopping my breath. I edged as far toward the window as possible, pulling my skirt tight around my legs and staring out, unseeing, at the green fields swimming alongside the train.

❦ 16 ❧

I CROSSED my arms over my chest, hiding my hands in my armpits.

"Why are you sitting like that?" Mama asked, pouring a second cup of coffee.

"Because."

Mama shrugged and held the cup for the woman, who was making her way across the aisle. Out of the corner of my eye and without turning away from the window, I could see her form approach.

"Sit there, beside Lark," Mama told her.

"Lark. What a pretty name," the woman said in her calm, rich voice when she was seated and had accepted the cup from Mama.

"What do you say, Lark?" Mama asked pointedly.

I shook my head and turned still further away from them.

"I guess the cat's got Lark's tongue," Mama told the woman.

"It's all right."

For several minutes, as they drank coffee, Mama and the woman spoke very little. Obliquely and with some subtlety, Mama was measuring the woman. The woman submitted as graciously as if she were being fitted for a new dress.

Finally, she spoke. "When I was little, I was so shy, the first week of school I sat with my back to everyone."

"Really?" Mama exclaimed.

The woman nodded. "We lived on a farm, and when I was five, I went to country school. There were eight other pupils, but I was the only one in first grade. I was the only one who couldn't read or print, and I was sure that I never would. Mama told me that if I cried, everyone would laugh, so I didn't cry. But I wouldn't let them look at me. I turned my chair away so that it faced the wall.

"At the end of the first week," she went on, "the teacher told us all to draw a self-portrait. I drew the back of my chair and the back of me sitting on it. The teacher didn't say a word.

"On Monday all the self-portraits were tacked up on the wall, and there they stayed for several weeks. I had a lot of time to see how I looked. I decided I looked like I was in jail. So I turned my chair around."

"Were you still scared of the children?" I asked, surprised to hear my voice.

"Oh my, yes. But it was easier to have them make fun of me than to be in jail."

"You're not shy anymore," I observed.

"Oh, but I *am*. Shy people are shy forever."

"Really?" This was bad news. I considered myself a shy person. I'd thought I'd outgrow it and be like Mama when I was big.

But, if the woman beside me was shy, how was she sitting here, talking to strangers? As if to enlighten me, she continued in her unhurried, gold-colored voice, "There are more shy people than any other kind. In fact, I've concluded that shy is normal."

"How come people don't *seem* shy?"

"They pretend. And they sympathize. Once you understand that almost everyone is as shy as you, and that they're hoping you'll say something first, you begin to feel . . . powerful. You have the power to make them easy."

She sipped her coffee, which must be getting cold. "It makes you feel grown-up."

Could that be true? My notebook was in my little brown pasteboard grip up on the rack. When we got to Aunt Betty's, I'd write down what the woman had told me.

"You live in Chicago?" Mama asked. Mama admired and envied people who lived in cities. Mama knew that if we lived in a city, she could find a job.

"Yes."

"Do you work? I mean, do you have a job?"

"I work at WCH."

"WCH?"

"A radio station."

"You work at a *radio* station?" Mama asked, lowering her voice, as if she'd been given a privileged bit of information. Mama didn't want anyone else to intrude on this thrilling new friendship until she had extracted for herself every possible clue or instruction for success. "What do you do there?"

"I have a fifteen-minute program in the morning and another in the afternoon. I ask women about their work."

"What kind of women? What kind of work?"

"Any kind of women, and any kind of work. Each day I have one woman on with me—a dancer, a housewife, whatever—and I ask her about what she does. You'd be amazed how much wisdom women have that they didn't know they had."

"No, I wouldn't."

"Women at home who listen tell me they learn something they can use almost every day."

"My God, you're lucky," Mama breathed.

"Yes." The woman understood perfectly what Mama meant.

Mama was deeply agitated. Absently she held up the lunch box. "Are you sure you wouldn't like a meat loaf sandwich?"

"No. Thank you."

In a trance, Mama unwrapped the waxed paper from a sandwich and began nibbling. "You lived around here?"

"Five miles west of Weed Lake. Papa lost the farm some years back."

I'd been right. Now, what about Earl Samson? I couldn't ask her. Like Mama, I'd been quelled into quivery quiet. Being on the radio was like being a movie star. I was sitting next to someone who was like a movie star. And she was very beautiful, even up close.

The woman lapsed into silence. Something serious was on her mind. It had been on her mind ever since I saw her on the platform. She had forced herself to come sit with Mama and me. Why?

"Have you been visiting your family?" Mama asked.

"I came for Papa's funeral."

"Oh," Mama said, "I'm sorry. I'm really sorry." She set her sandwich aside and wiped her hands. "Had he been sick long?"

"He shot himself. They found him in the alley behind the house. He'd blown his head off with a twelve-gauge shotgun." She suddenly recalled herself. "I'm sorry," she told Mama. "That was a terrible thing to say in front of your daughter. I'm sorry."

"It's all right," I told her. "I've heard of people doing that before."

"You have?" Mama asked.

"Grandpa Erhardt knew a man whose wife ran off, and he shot his own head off. There were brains all over his back porch, they said, and the dog—"

"Lark, shut up," Mama snapped.

I flushed hotly and sank into the corner of the seat as close to the window as I could get.

"Papa was worried about money. But he wouldn't take any from me," she said, more to herself than to us.

"Is your mother alive?" Mama asked.

"She's gone to live with my sister in Mankato," the woman replied, preoccupied. Her papa's not taking money from her, that would be in her thoughts and dreams a long time.

"It was cruel, his not taking the money," she said.

Mama folded her napkin, smoothing it on her knees. "What did your papa do, after he lost the farm?"

"He tried doing mechanic's work at the implement dealer's, but there wasn't enough work. People around here can't afford to hire to have things fixed. They fix them themselves or stop using them. And Papa would have starved before he went on WPA." Or blown his head off.

Mama nodded. Some thought WPA and the county poor farm were the same. Mama said they weren't. Not by a damn sight, she said. And anyway, it was wickedness to refuse help if you needed it. It was the kind of pride that goes before a fall.

My mama and papa disagreed about WPA. Papa was a good Democrat, but he said WPA was dole for loafers. Mama said if Papa was out of work and the cupboard was empty, his belly would soon make a better Democrat of him.

Grandpa Browning, who was a Republican and a steadfast admirer of Herbert Hoover, said Mama was a freethinker. It sounded like something I'd like to be, but it was clear that Grandpa Browning lumped freethinkers in with Bolsheviks, gypsies, and fairies. I knew nothing about Bolsheviks and little about gypsies, but fairies were our friends, I knew that. It seemed one of those unreasonable perversities of grown-ups that Grandpa Browning should despise fairies.

"Twenty minutes to Morgan Lake," the conductor told Mama as he passed, checking ticket stubs.

We would have to leave the woman behind, all her troubles unsolved. Mama looked concerned, as if she were tempted to stay on the train. But Aunt Betty, who was sick most of the time, was waiting for us in her little house near the edge of town.

Mama leaned forward and put a hand on the woman's. "My name is Arlene Erhardt," she said. "I live in Harvester. I'm going to stay with my sister Betty in Morgan Lake because she's expecting sometime around the first of July. She's sick all the time, and her husband's on the road. But if I can help you, will you call me or drop me a line?"

Mama grabbed her purse and rummaged impatiently in it, coming up with a pencil and a little book of addresses. Tearing an empty page from the book, she wrote her name and address and our telephone number, 139, on it. She tucked the slip of paper into the woman's hand. "I know we're strangers," she said, "but sometimes it's easier that way."

The woman clutched the paper and closed her eyes, as if she might cry. There was a slight heaving of her chest as she breathed, quelling her hysteria, pushing it down, out of her chest, into her belly, where after a while, it would make her sick.

"I have aspirin in my bag," Mama told her. "Would you like some?"

The woman shook her head.

Mama began talking about this and that. Mama was very good at the kind of talking where the other person didn't have to answer or even listen if they didn't want to.

"You need a good vacation," she advised the woman. "Not the kind where you visit your aunt in St. Paul. You need a vacation where everything is new and different, like California. I have a cousin, Lloyd, who went broke farming out in South Dakota. Didn't have a pot to pee in. He packed up his wife, and they drove to southern California. He had to borrow fifty dollars from my mother's Aunt Carrie in Marshalltown, Iowa, in order to make it to Los Angeles."

I hadn't known that Cousin Lloyd and his wife, Marlis, hadn't had a pot to pee in. I guess that there were some things Mama didn't tell me when I was little.

"The first work they found in California was picking oranges. Then Marlis landed a wonderful job as housekeeper for the widow of some big Hollywood producer. The woman said she hired Marlis because she'd never heard of a crook from South Dakota. That's because she'd never heard of *anybody* from South Dakota. Anyway, the woman got Lloyd a job painting sets, and that's what he does to this day. Crazy about it. Has a real talent for it, Marlis says. They are nuts about southern California. On Marlis's day off, they go to the beach. A couple of times they've driven to Mexico.

"They live free in a little cottage back of this woman's house, and they've got an orange tree and a banana tree right outside the door. It's hard to believe, isn't it?

"Next year maybe Lark and I will head out there for a visit. My husband works for the railroad, so we get passes to travel. We go in the summer because I don't like to take Lark out of school. Last summer we went to Corpus Christi, Texas. Normally I wouldn't go that far south in the summer. Hotter than a gangster's pistol down there, but a cousin on my papa's side was terribly sick, looking for work, so Lark and I went down and nursed him for a while and brought him back north.

"This summer we're sticking closer to home. We're on our way to my sister's. She's expecting her first almost any day, and she's had a hard time, so we're going to help out a little. Also, we're saving our money to build a new house. Lark's got one all picked out called the Cape Ann.

"But I started to say, if you haven't been to California, you should buy a ticket and hop on a train. Who knows, a director or—what do they call them?—or a talent agent, might spot you, and the next thing you know, you'd be playing opposite John Barrymore."

A few minutes later, Mama was handing me down my pasteboard grip. She pulled her own suitcase from behind the seat.

"Here, Mrs. Erhardt," the conductor said, "let me help you with that." And he carried the big bag toward the door.

Mama hesitated before the beautiful woman, who was still sitting with us. "Remember," Mama told her, "there's Lark and me. Call if you need us." She lay a hand on the woman's shoulder. "Your papa has gone to a place where he'll find out the reasons for everything. Be happy for him." She patted the shoulder and moved down the aisle. "Come on, Lark," she called behind her.

But I couldn't bear to leave without knowing. What if we never met the woman again? Shifting the grip to my other hand, I bent

toward her cheek, which smelled of delicate, flower-scented perfume. "Did you ever have a man named Earl Samson working on
your papa's farm? Did he write to you?" I asked.

"No," she said. "Is he a friend of yours?"

"Yes. And I hope you meet him sometime."

"Lark," Mama called impatiently.

I hurried along, bumping my grip on the arms of the seats,
turning at the end of the car to smile at the woman. Her beauty
was a light that shone in my mind when I thought of her, and I
thought of her often.

I couldn't leave the depot platform until the train was out of
sight. With our bags beside us, we stood waving, first to the
woman and then to the disappearing train itself.

"What was her name, Mama?"

"I don't know."

"Why didn't you ask her?"

"I didn't want her to feel hounded."

"What do you *think* her name was?"

"Something pretty," Mama said, hefting her heavy bag. "What
do you think it was?"

I considered this for a moment. "Angela."

"Pretty. Angela what?"

"Roosevelt."

☙ 17 ☙

THE DOWNTOWN of Morgan Lake was only a block long. At
the end of that block, the businesses ran out and so did the
sidewalk. Poor Mama, in her high-heeled, white pumps, teetered
precariously on the sharp gravel stones and deep ruts in the street.
Fortunately, Aunt Betty and Uncle Stan's house was just a block
beyond the Skelly station.

The yard was dusty and unwatered, the plantings around the
porch limp and scraggly. Several pieces of newspaper had drifted
into the yard, lodging themselves at the base of the lilac bushes.

The hinges on the screen door were loose when Mama opened it, and she breathed sharply with mild impatience. It was sad to see the little place unattended. Every house, however humble, deserved respect. Of course, Aunt Betty wasn't able, in her condition, and Uncle Stan was on the road during the week. It was up to Mama and me to lend a hand.

The inside door stood open. "Betty?" Mama called. "Betty?" She plunged ahead into the dim living room and set down her suitcase. To the right, off the living room, was the front bedroom, without a door, but with a sickly green, jacquard-weave drape hung on a wooden pole to provide privacy.

Mama pulled the drape aside. "Betty?" I followed. "There you are. Did I wake you?"

Aunt Betty lay, bloated and dusty looking, on the iron bed. Her face, normally merry and quite rosy, even at age thirty, was gray and swollen and lacking animation.

Mama crossed the room and sat on the edge of the bed. The springs squeaked shrilly, and the thin mattress collapsed perilously on that side. Mama paid it no mind, but studied Aunt Betty, gently brushing loose strands of golden red hair back from Betty's face.

"Feeling pretty bad?" Mama asked.

"I'll live," Aunt Betty told her quietly. A weak smile flickered in her eyes, then went out.

"Well, you mustn't worry about anything now. Lark and I are here to look after you and take care of business."

"My business is a mess," Aunt Betty observed dryly, stirring herself a little to glance about the dim room. The living room had merely been dusty and unsure looking, the way rooms were when men were housekeeping. The bedroom was awash in disorder. There were dirty dishes on the table, books and magazines lying everywhere, nighties and underwear discarded in odd places.

"I was going to pick up," Aunt Betty said, "but when I bent over, I started to faint, so I laid on the floor awhile until I could get up again. I asked Stan to pick up in here yesterday, but he was called away in the afternoon." Breathless, she rested a moment. "George Stamp cut off two fingers in a machine, and Stan had to drive him to Mankato."

Aunt Betty laid her fingertips on her lips and closed her eyes. She was feeling nauseated. Mama looked around for a bowl.

"Run to the kitchen, Lark, and get a bowl or pan."

Aunt Betty shook her head slightly and pointed under the bed. Mama pulled up the covers and found an old, chipped, blue mixing bowl. Pulling it out, she told Aunt Betty, "You can't lift this heavy thing. We'll find something lighter and keep it on a chair where it's handy. Why do you have it under the bed?"

"Stan can't look at it anymore. He's been through eight and a half months of vomit."

"Maybe he'll volunteer to have the next baby while you go out on the road."

"At my age, I doubt there'll be a next baby."

"Don't be too sure. This one may turn out to be the first olive out of the bottle."

"I couldn't go through this again."

"Most cases, it's only the first that makes you so sick," Mama said authoritatively.

Suddenly Aunt Betty clutched the heavy blue bowl and her whole body heaved in a great spasm of retching. Mama stood beside the bed and held her sister's forehead. "Go wring out a washcloth and bring it, Lark."

I ran to the bathroom off the kitchen, grabbed the cleanest-looking cloth, and wet it under the cold water tap. I tried not to notice the scummy gray sink and tub, the sour-smelling heap of towels and cloths behind the door, the stained linoleum around the toilet.

Hurrying back to the bedroom, I handed Mama the cloth. Aunt Betty's head lay back against soiled-looking pillows. Her eyes were closed, and she held herself so still, she seemed to be dead. Mama took the cloth and wiped Aunt Betty's face and hands.

"Christ," Mama said, under her breath, "this cloth doesn't smell clean." She turned her head. "Was this the best you could do?"

I nodded.

"Find another bowl or pan," Mama told me.

Off I flew to the kitchen. All Aunt Betty's pans and bowls were dirty. I found a blue spattered-enamel bowl that was somewhat less encrusted than the rest, and scrubbed it out with a tea towel, since the dishcloth had gone sour.

Above the sink a blue spattered-enamel cup hung on a hook. This I scrubbed as well, filling it with cool water from the tap.

"Here, Mama. Here's a bowl and a cup of water so Aunt Betty can rinse her mouth."

Mama handed me the other bowl and told me to empty it in the toilet. It was a good thing I'd had experience carrying vomit bowls last summer in Corpus Christi, or I'd be queasy now. When I'd emptied this one, I looked around the kitchen and tried to think what Mama would do. Filling the tea kettle and a big, battered soup kettle with water, I set them on the stove. I knew how to light our bottled gas stove at home, though Mama never let me. Now I removed a wooden match from the tin container and struck it on the burner, turning the handle for the burner under the tea kettle. The flame jumped up obediently, and I lit the second one.

While the water heated, I pulled the little table that stood by the window, across the room and stacked all of the dirty dishes on it. A big enamel dish pan hung on the wall. Climbing on a chair, I reached it down and put it in the sink. There were no clean dishcloths or tea towels to be found. Well, I would scrub the dishes with a dirty tea towel I'd used before.

Aunt Betty's broom and dustpan were in the cellarway. When I'd swept the linoleum and dumped the sweepings into the waste-basket, the water in the kettles was steaming. Grasping the handle of the tea kettle with a towel, as I'd seen Mama do, I carried it to the sink and half-filled the dishpan, adding cold water from the tap. There was only a little soap left in the Ivory flakes box under the sink. We would have to buy more.

Dish washing was one task at which I felt reasonably expert, and I set to it, singing "The Old Gray Mare," as Mama and I often did at home. I saw myself as a six-year-old good angel, come to put Aunt Betty's life to rights and to save her baby, dropped from the sky by a careless stork.

As I labored in Aunt Betty's kitchen, filling the cupboard with clean dishes, scrubbing the countertop and scraping off the stove, I grew light and happy and, possibly, pretty.

"Lark," Mama called. I dried my hands. "Lark." Wouldn't she be happy when she saw what I'd done? She'd tell me I was a good angel. She was at the kitchen door, the blue bowl in her hands. Her face was closed off with worry.

"Lark, I want you to go next door and ask if we can borrow a change of linen for the bed. Just until I can wash Betty's. Two sheets for a double bed, and two pillow slips." She called after me, "Tell them who you are."

Immediately to the south of Aunt Betty's house was a vacant lot, so I assumed that Mama meant me to go to the house on the north. The yard there looked as though it had come out of a bandbox. Even the dirt around the foundation plantings was clean. The grass was clean. All the edges were neat, and the bushes stood at attention.

The two wooden steps leading to the screened porch were scrubbed, as was the sidewalk before them. The very clapboards on the house appeared to have felt a brush recently.

I glanced down at my dress, in which I'd been cleaning Aunt Betty's kitchen. The best I could do was smooth it with my hands and keep my arms crossed in front of the worst.

My shoes were dusty. I pulled up my socks, patted my disordered hair, and knocked on the frame of the screen door. I could see that the inner door was open. "Hello, Mrs. . . . ?"

As though she'd been shot from a slingshot, the woman of the house appeared at the inner door and, in an instant, at the screen door. She was at least as tidy as her front yard. Her starched housedress whispered as she strided toward me, wearing tie-up black shoes with two-inch heels and a mirror shine. Her figure was tall and well-proportioned, and her dress, which she must have sewn since it was too nicely fitted to have come from the catalog, was contoured to a robust body, firm as new apples. Above the white collar, her neck was ruddy, as was her even-featured but plain face, innocent of makeup. In the ruddiness of their surroundings, her eyes were a jarringly clear and intense blue, like two blue "purey" marbles. Around her head, her hair was pulled tightly into a single, unbroken roll, built over a rat.

Even if I'd been clever at judging such matters, I couldn't have said how old this woman was. She left no clues.

"Yah?" she inquired, the single word German accented. Without giving any indication that I should step in, she opened the screen door.

"Aunt Betty lives next door," I explained, nodding vaguely in that direction. "She's sick. Mama and I have come to help her. Mama said to ask if we could borrow two sheets for a double bed and two pillow slips." I hastened to add, "Just until Mama gets Aunt Betty's washed." The only thing that held me on that doorstep was the certain knowledge that Mama would skin me alive if I returned empty-handed.

"Vell," the woman exclaimed sharply, as if my request were outrageous, but no more than she might have expected. "Vell," she repeated, still more sharply. At length, pointing with her finger to the spot where I stood, she ordered, "You shtay *here*," and turning precisely on her heel, she disappeared into the shadows of the house.

I hugged myself and wished that I were scrubbing the bathtub at Aunt Betty's, even though it had looked disgusting: full of gray soap scum all the way up to the overflow hole, and those little curly hairs that were always turning up in bathtubs even when nobody in the family had short curly hair. Another of life's unsolved mysteries.

While I waited for the German Woman, I studied her screened porch. The painted, gray floor shone, cool and unscarred. A dark home-braided rug covered the area between the screen door and the inner door. It looked thick and cozy. Two rockers, one at either end of the little porch, faced the street. Beside one was a basket of knitting; beside the other a smoking stand, nary an ash sullying the ashtray. The room was otherwise bare. Not a book or magazine, coffee cup or bobby pin softened its perfection.

As I gaped through the screen, hands cupped around my eyes, the German Woman materialized, startling and shaming me. It was not polite to pay too close attention to other people's possessions. I took the liberty of opening the screen, since the woman's hands were full.

"Schtay here," she commanded.

Instantly I let go of the door and it slammed in her face. Would she decide to withhold her bed linens? I would then have to repeat all this at another neighbor's.

"I didn't mean to slam the door."

"Ffor heffen's sake, don't chust shtand dere. Open za door."

I opened it and took the sheets and pillow slips. "Thank you very much."

"You are not to *keep* zem," she called as I hurried away as fast as my legs would carry me without actually breaking into a run.

Mama, standing on the porch step at Aunt Betty's, huffed, "I vouldn't dream of keeping zem." In return for the linens, she handed me a shopping list and her coin purse, stuffed with small bills.

"Give the list to the people at the store and let them make up the order. Be sure to get a receipt so I can check their arithmetic."

I didn't need to ask which store. There was only one that sold groceries.

The Main Street of Morgan Lake was bright and quiet. A

number of its little frame buildings were boarded up. Two cars stood at the curb, both held together with baling wire and rags, one in front of the tavern, and one in front of the creamery.

I passed the Skelly station. Across the street, in front of the implement dealer, a breeze gathered a dust devil unto itself. Further along, on that same side, was the creamery. There were vacant spaces between several of the buildings. No one maintained them, so they were filled with mustard and dandelion and foxtail and cast off lard pails and broken furniture. Mama said it was a disgrace. No one would come to live in a place where Main Street was allowed to go to seed. They'd take one look and stay right on the train. Mama saw every village as a potentially thriving city, if only people would pull up their socks and get to work.

I was of two minds about that. It would be pleasant if someone mowed the vacant lots, put out petunias, and installed a bench or two. But on the other hand, there was minor adventure and even mystery to be found in the untamed spaces.

In such a scraggly space as these, beside the hotel in New Frankfurt, where Grandpa and Grandma Erhardt lived, I'd found a pocket watch which didn't keep time and a pair of silk panties with deep lace trim on the legs. Mama had washed the panties and kept them for herself, but she'd let me keep the watch after we'd made inquiries at the hotel and I'd gone house to house in the village to inquire if it belonged to anyone.

Inside the case was engraved, "To Bub, From Mama. 1923." Like my darling Earl Samson, Bub became a long-lost friend with whom I would one day be joyfully reunited. Mama kept the watch for me, in the drawer with the letter from Earl Samson. I didn't yet trust myself not to lose them if they were in my care. And they were my most important possessions.

The letters on the window said Boomer's Tavern. As I passed, I looked in. The man behind the bar was probably Mr. Boomer. By a table a woman stood, one hand on her hip, the other holding a rag. Mrs. Boomer. Another man and woman sat at the table, drinking glasses of beer or, at any rate, sitting in front of them, passing time.

I loved taverns. I loved hotels, too, but I loved taverns more. When I told her that, Mama laughed and said I should keep it to myself. One of the best things about a little place like Morgan Lake or New Frankfurt was that, there being no restaurant or candy store, the saloon usually served sandwiches and sold ice cream and candy. And for this reason, children were allowed, by custom if not by law, to go inside—if their parents didn't forbid it.

Mama was not keen to have me spending all my time in the tavern, which I might have done, but stopping for an ice cream cone now and then or accompanying Grandpa Erhardt while he visited over a beer was all right. Movies were a rare and considerable treat, but not so considerable as sitting in a tavern.

For one thing, everybody made a fuss over a little girl in a tavern, admiring her dress and her hair bow and the color of her eyes, and remarking how much she resembled some distant and beautiful cousin they remembered who used to live hereabouts.

For another, the smell of beer was more delicious than the smell of pumpkin pie or Mama's perfume. In my mind it was inextricably tied up with people laughing together and sharing stories, each of which began, "D'ya remember the time . . . ?" "D'ya remember the time that Mick O'Neill surprised the skunk in the outhouse?" Or "D'ya remember the time that Harriet Good ran back into the burning house to get her teeth? Damned near perished of vanity."

On Saturday night the town was richly populated with colorful citizens who came back in story. The past and present were woven together as men and women, many of them long ago passed on, showed up to drive their new roadster into the chicken coop or to lose their bloomers on the dance floor over at the hotel.

And since many of the tavern stories concerned folks now lying beneath the sweet grass in St. Ambrose Cemetery outside Morgan Lake, or St. Leo's Cemetery on the edge of New Frankfurt, what was more natural than that ghosts should creep into the recitations?

It was because of the ghosts, more than anything, that Mama was reluctant to have me in the tavern. Grandpa Erhardt knew more ghost stories than anyone, and he believed in common ghosts as devoutly as he believed in the *Holy* Ghost. Ghosts were a simple fact of life. Or death. What was the fuss about?

Mama blamed the Old Country for Grandpa Erhardt's belief. He'd come to America when he was twelve. What you learned before twelve, you never put aside, Mama said. It was easier for her to blame the Old Country than to blame Grandpa personally. She dearly loved her father-in-law and couldn't bear to fault him. All the same, she didn't like me listening to ghost stories.

Grandpa believed in ghosts. Mama didn't, or said she didn't. I'd never seen a ghost, but there was in my nature a chink of willingness to suffer. Ghosts and bogeymen sidled in to plague me at odd moments, occasionally in the brightness of a summer afternoon.

Suddenly one of Grandpa's ghosts, the ghost of Lena Bauer, streaked, screaming, across my mind. I halted in my steps. It had been a cold December, without enough snow to cover the dead ground, when Lena bolted, a ball of fire, out of her kitchen into the barnyard, heading toward the watering trough beside the windmill. Her hair and dress and apron and woolen stockings, and her face and arms were in flames. Lena collapsed at the foot of the windmill, less than a yard from the water.

Sometimes on clear, cold winter nights, Lena dashed again to her death, a ball of fire consuming itself below the windmill. Old Al, long dead now himself, was supposed to have fixed—what was it, a kerosene stove?—that he had neglected, as he neglected so many things. But Lena, who never neglected anything, did not neglect to damn Al with her fiery ghost on winter nights, bringing light without warmth to the sore and dying barnyard.

I sat down at the edge of the sidewalk, there being no true curb on Main Street in Morgan Lake. I was as cold as the inside of a cistern, and a beading of perspiration lay on my upper lip. "Hail Mary, full of grace. Hallowed be thy name," I prayed, as Father Delias had advised children to do when they were in trouble or afraid.

On the movie screen of my mind, I sent the Blessed Virgin into the barnyard to purge the ghost of Lena Bauer. Out from the barn, where her baby lay in the manger, floated the Virgin, beautiful, ethereal, spectral. Lena Bauer waited, like captured lightning, beneath the windmill, her face a horrid grimace of pain and wrath.

Slowly the Virgin advanced. "Blessed art Thou amongst women, And blessed is the fruit of Thy womb, Jesus." The light fabric covering Her head fluttered and billowed as She approached. Lena stood her ground, as though the Virgin Herself could not move the force of such pain.

My heart pounded high in my chest. My hands gripped Mama's coin purse as if it alone anchored me to Main Street.

Mother Mary was quite near Lena now. A soft, white hand was outstretched toward the flaming wraith. "Holy Mary, Mother of God, pray for us sinners . . ." Closer, closer. Both white hands were raised to Lena. ". . . now and at the hour of our death."

The Virgin's arms embraced Lena. Slowly, as if simultaneously recalling something, their heads turned toward me. But in place of the Virgin's pale, beautiful face, a terrible, grinning skull opened its fleshless jaws and laughed. The two specters, arms around each other, burned holes of laughing hatred into me.

Then I fell asleep, right on Main Street. Sound asleep. I hit my head on the sidewalk, but I didn't know that until later, when I found the raised blue bump on my temple.

"Lark Ann Erhardt," Mama's voice, hissing angry, summoned me. I struggled through a dark tunnel, trying to reach her. A hand sharply gripped my shoulder, shaking me. I heard myself scream.

"What on earth's the matter with you, young lady? Stop that this minute. Wake up, now."

Through the tunnel I crawled, at length spying blue sky, a perfect, sunset blue, the color of the Virgin's scarf. Mama's face, looking not at all like the Virgin's, scowled at me, angry and worried.

"Do you know what time it is?" she demanded.

I moved my head slowly to indicate that I did not. Pain sprang into my temple.

"It's nearly five, for God's sake. I've been waiting and waiting. You left Aunt Betty's at three o'clock," she said, pointing to her watch, "and you haven't even been to the store yet." She hauled me roughly to my feet. "Look at your dress."

Five o'clock in the afternoon? And what day? Could it still be Monday? What a long day it had been, without yet being over. I stumbled up the wooden steps into Esterly's Groceries and General Merchandise, Mama pulling me along like an untrained puppy. I'd been in Esterly's before, when we visited Aunt Betty and Uncle Stan. Dry goods were on the right, groceries on the left, the post office along the back wall. The place smelled of onions and pickles and raw meat and new overalls and leather work gloves.

Still groggy, I stood leaning against the cool meat case while Mama, relieving me of the shopping list and coin purse, did business with Mr. Esterly.

"My sister, Mrs. Weller, is down in bed, so I'm looking after things for a few days," she confided. "Do you deliver?"

"If you can wait till we close, I do deliver, some. That'd be after six o'clock, you understand."

"That's fine. I'll take what we need right now, and you can deliver the rest." She recalled my dazed presence. "My little girl,

Lark—you've met her, I think—will be coming in for mail and odds and ends. Do the Wellers have an account here?"

There was a pause, the quality of which caused me to prick up my ears, like a dog listening to a sound too high for people to hear.

"Uh, no, no they don't." Mr. Esterly wiped his hands on his apron, adjusted the pencil behind his ear, and looked out the front window as if there were something of interest in the street, which of course there wasn't. Nothing and no one was in the street.

So Uncle Stan didn't pay his bills. At least not his grocery bills. And if you didn't pay your grocery bills, you probably didn't pay others. A swirling, churning, sick feeling came over me. Poverty made me feel weak, as if I were coming down with an awful, debilitating, communicable disease—the disease of being without money. Instead of going to the hospital, you went to the poor farm. The difference was, you never got well at the poor farm.

The pennilessness of the hoboes in the hobo jungle didn't have quite the same effect on me. I felt very sorry for them, but they didn't seem to require much: a meal, a pair of cast-off trousers, a dime. But people in houses had bills. Mama had explained all this to me when I asked why we couldn't charge a new tricycle and a bride doll and a doll house. I hadn't understood that you had to *pay* for things you charged.

How did Aunt Betty and Uncle Stan live if they couldn't pay their bills? I turned, laying my temple against the meat case. The news of Uncle Stan and Aunt Betty's poverty filled me with unnamed fears, which I would now begin to identify. This would not rob them of their power, but it would lend some order to them.

First, how were they going to feed the baby if Mr. Esterly wouldn't let them charge? Had they been paying their rent? Since we paid no rent in the depot, I was always curious about other people. "How much would you pay for that size house, Mama?" I would ask, estimating whether we might get ourselves into a house in this way. Mama had told me that Uncle Stan and Aunt Betty paid fifteen dollars a month. That was a lot of money, but an amount I thought maybe we could manage. But Papa had a steady paycheck. Uncle Stan worked on commission.

When Mama had considered going to work for the Spenser Corset Company, she'd explained that commission was the money you got from the Spenser Company when you actually sold a corset or girdle or brassiere. The Spenser Corset Company wasn't going to pay you anything if you weren't making them any money. This didn't seem altogether fair, since you probably worked just as hard when the customer didn't buy a corset as when they did, but Mama said the Spenser people would go broke if they paid sales-ladies for not selling corsets.

If Uncle Stan wasn't making any commission, there was the baby to worry about, and the rent. And what about Uncle Stan's car, which he drove all over southern Minnesota? Was that paid for? It was so old, surely it must be paid up. Our Oldsmobile wasn't paid up, but that was almost brand new.

"Yes," Mama answered, as many thoughts or more raced through her mind as were racing through mine, "that's all right. I'll be paying cash." She smoothed the wadded list I'd held in my hand. "Can you read this, Mr. Esterly? It's smudged."

The balding, round-faced grocer bent over the piece of paper lying on the counter. "Milk. Eggs. Chicken," he began reading. "Yes, I can read this," he murmured, relieved to be finished talking about Aunt Betty and Uncle Stan's canceled credit.

Before we left the store, Mama said to Mr. Esterly, "I wonder if I could find out how much the Wellers owe you?"

"Oh, dear," he said, at a loss. "Well, it's just . . . the accounts receivable are . . . confidential."

"Of course they are," Mama concurred. "I just thought maybe I could talk to Mrs. Weller's family. We're sisters, you know. Our mama and papa might be able to help."

Mr. Esterly was torn. At length he reached for a five-by-seven card file on the counter beside the cash register. From the W's he pulled a card labeled "Weller." He said nothing, but held it for Mama to read the total.

"Thank you," Mama said. "I'll see what I can do."

The grocer hurried to the door, holding it for Mama and me as we left. "I'll bring the other groceries on my way home," he assured Mama deferentially. "I'll be closing soon now. Six. I close at six."

"It's not his fault," Mama observed as we stepped along Main Street, past Boomer's Tavern, where the same couple sat, over the same beers perhaps. "Mr. Esterly has to pay his bills, too."

But Mama was worried, so worried she forgot to bring up the matter of my falling asleep on Main Street and her leaving Aunt Betty alone to come find me. How much did Aunt Betty and

Uncle Stan owe the grocer? And how could Grandma and Grandpa
Browning possibly pay the bill when they themselves were just
scraping by? There were so many things to worry about! I was
going to have to make a list and number them.

☙ 18 ☙

BUT WHEN Mama tucked me in on the living room couch
where I was to sleep, instead of reviewing my list of worries and
sorting them out, I lay gazing out the window at the pinkish sky
over the German Woman's roof and listening to the low voices of
Mama and Aunt Betty, beyond the curtained bedroom doorway.
There they sat in the half-light, by turns upsetting and reassuring
each other, as sisters do.

"Why didn't you tell me Stan wasn't making anything?" Mama
asked in a kindly voice.

"He doesn't want anyone to know," Aunt Betty replied. "He's
going crazy trying to find money."

"How does he pay for his room when he's traveling?"

"He stays with relations. If there's no one, he sleeps in the car."

"Umph," Mama grunted, moved by this information. "He's
never stayed with us."

"He's afraid you'll think he's a bum."

"That hurts me."

"He's afraid of you," Aunt Betty admitted, and giggled.

Uncle Stan afraid of Mama? That was one of the most interesting ideas I'd ever heard. Why would he be afraid? She'd never hit
him with a ketchup bottle, or even raised her voice to him that I
was aware.

"Meantime, you're laying here starving," Mama said.

"Don't be silly," Aunt Betty responded impatiently. "I haven't
been able to keep anything down. You know that."

Later Mama said, "I'm teaching myself to type."

"Why?"

Now it was Mama's turn to be impatient. "So I'll be able to get
a job."

"A job? Where would you get a job?"

"I don't know yet, but I'm going to be ready. When I can type fast enough, I'm going to take the civil service test."

"But are there any civil service jobs in Harvester?"

"Only at the post office."

"Aren't those jobs taken?"

"You never know what's going to happen."

It unsettled me when Mama talked that way. Our future was settled. We were going to build #127—The Cape Ann. Papa was going to become the depot agent when Art Bigelow retired. And Mama was going to have a wonderful garden with a strawberry patch and raspberry bushes and flowers all the way around.

The plush of the couch was stiff and prickly. There had been no clean sheet to put under me. But, despite the minor discomfort, I fell asleep about eight o'clock.

In my dreams that night, I was riding the train again, and Angela Roosevelt was seated kitty-corner down the aisle from me. Staring out the window at the passing farms, she wept for them. Quietly and intensely, but without seeming aware of the tears, she sat straight against the tall seat and wept.

I wanted to go to her and comfort her. I wanted to tell her that Earl Samson remembered her and still loved her, for I was certain in my dream that she *did* know Earl and that some shyness and deep regard for his privacy had been at the bottom of her denial.

At last she rose and moved away up the aisle, her back to me. I thought she was going to get a paper cup of water, but she passed the fountain and reached the heavy door. Bracing herself, she pulled it open and stepped out of the car.

Released from my paralyzing bashfulness, I jumped up and ran after her. Tugging open the difficult door, I discovered beyond it the blank face of a boxcar. Angela was gone, disappeared into thin air.

Waking in the dark, shivering, I searched for the old, velveteen crazy quilt Mama had tossed over me. In the warm early evening, I had thrown it off. Now I was chilly.

Arranging it over me, I decided that someday I would look up Angela Roosevelt in Chicago. I hoped to find her married to Earl Samson. Was there any way I could help bring that about? Could I put a sign down in the jungle, telling everyone who came there that I needed help finding Earl Samson? Would Mama let me do that?

When I found Earl Samson, I would tell him that his love had moved to Chicago and was on the radio there. It shouldn't be too difficult for him to find her. Everyone in Chicago must listen to her program.

A dim light shone from the kitchen door, beyond the little dining room: Mama had left the bathroom light burning so I could find my way. I needed to go, but I lay there for a long time, putting it off, not wanting to cross the dark living room and dining room. When I could hold it no longer, and knowing Mama would spank me if I wet Aunt Betty's couch, I threw off the cover and scurried as fast as I could, looking neither left nor right, but heading straight for the light.

In the bathroom, I hooked the door and clambered up onto the toilet. Cold against my thighs, the seat momentarily froze the contents of my bladder. After a minute, it thawed, and I relieved myself and sprinted back to the couch, noting from the corner of my eye that the door to the tiny bedroom off the kitchen was closed. No light shone beneath it. Mama was asleep on the cot. It must be very late.

Back on the prickly couch, under the crazy quilt, I hugged myself and studied the night sky outside. If Papa was still awake, he could see the same stars I saw. Wasn't that unbelievable after a hundred-mile trip? But it was true.

I'm looking real hard at the big star just above the chimney of the German Woman's house. Are you looking at that same star, Papa?

Then I noticed that lights were glowing behind the drawn shades in a back room in the German Woman's house. She must be reading, or maybe she was braiding rugs. Her windows were open. The nearest lighted one was maybe thirty-five feet from where I lay. The night was utterly silent. I heard the German Woman cough behind her shade. I fell asleep.

When I woke at dawn, her shades were already up. She was a go-getter like Mama. In the kitchen and back hall, I heard Mama's feet on the linoleum: tap, tap, tap to the kitchen sink to run water into kettles, which pinged as they struck the lip of the sink; tap, tap, tap to the stove to set the kettles to heating; tap, tap to the back hall, where she was scrubbing and rinsing laundry in a pair of galvanized tubs.

At home we had no place to do wash, so Mr. Borman came once a week and picked it up and brought it back later, except for items like my dresses, which Mama didn't trust to Mrs. Borman.

Those Mama did by hand in a basin. "I can't wait till we have a place of our own, with a basement where I can do my own laundry. Think of it, Lark. We'll have a Maytag like Grandma Browning's, and lots of lines so we can hang the laundry in the basement in bad weather."

Because she was always putting up indigent cousins from Sioux City or Fargo or Helena, and sometimes taking paid boarders as well, Grandma Browning had insisted on a Maytag. She spoke of it as her one extravagance. In addition to the Maytag, she had *two* rinse tubs, the first filled with hot water, the second with cold.

Aunt Betty didn't have a Maytag. She had two galvanized tubs on a base that rolled around so she could bring the whole business into the kitchen in the winter. One tub was the washtub, and in this was standing a rippling washboard, on which Mama was scrubbing sheets. The other tub was the rinse tub, which must continually be emptied and refilled as the water grew soapy.

A hand-cranked wringer was attached first to the washtub, so most of the soapy water might be wrung from the laundry before it went into the rinse, and then to the rinse rub, so the clothes weren't dripping wet when they dropped into the laundry basket.

Wrapping myself in the crazy quilt like an Indian chief, I hobbled in short steps to the kitchen, arranging myself on a chair at the table by the window. I saw Mama in the backyard, wiping the wire clotheslines with a rag dipped in gasoline, removing any grime or rust that might have collected on them. When she had cleaned them all, she tossed the rag in the old, oil-drum incinerator out by the alley.

Garbed in one of her fancier housedresses, a red one with white marguerite daisies sprinkled on it, Mama began hanging sheets on the line. A bag of clothespins swung ahead of her as she worked. She filled her pocket with pins, and when she'd used them all, she refilled it from the bag. In the heavily dewed grass, her high-heeled pumps were getting wet. Smoothing the last sheet, pulling wrinkles from it, she returned to the house, tap-tap-tapping across the back hall.

"You look pretty, Mama. How come you're wearing high heels to do the wash?"

"I want the neighbors to understand that the Browning sisters are not Okies or down-and-outers. We're from good family." She flounced across the kitchen, removed a kettle from the stove, carried it to the back hall, and dumped its contents into the washtub. Pausing in the doorway, she asked, "Did you know, Lark, that my great-great-grandmother—your great-great-great-grandmother—was a lady-in-waiting in the English Court?"

"What's a lady-in-waiting?"

"I'm not sure, but it's important."

"What's an English Court?"

"It's where the king and queen live."

"How do you know she was?"

"My grandmother told me. Granny was very fine herself, although they'd lost their money. You never knew her. She died before you were born. She had beautiful manners."

What had brought all this on? I wondered. Aunt Betty and Uncle Stan must be in very dire straits, indeed. Setting the empty kettle down beside the sink, Mama began preparing a big, gray enamel coffee pot for the stove. Soon it was percolating, filling the little house with its perfume. Sunlight streamed across the faded linoleum, and Mama made me hot milk toast with a dash of cinnamon and sugar on top.

Waiting for lines full of wash to dry, Mama dusted, swept, and ran the carpet sweeper. Then, as the laundry reached damp-dry, she hauled it in by the basket load and set up the old, wooden ironing board in the kitchen by the stove. Now the house smelled of clean laundry and ironing.

When I wasn't carrying trays to Aunt Betty or straightening up the kitchen drawers, Mama had me drawing water from the cistern beside the house and watering the scraggly, dry plantings around the front porch.

"And when you've given them all a good watering, you can pull out those weeds around the flowers."

As I worked, I kept an eye on the German Woman's house, hoping she wouldn't appear. I wasn't eager to cross paths with her. About one-thirty she emerged from the inner door, looked to see what I was at, said nothing, and settled herself in her rocker on the screened porch. Knitting needles commenced to click, but I could feel her eyes on me. I worked hard, afraid she might criticize if I left a crabgrass root in the ground.

Before Mama came to fetch me for my nap, the German Woman called to me, "Ven you haf finished der, you can come ofer here unt do mine."

I didn't know what to say, so I said nothing. Did she mean what she said? Did she want me to come over and work in her yard? I didn't want to find myself on the other side of the raspberry bushes encircling her backyard. Not ever. I pretended I hadn't heard.

On my previous visits to Aunt Betty's, there'd been no German Woman next door. A very old, bent-over woman with an ear trumpet had lived there. What had become of her? I wondered. She had skated around on ancient leather carpet slippers, but she hadn't been rude or scary. She didn't remind me of the witch in "Hansel and Gretel."

After my nap, I was dispatched, protesting, to the German Woman's, my arms loaded with meticulously ironed bed linens and, on top of these, wrapped neatly in waxed paper, a large slice of Mama's famous spice cake with penuche frosting, which she had baked while I weeded.

"Tell her thank you very much," Mama instructed me tersely.

I would rather have weeded for three days then return the sheets and pillow slips to the German Woman. But Mama was convinced that these compulsory social experiences were building my character and breaking down my shyness.

Now, here I was, smelling of Swan soap, dressed in my favorite sunsuit—a green-and-white-striped seersucker—and wearing fresh white anklets and my shoes that Sheila Grubb's dog had gotten his sharp little teeth into, trudging down the street to the house next door. I would never have dreamed of walking on the German Woman's grass, and there was no sidewalk running between the two houses.

There was a sidewalk leading from Aunt Betty's porch to the street and another from the street to the German Woman's door, where I found myself all too quickly. She was not seated in her rocker as earlier. I couldn't let go of the linens to knock, so I called, putting my face to the screen, "Hello. I've brought your sheets. Hello. Are you home?"

The house was so still, I could hear a clock ticking in the living room or what was presumably the living room. Again I called, "I've brought your sheets," adding, "and a piece of spice cake." My anxious heart and the ticking clock were all I could hear.

Then suddenly, soundlessly, she loomed in the inner doorway, tall and displeased, and if she were a child, I would have said, sly. What was there about me to which she had taken such an instant dislike? Why did she not want me at her door? I'd think she'd be happy to have her linens quickly returned and smelling so fine.

Unhooking the screen, she relieved me of my burden, informing

me, "Dey are folted wrong. I vill haff to folt dem again." She
pressed her lips tightly together, rehooked the screen, and turned
immediately away.

"Thank you very much," I called after her. No response but the
ticking clock. I stood rooted to the step. Finally I fled, dashing
headlong. In the dusty street, I stopped and swung around, panting and staring at the small house, sheathed in shining white
clapboard but looking dark and full of warning.

❧ 19 ❧

WEDNESDAY MORNING, early, Aunt Betty was very sick. I
woke to see Mama hurrying to her room with a wet towel and a
clean bowl.

"Stay in bed," she told me.

I sat up, pulling the quilt around me. The sun was over the
horizon, and the German Woman was out, moving slowly around
her yard, plucking a dead blossom, straightening a stake, rooting
up a dandelion, and, perhaps I imagined it, listening. Her tightly
coiffed head seemed to incline slightly in our direction.

"I'm going to call the doctor," Mama told her older sister.

"No," Aunt Betty cried, beyond the green drape. "No. I won't
have him."

"Because of the cost? Don't be a fool."

"I won't see him," my aunt screamed.

"What if this is uremic poisoning? You could die," Mama
warned her.

"I won't see the doctor! I don't have uremic poisoning. You get
those ideas from Mama. A woman gets the least sick, Mama cries,
'uremic poisoning.' I'll be fine. This happens all the time, and I'm
not dead yet."

"I'll pay for the doctor."

"No, no, no, no," Aunt Betty screamed hysterically, and threw
something which hit the wall, causing me to jump. Then she
began to retch again, but there was nothing left to come up, and

she simply made painful choking sounds. "If you call the doctor," she sobbed, "you'll never be my sister again."

What *was* the matter with Aunt Betty? I wondered. She'd gotten very fat, it was true, but that didn't make people sick, did it? When the stork brought the baby, how would she be able to take care of it if she didn't get well? Mama had said the stork would be bringing the baby any day. How did Mama know that? Who had told her?

If Uncle Stan wasn't making any money and they were practically starving, would they let Mama and me take the baby home and keep it until times got better? What was to become of them? Would they go to live on the poor farm? Surely they wouldn't take the baby there.

Throwing off the quilt, I dressed myself in my sunsuit and pulled on my shoes and socks. The house still smelled of clean laundry, much of which sat in ironed, folded piles on the dining room table. In the kitchen, I buttered a slice of bread and carried it out to the back step. The step was wet with dew, but I sat down anyway.

If the stork came from the southeast, as he had in my dream, this would be a good place to watch for him. I watched the sky until my neck ached and the sun lay on top of the garage roof. Then I examined my hands, discovering with a pleasant shock that this was the third day in which I had not bitten my nails.

"Mama," I called, racing through the house and into Aunt Betty's bedroom, "Mama, my nails are growing."

"Lark, get out of here," Mama said, wringing out a washcloth. Aunt Betty had removed her nightie, and Mama was helping her wash herself. I stood staring at my aunt, who sat with her legs hanging over the edge of the bed.

There certainly was something wrong with her. Her stomach looked as if she'd swallowed a canning kettle. I'd never seen anything so grotesque. The belly button was ready to pop right off and fall on the floor. What if Aunt Betty exploded? I agreed with Mama, we ought to call the doctor right away and find out what could be done. Maybe Aunt Betty needed to pass wind, as Grandma Browning would say. It was hardly any wonder she felt sick to her stomach all the time.

I backed out of the room and dropped onto the sofa, pulling the quilt over me. I could hear them in there.

"Have you told the folks that you don't have any money?"

"No. And don't you dare tell them."

"Do you know how mad Mama would be if she found out how you're living?"

"My loyalty's to my husband," Aunt Betty replied stiffly.

"What kind of husband expects his pregnant wife to starve rather than ask her family for help?"

"Stan never told me I couldn't ask. But it would kill him. You don't understand. Wait'll you see him, Arlene. He's not the man he was when he was working for salary."

Uncle Stan used to be a bookkeeper over in Mankato, at a big implement dealer there. He drove back and forth to work from Morgan Lake because it was cheaper living in the smaller town. But that dealer couldn't afford to keep him on salary, so now he was on the road.

A sweet-natured man, Uncle Stan had a smiling, childlike way about him that made you want to protect him. I understood Aunt Betty's silence.

But Mama sounded disgusted. "You've got a loyalty to this baby now, and don't you forget it."

"I wish I could be hard like you, Arlene."

I could hear the intake of Mama's breath all the way in the living room. "That is the meanest thing you ever said to me, Betty."

"I'm sorry."

"If you were sorry, you wouldn't say it. You're jealous. And you say awful things to get back at me."

"Jealous of *what?*" Aunt Betty asked sarcastically.

"Jealous that I have enough money to come here and work till I drop and put groceries in your empty cupboard."

"You're the one who's jealous. You never could stand it that Stan and I were happily married. You'd like everybody to be as miserable as you are. Since you think you're doing me a big favor, take your damned groceries and go home. I'm not going to eat them. I'd rather starve." Aunt Betty was screaming now.

I couldn't bear to listen. I saw that I was biting the nail on my right index finger, and I started to cry. Running from the house, I heard Mama scream, "When you've got a baby that's starving, too, tell me how much you hate my charity."

I ran out to the street, but I could still hear them, so I started downtown, past the German Woman's house. She was nowhere in sight. Although Aunt Betty's bedroom was on the opposite side of the house from the German Woman, that stern, listening neighbor could hear every word if she half tried. A spasm of shame shook me, and I broke into a full sprint. It was too awful to think that she might be hearing the cruel things Mama and Aunt Betty were saying. My face burned.

When the German Woman's house was out of sight, I slowed to a walk. Even here, near the Skelly station, Mama and Aunt Betty's words kept striking my brain like little hammer blows. "I wish I could be hard like you, Arlene." Mama hard? Mama was one of the kindest people I knew. It was true she stood up for herself. She didn't let people, not even men, "step all over her," as she would say, but she was Johnny-on-the-spot when someone was down on their luck.

Of course, Mama shouldn't have said that Aunt Betty was jealous because we could buy groceries. That made Uncle Stan look bad, and it wasn't his fault he was poor.

But the worst was Aunt Betty saying Mama wanted everybody to be as miserable as she was. That was a snake that would lay eggs in my brain. Was Mama unhappy, and I hadn't known or understood? Frightened, I sat down on the steps of Boomer's Tavern. I was as much unnerved by my own possible blindness as by Mama's supposed misery. Was it because I was a child that I hadn't understood? Maybe it was because Mama was good at hiding her troubles? Maybe I hadn't wanted to know, or maybe—and I prayed to St. Ann that this was true—maybe Aunt Betty was wrong. That had to be the answer. That Mama might in fact be miserable, that life might not be what it seemed, was unthinkable. I put my hands tight over my ears as if someone were speaking vile truths to me, things a child shouldn't hear.

"Little girl," I heard at last, "little girl, have you lost your ice cream money?"

Before me on the crumbling sidewalk stood an old man dressed in clean, striped overalls and a clean, blue work shirt. His hair was snow white like Santa's, and his cheeks were round and pink. I stared at him. If he'd had a beard, I would have thought Santa had materialized out of season, wearing the clothes he wore while working in the toy shop. I studied him. He was plump and his blue eyes did twinkle, didn't they? I didn't know what a droll little mouth was, but this man's mouth did look sort of like a bow when he smiled, one that had been perked up on the ends.

"Come along," he said, climbing the steps, "I'll buy you an ice cream." I followed him into the tavern. "Mike," he called to Mr. Boomer, "this little girl would like an ice cream." Turning to me, he lifted me onto a high stool.

"Vanilla or chocolate?" Mr. Boomer asked.

"Chocolate," I told him, dazed by my good fortune.

"Two," said the old man, who had himself come to enjoy an ice cream.

"Whose little girl are you?" Mr. Boomer inquired, handing me a chocolate ice cream cone.

"Thank you for the ice cream," I told the white-haired man. "Arlene and Willie Erhardt's."

"Ain't your mama sister to Mrs. Weller?"

"Yes." Then, remembering myself, "Yes, *sir.*"

"Mrs. Weller had her baby yet?"

"Not yet, but I've been sitting out in the yard watching for it. Mama says any day now."

"You've been sitting in the yard watching for it?" Mr. Boomer asked.

"Yes. If the stork drops the baby, I'm going to catch it."

The two men exchanged glances. Did they think I was too small to catch the baby?

"I'm stronger than I look," I assured them.

"What if the baby comes now, while you're eating ice cream?" Mr. Boomer asked.

I'd run off, forgetting about the baby! I started to climb down from the stool.

"Now, wait a minute," Santa said. "Look at the time. The stork never comes at noon. That's when he eats his dinner. You just sit right there and enjoy your ice cream, little lady, and never mind what Mike Boomer tells you. He's full of malarkey. You know what that means?"

I nodded. "Republicans are full of malarkey. My papa says we've got to trust in Roosevelt, and never mind Republican malarkey."

Santa laughed. Mr. Boomer said, "Your pa sounds like a fountain of wisdom. He work for the railroad?"

I nodded.

"Thought so. He was in here once or twice with Stan Weller," he explained to my benefactor. "Works for the railroad out the west part of the state." He asked me, "Where was that again?"

"Harvester."

"That's it. McPhee here works for the railroad, too."

"Deliver a little freight is all," Santa said. "Fact is, I gotta get down there now and see what come in last night." He turned to me. "You like to pal along with me down to the depot?"

"Yes." I climbed down from the stool and bid good-bye to Mr. Boomer.

"Come back tomorrow so I know if the stork dropped the baby," he called after me.

Outside the tavern Mr. McPhee and I turned right, heading toward the tracks. McPhee walked with his hands clasped low behind his back. Out of deference, I did the same.

"You have any brothers or sisters?" he asked.

"No. Mama says I'll do."

He nodded.

"Do you have any children?"

"A boy. Lives over to Mankato."

"How old is he?"

"Forty-five."

"Pretty old."

"Yes."

"Does he have any children?"

"Two, a boy and a girl. They're grown up and moved to Minneapolis. Every generation goes someplace bigger," he observed. "Someday there won't be anybody here. They'll all be there."

"Did you ever want to move?"

He shook his head. "Somebody's got to stay home. If somebody don't stay home, my ma used to say, there ain't a home, and I believe she was right. She never wanted to leave Galway, and when she got settled in Boston and had a good job in a kitchen, she didn't want to leave there. But she met Pa and that settled her hash, she said.

"He come over from Tralee in '50. They was married in '60. And he got into a little trouble in '68, so he packed 'em both off, halfway across the land."

"What kind of trouble did he get into?"

"Nothing much. A bit of gambling and something to do with a fighter named Kelly. But here they were, on the prairie, where there wasn't any big kitchens or houses grand enough for a maid, so what was Ma to do? She took in wash and kept a big garden and delivered babies."

"And your pa?"

"He had trouble finding work suited to his talents."

"What were his talents?"

"He was sociable, that was one. And he was willing, that was another. But he didn't have any skill he could put his hand to. He was off to St. Paul and then Dakota and finally the Yukon. It was always his plan to come back with money. Ma wouldn't go. Said she'd come far enough from Galway. Said the world shouldn't think we was all peddlers and pugs and potato bugs with no decent pillow to lay our heads on."

"What's a pug?"

"A prize fighter. Like Mr. Jack Dempsey and Mr. Gene Tunney."

"And Mr. Billy Conn?"

"Where'd you hear about him?" McPhee laughed.

"Papa."

We had reached the depot. The eastbound passenger had been and gone, and a few cartons were piled on a low freight wagon. The agent saw us approaching and came out to meet us.

"Got some freight for you, Paddy. See you got company."

"This is . . ."

"Lark Ann Erhardt."

"How d'ya do? You and your ma come in from Harvester Monday."

"Yes."

"Your pa's Willie Erhardt. I know him. He still play softball?"

"No, sir."

"Used to play softball every chance he got. Played for the New Frankfurt team. I played second base for Morgan Lake. Got rheumatism in the shoulder now. Can't play no more. Remember me to your pa. Harold Arndt."

Mr. McPhee and I set out to deliver the freight. McPhee pulled the wagon, which bumped and clattered along the broken street. The first stop was Esterly's Groceries and General Merchandise, where we dropped off the incoming mail pouch and picked up an outgoing one.

"Mrs. Kraus was in here fifteen minutes ago, looking for the mail," Mr. Esterly told us. " 'Der train vass here haff an hour already,' " he mimicked. " 'Now I am here. Vare iss my mail?' "

"She's a corker," McPhee agreed. "I got a package on the wagon came for her from Monkey Ward. That oughta hold her."

Could Mrs. Kraus be the German Woman? I wondered as Mr. McPhee and I waved to Mr. Esterly and went on our way. Across the street and down to the corner we thumped and crunched, halting outside the implement dealership. Through the big window, I saw a salesman sitting with his feet up on a desk, straw hat pulled down over his eyes. On the wall beside the desk hung a calendar, and above the month of July, a very attractive young woman wearing bib overalls like Mr. McPhee's only a good deal more fitted, drove a tractor pulling a cultivator through a field of corn.

Mr. McPhee left the box of tractor parts on the desk, but did not wake the sleeping salesman. On we rolled, down a nameless street without paving and with almost no gravel to conceal its washboard surface. The two remaining packages jounced like spit on a griddle, and I minded them to make sure they didn't fall off. We pulled up before a house so small and tidy, I expected midget German Lutherans to greet us. Out instead came a plump, middle-aged woman with a toothless smile and a Slovak slant to her cheeks.

Holding aloft the package we had delivered and laughing as though a wonderful joke were wrapped in the brown paper, she explained that her father's truss was in the box sent out from St. Paul. Being without teeth, she had difficulty with the word "truss," and she screwed her mouth up carefully, but still managed to spit on her chin. At this she fairly danced with amusement, wiping her chin on her apron.

Could we stop for kolaches and coffee, she wanted to know when she had calmed herself. McPhee said that we had a minute to spare, and we followed as she flurried away ahead of us to a profoundly spotless kitchen, fishing dentures from a cup beside the sink and popping them into her mouth.

Giggling, she turned and motioned us to chairs pulled up around an oilcloth-cool table. Through the open window wafted the perfume of sweet peas, coaxed up chicken wire to the sill. The smell of sweet peas mingled insouciantly with garlic and liverwurst and red wine, and prune kolaches, which were cooling on the counter.

In the backyard a gnarled little man sat dozing on a bench under a grape arbor. Her papa, whose truss we had delivered. She poured delicate china cups full of coffee and milk, and set them before us on matching saucers. From the cupboard she took down china plates from the old country, each hand-painted with fruit and flowers. On these she served our kolaches. Out of a drawer came real linen napkins, elaborately worked with hemstitching.

Tucking the napkin into the neck of my sunsuit and folding my hands in my lap, I waited for our hostess to be seated. The warm kolache, which nearly covered the plate, sent up messages of buttery flakiness and sweet, oozing prune filling that were painful to ignore. But when you were being so finely served, you must have the character to respond in kind. Therefore, I controlled my impulses while the plump and jolly lady inquired through the back screen whether Papa wanted a kolache and coffee.

"He's asleep," she told us, returning to the table and seating herself between McPhee and me. "He went out with the dowsing stick, but the sun made him sleepy." She spoke beautiful English, with the smallest trace of accent, like a bit of lace, around the edge. What an odd mix of elegance and earthiness she was.

I couldn't help remarking, "But you've already got a well out back." The pump was in plain view. "Did it go dry?"

"Papa keeps in practice," she explained. "If he doesn't practice and somebody calls him to find water, it takes him longer. He has pride. He's an artist, so he practices." She smiled. "Eat."

I held my head over the plate for fear of spilling prune filling on the beautiful napkin. This was the best kolache I had ever tasted, possibly the best that had ever been produced. The apple of a woman, like her papa, was an artist.

When I had devoured every morsel, and only the severest self-control had restrained me from licking all my fingers, my hostess beamed, "More?"

But I was so full, another kolache would have meant getting sick. Still, I debated. "No, thank you," I answered finally. "They're the best I ever had, but I don't have any more room."

"You are a good girl," she exclaimed, squeezing my sticky hand. "I can tell good girls, just like that," she said, snapping her fingers.

"Really?" I asked, taking her at her word. "How?"

"I have my ways," she said mysteriously. Like dowsing and baking, it was an art.

A thrill went through me. There was magic here, magic in this house. She threw people off the scent with tricks of commonality, like keeping her teeth in a cup, then popping them in, in plain sight of company. But her emanations were too strong to be ignored. Just now, with her hand over mine, they had jumped, like an arcing electrical current, galvanizing me. A tremor ran up my arm, and the hairs on the back of my neck stood up.

"Papa is awake now," she noted. "Would you like to learn how to use the stick?" she asked me.

I nodded.

"Come," she told me, rising and heading to the back door. Out into the yard she led me, past the pump to the arbor, where the old man shuffled along, bent over the forked stick. "Papa," she said, speaking a little louder, "Papa, this little girl would like to know how you find water." The black braids, wound around her head like a crown, glistened in the light, as though diamonds were set amongst the plaited strands.

"Sure," he said, studying me, "sure." He pronounced the word "shooor," not "sher," as others did. His pronunciation lent it gravity and certainty.

The daughter smiled proudly on me, as if she were delivering to her papa an especially apt pupil. Her hand on my shoulder carried messages: You are a child who could learn these many things we know, if you would let yourself, if you would trust.

She knew that I was frightened. Did she know also that I was caught? That I would find my way back here? She walked away, leaving me with the old man, who smelled of garlic and tobacco and something else, something a little acrid but not at all unpleasant.

Grasping the forked divining rod in spotted, brown hands, whose veins were enormous and greatly articulated, he began again to make his way unhurriedly, methodically, up and down the backyard, which was considerable and almost completely given over to cultivated garden and grape arbor. As he shuffled along, he moved the rod slowly from side to side, yet holding it loosely, giving it its way, as one might give a horse its way, confident that it knows the trail, where the burrows and sharp rocks are hidden.

From time to time, the old man cast a look sideways to see if I was observing the rod. Hugging his steps on his left, I kept my eyes fixed on the stick, only darting a swift glance now and then to be certain I wouldn't mow down a row of tomato plants. Determined to catch any significant movement, to learn its secrets, I was as intent upon the dowsing rod as a scientist upon his microscope.

In the far, back corner of the yard, in the shadow of a wire fence where another variety of grape climbed and clung, the rod dipped as though an invisible hand had reached out of the earth and pulled it. Startled, I yelped and sprang back. The old man laughed, and his eyes nearly disappeared into leathery creases.

When finally he stopped laughing and wiped his face on the back of his sleeve, he said, "You are mad at me?"

Still quaking inside from the dip of the rod, the sudden and unexplainable sorcery of it, and chilled by tiny feathers that seemed to brush up and down my skin, I *was* angry at him for laughing, but how did he know that? I wanted to run away, back to Aunt Betty's, but I wanted also to learn the divining rod.

"Don't be mad," he said, not unsympathetically, "or the stick won't work." He handed it to me. It felt as I imagined the old man's face must feel. "Don't hold it too tight," he warned. "Let it talk to you."

Slowly and with continued advice about my hands, we began making our way back toward the house. The sun beat down upon my back, warming my skin, but leaving my insides cold with wonderment. As the old man bent near, I realized that the sharp, not unpleasant smell I had detected earlier reminded me of Grandma Browning's medicine cupboard, which was taller than Grandpa and contained many bottles with homemade labels and small paper bags filled with dried leaves and strange powders. When Grandma opened the cupboard, it gave off a cloud of evocation.

The dowsing stick was doing nothing unusual. It lay loosely yet securely in my grasp, but unexcited, so far as I could tell, by the earth below it. I did not have the magic. In my hands it was only a stick. I felt failed and foolish beneath the old man's intent gaze.

When we reached the back steps, I handed the rod to him. "I'm sorry," I said. Again he laughed, and I thought he was rude. Opening the screen door, he followed me into the kitchen, where his daughter and McPhee still sat at the table.

"She is all right," he said to his daughter, lowering himself onto a chair while she fetched him coffee. "She could learn."

"The stick didn't do anything," I reminded him.

"There was no water. The only water is in the well," he said, gesturing toward the pump beyond the window, "and out in the back corner."

"Then why did we look in those other places?"

"For good reason," he said. "For good reason."

I didn't understand, but timidity prevented me pressing.

"She's a good girl," his daughter observed. She lay a hand lightly on my head. "Like one of us. She could be one of us."

By "one of us," did she mean one of their family or their

nationality or something else? There was a great deal to ponder in these people and their meanings.

"Well," McPhee began, rising from the table, "I have more freight on the wagon." He shook hands with the old man, who was not much his elder and, indeed, had less white hair than McPhee. "Don't get up. Your truss come on the train. I expect you'll be out for horseshoes on Sunday."

"My truss, ah good. I'm no man without my truss."

"Thank you," I told my gnarled tutor, "for teaching me to hold the stick."

He took my hand as if for warmth on a cold day. "Yes, yes," he said. "You'll come back." His black eyes extracted a promise.

"Take these home," the daughter commanded, handing me three kolaches wrapped in waxed paper.

As McPhee and I descended the porch steps, the woman probed, "You like us?" She wasn't anxious, she was curious. Her gaze forced me to look her in the eye.

"Yes."

"I thought so," she said, and watched us rumble down the street.

McPhee made no mention of the pair we'd left behind. He had doubtless been acquainted with them for years and understood them or at least ceased puzzling over them. For surely they were puzzling. I couldn't be the only person who found them exotic, could I?

Back to Main Street we rolled, and there turned right toward Aunt Betty's house. As we made the turn, I was suddenly apprehensive. What time was it? How long had I been gone? I had a recollection of the bells ringing at St. Ambrose Catholic Church some while earlier, so it was past noon. Had Mama been out scouring the countryside for me? She was probably waiting with a switch in her hand. The skin on the back of my legs prickled in unhappy anticipation.

When we drew up in front of the German Woman's house, McPhee stopped the wagon and hefted the last package. There remained only the mailbag, which would be delivered to the depot.

"Well," he said, "wish me luck with the Widow Kraus. There won't be any kolaches *here*."

I sat down on the edge of the wagon and urged myself to go home. The sooner I made an appearance, the less punishment would be waiting for me.

"Da train vas here hours ago," the Widow Kraus complained loudly, as if McPhee were a naughty child. "Vair vere you all dis time? I vill report you. You are vorse dan dat chilt," she said, pointing at me. When she had finished with him, she hooked the screen and turned abruptly away without a thank-you or good-bye.

McPhee whistled down the walk, hands clasped low behind his back, retreating in a markedly untroubled way.

Tiptoeing across Aunt Betty's porch, I opened the screen an inch at a time, sliding through the narrowest possible opening. Inside I stood stock still, listening. Beyond the green drape, Aunt Betty was moaning the way people moan when they have been sick too long and have lost their concentration and determination.

"I'll be right back," Mama promised. "Lark will stay with you till I come back."

Pushing aside the drape, Mama said in a low voice, "Sit beside the bed where she can see you. Talk to her. I'm going next door to call the doctor." Mama was not really looking at me. She was looking into her own head. She did not realize that I had been gone. Was Aunt Betty dying?

Mama hurried out, and I went into the bedroom and sat on the straight chair that had been drawn up near the bed. Laying the kolaches aside, I watched Aunt Betty moving restlessly beneath the sheet, as though she were trying to climb out of her body. She was not a person with whom I could associate pain. What was happening was a mistake. My aunt was a person who laughed strongly and told funny stories that made the whole house gay and cozy. If she were well, she would weave silly tales about the Widow Kraus, plucking that woman's stinger so we could look at her without fear and dread.

Scooting the chair over a couple of inches so that it was flush against the bed, and laying a hand on Aunt Betty's feverish arm, I asked, "Would you like me to tell you a story, Aunt Betty?"

❧ 20 ❧

"ONCE UPON a time there was a beautiful princess with golden red hair, and her name was . . . Elizabeth. She lived with her mama and papa, and her sister, Arlene, in a kingdom called Blue Lake.

"One night at a dance, in a real pretty place called the Lakeview Ballroom, the beautiful Princess Elizabeth met a handsome prince, who was visiting from another kingdom.

"The prince said to Princess Elizabeth, 'My name is Stanley Weller, and I'm from Red Wing, but I work in Mankato for an implement dealer, and I'm here visiting my aunt and uncle.'

"Beautiful Princess Elizabeth laughed real hard at his long introduction and said, 'We're not getting married, we're just going to dance.'

"And Prince Stanley said, 'If we were getting married, I'd have mentioned my wooden leg.'

"Princess Elizabeth fell in love right there, and three months later they got married and moved to Morgan Lake. They settled down in a little castle on Main Street, two blocks from the Skelly station.

"Then, what should happen but a wicked witch moved into the castle next door, and she was very jealous of Princess Elizabeth because the princess was happy and had a handsome husband. The witch was a widow lady, and she didn't want anybody to be happy.

"One day the princess got a letter from the stork. He told her that he was going to bring her a baby, and she should name the baby Lar . . . she should name the baby Ann. When the wicked witch heard this news, she got so mad, she started planning bad things for the beautiful Princess Elizabeth.

"The first spell made Princess Elizabeth's stomach grow real big while the rest of her got skinny. And when she went out among the citizens of Morgan Lake, people wondered what had happened, and they whispered to each other, 'It looks like Princess Elizabeth is carrying a peck of potatoes under her dress.'

"The second spell that the witch worked on the princess made her sick, so that she had to stay in bed all the time. One or two people in the kingdom knew that a witch lived in the castle next to Princess Elizabeth. One person who knew was Duke McPhee. And another was Princess Myrna Loy of Harvester.

"The wicked witch didn't know that Princess Myrna Loy had recognized her, so she went right on with her evil plan to shoot the stork who was bringing Princess Elizabeth's baby. But a good fairy had sent Princess Myrna Loy a dream showing her this and telling her to catch the baby when it fell."

Aunt Betty whimpered and her face grimaced in pain. I thought that I'd better get to the happy ending.

"Princess Myrna Loy waited faithfully on the back steps of the castle, watching for the stork. And one morning she saw a little speck in the sky, a long way off.

"Princess Myrna Loy ran across the back alley, climbed over the fence, and hurried as fast as she could out into the middle of the pasture. All of a sudden, just like in her dream, the stork let go of the blanket, and the baby princess began to fall through the air. Princess Myrna Loy ran faster than she had ever run in her life and held out her arms, and the little pink baby fell right into them. And the baby smiled at her.

"And the stork fell out of the sky, too, and landed at Princess Myrna Loy's feet, a poison arrow in its heart.

"When Prince Stanley came home, he went next door and told the witch that she would have to pack her things and get out.

"When she heard that Princess Myrna Loy had saved the baby, the witch got so mad, she started to burn. Her black shoes caught fire, and then her hair, which was rolled up tight around her head. In a few minutes, she had completely burned up in the flames of her bad temper.

"Then, all the witch's poisons and potions dried up and blew away, and the beautiful Princess Elizabeth got well. She and Prince Stanley and Princess Ann lived together happily ever after. Amen."

Aunt Betty lay twitching in her sleep. She breathed heavily, and now and then her breath came out in a soft moan.

I heard Mama's step on the porch, and I went to tell her that Aunt Betty was asleep. Mama tiptoed to the kitchen, and I followed.

"That woman next door is a witch," Mama said angrily. " 'It's long distance to call Mankato,' she told me, as if I didn't know. 'You have money?' 'My sister may be dying,' I told her, 'and you're standing there asking if I have money to call Mankato for a doctor? What kind of person are you?' As it happened, I had taken money with me. I threw it at her, I was so mad."

"Did you talk to a doctor?" I asked.

She nodded. "He's coming out tonight." Mama slipped down onto a chair at the kitchen table, put her head down on her arms, and started to cry.

I couldn't stand to see Mama cry. When Mama cried, it seemed that maybe Aunt Betty *would* die, and maybe I wouldn't be there to catch the baby.

≥ 21 ≤

MAMA REMOVED her high-heeled shoes and put on bedroom slippers so that the sound of heels on the floor wouldn't disturb Aunt Betty. "The sleep is helping her fight the poisons," Mama said.

But when Aunt Betty continued sleeping restlessly hour after hour, Mama had increasing difficulty controlling her fears. For our supper she heated a can of soup and tried to make toast in the old toaster which sat on the stove burner and took its heat from the flame. But she didn't have the trick of it, and the toast started to burn.

"Oh God, oh God," Mama cried, grabbing a dish towel, wetting it at the sink, and waving it wildly in the air to flush the smoke out the window. "Betty doesn't need smoke in her lungs. Help me, Lark. Get a towel and wet it. Hurry."

I wet two and began flinging them around my head, hurling water around the kitchen.

"Wring them out!" Mama shrieked. "What's the matter with you? Can't you do anything right?"

Then the soup boiled over on the stove, and Mama began to cry again.

After supper I went out to sit on the back steps, trying to salvage a sense of contributing to Aunt Betty's welfare. I could at least watch for the stork, a duty I had neglected earlier.

"Mama," I called, suddenly remembering the woman who had given me the kolaches, "there's kolaches on the table beside Aunt Betty's bed." The kolache woman, with her black eyes that pulled everything to them, was magic. And so was her ancient papa, and so was their tidy little house, filled with foreign smells and dark furniture and elegant china.

Did that woman have any magic to help Aunt Betty? A tiny current of possibility began trickling through me. Why not? In "The Castle Behind the Clouds," a tale from *Happy Stories for Bedtime*, the good witch saved Celestina with a magic antidote. Tomorrow morning, first thing, if Aunt Betty wasn't greatly improved, I was going to find my way back to that house and ask for an antidote.

At the same time, I doubted my ability to carry out this plan. Even with McPhee at my side, I had been shy and afraid with the kolache woman and her papa. I would never have the Beverly Ridza sort of spunk necessary to ask for their help. I sighed deeply and stared at the mauve-lavender southeastern sky. Although crows convened on the pasture fence, quarreling seriously, no stork could be seen anywhere.

I was already asleep on the couch when the doctor arrived, so I don't know the time. I woke to the sound of low voices, Mama's and the doctor's, coming from Aunt Betty's room. Aunt Betty's voice was silent.

I heard a snapping sound, as of a doctor's bag closing, and then Mama and the doctor emerged from the bedroom, Mama with tears on her face and a wadded handkerchief in her hand, the doctor with professional concern on his thin face.

"I'll be back tomorrow night," he said as Mama opened the screen door for him and followed him to his car.

When she returned, I asked, "Is Aunt Betty going to be all right? What did the doctor say? Did he give her medicine?"

"He left medicine, but he doesn't know. It depends on her general strength, he said. Go to sleep now." Mama's shoulders hung low as she pulled aside the green drape and slipped into Aunt Betty's room.

The next morning, which was Thursday, Aunt Betty seemed some better. She sat up in bed, drank tea, and nibbled half a slice of toast. She wore a thin, dimity nightie, and her shoulder bones looked as though they would stab right through the fabric, but she was more spirited and even joked a little with Mama about the previous day's quarrel.

I was greatly relieved. I was still fainthearted at the notion of going to the kolache woman, pouring out our problems, and asking for help. I could imagine her saying, "What gave you the idea that I could help? I'm not a doctor."

Thursday afternoon Aunt Betty began to slip away from us again. Mama said her fever was rising. Her eyes were glassy, and she trembled with chill. I fetched an extra blanket and sat with Mama in the bedroom all afternoon, taking my nap on the floor. There were times now when Mama's fear made her seem like a little girl.

"Where did the kolaches come from?" Mama asked during our vigil.

"A lady. Her papa showed me how to use the dowsing rod."

Mama nodded. "They were good. I had them with tea last night."

That evening when the doctor came, Mama asked, "Shouldn't I put her in the hospital in Mankato?"

"There's nothing we can do there that you aren't doing here, at least until she goes into labor. And it would be more expensive."

After the doctor left, Mama sat down on the couch by me and said, "I don't know if I'm doing the right thing. Should I put her in the hospital?"

Mama's self-doubt distressed me. She always knew just what to do.

"Uncle Stan doesn't have any money, so how can we take Aunt Betty to the hospital? Anyway, she probably wouldn't go. She'd fight and cry."

"Yes," Mama said, more to herself than to me. We sat, not speaking, while Mama wrestled in her mind. "I haven't called Grandma," she said. "If anything happens, she won't forgive me."

"Call her tomorrow."

"Maybe," Mama said. "I won't tell Betty."

"How come?"

"She doesn't want anybody to know how poor she and Stan are," Mama said softly. "It would kill her if Mama came and saw how things are."

"Why shouldn't people know if you're poor?" I asked.

"It's Uncle Stan. He's ashamed."

I couldn't understand. After a long silence, I asked Mama another question that had bothered me since we got to Morgan Lake. "Doesn't Aunt Betty have any friends? Nobody comes to see her."

"I don't know. Maybe she sent them away."

She used to have a lot of friends.

I helped Mama drag the armchair into Aunt Betty's room. "I'll sit with her tonight," Mama said.

We settled down: Mama speaking soft, soothing words when Aunt Betty churned and moaned and sometimes cried out unintelligible entreaties in her sleep; me stiff with fear and theological considerations of guilt. If Aunt Betty died because I was afraid to ask the kolache woman for help, would I have committed murder?

I couldn't get comfortable on the couch. Corners of guilt poked me however I arranged myself. I lay, staring out the window at heaven, which was receding from me. I prayed to God not to let Aunt Betty die.

I got up and went to the bathroom. When I returned, Mama pulled aside the green drape. "Are you all right?"

"Yes. I just went to the bathroom."

"You're not getting sick?"

"No. My cold's almost gone."

Here was Mama, worrying about everyone, and all I could do was worry about my own soul. Tomorrow, if Aunt Betty was alive, I would go to the kolache woman.

Across the way the light burned in Witch Kraus's back bedroom. As I watched, I saw her shadow move across the drawn shade. In a few minutes, her toilet flushed, and a minute later, her shadow again crossed before the shade, and the bedsprings complained as she resumed her plotting against Aunt Betty.

In the morning, Mama sent me to the store for bread and milk and the mail.

"Can I stop and say hello to the kolache lady?"

"On the way to the store," Mama advised. "I don't want sour milk when you get home."

I think Mama wanted me out of the house for a while, so she could think. Aunt Betty was weaker than yesterday morning. "Stan'll be home today," Mama said aloud. "I'll let him decide what to do." Then, "But what does he know? He's the one who let this happen."

When I was dressed, I buttered a slice of bread and slipped away, half a dollar in my pocket. A block from the kolache woman's house, dread grabbed me by the throat. I didn't know these people. Maybe the woman and her papa would kidnap me and chain me up in their shed, holding me for ransom.

The kolache woman's front door was ajar. From the kitchen came sounds of dishes being washed. Maybe I should go downtown and see if McPhee had any packages to deliver.

"Good morning." It was the old man. He had come around the corner of the house, carrying a hammer, his shirt pocket heavy with nails. "I have to fix the loose step," he said, indicating the one on which I sat.

"Maria!" he called through the front door. "The little girl is here."

Before I was ready, I was being swept into the house, through the dark living room that smelled of garlic and furniture polish, and into the kitchen, which still smelled of strong breakfast coffee.

"Sit," Maria invited, leading me to the chair by the window, where you could smell sweet peas. On the table a loaf of coarse homemade bread sat on a board beside a bowl of butter. Maria got down a plate and set it on the table in front of me. Slicing off two thick slices of bread, she buttered them lavishly and put them on the plate. "Wait," she admonished, fetching a jar of her own strawberry jam. With a tablespoon, she spooned out thick red preserves onto the bread, then handed me a knife.

Before I had spread the preserves from crust to crust, she'd poured me a cup of coffee and milk. "Now," she said, meaning I should begin to eat, which I did. "Wait," she said again, laughing at herself and hurrying to the icebox, to return with a big hunk of homemade cheese, from which she hacked off a good size chunk for me.

While I ate, she poured herself a cup of coffee and sat down opposite me to watch. She enjoyed watching me eat, her eyes following the bread to my mouth, then the cheese, her head nodding slightly as if I were a pupil performing a routine which she had taught me.

It didn't bother me to have her watch, since she didn't criticize, but rather, barely restrained herself from clapping as I finished one slice of bread and took a bite from the cheese. I was casting about for a way to introduce Aunt Betty's problem.

When I had drunk my coffee, Maria asked, "Your auntie is sick?"

"She might die."

"A baby's coming?"

I nodded. How had she known all this?

"Aunt Betty vomits all the time," I told Maria. "And she's running a fever. Mama doesn't know what we're going to do."

High up, in a cupboard near the ceiling, behind glass doors, I saw dozens of little bottles with hand-written labels and many little sacks filled, I was sure, with strange, dry, acrid-smelling ingredients, like those in Grandma Browning's tall medicine cupboard.

"The doctor has come," Maria observed.

"He gave her medicine, but it didn't help."

"Yes," she said, as if that were to be expected.

She asked several further questions regarding Aunt Betty's illness, some of whose answers I knew, some I didn't. At last she said, "Your aunt would like a caller." She gave me a long look from which I tried not to retreat, and this sealed our agreement.

Relieved, I climbed down from the chair. "I have to go to Esterly's now," I said.

"After papa eats, I will come," Maria promised, following me to the front door. "I will bring tea."

On the wall above the living room couch were two portraits in heavy gilt frames. One was Maria's papa wearing a colorful uniform, his hair black and glossy, his face unlined and merry. The other was a woman whose hair was wound like Maria's in circling plaits. Her nose was long and straight, her mouth wide and unsmiling. A woman of strong magic. Maria came of formidable blood.

22

RETURNING TO Aunt Betty's from Esterly's, I'd gone out back to sit on the steps and watch for the stork. Shielding her eyes against the midday glare, Mama joined me, gazing out at the pasture and the eastern sky as if she, too, expected to see a stork.

"It's good to be outside," she said. Except for hanging clothes and coming to fetch me from the sidewalk in front of Boomer's Tavern, Mama hadn't been out of the house since we'd arrived. Mama wasn't used to such confinement.

"The kolache lady's coming after lunch," I informed her.

"Why didn't you tell me that before?"

"I don't know."

"I'll have to bake something. I wish you'd told me before. It's almost noon," she said impatiently, turning on her heel and flustering into the house. "What on earth can I make?"

I hadn't told Mama that Maria was coming because I'd already begun to have second thoughts by the time I arrived at Esterly's. In all my vague plans to secure Maria's magic for Aunt Betty, I'd ignored what Sister Mary Frances had told the catechism class about magic: mainly, that it was a sin. She had warned us against ever uttering the words "hocus-pocus." The day she came upon Ronald Oster trying to turn Beverly Ridza into a jackass, waving his arms and hocus-pocussing over her, Sister had grabbed him by the ear, canceled our little recess, and indignantly herded us back to our pews, explaining, as she crossed herself, that hocus-pocus stood for *hoc est meus corpus*—"this is My body." To practice magic was to contradict the will of God, she assured us.

Why did God mind so much, I wondered. I could understand if you were doing *bad* with your magic. But why did He mind people doing good with it? The Bible said that He was a jealous God. That could explain it. But jealousy was a sin. He expected *us* to be perfect. It wasn't fair.

I didn't see how God could help loving Maria. She was warm and generous. Also, she was Catholic. And where had her power come from, if not from God? My brain ached with the weight of these thoughts.

I was sitting on the front porch, when I spotted Maria striding down the middle of the street in her sensible black pumps. She was smoothly girdled and wearing a dark challis print with a white-collared vee-neck. How righteously her coronet glistened in the sun! She looked like the head of the Methodist Ladies Aide.

Under her right arm was clutched a very large, black handbag. That was where she carried the magic tea and whatever other antidotes she had brought to cure Aunt Betty.

Witch Kraus was sitting on her front porch, hooking a rug. Punch, punch, punch, the hook went angrily in and out of the canvas. Did I only imagine that her hands clenched the hook as if it were a dagger?

As Maria drew abreast of the Witch's house, Witch Kraus called in greeting, "*Miss* Zelena." Maria nodded properly but formally in the Witch's direction and did not break stride in her advance toward Aunt Betty's beleaguered castle.

"I have come to see how is your sister," Maria told Mama when the two of them met, Maria grasping Mama's hand in a firm clasp. "And you, how are you, I want to know."

"I'm fine," Mama lied, leading Maria into the living room. "My sister's in there," Mama explained, pointing to the green drape, "but she's asleep."

"Sure, sure," Maria said, pronouncing the word as her papa did—"shooor." "We can sit in the kitchen, where we won't bother her."

Mama led Maria toward the kitchen and the hastily baked crumb cake sitting on the counter, fresh out of the oven. "Have a chair," Mama invited Maria, "and I'll get the coffee."

When they were both settled at the rickety little table, Maria said, "I am Maria Zelena. I am hearing from your little girl that your sister is sick. I am good at helping sick people. I learn things from my mama, who was well known, even in America, for curing sickness."

"We don't know what it is," Mama said.

"It's everything," Maria said. "Worry and sadness open the door, and evil flies in." Seeing that Mama was startled by the word "evil," she amended, "evil . . . germs fly in." Despite the revision, there remained in her eye a cast which spoke to Mama's instincts.

Mama rose from the table. "Lark, find your *Happy Stories for Bedtime,*" she instructed, "and take it out on the front porch."

I would rather have had a licking with the brush than leave that room, but it was pointless appealing Mama's decision. I retrieved *Happy Stories for Bedtime* from beneath the couch, and let myself out the screen door, closing it softly.

I sat, legs stretched out before me, leaning against the clapboard porch wall, the book on my lap. Its familiar cover brought Harvester to my mind, and I realized with a shock that I hadn't thought of Hilly or Sally or even Papa for several days. Aunt Betty's illness had driven them out of my thoughts. Now I began to worry about Hilly, who did not have Mama and me close to keep an eye on him, but only Mrs. Stillman, who was old and unable to follow him to those places where he might get into trouble, places like cemetery road. Would Sally's mama look after him? She could barely look after herself.

I began to drowse, and once I nearly fell over on the porch floor. Sneaking back into the house, I lay down on the couch. From the kitchen drifted the low, intent voices of Mama and Maria, but I was too sleepy to concentrate on their words or on the sharp smell, vaguely familiar to me, which drifted from that direction as well. Maria was brewing her magic tisane, and I was missing the entire ceremony.

I woke later to the hypnotic sound of Maria's voice, coming from beyond the green drape. "Yes, yes," she crooned, "it does not taste good, little girl, but it does not taste bad, you will see, and it will make you better. That's right, little girl, I will hold the cup. Yes, yes, I will hold the cup. You drink. It won't come up, you will see. Your sister is holding a bowl, but it won't come up. It will stay down. You are needing this, little girl, and your body will not throw it up." And on she crooned, Aunt Betty apparently sipping the healing elixir.

Later I heard Maria say to Mama, "We'll fold the sheet back."

"She won't take a chill?" Mama asked.

"In this heat?" There was a rustling of cloth as the sheet was folded back. "Is there a fan around, you know, one from church?"

This was a cue for me to help. I ran to the dining room and fetched the two I'd seen lying on the built-in sideboard. They were round pieces of lightweight cardboard, glued to a stick. These particular specimens had pictures of Mary and Baby Jesus on them and, below the picture, "Compliments of Kinder Mortuary, Mankato, Minnesota. Telephone 283."

"Good," Maria said as I handed them to her, and she passed

one to Mama. For an hour, until Aunt Betty fell into a deep sleep, Maria and Mama stood, one on either side of the bed, and kept the air moving over her face and exposed arms.

Before she left, Maria praised Mama for her hard work and gave her instructions for the night ahead. "Plenty of ice?" she asked.

Mama nodded. "The iceman comes again tomorrow."

"If the fever goes . . ." Maria gestured upward with her hand. ". . . then you start the cold cloths. Tonight, more tea. And more tea. For the kidneys. It is hard work. The little girl can empty the pot for you," she suggested, referring to the gray enamel chamber pot Aunt Betty was using. "All night give her tea when she is awake. The kidneys." Maria looked sharply at Mama. "Come outside," she said, tucking her great, black handbag under her arm.

I crept to the screen door and strained to hear as Mama and Maria stood together on the sidewalk, conferring.

"It is bad," Maria said, uncompromisingly.

Mama's head jerked to the side as if she'd been slapped. "Is she going to die?"

"Maybe," Maria said, making two words of the one—may be. "You and your little girl, talk good words to her," she advised enigmatically. "I will come tomorrow at the same time. If it is very bad, send someone for me. Maria Zelena. Papa is Ladislau Zelena."

As Maria retreated up the street, Uncle Stan's old black Ford passed her, bouncing and rattling as if the doors would fall off. Mama waited on the sidewalk for him, her arms at her sides now, her back straight. As the car pulled up in front of the house, I ran out the door and past Mama.

"Uncle Stan!" I called, throwing my arms out to hug him. Whatever his faults, I was very fond of Uncle Stan.

Slamming the car door, he waited for me, smiling a smile that was worn thin by the week out on the road. I flung myself at him, and he picked me up, holding me in his left arm.

"Are you glad to see us, Uncle Stan?" I asked him, laying my head against his rough cheek.

"You bet," he answered, his voice as tired as his face. Up the walk he carried me. "Arlene," he said, nodding to Mama and carrying me into the house, letting the door slam behind us.

"Shhhhh," Mama reprimanded, following us into the house. "We just got Betty to sleep."

Uncle Stan set me down on the couch and lowered himself wearily beside me. He was a good-looking man. Some might have said handsome, in an Irish way. I know a little about Irish ways because, though Papa's name is German and Mama's English, there was intermarrying with Irish on both sides, resulting in O'Neill and Murphy and O'Connor branches. My own Grandma Erhardt was a Sullivan. I contained about a third Irish blood, Mama said, though she explained that, when you saw the blood, as I did when I fell and scraped a knee, you couldn't tell what kind it was. For Uncle Stan, it was the same as for me; his mother had been a Monahan.

Uncle Stan had the straight, pinched nose, the well-shaped but thin lips, the high forehead and fine cheek bones of an Irish aesthete. But, as so often happens, he had the puckish brows and roguish blue eyes of a barkeep. His brown curls he kept close cropped, in order to resemble an altar boy somewhat less. His skin was palely freckled so that you had to get close to notice. It was easy to understand how Aunt Betty had found Uncle Stan irresistible.

But there appeared to be a streak of Irish hard luck in Stan. It wasn't just his job—he was lucky to have one at all—but his bad luck at cards and horseshoes and almost anything where chance played a part. Most men with Stan's ill fortune would have turned dour, but he had learned to laugh when the crucial horseshoe fell wide or his three aces were bettered by four kings.

"Oh, my God," he would say with a laugh, "do you believe it? What am I? Fortune's stepchild?"

People loved Uncle Stan for laughing at his hardship, and none loved him for it more than Aunt Betty. "Laughing at bad luck is noble," she had made the mistake of commenting to Mama. "It's easy to see, Stan's descended from kings."

"And we all know how well the Irish kings have fared," Mama could not resist responding.

But underneath Uncle Stan's laughter was a perplexed sadness, which made me feel protective toward him. And if *I* felt protective, what must Aunt Betty feel? Little wonder she was ready to die rather than expose their poverty.

"Get Uncle Stan a glass of iced tea," Mama told me in order to get me out of the room for a minute.

"I don't suppose there's beer?" he asked.

"You know there isn't," Mama said, not without patience.

"Iced tea, then," he conceded.

Mama lowered her voice to a near whisper as I departed, but I knew almost everything she was going to tell Stan: Aunt Betty was near death. The doctor had been called. He had advised not taking Aunt Betty to the hospital in Mankato since there was no money. Would Mama tell Stan about Maria and her magic?

"And Esterlys wouldn't give us credit," Mama was recounting as I entered the room, carrying a glass of iced tea and a piece of crumb cake for Uncle Stan.

Surely he had already known about the credit. Why had Mama brought that up when the rest of her report was enough to sink a battleship? Because Mama believed in "getting all the cards on the table." "If you know the worst," she'd say, "everything else is less than the worst." But Uncle Stan looked as though he'd been shot. The color was drained from his face, and though from habit he reached for a smile, he came up empty. His face crumpled and he put his head in his hands. His shoulders shook with soundless sobs.

Mama took the tea and cake from me and headed toward the kitchen. "Help me get supper on, Lark," she said, leaving Uncle Stan to pull himself together in private.

Mama made scalloped potatoes with slices of ring bologna, like coins, folded in among the creamy potatoes. With this we had canned peas and, for dessert, crumb cake. I was the only one who ate substantially. Uncle Stan remained at the table only long enough to be polite. Then he left us for Aunt Betty. She was sleeping deeply, but her cheeks were the color of dusky roses, not a good sign in a redhead.

When the dishes were dried, I went out back and took up my watch on the step. Pulling the string to extinguish the kitchen light, Mama followed, bringing me a glass of iced tea and milk.

"If Aunt Betty gets well," Mama told me, "I'm not going to let her stay here and starve."

"What will you do?"

"I'll make her go home."

"Can you do that?"

Mama didn't answer. Finally she said, "I'll tell Mama and Papa, and they'll come get her."

"She won't go," I warned, recalling the conversation I'd heard between Mama and Aunt Betty. "And she'll hate you."

"Oh, God," Mama despaired, throwing her arms tightly around

me, "what am I going to do?" Her body tensed with anger. *"He can't do anything! It's up to me."*

Who couldn't do anything, God or Uncle Stan?

☙ 23 ❧

UNCLE STAN sat for three hours with Aunt Betty, but she didn't wake. Sometimes he'd get up from the big chair, walk wearily to the window, and stand with his back to the room, weeping.

Periodically Mama looked in, felt Aunt Betty's forehead, and shook her head. At nine-thirty Mama announced to Uncle Stan, "I'm going to have to put cold cloths on her, or she'll go into convulsions." She fetched a big bowl of water and added ice chips hacked from the disappearing block in the icebox. When she began stripping Aunt Betty's gown, Uncle Stan backed toward the door as if guilt constrained him from viewing his wife's body in its present unhappy condition.

"Help me with Aunt Betty's nightie, Lark." Mama's voice had a sharp edge that was meant for Uncle Stan, as if she were at the end of her patience with him.

"I'm going for a walk," he said. "I won't be long."

We heard the screen door close softly. "He'll walk as far as the tavern," Mama sniped. "Someone will feel sorry for him and buy him a beer." This was said as though she were disgusted by those who would pity him.

"Don't you feel sorry for him?" I ventured.

Mama sighed, not sure of the answer herself.

We worked together for an hour. At one point I was so drowsy, I nodded off in the middle of wringing out a cloth. Aunt Betty rose to the surface of consciousness a couple of times, complained of the cold, then, with eyes rolling upward, she fell back into stuporlike sleep.

At length Mama patted Aunt Betty all over with a towel and pulled the sheet up to her chin, not bothering to dress her again in the nightie. Dropping into the arm chair, she told me, "Get into your nightie and come give me a kiss when you're ready for bed."

But when I was ready for bed, Mama was sound asleep in the chair, and I didn't wake her. Now that I was curled up on the couch, I was no longer sleepy. I remembered the letter I had meant to write Hilly. I would write it tomorrow night. By then the stork might have come.

I would tell Hilly about Maria and her magic tea that was going to make Aunt Betty well. I still had faith in Maria's magic, notwithstanding that Aunt Betty was near convulsions. And I would also tell Hilly about the Witch who lived next door to Aunt Betty.

Glancing across the narrow strip of yard, I saw the light burning in the Witch's back bedroom. Was she hooking her rug? No. I'd be able to hear the hook. The bedsprings whined. Was she going to get up and go to the bathroom?

A figure passed before the window shade, moving from left (where a door led to the hall and bathroom) to right (where the head of the bed was pressed against the outside wall, near the window). It was not the figure of Witch Kraus. It was taller and moved like a man.

"Gott im Himmel," the Witch cried, and the light was immediately extinguished.

Then, while the bedsprings were responding to the arrival of this second person, the Witch whispered angrily, words I couldn't distinguish. For several minutes, only the muted yielding of springs floated across the dark sea to my window. The Witch and her friend were getting comfortable. I had hoped they would talk out loud so I could listen.

I recommenced thinking of Hilly. How long would it be until #127—The Cape Ann was built, and Hilly could work in the garden with me? Mama would buy me a big galvanized steel watering can like Aunt Betty's, and Hilly and I would take turns filling it and carrying it up and down the rows of flowers and vegetables. . . . A new sound reached me from the Witch's bedroom. It was a sort of sighing and murmuring at the same time. Then there was whispering—I couldn't tell whose—not urgent or angry, but muffled, mixed sometimes with giggles which were obviously the Witch's.

I couldn't imagine what the Witch and her friend were up to, although the sounds reminded me of some I'd heard once or twice at home, when I'd wakened in the middle of the night, needing to use the potty.

"Put it in your mouth," said the man.

"For Gott's sakes, be qviet," the Witch hissed. "You want effrybotty to hear?"

What did the man want her to put in her mouth? Were they eating in the dark in bed? Why not turn on the light so you wouldn't get crumbs in bed?

"Yes, yes," he was groaning happily.

"More, more," he said, but she said, "No, it's time," and they began bouncing up and down on the bed like children. If I bounced on the bed that hard, Mama would come and make me stop. Any minute I expected to hear the bed fall down with a crash. That had happened when I and two of my cousins jumped up and down on the bed at Grandma Browning's.

Before long, the man cried out, as if the Witch had stabbed him, then he whimpered like a balloon losing air and fell silent. My heart stopped. Had she killed him? Moments later, in a different room, light appeared at the window. Water ran from a faucet. The toilet flushed. The lighted window went black, and presently someone—it could only be the Witch—was whispering behind the drawn bedroom shade.

Her whispers were at first calm, almost indifferent, but as she persisted speaking over the dead body, the Witch gathered passion, and the final phrases of her incantation were frenzied, even hysterical.

From the bed, the mumbling of someone returning from the dead answered the Witch's conjury. She had brought him back to life. And I had heard the whole thing. Too weak to hold my head up, I slumped in a boneless heap on the couch.

How long I lay in that trancelike condition I don't know, but I was shot from it by screams exploding from Aunt Betty's room. I threw my arms over my head. Never had I heard such screams, not even on "Suspense." Clapping hands over my ears, I turned my back to the sound and stared out the window into the purple-gray antedawn, where trees switched in nervous anticipation of the light.

The porch screen opened at the Witch's house. With hurried stealth, a white-shirted, dark-trousered figure emerged onto the sidewalk. Making his way across the grass, he seemed buffeted by the screams from our house, as though a storm lashed him, driving him backward. Putting his head down and leaning into the squall, he pushed on, up the step, across the porch, and into the living room. I kept my back turned, although I doubt he noticed me as he rushed headlong through the green drape.

When Aunt Betty's cries momentarily subsided, Mama asked Uncle Stan coldly, "Where have you been?"

"Sleeping in the car," he lied. "Is the baby coming?" he asked.

"Yes."

Dressing quickly, I padded to the kitchen, through the back hall, and out the back door, huddling on the step to wait and watch. How long would it be before I'd see the stork? How had Mama found out that he was on his way?

At a quarter to five, I went in and buttered a piece of bread. Mama was sending Uncle Stan to fetch Maria Zelena and then to call the doctor in Mankato.

"Do the Zelenas have a phone I can use?" he asked.

"How should I know? I called from next door," she told him. "Don't go *there*. That woman is a witch. Use the Zelenas, if they have one. Wait." From the sideboard in the dining room, Mama carried her handbag to the living room and rummaged in the coin purse while Stan, his face the color of unbleached muslin, waited, shifting feet and looking helpless and distraught. "Here. This is what it costs. Call person-to-person. Doctor Neumann. I don't have the number."

When Uncle Stan had gone, Mama filled the coffee pot and put it on the stove. "How long have you been up?" she asked.

I shrugged. "Since you told Uncle Stan the baby was coming. I've been out back, watching for the stork."

Mama turned from the stove and gave me a sharp, inquiring look, then she burst out laughing.

"What's so funny?"

She put a hand over her mouth, but her eyes were still laughing.

"What's so funny, Mama?"

"Nothing. I'm just tired. Sometimes people laugh at nothing when they're tired." Her face in the watery kitchen light was blue around the edges and under the eyes. Her lips looked bloodless. "Are you hungry?"

"I've got a piece of bread."

Mama took half a ring of bologna from the icebox and set it on the table. "Let's make you a sandwich," she said, fishing a butcher knife out of the drawer. When she'd cut several slices and laid them on my bread, she asked, "Onion?"

"Yes, please."

It was as though everything was all right. Then Aunt Betty screamed again. It was not the kind of sound you expected to hear from a human being, and I sat down on a kitchen chair as if someone had shoved me there.

Mama ran into the bedroom as a second wail broke over us. I heard her speaking calm, businesslike words, as if she were reading a set of instructions off the back of a box. I slipped from the chair and backed out of the house.

Outside, I lay down on the cellar door, which was wet, and put my hands over my ears. I couldn't exactly *hear* Aunt Betty, but every so often a pressure bore down on me, like someone laying a heavy featherbed over me, and I knew that she was screaming.

After a while I began to think about my sandwich, lying on the kitchen table, waiting for ketchup. I had had nothing to eat since last night's dinner, and not much then. My stomach was gurgling. I could smell coffee. Had Mama turned off the stove?

Without removing my hands from my ears, I got up and peered in the open kitchen window. The stove was off. Sunshine, slanting in the dining room windows, spilled through the kitchen doorway, throwing a warm path of gold across the linoleum, right up to the table where the sandwich lay.

Lifting the fingers from one ear, I listened, cautiously prepared to clamp them back on. Quiet. I skittered into the house, poured ketchup on the bologna and turned to escape, sandwich to my mouth. Voices, moving from Aunt Betty's room to the living room—Mama, Maria, and Uncle Stan.

"There are old towels, clean ones, to use?" Maria was asking.

"I'll get them," Mama told her.

"The baby will be here before the doctor," Maria explained.

"Oh, Christ," Uncle Stan groaned.

There was no time to be lost. I ran outside, letting the door slam, and dashed across the alleyway to the pasture.

Climbing over the fence, I waited, catching my breath, studying the sky, nibbling bread crust. The cows were gathered beneath a stand of cottonwoods, on the far side of the enclosure.

When I'd swallowed the last crumb of sandwich and licked the last trace of ketchup from my fingers, the sky was still empty of storks, so I set out walking beside the fence, around the perimeter of the pasture. I would walk as far as where the cows were grazing, and back.

As time drew close, I was increasingly nervous. I tested my legs by sprinting halfway to the south end of the field. I mustn't practice too much, however, or I'd get tired.

I hadn't spent much time in the company of cows. Once or twice I'd helped herd them from pasture to barn at the end of the day. My few experiences with herding cows into a barn, and watching while they were milked, did nothing to convince me of their intelligence. I never saw a farmer try to teach a cow tricks.

While I did not imagine them clever enough to conspire, I kept an eye on them, albeit an oblique one, since I must watch at the same time the endless, cloudless expanse of sky. From a distance, the cows were as benign as those in the picture over the dining room buffet at Grandma Browning's house.

The cows in Grandma's dining room lolled around a mud hole at the edge of a slowly meandering stream. These lazed about beneath trees, some grazing idly; others, overcome by torpor, reposing like pampered odalisques.

On closer observation, however, did these not seem to be slyly noting me, taking my measure? The one with her back to me, grazing, who turned her head all the way around to heed my approach—what was she thinking?

I edged closer to the fence. Another corner was coming up. I had told myself I would turn back at this point. Instead I decided to circle the meadow, passing the farmhouse and outbuildings on my way back to Aunt Betty's. Maria seemed to have been wrong about the baby's arrival. Maybe it wouldn't come until tomorrow.

Tomorrow was Sunday. Sunday was a good day to be born. I was born on Sunday, although I didn't remember it. Sometimes, when Mama talked about it, I thought I could remember being afraid, high in the air, rocking in a little flannel blanket, clutched in a stork's beak.

What would Aunt Betty's baby remember? If only babies could talk, they could tell us what God was like, before they forgot. If I asked Aunt Betty's baby easy questions about God, questions you could answer yes or no, maybe she could give me a sign. Maybe God sent babies into the world without words, precisely so they wouldn't reveal Him while they still remembered.

I was tramping down Aunt Betty's alley now, and still there was no sign of the stork. Could the stork come from more than one direction? Was there perhaps more than one stork? What direction was heaven?

Maybe the stork had come from the west, and I'd missed him. Maybe the baby had arrived. I began to sprint. Now was the time to ask the baby the questions. Just one or two: Would I like God if I knew Him? Could people recognize each other in heaven without their bodies? Tomorrow when the baby was rested, I would ask her one or two more. How many days would I have before she forgot?

"Mama, is the baby here?" I called, hurling myself into the back hall.

Mama was sitting alone at the table, hands folded, head tipped to one side as though she were asking a question. When I came running in with my own questions, she continued to stare for a moment, then turned slowly, looking at me as though she'd never seen me before. At length she said, "The baby is dead, Lark."

"Dead? You mean it hasn't been born yet, the stork hasn't come?"

"It was born dead," she said in a voice far too calm and unhurried. She seemed barely aware of me.

The stork had dropped the baby just as I had dreamed.

"I don't want the baby to be dead," I said.

"The baby is with God," Mama told me.

"No, it isn't," I said, remembering Sister Mary Clair. "The baby is in limbo, Mama."

She slapped me. "Don't you ever say that again."

"Mama!" I stumbled back against the table.

"Never again!" She loomed over me. "I never want to hear another word about limbo! The baby's in heaven." She grabbed my arm roughly. "Betty doesn't need any smarty-pants Catholic brat telling her the baby's in limbo. Do you understand?"

She let go of me suddenly, turning her back. She looked lonely, standing in the middle of the kitchen, shoulders hunched, nothing and no one to support her.

I crept toward her. "Mama? Can I see her?" I touched her arm. She was weeping. I threw my arms around her waist. "I won't ever say anything about limbo, I promise."

"Aunt Betty's asleep. Maria gave her tea, and she went to sleep."

"The baby. Can I see the baby?"

"Will you be quiet and not wake Aunt Betty?"

I nodded.

"The baby's—" She made a pass at her eyes with the hanky. "I almost said 'sleeping.' The baby's in a basket on the bureau. Come right out again as soon as you see her." Mama sounded like she was talking to a stranger, some little girl who belonged to someone else. It frightened me. I wanted to say, "You don't have to be ashamed of having me, just because Aunt Betty's baby died." I wanted Mama to hold me and say, "I'm sure glad I've got you."

The shades were drawn in Aunt Betty's room. It was dark and hot. The medicinal odor of Maria's tea hung in the closeness. In the big chair, Uncle Stan was asleep, head back, snoring softly.

A wicker laundry basket sat on the bureau. In it a bed pillow with a clean white pillow slip was arranged for a mattress. The baby lay on the pillow, dressed in a tiny white gown, which was nonetheless too big, embroidered with white rosebuds. On her head she wore a little white organdy bonnet, again far too big, decorated with roses made of satin and tied under the chin with satin ribbons.

She didn't look like a baby girl. She looked like a baby bird, fallen from the nest onto the grass. Where had the stork dropped her? I wondered. I wanted to touch her tiny hand, which seemed no larger than a quarter, but I was afraid her eyes would open and look at me accusingly.

24

MARIA'S MAGIC worked. Aunt Betty's fever went down. The sickness cast on her by the Witch ebbed from her body. Maria came each day for a week, preparing her tea, making certain that Aunt Betty drank it.

But while Aunt Betty's body grew stronger and freer of poison, her mind closed around her loss, and she was remote from everyone. I tried to stay out of her way altogether.

I watered plants. I picked up stray pieces of paper that blew into the yard. I swept the porch and the walk, and wiped off the dusty windowsills with a damp rag. Indoors I straightened up, polished furniture, and swept the floors. In the living room, I ran the carpet sweeper until Mama told me to stop because it made too much racket. I put it away and began picking lint from the rug on my hands and knees. However hard I worked, it mattered little. The sick, guilty feeling was going to be with me the rest of my life.

During the week following the baby's death, Maria took me home with her for several hours each day. Mr. Zelena let me feed the chickens, which were kept in a pen behind the shed, and he also let me water the garden and pull weeds. Maria taught me to embroider.

After my embroidery lesson and garden chores, I would take a nap on Maria's couch. I grew accustomed to the strangeness of the Zelena household: the heavy smell of garlic and herbs, the mystery that breathed silently, behind doors and around corners. And yet, perhaps not entirely accustomed, for I never opened a door or took a step without Maria's urging, for fear I would stumble on secrets not meant for me.

From a member of her sodality, Maria procured a roll-away bed for Grandma and Grandpa Browning, who had come from Blue Lake. At night the few furnishings in Aunt Betty's living room were shoved against the walls, and the rollaway was set up.

Sunday, which was Grandma and Grandpa's first night with us, as she tucked herself and Grandpa into the rollaway, inches from me, Grandma exclaimed, "We're like peas in a pod, aren't we?"

In Aunt Betty and Uncle Stan's room, there was no sound. They lay awake, not whispering. Since the baby's death, Aunt Betty spoke to no one. When Grandma had tried to talk with her, Aunt Betty had told her, "I don't want to talk, Mama. Just leave me alone."

Rising at four A.M. Monday and closing the door between kitchen and dining room, Mama began heating water to fill the big galvanized laundry tubs. All day she was bent over the washboard.

Before Maria came to brew Aunt Betty's tea and take me to her house for the afternoon, I helped Mama. She fed the clothes into the wringer, while I turned the crank. When the basket was full, I grabbed one of the handles and helped carry the wash to the clotheslines. I handed Mama shirts and dresses and towels, and she pinned them to the line. Together we shook the wrinkles from the sheets and straightened their edges.

How strange it seemed, when we carried the first load to the yard, that the basket that had cradled the dead baby now held a heap of wet laundry.

Late Saturday the undertaker from Kinder Mortuary had driven out from Mankato and taken the baby away. We would not see her again until the funeral at St. Ambrose Catholic Church on Tuesday.

I didn't mention to Mama that it was my fault the baby had fallen, nor did I ask where the stork had dropped her. Guilt and shame constrained me from talking about the baby. Also, I was afraid the punishment would start. That would probably come after the funeral. Right now, people were too shocked to think about punishment.

Between the baby's death on Saturday and the funeral Tuesday morning, Uncle Stan paced like a dog who has to go out. But he stayed home except for a little while Saturday afternoon, after the undertaker had gone, when he drove to the Zelenas' to call his family in Red Wing.

He would sit with Aunt Betty for a few minutes, trying now and then to talk with her.

"Don't you want to talk about it, honey? You know, I feel bad, too."

But Aunt Betty was wandering in dark fields of distraction. Uncle Stan would pace then, up and down the bedroom. I sat on the front porch, and I could hear him talking and pacing. Out the screen door he would explode, and plunging his hands deep into his pockets, he would march around the house, head down, trying to understand how everything had gone so wrong.

When he'd nearly worn a path in the grass, he hurled himself back into the house and threw himself violently down on a kitchen chair. "Is there coffee, Arlene?"

Mama poured him coffee, but withheld sympathy.

"You think it's my fault," he said, stirring sugar into his cup.

Maria, whose magic tea was warming on the stove, poured it through a strainer into a cup and, casting a disparaging glance at Uncle Stan, left the room, bearing the healing tea to her patient.

Mama emptied the drain pan under the icebox. "You didn't want anybody to know you weren't making any money," she accused.

"You think I'd let her starve, is that what you think?" he asked, offended.

"I think you managed not to notice."

"You're hard," he said, as if sorry to have to point it out.

"She's my sister."

"She's my wife."

"If I'd had to hit her over the head and deliver her to Mama in a gunnysack, I'd have done it, if she were *my* wife."

"You're hard," he repeated, as if this accusation were a shield against her contempt. Contempt was unwomanly. Arlene was unwomanly. "You don't understand men," he said, dismissing her blame.

"I understand some men too well," Mama told him.

He huffed out the back door, leaving the coffee on the table. In the garage, he slammed things around as if he were looking for something or were going to undertake a project, but he had nothing on his mind except confusion and anger.

After a while I followed to see what he was doing. A big cardboard box, broken flat, was spread on the floor. It was what Uncle Stan stretched out on when changing the oil in his car. Now he lay on it, legs pulled up fetally, arms wrapped around himself, sleeping. I tiptoed in and stood watching. Tears, not yet dry, clung to his long lashes like beads of dew. He looked like a hobo sleeping down in the hobo jungle. Seeing him like that made me fear for all of us.

❧ 25 ❧

THE BABY'S name, I learned at the funeral, was Marjorie Ann. If she'd grown up, she'd have been Margie Weller. Sitting in the front pew of St. Ambrose Catholic Church, I tried to imagine what someone named Margie Weller would look like when she was almost seven. Would I like her and want to play with her?

The sun through the vivid stained windows turned the folds of white satin in Margie's little coffin to pink and blue and green. With her beaky nose and pallid, waxy skin, Margie looked like an ugly porcelain doll. Her hands, unnaturally fine and slender for a baby, lay on a child's white, kid prayer book, whose pages were edged with gilt. Wrapped around one tiny wrist and spilling carefully onto the prayer book was a child's rosary, bitty little seed pearls strung along a fine gold chain, ending in a gold cross so delicate it resembled Maria's lace crochet work. Even a book and rosary this small were too large. And they were too beautiful. Their size and beauty made the baby look smaller and uglier. The white gown and bonnet that would have been her christening clothes were the same ones she had worn on Saturday. And they were too large and too fancy. I couldn't help thinking that Marjorie looked like Mrs. Astor's horse.

All of this touched a place in my conscience, which was lashed raw with guilt. I wept obscenely. Mama nudged me and gave me her handkerchief. I couldn't stop. Wherever I turned my mind, the ugly-faced baby, prayer book on her stomach, pricked me.

On Mama's other side was Aunt Betty, cold and gray, barely breathing, and beyond her, Uncle Stan, still looking confused and cross. Nothing would ever be the same between them and me.

Papa, who sat on my other side, poked me in the ribs, shaking his head and frowning. "Be quiet," he whispered. That made me cry more. Early that morning, Papa had driven from Harvester in the Oldsmobile. He was returning early tomorrow, before the morning trains.

Behind us sat Grandma and Grandpa Browning, and Uncle Stan's parents, Alf and Delia. Across the aisle from them were Grandma and Grandpa Erhardt, who lived only thirty miles from Morgan Lake and had come for Mama's sake. They had met Uncle Stan and Aunt Betty but once, at Mama and Papa's wedding. Early this morning, they'd arrived on the milk train with boxes of food. Papa was taking them home later.

In the pew behind Grandma and Grandpa Erhardt were Maria Zelena, her papa, and Mr. McPhee. No one else had come for the funeral except half a dozen anonymous old women in twenty-year-old print dresses and shapeless black hats, which were stitched to their heads with hat pins.

Papa pinched my leg and hissed, "You're putting on quite a show." I buried my face in Mama's skirt, creating big stains of tears and spittle.

"You'd better get her out of here," he told Mama, and slipped out of the pew to let us pass. Pulling me by the hand, Mama hurried me up the side aisle and out into the vestibule.

"What on earth is wrong with you?" Mama whispered sharply. As I could only stare at her and blubber, she took my hand again and hauled me out the door, which clanged behind us disclaimingly, like the righteous gates of heaven. I sat down on the top step, all the way to the side, in the shade cast by the banister wall.

Mama stood two steps below me, pocketbook gripped beneath her arm. "Now, young lady, you tell me what's wrong. Don't you think Aunt Betty feels bad enough, without you making a scene?" I was bent over with my face planted on my drawn-up knees. "Honey, you didn't *know* the baby, how can you be so sad?"

"I can't explain," I told her, my words muffled by my dress.

"Remember, the baby's in heaven, and it's never going to be hungry or tired or sad. Doesn't that make you happy?"

The baby was in limbo, and it was never going to see God.

"Lark, I can't stand here all day. Don't you see how selfish you're being? Aunt Betty needs me in there."

Mama wasn't yelling. She didn't sound angry. She was trying to make me see reason, and her very patience made matters worse. If she'd dragged me home, given me a spanking, and left me there alone, I'd have felt a little better.

"Lark, are you going to answer me?"

The cat had my tongue.

"All right, Lark, if that's the way you want it, you can sit here till after the service. But if you wander off, I'll take the brush to you."

I sat hunched against the banister wall, crying, until at last the tears ran dry, and there were only spasms of sighs left in me.

Mama and Uncle Stan were the first to emerge from the church, one on either side of Aunt Betty, supporting her. Aunt Betty was steady enough on her feet, but she looked like a sleepwalker about to step off a cliff.

Papa, Grandpa Browning, Alf Weller, and Ladislau Zelena carried the tiny coffin, which probably could have been transported by any two of them. Slowly, watching their feet, down the steps they came. Inside the church, the organist continued to wrench straining, wheezing chords from the pump organ.

Aunt Betty, along with Uncle Stan, was eased into the backseat of a black Chrysler chauffeured by the older of the two undertakers. Quietly and with ritual slowness, it glided away from the curb, following the hearse.

Behind the Chrysler Papa drove the Oldsmobile, Mama in the

front seat, Grandma and Grandpa Erhardt in the back, with me between them.

I touched Mama's shoulder. "Isn't the hearse beautiful, Mama? Almost as beautiful as the coffin."

"Oh, Lark," Mama sighed.

The sun flashed like little strokes of lightning from hood ornaments and grills and chromium appointments. All the cars were freshly washed, waxed, and buffed for the occasion. We were the most brilliant thing to pass down Main Street since the last funeral. I was disappointed that so few people saw us.

Mr. Esterly was sweeping the walk in front of the store. He paused, paying heed to our sorrow. On the brick platform, the depot agent, sorting through freight packages, looked up and stilled his hands until we had passed.

Arching the open gates of the cemetery, wrought iron letters, amidst lilies and flourishes, spelled, "St. Ambrose." The hearse turned in and wound along the path laid between weeping willow, cedar, and aspen, halting at length near the center of the graveyard.

Wordlessly, we piled out of cars and hiked across the grass to the open grave waiting for Baby Marjorie. Mindful of the dream in which I'd tumbled into such a pit as this, I backed away, a stone bench beckoning.

From where I sat, I could see Aunt Betty, between Uncle Stan and Mama. She looked as if she might never again speak or move except at someone else's bidding. Unseeing, she glanced my way. I dropped my eyes. Even the empty gaze with which she had swept the hillside was an accusation.

❧ 26 ❧

WHEN WE returned to Aunt Betty's, food was brought out and laid on the lace-covered dining room table. Everyone who had been at the funeral, including Father Dressler from St. Ambrose and the old women who sat in the back pew, came to the house to eat.

I stole into the little bedroom off the kitchen where Mama slept and closed the door. The room was clean and cool, and smelled of Mama's cologne and makeup. Voices murmured beneath the crab apple tree in the backyard, where the men had retreated to smoke. I listened without attention and fell asleep.

Waking, I saw that the afternoon had spent itself. The cot lay in a pool of downy shadow. In the kitchen, the food had been put away. I retrieved a slice of ham from the icebox and a dinner roll from the bread box. I heard the women in the living room talking quietly. Beyond them, out in front of the house, the men lounged on the grass and against the sides of their cars. Alf Weller sat on the running board of his Model A, which was nearly indistinguishable from his son, Stan's.

The Zelenas and McPhee had departed, as had the old ladies, who, Mama said, ate more than men and then proceeded to relate nightmare stories of dying babies and dying mothers, of women who went mad or blind giving birth and women whose babies were born horribly "marked."

Padding barefoot out the back door, I climbed the crab apple tree and sat among its branches, eating the sandwich. From there I discovered that I could see over the Witch's raspberry bushes and into her backyard.

She was kneeling on a cardboard mat, pulling weeds from around tomato plants. Now and then she cocked her head, listening to her own thoughts. After a while she stood. Throwing her work gloves on the back steps, she began to march up and down, up and down. Then she stopped and, with both hands, grabbed hold of the hair which she wore rolled tightly back from her face. She pulled at it frenziedly, as if to yank it out by the roots, and when it was torn from the hairpins that held it and flying wildly around her head, she threw her hands in the air and looked up at the sky. At length she ran into the house, forgetting the gloves lying on the step.

I finished my sandwich, climbed down from the tree, and wandered around the house to the front yard, where my two grandpas and Alf Weller still chewed the rag over President Roosevelt and Hitler. They'd been going on about Roosevelt and Hitler and Chamberlain most of the afternoon, I thought.

"Where's Papa?" I asked Grandpa Erhardt.

"Took Stan for a ride in the Oldsmobile. Said they wouldn't be gone long."

"When did they go?"

Grandpa took out his pocket watch and opened it. "What time did the boys go?" he asked Alf Weller. "About four, was it?"

"About that."

"Then they've been gone close to an hour and a half," Grandpa observed. "Should be back any minute now," he assured me, thinking I had some need of Papa.

In the house the women were again laying food on the table and brewing coffee. Delia Weller and Grandma Erhardt were talking about leaving as soon as supper was out of the way, before it got dark. They didn't like to be on the road when it was dark.

"One thing I'll say for Willy," Mama told Grandma Erhardt, "he's a good driver. You don't need to worry about that."

"Oh, yes, I know. Though sometimes I think he drives too fast," Grandma pointed out.

"I do think Stanley looks poorly," Delia Weller suddenly put in, as if they'd been talking about him all along.

"He's thin," Grandma Erhardt sympathized.

"Yes," Delia agreed. "He's working too hard. And it's worried him, I know, about the baby. These times are so bad. It's not a time for bringing children into the world."

"Well," Grandma Browning injected, "sometimes *God* decides when it's time." She was defending her daughter in case the gist of Delia Weller's conversation was that Aunt Betty ought to have waited until times were better.

"And now," Delia observed, "He's decided that the time wasn't right after all."

Grandma Browning said in a voice so reasonable, it was obvious that she was piqued, "I can't speak for God, but Betty's not getting any younger. If Stanley wants children, he has to consider that.

They've already waited too long, I think. Now Betty's risking her life."

"I wonder if the boys will be coming soon," Grandma Erhardt interrupted mildly. "Supper's nearly ready."

"Lark, go see if Aunt Betty's ready to get up. She should eat."

The bedroom was bathed in a peachy glow from the late afternoon sun. Wearing a cotton kimono, Aunt Betty was gathered into a ball on the bed. Her back was to me, and her spine and ribs pressed against the kimono fabric.

I touched her shoulder. "Aunt Betty?" She sighed in her sleep. "Aunt Betty."

Slowly she returned from the land of Nod and rolled onto her back, staring at the ceiling.

"It's almost time for supper. Mama says you should eat."

She continued to stare.

"Would you like me to brush your hair?"

She looked at me blankly.

"Do you want to put on your dress?" I tried to think of things to say to get her out of bed.

Mama brushed aside the drape and said matter-of-factly, "Time to get up, Betty. Everyone's waiting. We're going ahead without Willie and Stan. They're not back."

"Not back?"

"Willie took Stan for a ride in the Oldsmobile." Mama put her arm around Aunt Betty and helped her to sit. "Get your aunt's slippers from the closet, Lark." We slipped them on her feet.

"I suppose we should leave the boys' plates on the table," Grandma Erhardt said when supper was over, and the table was being cleared. "They'll come hungry."

"I'm starting to worry," Delia said. "It's not like Stanley to miss supper."

Grandma Erhardt assured her, "They've just lost track of time. You know how boys are."

"Yes," Delia agreed. "Still, I worry. The sun is down. Dad and I have to be on our way as soon as the dishes are washed."

"They'll be here, wait and see," Grandma Erhardt promised, tying on the fancy apron she'd brought with her on the train.

"What if they're in the ditch somewhere?" Delia continued, addressing Alf, who had settled himself on the living room couch and was tamping tobacco into his pipe. Referring to the pipe, Delia suggested, "I think you should take that outside."

"They're all right, Mother," he told her impatiently. "Get the dishes washed so we're ready to go."

The dishes were washed and put away, and the kitchen light extinguished when Grandpa Browning brought Aunt Betty back from their little walk around the outside of the house. Settling her in the corner of the sofa, he wandered outside, peeling a stick of Beechnut and folding it into his mouth. Alf was on the porch, smoking his pipe, sharing opinions with Grandpa Erhardt about the state government in St. Paul and how it had let people down.

Delia sat on a dining room chair in a posture of attention, ready to spring up at the sound of a car. "I don't know what to do," she told Grandma Erhardt, who stood nearby, removing her fancy apron and folding it carefully. "We've got to get home, Alf and I, but we can't leave without knowing that Stanley's all right."

Grandma Erhardt nodded. "How are you feeling?" she asked Aunt Betty. "Do you have pain?"

Grandma Browning said, "The baby was so small, Betty didn't have much tearing. That's what Arlene said, didn't you?"

"Yes," Mama answered. "But she had a lot of pain from the poisons."

Aunt Betty was looking out the open window into the near darkness of late twilight. Maybe she was thinking about Baby Marjorie, who was spending her first night in limbo. That's what I was thinking about as I hung on the periphery of the evening. And I pondered Grandma Browning's words about tearing. What, I wondered, did the baby's size have to do with Aunt Betty's pain?

"I remember how torn I was when Stanley was born," Delia told us. "It was three months before I was out of bed. He was a big baby. Eight pounds, nearly."

The headlights of a car appeared at the top of the block. Delia sprang from her chair.

"Not Willie," Grandpa Browning called out.

I pushed open the screen door.

"Don't stand with the door open," Grandma Browning told me. "You'll let the moths in."

Mama said, "I can't sit around waiting. It makes me nervous. Lark, you want to go for a walk?"

"What if Willie comes?" Grandma Browning asked.

"We're not going far."

On the porch Mama said, "I won't be long, Papa. I just need to walk." From the way she grabbed my hand and pulled me along, I knew Mama was mad.

"I've got a pain in my side," I told her as we neared the Skelly station, which was closed and dark, its windows giving back a faint, spectral reflection of Mama and me as we passed.

Nothing on downtown Main Street was open except Boomer's Tavern. In front of it, watery light lay in a pool on the sidewalk. A single car, not Papa's, was parked at the curb.

"Wait here," Mama ordered, leaving me on the steps while she went in to inquire. She was back in a minute, grabbing my hand. "He's not here," she told me. "He hasn't been here."

Down the street we continued, past Esterly's Groceries and General Merchandise, the barber shop, and finally, a tiny café, long ago out of business and abandoned. Barely visible through the streaked window, a few cheap wooden chairs and small tables waited for ghosts to sit down and order.

A light burned in the depot, and another outside illuminated the platform. "Have you seen Willie Erhardt or Stanley Weller?" Mama asked the agent through the open window of the office.

"No, ma'am."

So Mama and I tromped back to Aunt Betty's. The three men were still on the front porch. "No sign of them?" Grandpa Browning asked.

"No," Mama said, and opened the screen door. "Get your nightie on, Lark."

Delia was sitting at the dining room table quietly crying. "I know something's happened," she whimpered, dabbing her eyes.

Mama shepherded me into the bathroom to put on my nightie. "Do you think Papa's had an accident?" I asked.

"No."

"Why don't you?"

"I know your papa."

"Then what's he doing?"

"Drinking."

After she'd washed my face and hands, Mama put me in her bed, kissed me, and turned out the light. "Don't worry about your papa. God watches out for fools, children, and Democrats. Your papa qualifies for all three."

When I woke, it was growing light outside. Lying beside me on the narrow cot was Grandma Erhardt, still wearing her good flowered dress, though she'd removed her shoes and stockings.

Trying not to disturb her, I crawled to the foot of the daybed and climbed over the end. On the living room couch, Grandpa Erhardt was curled up, the crazy quilt tucked around his shoulders. Delia and Alf shared the rollaway.

Peeking into Aunt Betty's room, I discovered Mama and Grandma Browning squeezed into bed, still in their funeral clothes, one on either side of Aunt Betty. Grandpa Browning lay stretched out on the floor with a sofa pillow under his head. The room smelled of cigars and warm flesh.

The kitchen clock said four-thirty. I ate the last of the potato salad that was in the icebox and let myself out the back door. Laying a dark trail where my feet crushed the dewy grass, I made my way around the house to the front porch and sat down on the step to wait for Papa.

Within minutes the Oldsmobile appeared at the top of the block. Papa switched off the ignition and let the car coast to a stop.

"There he is," Mama said, her face obscured in shadow behind the screen door. Her cold voice made me shiver.

❧ 27 ❧

PAPA HESITATED. He must have considered driving away again.

I dashed across the street. "Papa, where *were* you? We thought you were in an accident."

"Ran out of gas," he said wearily, crossly, as if I had no right to ask, "and couldn't find anybody open."

Uncle Stan was flopped in the backseat, asleep, head thrown back, mouth agape, snoring. The car smelled strongly of alcohol.

"Why didn't you come home?"

"I told you, we ran out of gas."

"But before, when the gas stations were open, why didn't you come home then?"

"Leave me alone," he said, and reached into the backseat to shake Uncle Stan.

The house quickly filled with embarrassment as first Grandpa Browning, then Grandpa Erhardt, Delia, and Alf woke to discover that Papa and Uncle Stan had returned, not bloody or with any other good excuse, but with a silly story of running out of gas.

Both men headed toward the kitchen. "Any coffee? We haven't exactly had a swell time of it, you know, sitting out there in the country all night."

"Where'd you run out of gas?" Grandpa Erhardt wanted to know.

"Between Archer and Mankato," Papa told him.

"What took you to Mankato?" Alf inquired. Hitching up his trousers and tucking in his shirt, which had come out while he slept, he followed the men to the kitchen.

"Nothing in particular," Papa said, lifting the coffee pot, finding it empty, and slamming it down again. "Thought I'd show Stan how fast the Olds'll go. Got her up to a hundred between here and Farley."

Uncle Stan sat at the kitchen table, barely able to keep his bloodshot eyes from closing, letting Papa handle the explanations.

"Willie." It was Grandma Erhardt, small and angry, in the doorway of the little back bedroom. "You and Stan should have stayed to home. What about Betty, here alone?"

"Alone?" Papa snorted. "With twenty people hanging over her, including a bunch of batty old bitches I never saw before?"

"You be careful how you talk to your mother," Grandpa Erhardt told Papa.

Grandma Erhardt pursued. "You know what I mean, Willie. Stanley was needed here. His wife nearly died this past week."

Delia clung to the kitchen door, weak from the night's ordeal. "The two of you should be ashamed. You don't know what you've put us through. Your pa and me are not young, Stanley. You could've killed us. We thought you were dead someplace in a ditch."

"Instead of being drunk God knows where," Alf added, furiously shaking the change in his pocket.

Mama came into the kitchen and began running water into two coffee pots.

"How come you didn't walk to a farmhouse and borrow some gas?" Grandpa Browning, in his stocking feet, wandered into the kitchen, massaging the stubble on his jaw.

"It was too late to go waking people up."

"But where *were* you until it was too late?" Grandma Erhardt demanded.

"What the hell is this?" Papa asked. "A court of law?" Standing in the center of the room, he looked around at them with accusation and great self-concern, as if he were a dog surrounded by wolves.

"It's more than a court of law, Willie, it's your conscience," Grandma Erhardt told him.

"Your mother wants to know, where were you?" Grandpa Erhardt pressed.

"We went to Mankato. We had a couple of drinks. You gonna send us to prison?"

"How much money did he lose playing cards, Stan?" Mama's voice sliced quietly through Papa's drama.

"Not much," Stan said, closing his eyes and looking as though he might topple off the chair. He was experiencing a kind of second drunk.

"Stanley," his mother cried in horror, "*you* didn't gamble, did you?"

"Juss . . . juss twenny-five dollars Willie . . . Willie lent me." He put his hand on the table to steady himself.

"My God. That's a third of what your pa makes in a month. Stanley, what's becoming of you?" Delia shrieked.

"A man should never gamble what he can't afford to lose," Alf pronounced.

"F'chrissakes, I'm broke. I can't buy food. My wife's starving." Tears slipped from beneath his lids.

Suddenly Aunt Betty appeared in the doorway, dressed in her nightie. "You don't have to tell them," she cried, running to him, pressing his head against her body where the great swelling had been.

"Whassa use?" he asked. "Whassa use? We're at some kinda end here." He grabbed Aunt Betty's hand. "I thought I could make us some money tonight. I thought I could be your hero." He lifted his face to see if she understood.

Mama had seen and heard enough. Turning her back, she said, "You must be real proud, Willie."

Spinning her around, Papa slapped her face. "Don't you ever shame me in front of my folks," he yelled at her.

"What kind of man are you?" Grandpa Erhardt demanded, grabbing Papa's arm.

Papa swung around, pushing his father away. Thrown off balance, Grandpa flung out his arms to catch himself, but there was nothing to hold, and he fell to the linoleum, striking his head on the corner of the icebox.

Before Alf could reach her, Delia folded up in a sigh. Seeing what he'd done, Papa grabbed Grandpa Erhardt under the arms.

"Stan, give me a hand here," he said.

"I'm all right," Grandpa told him, but his head was bleeding.

Stan took Grandpa's legs, and he and Papa carried him to the couch.

"Pa, I'm sorry," Papa kept repeating.

Mama grabbed a clean dish towel from the drawer and held it against Grandpa Erhardt's head. Grandma Browning and Alf saw to Delia, who soon came around, weeping and telling them again and again, "We've got to talk about Stanley."

When Grandpa Erhardt's wound had stopped bleeding, and Mama had washed it, Grandpa said, "Annie, it's time we got home."

"Let me get you some breakfast before you leave," Mama said.

"No, no, Arlene," Grandma Erhardt demurred, "we'll be home before we know it. You have enough to do here."

When Grandpa and Grandma Erhardt were settled into the Oldsmobile and ready to leave, Papa tried to put his arm around Mama as they stood together on the porch. Mama pulled abruptly away.

"Did you see your sister in there?" Papa asked. "That's how a woman treats a man if she cares about him."

Mama looked dumbfounded.

At length she said coldly, disinterestedly, "You're going back to Harvester from New Frankfurt?"

Papa nodded, wincing and putting a hand to his forehead, where a headache had hold of him.

"I want to know how much money you lost last night," Mama said.

"You can't leave me alone, can you?"

"How much?"

"I wrote IOUs. I'll pay 'em off over the next few months."

"How much? I'm the one who pays the bills. I'm the one who's got to figure out how to feed us. I want to know where we stand."

Finally he seemed to cave in. "I lost a lot."

"More than two hundred?"

He nodded.

"Oh, God, Willie." Mama started to cry.

"Jesus, not where my folks can see you, Arlene."

"How much, Willie?"

"Four hundred and fifty."

Mama sank down on the porch step, her face in her hands, her shoulders heaving.

"It's going to be all right, Arlene. You'll see. I gotta go now." He began backing away. "When're you coming home?"

Mama didn't answer.

"Well, all right then. I gotta go." He turned and hurried across the street to the car.

As the Oldsmobile pulled away, Grandma Erhardt waved. She was worried about Mama, but she smiled and waved.

When the car had turned the corner and was gone, I said, "Don't cry, Mama. I love you. Don't cry." I dropped the five-dollar bill into her lap.

"Where did you get that?"

"Grandpa Erhardt told me to give it to you when they were gone."

Then Mama cried harder, and I was sorry I hadn't waited until later.

❦ 28 ❧

AFTER A WHILE Grandpa Browning came out on the porch and stood behind Mama. "What's the matter, Arlene?"

"Nothing, Papa."

"Willie lose a lot of money?"

"It's not anything, Papa. I'm just worried about Betty and Stan. What're they going to do?" She wiped her eyes on the back of her forearm.

"We'll work something out."

"What can we work out?" She wanted concrete answers, not "eyewash," as she called it.

"Your mama and Delia are in there fixing breakfast. We'll eat and then we'll talk," Grandpa told her.

After breakfast I helped Grandma Browning with the dishes while the others remained at the table, trying to work out a future for Uncle Stan and Aunt Betty.

It was Grandpa Browning's idea that Stan and Betty give up their little house. Aunt Betty, who was in delicate health, would stay with Grandpa and Grandma in Blue Lake while Stan, with a little money scraped together here and there, would head out in the Model A for California.

"No," Aunt Betty cried when she heard the last. "Stan isn't going anyplace without me! She grabbed hold of Stan's sleeve as if he were going to be plucked away then and there.

"There isn't any work here," Grandpa told her patiently. "What's Stan gonna do? Now, hear it to the end. As soon as Stan has work, he'll send for you. If we write to Cousin Lloyd, I know Stan can stay with him and Marlis till he finds something. Fact is, Lloyd might be able to get him on right there where *he* works for the movies."

Mama was stalwart and resourceful as they sat planning and discussing, businesslike, but positive and encouraging, too. She thought of people they could touch for a little money—a dollar or two here and there—to stake Stanley in his new life, his new adventure, as she put it.

"And we'll keep a record of everyone's name and the amount," she said. "And when you're on your feet, you'll pay them back, one by one, plus interest." They all liked that idea because it wasn't charity.

When the meeting in the dining room broke up, Alf and Delia climbed into their Model A, subdued and exhausted, saddened but convinced—at least Alf was—that what Stanley was doing was right and necessary.

Mama went as far as the front porch to see them off, while Aunt Betty and Uncle Stan accompanied them to the car. Grandpa Browning stood just outside the screen door, waving. Grandma had not tried to get up from the couch. Her leg was swollen and throbbing. It wasn't that long ago that the cast had come off her ankle.

Released from her in-laws, Aunt Betty climbed the porch steps. "You damned bitch," she spat at Mama.

"What're you—" Grandpa started to interrupt indignantly.

"You damned bitch," Aunt Betty repeated. "I don't want to look at you again as long as I live."

"Help me up from here, Lark," Grandma demanded.

"You stop that," I screamed at Aunt Betty and sprang out the door, knocking Grandpa out of the way. "Don't talk to my mama that way."

"Jim!" Grandma called, furious to be so helpless. "Help me up here!"

Ignoring Grandma's cries, Grandpa took a step toward Aunt Betty, grabbing her upper arm. "Girl . . ."

She wrenched away. "Who do you think you are," she hissed at Mama, "packing Stan off like he was a kid? You're so good at bossing people. You sure you're not a man?" she taunted, bending close to Mama, pulling on the bodice of Mama's dress.

Mama's hands flew to Aunt Betty's hair. "I don't care if you *did* lose your baby, you can't talk to me that way!"

At last Grandpa and Uncle Stan fell upon the sisters. Grandma, having struggled to her feet, stood horrified and helpless at the door. "Oh, my God. Oh, my God," she kept repeating.

29

I PEERED through the darkly streaked glass, into the dead café. Dust lay thick along the chipped and rotting windowsill where I leaned, and dust filmed the little counter and the few tables and chairs inside. The cardboard sign tacked on the wall showing a small blond girl eating Butter Nut bread was faded to sepia.

Nothing was ever going to happen again in the café. It was like limbo. Nothing good would happen and nothing bad. Everything was set in place as it would remain forever. Baby Marjorie was someplace like this.

"It's a good day for ice cream," McPhee remarked, startling me. He had approached from the depot, where he'd been checking the freight, finding none had arrived.

"What do you think it's like in limbo?" I asked McPhee when we were perched on the high stools at Boomer's Tavern.

He looked askance, considered for a moment, then replied, "Like Morgan Lake, I think." After a minute he asked, "What made you think of limbo?"

"Aunt Betty's baby. There wasn't a priest when Marjorie died, so she's gone to limbo."

"Maria Zelena tell you that?"

I shook my head.

"Don't you suppose Maria baptized Marjorie?"

"She's not a priest."

"Anybody can baptize a baby if it's an emergency. That I know." He turned to Boomer. "Ain't it so, Boomer? Anybody can baptize if it's an emergency?"

"That's my understanding," Boomer told us.

It wouldn't alter my responsibility for the baby's death, but it would make me feel some better to know that she was in heaven.

"Grandpa and Grandma Browning went home today."

"That so?"

"Monday I'm going on the train to stay with them."

"That so?"

"Mama's going to help Aunt Betty have a sale and get packed up."

As we emerged from Boomer's Tavern, a little before ten-thirty, I fell in step beside McPhee, hands clasped behind my back.

"Do you think Maria Zelena has the coffee on?" he asked.

As she opened the screen door and stood back to let us pass, McPhee told her, "We've come to find out if you baptized the Weller baby."

I followed him to the kitchen, girding myself for Maria's answer. How slowly she moved. How very many steps there suddenly were to serving coffee. Reaching down cups and saucers, arranging them at three separate places. Opening a drawer and withdrawing three spoons, laying each beside a cup and saucer, and so on.

When she had lowered herself onto her usual chair in the most unhurried way and tucked an errant strand of hair into the braided crown from which it had escaped, Maria picked up her spoon and held it poised above her cup.

"You want to know if I baptized your aunt's baby?"

I nodded.

"Is it so important?"

I cleared my throat. "Yes."

"Why should you worry about this?" she asked.

I couldn't tell her that I was the one who was supposed to catch the baby if the stork let it fall. I wanted Maria to think well of me.

"I want Marjorie to be happy and see God," I said, sounding very false.

Maria looked hard at me. "You think the baby won't see God if she's not baptized?"

"That's what Sister said," I explained.

"You mustn't believe everything you hear, little Lark."

"But the catechism says . . ."

"What kind of god would keep innocent babies out of heaven?" she asked. "A crazy god!"

"Don't say that!" The catechism had to be right. Without its rules there was no shape to life, no ground under my feet.

"Not everything in church is truth," Maria went on. "And not all truth turns up in church."

My chair knocked hard against the stove as I fled from the kitchen. Out the front door I galloped.

I hated Maria. We had become friends, and now she turned out to be a heretic.

30

AFTER DINNER Mama sat at the dining room table, compiling a list of people who might be willing to lend Uncle Stan a dollar or two for the "adventure." When the list was complete, she began writing letters to prospective donors.

"What do you think of this?" she asked, turning in her chair to read Aunt Betty her first effort.

Aunt Betty sat in the arm chair, obscured by thick twilight. The wan yellow from the dining room barely brushed her features, and she did not turn toward it as Mama read.

"Dear Cousin Geneva,

I am writing to let you know that my sister Betty's baby girl was born dead Saturday, June 24. Betty was very near death herself. It is a miracle that we have her with us. The baby, which was the image of Betty, was full term though very small. Betty named her Marjorie Ann, after our grandmother, Marjorie Ann Browning.

Times have been hard for Betty and Stan, but they are courageous and determined to get ahead. Stan is driving to California to find work, and Betty will stay with Mama and Papa until he sends for her.

I'm helping my sister get ready for a sale so she and Stan can clear up their debts and start fresh. What an adventure!

Many relations on both sides are contributing to the 'California Adventure.' One said, 'I'll pay for gas for the Model A.' Another told me, 'I'm buying Stan a night in a travel court.' It's thrilling, Geneva, the way people are jumping on the bandwagon.

I personally am making a record of everybody who contributes, so that we can let them know about Stan's progress and repay their generosity when he's on his feet again. I told Stan and Betty I was sure we could count on you to help them put tragedy behind them.

Well, Geneva, I must sign off now as Lark is calling.

Love to all,

Arlene"

"I'm not calling," I told Mama.

"Never mind," she hushed me. "What do you think, Betty?"

"I think Marjorie is just a free drinking glass in a box of soap flakes to you—something to sell your product."

"Which is?" Mama wanted to know.

"Stanley and me. You're selling us like soap flakes, Arlene. It's disgusting. You never heard from any cousins. This whole thing is cheap and trashy."

Wounded, Mama tried to hide her disappointment. "You've got to get people excited, Betty."

Stan, sitting at the kitchen table smoking a Lucky Strike, called,

"I like the part about 'courageous and determined to get ahead.' "

Aunt Betty went on, "Going to California and getting a job is what *you'd* like to do, Arlene." She left her chair, making her way to the table where Mama sat writing. "*I'd* like to stay here and just get by."

Mama looked at her in amazement. " 'Just get by'? You weren't just getting by. You were starving. Your baby died because you were starving. I'm sorry if that's something you don't want to hear, but don't tell me you were getting by."

Aunt Betty stared daggers at Mama. "That's not true, Stanley," she assured him, crossing to the kitchen door, her voice tearful. "I wasn't starving, honey."

But Uncle Stanley was not in the kitchen. He had vanished, maybe to the alley to finish his Lucky Strike in peace.

"Now look what you've done," Aunt Betty cried, turning to Mama. "Driven Stanley out of his own house. When am I going to be rid of you?"

"In the morning, you silly bitch." Springing to her feet, Mama threw the letter on the table and hurtled past Aunt Betty, through the kitchen to the little back bedroom.

Slumping against the doorjamb, Aunt Betty rubbed her brow with her fingertips, working her lips savagely. At length her hand dropped to her side. She surveyed the tiny rooms with a tormented, devouring gaze.

In the living room I lay on the couch, pretending to be asleep although I still wore my sunsuit and shoes. Through quivering, slitted eyelids, I watched Aunt Betty. She was like a sad old woman, dry and cold and full of pains. Last Christmas at Grandma Browning's, she'd been pretty and gay.

But that was Christmas. Uncle Stan was still a bookkeeper then. It was after January inventory that they had put him on the road. At Christmas he was making fifty dollars a month and they were only scraping by, but it was fifty *sure* dollars and they weren't starving.

Clasping her arms across her belly, Aunt Betty drifted, ghost-like, across the dining room, through the living room, out the complaining screen door, and down the steps.

I sat up, peeking out the lace curtains to watch her glide along the narrow walk to Uncle Stan's dusty Model A parked on the street. Up into the dark behemoth she climbed and laid her head against the seat. In the deepening twilight of nine-thirty, it was only just possible to see her white hands caress the black steering wheel.

Much later, maybe an hour, the screen door squawked like a parrot, and I turned onto my side, jabbing myself with the corner of *Happy Stories for Bedtime*.

Aunt Betty slipped into the house and stood hugging herself as if she were cold.

Mama appeared at the kitchen door. "You were out there so long," she said, "I thought you'd fallen asleep."

"I've been thinking."

"I poured myself a glass of iced tea. Would you like one?"

As Aunt Betty moved across the dining room, she and Mama both said, "I've been thinking," at exactly the same time. They burst out laughing and fell into each other's arms.

"Let me talk first," Mama said.

"No, let *me* talk first," Aunt Betty insisted.

Mama led Aunt Betty to the little table by the window, then fetched a second glass from the cupboard. I sat up, repositioning myself so that I could see them.

Mama opened the icebox and removed the pitcher of iced tea.

"You're only trying to help Stanley and me," Aunt Betty conceded. "I see that. It's just that when you try to think for me, you think up things I never would, like going to California."

"But don't you see—"

"Let me finish. I know I *should* want to go, but I'm not done with *this* place. I haven't finished the thinking and crying that needs to be done here before I can root myself up. It's been less than a week since the baby was born. I'm still walking funny."

Mama filled Betty's glass and sat down opposite her at the table. "I understand, I do. I wish there was time for you to say good-bye properly. But every week that you stay, is a week deeper in debt."

"You don't know how hard it is to leave the baby."

"Has Stan tried WPA?" Mama asked. Maybe there was yet a way for Uncle Stanley and Aunt Betty to stay here.

"Relief?" Aunt Betty replied, shocked that her sister could ask.

"From all accounts, it's better than starving."

"No, it's not. This isn't pride talking, Arlene. WPAers are treated worse than crooks around here. We could never hold our heads up."

Mama went to Aunt Betty and knelt beside her chair, stroking her sister's pale, curly hair, which she had always envied. "Then there's just one answer, isn't there?" she said, brushing the hair back from Aunt Betty's hollow, feverish face. "And when you get to California, you're going to have another baby. I predict it."

"I don't think God wants me to have a baby."

"God doesn't know what He wants. He's always giving with one hand and taking with the other."

"I needed *this* baby." Aunt Betty spoke softly and looked directly into Mama's eyes. "It was going to be my reward for being good and doing without."

No one was ever going to forget that I let that baby fall.

☙ 31 ❧

THE FOLLOWING Monday morning, before he went out on the road, Uncle Stanley drove Mama and me to the depot in his Model A. I was leaving for Grandma Browning's.

Coming out the door at Aunt Betty's at nine-thirty into the already heavy and somnolent day, Mama observed to me, "You probably won't be back here. Take a good look around."

The thought hadn't occurred to me. For the first time, I was pierced by the little panic and tristesse occasioned by small things passing irrevocably from view.

Clambering into the backseat, I waved to Aunt Betty and looked around at the street, the houses, the trees, and even the old yellow dog lifting his leg on an elm in front of the Witch's house.

Glancing again toward the porch, I waved once more, but Aunt Betty was gone. We hadn't pulled away yet, and she was done with me. You shouldn't do that. When someone was leaving, you shouldn't go in the house until they'd disappeared, with you waving them out of sight. But I was the one who let the baby fall.

Belching and kicking up dust, Uncle Stanley's car bounced

down Main Street, past the Skelly station and Boomer's Tavern, Esterly's Groceries and General Merchandise, and the dead café. At the depot Uncle Stanley went in with Mama to get my ticket. We had nearly half an hour until train time, so I wandered down to the dead café for one last look, a farewell to Baby Marjorie.

Its unaltered condition fascinated me and provoked a sort of disbelief. I studied the room intently, trying to catch it in some small modification. But each chair was precisely as it had been, each dead fly on the interior window sill lay moldering in the very spot it had yesterday. Wasn't there *something*? Not that I could find. I was strangely comforted by that, and I turned away before Mama had to call me to come.

McPhee, wearing his same striped overalls, was pulling the freight wagon out of the freight room. "So you're leaving us," he said.

I nodded. After running out of Maria's kitchen on Thursday, I was embarrassed to see him. I would do the same again, but it was still a skunk lying in the road between us.

"We'll miss you."

People said things like that without meaning them, but I appreciated the kindness. I would miss McPhee. "Do you think you might come to Harvester some time?" I asked.

He leaned on the freight wagon. "Well, I might," he said.

"If you do, knock on the depot door that's near the parking lot. That's where I live."

"I'll do that." He gazed off across the tracks in the direction of the cemetery. "Maria Zelena was sorry that you had to leave all of a sudden that way," he told me. "She took a shine to you."

I said nothing. My face was growing warm. I wished he hadn't brought up Maria Zelena.

"Maria's got an idea that you worry too much," he observed, eyeing me sideways while pretending to study the distance.

Why was he embarrassing me when I was leaving? Now was the time to make idle talk and send me away with a smile. Instead, McPhee was stirring everything inside me that I wanted left sleeping. He didn't know that I had killed the baby. I stood there, dumb as a doorknob.

McPhee looked me up and down. "I said to Maria, 'The girl's a deep thinker. She's not so much a worrier as a deep thinker.' You're not worrying yourself about that baby being in limbo, are you?"

"Not if Maria baptized her." I watched him closely.

"She told me she did," he said.

He was lying, and his lying was evidence that limbo was bad business. He took one of my hands and shook it. It lay limp in his.

"Whatever they tell you, deep thinker, God loves us all. Me, you, and your aunt's baby." Wouldn't it be lovely if God was that simple? Like McPhee and like Santa Claus. McPhee let go of my hand and lifted the tongue of the freight wagon, pulling it down the brick platform toward Main Street.

Mama emerged from the depot with Uncle Stanley close behind, tucking a couple of dollar bills into his wallet, confusion and a desire for confidence fighting each other for control of his features. What had Mama said to him? Her own face wore a take-charge expression. Mama had my grip in her right hand, a bag of lunch in her left, and *Happy Stories for Bedtime* tucked under her left arm.

Uncle Stanley swept me up in his arms and asked, "Are you still my best girl?" I hugged him because I knew no better. "That's my girl. You won't forget your Uncle Stanley, will you?"

I shook my head. He clung to me oddly, squeezing me too tightly, as if it really mattered that I was his girl.

"How about a good-bye kiss?" he asked. I planted one solidly on his cheek. He was hurting my ribs with his hug, but I kept quiet, mindful that I would soon be back on the platform. "That's just what I needed," he said, setting me down. "I won't wash my cheek till I see you again." He winked at me.

Turning to Mama, Uncle Stanley said, "Well, Arlene, I'll see you on Friday then. When d'ya think we'll have the sale? I have to give them notice at work."

"A week from next Saturday. And the week after that you'll be on your way to California."

"Well, I'll see you on Friday then," he said again, and took my hand. We walked together to his car. He didn't want to drive to Mankato and give his notice. He didn't want to go back out on the road, smiling and shaking hands and not selling anything, staying with aunts and cousins because he couldn't afford a rooming house. I could feel that sickening reluctance in the grip of his hand. He wanted . . . what? To climb into bed in a half-lit room with the sheet up around his head.

Pulling himself up into the car, he said, "Wish me luck."

"Good luck, Uncle Stanley. You'll sell a lot of machines this week. But it doesn't matter, come home anyway."

Hurriedly he put the car into reverse, backed up, then headed out to the street and away. I waved to him although he did not look back.

From the open window of the withdrawing train, I waved and blew Mama kisses until she was out of sight. She, on the platform, did the same until I was gone. Then I pulled a hanky from one pocket and my ticket from the other, laying the ticket on the seat and clandestinely dabbing my eyes with the hanky. Soon the last of the houses and sheds and rubber tire swings and broken cars disappeared. Now Mama was *there*, and I was someplace entirely else. Many times before I had visited Grandma and Grandpa Browning alone. I nevertheless felt an emptiness inside my chest, as if, quite literally, I had gone and left my heart.

When the conductor had punched my ticket and slipped the stub into the metal clip between the windows, I dragged the grip out from behind the seat and hoisted it onto the empty seat opposite mine. Releasing the metal hasps, I opened the flimsy suitcase and extracted from beneath my dresses and underwear the tablet and pencil I had tucked in there while Mama was packing. The sin notebook.

Mama had taught me to write numbers up to one hundred. When I had entered sin one hundred in the notebook, I hadn't the temerity to tell her that I needed bigger numbers, so I started over with one. Now I flipped the pages to the most recent entries. I was up to thirty-four for the third time. With the use-blunted lead I printed: "34—killed a baby." Hastily returning the tablet and pencil to the grip, I closed the case and hauled it back, behind the seat.

Laying my head down and closing my eyes, I covered my heart with my fist so that no one passing in the aisle could see its wild beating.

32

WITH THE remains of ten years of marriage packed into two, cheap pasteboard grips and two cardboard boxes tied with twine, Aunt Betty stepped down from the westbound train in Blue Lake on Monday of the third week in July, Mama right behind her.

Aunt Betty screwed up her eyes against the sun. "It's so hot and dusty here," she said. "And the wind's always blowing grit in your face."

"It's no hotter here than in Morgan Lake," Mama told her, grabbing me and giving me a big hug.

"Oh, it *is*. Stanley always said Blue Lake was the hottest spot in the state in July and the coldest in January." She stood on the platform, looking around. "The prairie's so flat, it's like living on top of the dining room table." She hadn't even said hello to Grandpa and me. "For God's sake, don't let them bury me here."

"We have to be patient," Grandma advised Mama on Tuesday.

"*You* have to be patient," Mama replied. "*I'm* taking Lark and going home. I've got my own life to tend to."

Upstairs Aunt Betty rested, the oscillating fan on the bureau trained on her. Mama sat at the dining room table, paging through *Life* magazine, while Grandma perched on a high stool, ironing Grandpa's undershirts.

"Did you see this about Japan?" Mama asked idly, continuing to read. "Everybody's in the army it looks like, except the old men. I'd hate to live there."

"It's the Germans that bother me," Grandma said. "Did you read the piece about the English? They're getting ready for another war, it says. I don't know why countries can't get along." She folded the undershirt and added it to a growing pile of ironed underwear lying on the table. "When do you leave?" she asked Mama.

"Tomorrow."

"That soon? I thought I'd have the Dugans and Standishes for Sunday dinner. They'd like to see you."

"I have to get home. I hate to think what the place looks like with Willie baching so long."

"A few more days wouldn't hurt."

"There's business to tend to," Mama said, closing the discussion.

On the train home the following morning, Mama grabbed my hands in hers and held them up. "Look, Lark, your nails! Look how long they are."

It was the first time in memory that my nails had grown beyond the quick and had whitish tips like other people's. Despite the guilts and worries of the past three weeks, I had not bitten them.

Now I withdrew them, tucking them under me, grinning imbecilically and staring out the window at nothing, filled with embarrassment and pride.

"I'm proud of you," Mama went on. "This afternoon you can walk down to Eggers's Drug Store and buy a bottle of LaCross fingernail polish. What color would you like?"

"Pink."

"Pink it is."

I wished that Angela Roosevelt could see my long nails.

That afternoon when we stepped across the threshold, Mama halted so suddenly that I ran into her. "My God," she blurted, surveying the ravages of Papa's three weeks of keeping house.

Dirty dishes littered every surface. Precarious towers of plates and cereal bowls teetered, held in bizarre constructions by the glue of hardened vegetable matter and the mucilage of old oatmeal. On the stove, hamburger barnacles encrusted the blackened skillet. Gingerly Mama stepped across the room to the sink and pulled back the curtain concealing the slop pail.

Seeing that the pails had spilled over, she cried, "Willie, you sonofabitch." But Papa was away down at the freight room, storing cartons.

Mama dropped down onto a kitchen chair. "Welcome home," she said to no one in particular.

Papa did not show up at his usual lunch hour. I was relieved. When the mess was cleaned up, maybe Mama would calm down. We scrubbed and scraped and washed and dried and wiped up and sorted out. Betweentimes we hauled slops across the tracks.

"I see what he's up to," Mama said.

"What's he up to, Mama?"

"If he makes coming home bad enough, he thinks I won't go. My own sister nearly dying, and he's punishing me."

After two hours our furious labors in the kitchen were done. Now Mama turned toward the living room, where Papa's socks and underwear and shirts were draped over the furniture and strewn across the floor. Ashtrays overflowed. On the arm of the sofa, a brown wound about the size of a dime revealed pale stuffing.

It was twenty past four when we finished bringing order out of the chaos. Mama lay on the living room couch with a cold cloth on her forehead, a knife pain stabbing her from temple to temple. The drapes were drawn.

"Bring my purse," she said. "It's on the bureau." From its varied and sweet-smelling contents, she extracted two dimes. "Go get your nail polish. Don't lose the change, and don't dawdle."

I dawdled a little. While the big clock above the prescription counter pulled the moments to it with a tick and pushed them away with a tock, and Mr. Eggers puttered, measuring and mixing, glancing up occasionally to make certain I wasn't pouring Evening in Paris talcum into my palm or removing breast pumps from their boxes, I lingered before the Coty's display, intoxicating myself with the potentiality of being beautiful and smelling of crushed peaches and sandalwood.

"Was there something you wanted?" the druggist inquired, calling from the chest-high space where he worked with the mortar and pestle.

"Fingernail polish. Pink."

All the way home I caressed the little bottle, turning it upside down and right side up to observe the thick, lush flow of the enamel. In the kitchen I set the bottle on the table. "It's called Precious Pink."

"Put it on my bureau," Mama told me, pouring mayonnaise dressing over macaroni and tuna salad, a favorite, hot-weather dinner of hers but one which Papa called "Fairy Salad."

"Can't we paint my nails now?"

"Do you see the time?" she asked, indicating the electric clock. It was five-thirty. "I told you not to dawdle. It's almost supper time."

"Did your headache go away?" I asked, setting the polish on Mama's bureau beside her perfumes.

"No such luck."

"Is it a migraine?"

"Not yet."

"What's a breast pump?" I asked, sitting down at the table. "They've got breast pumps at Eggers's."

Papa opened the screen door. "What difference is it to you what a breast pump is?"

"They've got them at Eggers's."

"They've got plenty of things at Eggers's that are none of your business."

Stirring the mayonnaise into the salad with a big spoon, Mama said, "A breast pump is something—"

"I said it was none of her business, Arlene," Papa interrupted.

"There's no reason the child shouldn't know what a breast pump is."

Papa closed the inner door and stood before it.

"It's too hot to have the door closed," Mama said. "I've got a headache. Please open it."

"I don't want the whole world hearing us arguing about breast pumps."

"If you don't argue, they won't hear us," Mama told him, crossing to the refrigerator. "Do you want iced tea?"

"You know I don't drink that slop." Ignoring Mama's request that he open the door, Papa sat down at his place and, smiling, said, "Let's not fight."

Mama slammed the refrigerator door and set the cold tea pitcher on the table. Papa grabbed her wrist, pulling her down on his lap. "I'm glad you're home. I missed you."

"If you missed me so much, why didn't you pick the place up before I got home?" Mama asked coldly.

"I was going to. I thought you were coming tomorrow," he said.

"I told you when I was coming."

Mama pulled away and went to fetch bread from the cupboard. "Lark and I worked from the time we got off the train till after four o'clock, cleaning up your mess."

"I'm sorry, honey. I was going to clean it up. I've been so damned busy. Art's been out sick two days this week. I've been running my ass off keeping up."

"In case you haven't noticed, it's over ninety degrees." She poured herself a glass of tea and put it to her temple. "Not the kind of weather when you want to come home and start scrubbing floors."

"Why didn't you leave it till later?" Papa asked.

Mama set her glass down hard on the table. "You're making me crazy with your lying innocence," she told Papa and hurried into the bedroom.

Papa sprang up and followed. "You're calling me a liar?" he demanded.

Slipping down from the kitchen chair and passing behind Papa into the living room, I hunched myself into the corner of the couch.

"I'm working my tail off every day, getting by on hamburger every night, and you come home complaining and calling me a liar."

"Your ma and pa are happy to have hamburger. How'd you get to be so special?" Mama wanted to know.

"You leave my ma and pa out of this, bitch."

"All right, Willie, let's just talk about *us*," Mama shouted. "What about the four hundred and fifty dollars we don't have that you lost at poker? Where are we going to get that?"

"I knew you'd come home screaming about that. I said to myself, 'The first thing Arlene's gonna do is throw that four hundred and fifty dollars up to me.' And, by God, I was right."

"Oh, no, you don't, Willie. You're not going to make me the villain." Mama's voice had the fuzzy sound it took on when she had a migraine. "*I* didn't lose the money."

"If we've got money to support your sister," Papa spat at her, "we've got money for poker. And it's none of your business how I pay my debts. I'll take care of them my way." He barged through the kitchen, knocking over Mama's chair, and out the door, slamming it behind him.

I ran to the living room window and pulled the drape aside. Papa climbed into the pickup and drove away, spraying parking-lot gravel behind him. I guessed that he was going downtown to eat at the Loon Cafe, where Dora Noonan and Magdalen Haggerty would laugh at his jokes and serve him extra vanilla ice cream on his pie.

From the bedroom Mama's voice was faint. "Lark," she called. I went to her.

"Put the macaroni in the refrigerator," she told me.

"Mama, where's our car?"

"What?"

"Where's the Oldsmobile?"

"It's not in the parking lot?" She opened her eyes to a slit to look at me.

I shook my head.

"My God," she said.

"Where is it, Mama?"

"He's sold it."

I put the macaroni in the refrigerator, then tiptoed into the bedroom and removed the nail polish from Mama's bureau. Sitting down at the kitchen table, I pushed aside a plate and studied my hands, examining the ragged nails, bitten back to the quick now. Opening the bottle of polish, I began to paint my fingers, nails and skin, up to the first knuckle. When I had finished, I poured the remaining polish on Papa's chair and went to bed.

33

SEPTEMBER TOOK me by surprise. When Mama said, "School starts next week," I was dumbfounded.

Arithmetic and the Monkey Ward Christmas catalog were the best things about that autumn. Arithmetic I did not love for itself, but for what it symbolized: another giant step toward adulthood. I longed for third grade, when we would learn handwriting. Then I would have the basic skills to escape from childhood. I half imagined that someone would give me paid work when I could write longhand.

During kindergarten and first grade, I enjoyed playing "house" or "school" with my friends. Now I wanted to play "office" or "store" or, sometimes, "college," although I didn't know much about that. I could only predicate it by saying, "Imagine there are books *all* around. Books and books and books." To which Beverly Ridza, if she were playing, would complain, "Godsakes, that sounds awful."

I played with Beverly more in second grade than I had in first.

Sally was still my best friend, but Beverly had taught me to swim. Now, when school let out at three, Sally and I and Beverly left together. Sally lived closest to school. I was next, and Beverly lived a block beyond Rayzeen's Lumberyard in a one-room tar paper shack on the falling-down outskirts of town.

On Friday afternoons the three of us alternated stopping at Sally's to study catechism or coming to my house. Mama saw at once that Beverly's problem with catechism was poor reading. Out came the flash cards she'd made for me and new ones which she made up just for Beverly. Oddly enough, Beverly didn't seem to mind. She was flattered by the attention and time Mama gave her, especially as Mama did not patronize her or, worse, pity her. The truth was, however, that twice after Beverly left, Mama cried.

Now that I was in second grade, time seemed to evaporate. My seventh birthday, late in September, flew by before I knew what hit me. Lucky thing I had the new roller skates to remember it by. The fall bazaar at St. Boniface Catholic Church came and went with the same reckless haste.

The bazaar was held in the church basement in early November. As with the Knights of Columbus picnic, there were booths of baked goods and handiwork and white elephant objects. Games of skill, like ring toss; and games of chance, like bingo; and an enormous wheel of fortune were part of the festivities.

At the kitchen end of the room, folding tables were set up in a long row and for twenty-five cents you were served a plate heaped with fried chicken, mashed potatoes and gravy, Jell-O salad, and baked beans. When you got around all of that, there was pie or cake for dessert.

This year Mama let the girls in the catechism class serve the dessert. She made each of us a fancy apron like those she had sewn for the handiwork booth. Sally and I and Beverly, sporting our ruffled aprons, passed up and down the row of tables, carrying plates of dessert, serving from the left and clearing away from the right, and impressing even Sisters Mary Frances and Mary Clair despite themselves.

For the first time in years, Mrs. Stillman and Hilly did not attend the bazaar. Nor had Hilly come to the door at Halloween to see the children's costumes. The day after the bazaar was Sunday. Following Mass, Mama and I went calling on the Stillmans with a pumpkin pie.

"We'll tell her it's left over from the bazaar," said Mama, who had risen early that morning to bake it.

"Why?"

"So she won't be embarrassed," Mama explained.

Mama drove the pickup, and I sat beside her holding the pie. The day was gray and windswept, with grit and moldering leaves in the air, but the Stillman apartment was cozy.

"We can only stay a minute," Mama told Mrs. Stillman, who insisted that we come in and take off our coats. "We have to get home and start dinner." That was true. We always sat down to Sunday dinner about two, and it was now nearly noon.

"I'll call Hillyard," Mrs. Stillman said. She turned at the door. "He's in his pajamas and robe, I'm afraid. He doesn't want to get dressed anymore. I hope you won't mind."

I had not seen Hilly since late September when we had taken him and Mrs. Stillman slices of my birthday cake. Hilly had misunderstood, thinking it was his birthday, so we all sang "Happy Birthday" to him.

I was startled now to see the difference a few weeks could make. His robe and pajamas hung on him. The insteps of his feet in the brown felt house slippers looked thin and bony, as did his wrists below the sleeves. Adding to the sorry picture was the condition of his robe, worn and laundered to the weight of a dish towel, and with elbows so threadbare, his pajamas sleeves poked through.

Curiosity flickered in Hilly's eyes, then disappeared. Gone entirely was his old happiness at seeing me.

"Do you like pumpkin pie, Hilly?"

He roused himself and studied me.

"It's Lark," his mother told him.

"Lark?"

"That's right."

But I could see that he was still not sure.

"Lark and Mrs. Erhardt have brought us a delicious pumpkin pie. You know how you love pumpkin pie." She seemed to draw from a bottomless well of patience.

Hilly smiled an unsure smile, his eyes darting from one of us to the other.

"Would you like me to come after school and read to you someday?" I asked.

"That would be very nice," Mrs. Stillman said. "I think Hilly

needs his friends right now." She spoke of him as though he were
not present, and indeed he seemed not to be.

"What's wrong with Hilly?" I asked Mama when we were
outside.

"I don't know," she said thoughtfully. "Maybe his sanity is
coming back."

"I don't like him to be this way."

Mama told me again the story of Hilly going to war and being
decorated for bravery by two governments, of his being wounded
and sent home a shell-shocked hero no one wanted except his
mother. "If Hilly's getting well, we should be happy. It's not his
duty to be your playmate."

ℵ 34 ℤ

BACK IN late July, when Mama saw that I had chewed my nails
down to raw flesh, she sat down and cried. And when Papa
examined my hands, she told him, "If you take her to the cemetery, I'll pack up our things, and Lark and I'll go to my folks. You
can sit here in your filth until hell freezes over."

"You try that, lady, you just try that," he said. "And you see
how far you get."

But he didn't take me to the cemetery. The determination and
passion he had invested in my fingernails because they were a
symbol of my femininity, he now transferred to my catechetical
scholarship, because it was a symbol of my piety. If I couldn't be
beautiful, I *could* be holy.

He began reviewing the catechism book with me, not asking
what lesson we were studying, but opening it at random and
questioning me in that fashion.

"But we haven't had that lesson yet," I told him when he asked,
quoting from the book, " 'What is the judgment called which we
have to undergo immediately after death?' " Looking up from the
book, he said, "You should have read it all even if Sister didn't
assign it. Don't you want to be smarter than the others?"

"I'm already smarter than the others."

"We're pretty stuck on ourselves, aren't we?" He closed the book, keeping his index finger in the place where he'd read.

"I just meant, I always get a holy medal or a saint's picture for knowing the lesson, that's all. I'm the only one who's gotten one every week. I'm *not* stuck on myself."

"Do the sisters know how you smart-talk your pa?"

This scene took place one night in September while Mama was at bridge club. I didn't tell her. If I did, Papa might tell the sisters that I was sassy. The sisters already mistrusted my piety, due to Mama's being a convert.

Two weeks earlier Sister Mary Frances, presenting me a picture of St. Veronica with her veil, pointed out, "Knowing our catechism and reciting it is not a game. If learning about God and His church is only a game, we will never see heaven. We study catechism in order to please God, not to win prizes." I had wondered at the time, did that mean she wanted me to answer incorrectly now and then? Would that prove that I was sincere?

I rejected the idea for two reasons: It would be a lie, and more important, I was proud of knowing all the answers. I didn't want to humble myself. I had little enough purchase in this class where the parents of the other children (except for Sally) were all born Catholics. I wouldn't pretend to be stupid.

Every second Friday now, when Mama left for bridge club, Papa babysat me, and together we reviewed my catechism. Mama was pleased that Papa so willingly stayed at home with me. She didn't question him about his reasons, but imagined, perhaps, that he was making amends for the loss of our Oldsmobile. And Papa told me that the lessons would be "our little secret," a surprise for Mama. I began studying catechism each night before bed so that I would know the entire book.

Friday afternoons after school were traditionally the time when Sally and I studied catechism. Now we included Beverly in the ritual. Every second Friday I had a double dose: catechism with my friends and catechism with Papa.

I knew exactly what to expect with my friends: cookies and milk and giggling and getting off the subject ("Doesn't it make you sick the way Leroy Mosely picks his nose and puts it in his mouth?") and Mama nudging us back ("When you girls are ready, I'll hear your *Confiteors*").

I never knew what to expect with Papa, except that we would sit

at the kitchen table and he would bring out a little half-pint bottle
of bourbon whiskey he had stashed away somewhere, setting it on
the table and reminding me conspiratorially that this, too, was
"our little secret." Since Mama had a highball at bridge club, she
didn't notice the smell of bourbon when she returned. And if she
had noticed, it's not likely she would have complained. She was
grateful that Papa wasn't out God-knew-where, playing poker.

Mama made us a big bowl of popcorn before she left for bridge.
"You two have a good time," she'd say, slipping into her wine-
colored bouclé coat and easing on black kid gloves, massaging the
leather fingers over her own.

She kissed me good-bye, leaving a soupçon of fruity tasting
lipstick on my mouth and a hint of her spicy perfume on my
cheek. Mama was a party dessert on bridge nights.

"Are you ready?" Papa would ask, rubbing his hands and pouring himself a drink when we had heard Mama drive off in the
pickup. It was as if we were going to put on boxing gloves and step
into the ring.

Sometimes Papa was in a jolly mood and only asked me to
recite the prayers in the first pages of the *Baltimore Catechism:* the
Lord's Prayer, the Angelical Salutation (which most people called
"Hail, Mary"), the Apostles' Creed, the *Confiteor,* the Acts of
Faith, Hope, Love, and Contrition, the Blessing Before Meals and
the Grace After Meals.

I knew the prayers letter-perfect. Sometimes, when I had reeled
off the Apostles' Creed or maybe the *Confiteor,* Papa would say,
"Now do it with some feeling." I closed my eyes then and tried to
speak like a God-fearing child. One night I asked Papa why God
wanted me to fear Him.

"So you'll be good," he said, drinking the last of his bourbon
and water.

"Wouldn't I be better if I loved Him?"

"You're supposed to love Him *and* fear Him."

"That's hard," I said.

"If you loved God, but weren't scared of Him," Papa said,
"you'd go around doing all kinds of bad things and not worrying
about Him getting mad."

"No, I wouldn't."

"I'm telling you, you would. I've lived a lot longer than you,
and I know people need the fear of God put in 'em."

Papa was suddenly angry. "God is our heavenly Father," he said.

I nodded, extremely sorry I had brought the subject up.

"Just like I'm your earthly father."

He looked hard at me across the oilcloth-covered table, his stomach pressed against the table's edge. I looked into his eyes and tried not to blink. I must appear as sincere, attentive, and God-fearing as I was able.

"You love *me*, don't you?" he asked.

"Yes."

"And you're afraid of me, too, aren't you?"

"Yes."

"That's right. Now, *when* are you afraid of me?"

"When?"

"You're afraid of me when you're bad," he explained. "If you weren't afraid of me, you'd be lying and stealing all the time."

I felt as though Papa had shoved me right off my chair. "No, I wouldn't!" I cried.

"Of course you would. Why can't you see that?" he pursued. "Tell me why you aren't bad all the time, just tell me that."

"Because I love Mama!" I screamed, running into the bedroom and climbing into the crib. I pulled the quilt over my head, blubbering into my pillow. People were good because they loved somebody.

Papa poured another drink and carried it into the living room. His shoes made no sound on the linoleum as he paused at the bedroom door, stood for a minute, then moved on, cracking across the living room linoleum, padding across the big, shag throw rug in the middle of the room, then cracking again on the cold linoleum as he settled himself in the armchair by the stove. After a while the newspaper rattled and sighed as he turned the pages.

Much later, when I was sleeping soundly, Papa came and stood at the bedroom door. "Do you still love me?" he asked, and I seemed to hear him in a dream. "Do you still love me?" he repeated. He was weeping.

❧ 35 ❧

MAMA WAS sewing a pair of pajamas and a robe for Hilly. In the past we hadn't given him a Christmas present. "But this year," Mama said, "Hilly needs bucking up."

When Mama's friend Bernice McGivern went to Minneapolis right after Thanksgiving, Mama instructed her to buy several yards of blanket fabric, so Hilly's robe would be warm and soft. Bernice returned with a piece of red-and-blue plaid that was perfect. Hilly would be cozy all winter, and the red of the plaid would bring out his dark eyes. Mama then sent away to Monkey Wards for dark blue cotton flannel for the pajamas.

The robe was finished, down to the last bit of topstitching, and looked just as though we'd bought it at Dayton's in Minneapolis. The pajama bottoms were complete as well, ironed and folded into the tissue-paper-lined box in which they would be given. Now Mama was embroidering with red floss in satin stitch a fancy letter *H* on the pocket of the pajama top. How elegant Hilly was going to look. Like William Powell.

"Nobody wants to get *just* clothes for Christmas," Mama told me, "so we'll have to think of a toy for Hilly."

"A toy?"

"Something just for fun, like the ocarina that we gave him last spring." The early freight train was pulling in, and Mama waited until she could be heard above the roar to add, "I'll leave that to you. Think of something to help Hilly pass the time."

I'd been spending a good deal of time with the Monkey Wards Christmas catalog, making out a Santa Claus list, so I began now to pore over that with Hilly in mind. The gift couldn't be expensive. We were already over our Christmas budget, Mama said, on account of the pajamas and robe. "A dollar is the limit," she told me.

For several evenings in early December, I scoured the children's pages of the catalog. Each time, the little red leatherette rocking chair jumped off the page at me. I had written it at the top of the Santa list, although Mama said the price tag of $7.49 was a lot to ask of Santa in hard times. I didn't understand why Santa, who lived at the North Pole, was affected by hard times in Minnesota.

But Mama said it was hard times everywhere except Hollywood, where Uncle Stan had gotten a job as a carpenter's helper at a movie studio and was getting back on his feet.

Uncle Stan hadn't sent for Aunt Betty yet, but Mama was hopeful he'd surprise her with a bus ticket at Christmas. We were spending Christmas at Grandma and Grandpa Browning's this year so Mama could cheer Betty up if "Fortune's Stepchild doesn't come through with the fare to California."

After the third session with the catalog, I spied the perfect toy for Hilly. "Mama, look at this." She was pressing Hilly's pajama top. The red *H* was beautiful, smooth and full and slippery under the fingers, like satin. Mama said a little old Chinese lady couldn't have done better, and she was right. "Here's what we should get Hilly. Another book by Minerva Baldwin Arbuthnot. See?"

"Minerva who?"

"The lady who wrote *Happy Stories for Bedtime*. This one's called *Stories for Rainy Afternoons*. Isn't that perfect? And it's ninety-eight cents."

Mama sent away for it immediately, and it was at the post office Friday, December 15, when she dropped by to collect the mail. It put her in a fit of Christmas, she said, when she saw what a pretty book it was, and she came right home and stirred up a big batch of her famous divinity candy.

The next morning while I was at catechism class, she cooked her equally famous fudge, and after lunch the two of us baked cookies: chocolate cookies with walnuts inside and rich chocolate frosting on top, and sugar cookies in the shapes of stars and bells, red-and-green-colored sugar sprinkled lightly over them.

While Mama washed up cookie pans and bowls, I wrapped *Stories for Rainy Afternoons*. I was very slow and when I was finished, it was not to my satisfaction, the paper having wrinkled and torn, but Mama said it was all right and Hilly would not mind. I made him a Christmas card with stars and angels, and three camels that looked like rat terriers.

After supper that evening, Mama and I set out in the truck for the Stillmans'. Piled on my lap were the big box containing Hilly's robe and pajamas, *Stories for Rainy Afternoons*, and a box of homemade candy and cookies.

"I know it's still nine days till Christmas," Mama said, "but I couldn't wait to deliver these, could you?"

"We don't have anything for Mrs. Stillman," I told Mama.

"I have a little present in my purse," she said.

"What is it?"

"My brooch."

I couldn't believe it. "The one with all different colored stones? You're not giving that away, are you?"

Mrs. Stillman didn't answer the door at once. I knocked again.

"I'm sorry," she apologized, pushing the storm door open. "I was in Hillyard's room, and I didn't hear you." She ushered us in. "Those aren't for us!" she exclaimed over the boxes we carried. "You shouldn't." She set Hilly's presents on a chair.

"The red box has cookies and candy in it," Mama told her.

"I'll make tea and we'll sample them," Mrs. Stillman said, taking our coats while we pulled off our boots and set them on the newspaper by the door. "Hillyard has been in bed with a cold that's settled in his chest," she went on, "but maybe he'll come out to say hello and have some tea and Christmas treats."

She carried our coats to her bedroom. "Hillyard and I went for a walk one night," she said, returning. "He rarely wants to go out anymore. But he did that night. There was new snow and he was very excited. We walked a good many blocks.

"A most unusual thing happened." She stood behind the green wicker chair, running her hands over the back of it. "He said, quite clearly, 'I built a snow house that year, Mama. Do you remember?'"

"A snow house, he said?" Mama asked.

"When the snow was deep, he liked to make a cave in it. A house, he called it. That was when he was eight or ten and we lived in the Appledorn house, by the Lutheran Church."

"That's remarkable," Mama said, "that he remembered like that."

"That he remembered and that he expressed himself so clearly. Yes. But I'm afraid he took a chill that night." Reaching for the box of candy and cookies, she left us to start tea.

Mama dug in her purse for the little box containing the brooch and set it beside the Christmas tree, on the table by the davenport. The small tree had no lights, but was wrapped around and around with paper chains and popcorn strings. Pictures had been cut from magazines and tied to branches with thread, happy pictures of people driving cars and children riding bicycles. Near the top of the tree was a picture of a smiling Mrs. Roosevelt and another of

Joe DiMaggio, kissing his bride, Dorothy Arnold. It was a strange and wonderful tree.

"Hillyard decorated the tree," Mrs. Stillman told us, appearing in the kitchen doorway, tying an apron around her waist. "I'll see if he feels up to joining us."

Emerging from the hall, Mrs. Stillman said, "Hillyard will be out in a few minutes. He's combing his hair. He can part it himself now." She disappeared once more into the kitchen, and shortly returned, bearing a tea tray.

"Hillyard?" she called.

And there was Hilly, with his hair combed and neatly parted, looking deliberative and reasoning. He was wearing a pair of gray woolen trousers, much too big for him, slack and cinched in at the waist with a leather belt; a white shirt, open at the neck; and a gray jacket-sweater, mended at the elbows. On his feet were the same brown house slippers as before.

Mama said Hilly was about forty years old, but he had always looked young. Now a dusting of gray had stolen into his thick brown hair, turning him middle-aged.

His mother said, "Hillyard, dear, sit here in the green chair so Lark and Mrs. Erhardt don't catch your cold."

He sat, not looking directly at us but at his feet and hands, and at his mother who was pouring tea. It was as if we were strangers, and he was ill at ease. There was no sign of the guffawing, jigging friend who welcomed me with open-mouthed smiles and garbled greetings. There was only this old man I didn't know who never laughed or said strange things. The saner he got, the sadder Hilly seemed to become.

"Can Hilly open my present now?" I asked Mrs. Stillman. "He can save Mama's for Christmas."

Mrs. Stillman looked at Hilly. "Would you like to open Lark's present?"

He looked unsure.

"It's all right," his mother told him. "It's all right to open one present before Christmas. Many people do that."

His face lightened, and I fetched the book. The wrapping had not weathered the trip from home intact. Hilly had no difficulty removing the paper and ribbon.

"Can you read the card?" Mrs. Stillman asked. She crossed to the green chair and studied over Hilly's shoulder the card I had made. Hilly opened it and stared at the greeting. "Can you read it?" his mother repeated.

Again he knitted his brows. His left hand played with the wrappings. He looked up at his mother and down at the home-made card lying on the book.

"What's the first word?" Mrs. Stillman asked.

" 'Dear'?" He searched her face.

"That's right. And the next?"

" 'Hilly.' "

"Very good. Can you read the rest?"

" 'I love you'?"

"And who is it from?"

" 'Lark Ann Er . . . Er . . .' "

"Erhardt."

" 'Lark Ann Erhardt.' "

I was thunderstruck. He was getting his sanity back.

"Hillyard is doing very well, don't you think?" his mother asked, looking at Mama and me.

"It's wonderful, Hilly," Mama told him.

Some small formality in the tone of Mama's voice told me that she, too, felt that Hilly was an entirely different person than he had been months earlier.

Mrs. Stillman took the card and stood it up beside the Christmas tree. "That is a beautiful card. We will treasure it."

Hilly studied the book in his hands, *Stories for Rainy Afternoons* printed across the top in heavy gold letters, Minerva Baldwin Arbuthnot spelled in smaller letters at the bottom, and in between, an illustration of a mother sitting in a wing chair beside a window, a boy and girl gathered on the floor beside her, listening to a story while outside, rain formed delicate, lacy streams down the windowpanes. Hilly glanced up at me, then down at the book. He opened it and began turning the pages, not with the ardor I had envisioned but with mild curiosity, a desire to be polite, and a sort of perplexed ruefulness.

"What a thoughtful present," Mrs. Stillman said. "You remembered how much Hillyard enjoyed the stories you read him. Now *he* can read stories, too." She passed a plate of cookies and candy. "I'm afraid our tea has gotten cold. Let me add some warm." Mrs. Stillman was chattering to cover Hilly's perplexity over the book. "If you have the time, maybe Hillyard could read something from his new book to you, Lark. That would be a turnabout, wouldn't it?" she tittered, and tipped the teapot up, pouring fresh tea into our cups.

Mrs. Stillman was unsettled by Hilly's new condition, his gradual but evident return to reason. It was another enormous adjustment, and she was not young. She had grown used to Hilly's derangement. Its attendant problems and embarrassments were familiar. But what would be the pitfalls of sanity, and how could she protect Hilly from them? The challenge for which she had prayed all these years had come too late in her life. These insights were not mine but Mama's.

"We'll have our tea and these delicious treats, and then maybe a little read from the book," Mrs. Stillman suggested, wishing to make a complimentary fuss over the gift.

I had two pieces of candy, one fudge and one divinity, and a chocolate cookie. Mama had shot me a meaningful expression, but Mrs. Stillman had insisted. We sat sipping and munching for several minutes, our conversation desultory.

Mrs. Stillman asked me, "Are you ready for Santa?"

"I made a list, but I didn't write the letter."

"And what are you hoping for?"

"A red leatherette rocking chair, majorette boots, and a silver-colored baton. Also some books."

"I'll drop Santa a note and put in a good word for you."

No one had done that before. Maybe Santa would bring the rocking chair after all.

When we had finished our tea, Mrs. Stillman said, "Shall we have a short reading?" She looked at Hilly.

Hilly got up, crossed the room, and gave me the book. Since I was the child present, he doubtless reasoned, it was appropriate for me to read the children's book which he, strangely, had been given.

Mama checked her watch. "It's getting late," she pointed out. "Is there a very short piece?"

"There's a poem at the beginning," I said. "It's called 'For Ned, Then and Now.' " I opened the book to the little rhymed dedication and read:

> "For Ned, Then and Now
>
> Then:
> Neddy in the garden
> And Neddy on the stairs,

Wrestling mohair crocodiles,
Trapping velvet bears.

Now:
Marching bravely into
The worldly thoroughfares,
Pray, shun the wily crocodiles,
Eschew the grizzly bears."

"Eschew means to keep away from something," I explained to Hilly. Mama and I had looked it up last night when we were glancing through Hilly's gift. "Keep away from crocodiles and grizzly bears, Hilly," I told him, giggling. Hilly's gaze was level and serious, and I was embarrassed by my failed attempt at levity.

When Mrs. Stillman opened the door to see us out, there was snow piled in a downy drift on the landing and in mounded pillows on the steps leading to the street.

"Isn't it pretty?" she cried. "Just like a Christmas card."

Trouser legs flapping about his ankles, Hilly stood in the doorway, staring after us, trying to figure out what the evening had been about.

"Is it going to blizzard?" I asked as we tramped to the truck, our boots making the hollow, crunching sound of someone munching Grape-Nuts.

"I don't think so."

Mama fussed with the reluctant truck. Her right hand played with the choke and the starter, while her right foot skillfully worked the gas pedal. The engine coughed and caught, and Mama nursed it along until the clitter-clutter steadied and we joggled rhythmically in our seats. As she put the truck in gear, I asked, "Can we drive around town once?" The night was too perfect to abandon. It was the sort of night when you think you could lie in the snow until morning and never get cold.

"Hilly's not my old friend anymore," I told Mama as we passed St. Boniface.

"He's not your old friend anymore. He's your new friend."

Her words didn't buck me up as they were intended. I wanted the old Hilly back.

"Don't be sad," Mama said. "Santa is coming. In . . . nine days."

She was right. Santa was coming. This year I was going to take a long nap the day before Christmas. When we came home from midnight Mass, I was going to stay up with the grown-ups until Santa came.

I was going to thank him for coming every year. There were very few things in life that didn't change or break or grow up. I was grateful for Santa's constancy.

36

FRIDAY AFTERNOON after school, Sally and Beverly and I trudged through dirty snow to my house to study catechism. When we were gathered around the kitchen table, half on and half off our chairs, and Mama had made us cocoa and cinnamon toast, Sally wanted to know, "What did you ask for, for Christmas?"

"Shoes," Beverly answered, dipping toast into her cocoa and sucking the liquid out of the bread. "Shoes and a gun."

"A gun?" Sally whispered, frightened by the word. It was a heavy, anxious word.

"So's I can shoot my pa if he ever comes around," Beverly explained matter-of-factly.

"Why?" I asked.

"He's no good."

"What did he do?" Sally wanted to know.

"Lots."

"Like what?"

"Godsakes you're nosy," Beverly complained, but she continued. "He beat my ma."

Papa had done that.

"And he burned Charlie with a cigarette on purpose when Charlie was crying."

Papa had never done that.

"No," Sally said, deeply shocked.

"He did too. And then Charlie couldn't stop crying 'cuz he was still wearing diapers so Pa burned him again." A big chunk of toast fell into the cup, and she fished it out with her fingers and ate it, cocoa dribbling down her chin.

I was subdued and somewhat awed by Beverly's feelings toward her papa. She was the first person I'd ever met who didn't love both their parents.

"Don't you want Santa to bring you any toys?" Sally asked her.

"Santa?" Beverly nearly choked on her toast. "You kidding me?"

Sally shook her head.

"Godsakes, you're seven years old, ain't you?"

"Don't say ain't, Beverly," I reproved.

"Maybe I say ain't, but I ain't no baby. I leastways know there's no Santa Claus," she continued.

Sally and I stared at her.

"What do you mean?" I pressed.

"What I said. There ain't no such person as Santa Claus. It's just your folks that put the presents out. I'm sorry if you didn't know that. I thought you was kidding me. How do you think one old man is going to fly all over the world," she asked, spreading her arms to indicate the enormity of the task, "in *one* night?" She added, "And teach them dumb reindeers to fly?"

Sally flared, "You're wrong, Beverly Ridza. And you're stupid."

"I may be stupid, but I ain't wrong," Beverly told her, taking another slice of toast and dunking it in her cocoa, which was already soupy with bits and pieces of bread.

"Santa doesn't come to your house because you're naughty and you swear all the time and say ain't," Sally parried wildly. "Anybody knows he only comes to good children. And you don't know your catechism, besides," she added for good measure. "You're going to hell."

"Godsakes, if I'd known you was still babies, I wouldn't of told you. Even Charlie knows about Santa Claus."

Who else knew? Did *everybody* except me and Sally? I wondered, for I believed with absolute certainty from the moment Beverly had said, "Santa?" that she was in on the truth, and Sally and I had been living in a fool's paradise. I pushed aside my toast and cocoa.

"If you don't want yours," Beverly told me, "I'll take it. This is good toast and cocoa."

Sally started to cry, quietly and without fuss. We didn't have a bathroom she could go to, and Mama was in the living room talking on the phone with Bernice McGivern, so Sally got up from the table and walked into the bedroom. There was not even a door she could close. She stood just inside the bedroom doorway, nobly, her back to us, hands at her sides, like a tragic princess.

I picked up my *Baltimore Catechism* and pretended to read. Pretty soon Mama hung up the phone and came out in the kitchen. Right away she observed that Sally wasn't with us, that she was standing in the bedroom.

"I'm sorry I was on the phone so long," she said, fetching another chair from the living room and sitting down at the table. "Well, now, let's see where we are. What's the lesson?" she asked rhetorically, riffling through Sally's catechism. "Here it is. Number Twenty-two: the Sacrament of Matrimony."

"What's matrimony?" Beverly asked.

"Marriage."

"Oh. That."

"I'll make a flash card for matrimony," Mama said.

"Don't make a difference to me if I don't remember that one," Beverly told her.

Mama laughed hard. Beverly looked puzzled, then, slowly, pleased with herself, as if she'd told a successful joke. She glanced my way to be certain I'd noticed.

"Don't you ever want to get married?" Mama asked Beverly.

"Godsakes, no."

"You don't ever want to have a baby?"

"They're just trouble and they cost a lot of money."

"What if *your* mama thought that?" Mama asked.

"She does."

Mama studied the catechism page. "Lark, 'which are the effects of the Sacrament of Matrimony?' " she asked, reading from the book.

" 'The effects of the Sacrament of Matrimony are: first, to sanctify the love of husband and wife; second, to give them grace to bear with each other's weaknesses; third, to enable them to bring up their children in the fear and love of God.' " Papa had been right. God *did* want me to be afraid of Him.

Silently Sally stole back into the kitchen, slipping into her place at the table. Her cheeks were damp.

"Sally, 'To receive the Sacrament of Matrimony worthily is it necessary to be in the state of grace?' " Mama asked as though Sally had been beside her throughout.

When Mama drove Beverly and Sally home, I unbuckled my shoes and climbed into the crib, cold and tired. Sitting at the kitchen table, reciting catechism, I had hardly been able to breathe, sadness squeezed me so hard.

What else was going to be a lie? I had believed in Santa Claus more than in God. I liked him better, too. Santa didn't ask me to be afraid of him. Now it turned out he was pretend. Was God pretend as well?

I longed to believe that Beverly was lying, but I knew she wasn't. Then I hoped that I was asleep and this was a dream, but I knew that was not true.

I jumped to my feet and kicked the sides of the crib. It rattled and shook as if it were going to fly apart. I kicked it some more.

37

THE PALL OF Santa's death lay over Christmas. And the appearance of the little red leatherette rocker under the tree at Grandma Browning's only furnished me a child-size place to sit and rock and gaze wistfully backward at childhood and ignorance. If this was what it was like to be seven, I wanted to be five again and back in kindergarten. Those had been the days, the days of reindeer and elves.

In those days a gabbling, childlike Hilly understood me and was glad to see me. Although he was relatively coherent now, Hilly had little to talk about except, occasionally, something he'd seen in a magazine. Most of the time he was quiet. In 1918 he'd been hurled into a sea of shell-shock. In 1939 he was climbing out onto a tiny island of sanity, only to find himself again in a world of Huns.

I brought him our copies of *Life* when we were done reading them, but they disturbed him because of the many stories about the war in Europe. He burst into tears one day in February at the sight of Swedish aviators preparing to climb into their planes.

As winter dragged into spring, we heard increasing news on the radio and in the newspaper about the war. Men argued around Navarin's Sinclair station about whether we would get into the fighting. They were pretty evenly divided yes and no. Mama said the Germans in Harvester were snappish when asked about yet another war begun by their people. "*We* didn't invent Mr. Hitler," they said. "We're Americans." But there were those in town who called them goose-steppers and krauts behind their backs.

Our last name was German, but no one ever directed any comments to me or, so far as I knew, to Mama or Papa, maybe because Papa was so outspokenly anti-German. When he dropped into Navarin's station, which he often did in the evenings before Mr. Navarin closed up and before the freight came through, he talked war with Mr. Navarin and Sonny Steen and Axel Nelson and whoever was hanging around.

"If it wasn't for my bad leg," Papa told them, "I wouldn't mind bein' over there, carrying a gun against the Heinies. We're gonna fight 'em later. Might as well fight 'em sooner and get it over with."

I thought about the Witch, Ilsa Kraus, in Morgan Lake. Were people calling her a Heinie? I wondered if she ever heard from Uncle Stan, who was working in Hollywood?

At Christmas he had called Aunt Betty long-distance and told her it wouldn't be long before he had the money to send for her and set up housekeeping. It had taken more time than he'd expected because the car had broken down and cost him a good deal of money. It was necessary to have a car in California, he assured her.

Aunt Betty had worked as temporary Christmas help at the Ben Franklin Five and Dime in Blue Lake, and after Christmas the owner, a Mr. Miller, had asked her to stay on. She hadn't told Uncle Stan about this development, as she was determined to save her wages for the fare to California, turning up in Hollywood one day to surprise the socks off Uncle Stan.

I loved to imagine it: Uncle Stan, after work, returning to Cousin Lloyd's house from the movie studio and sitting on the front steps. Pulling off his shoes because his feet hurt from standing all day, he'd sit in his stocking feet, smoking a Lucky Strike. Up the street, carrying her grip and looking very smart, would march Aunt Betty, jaunty and tickled, anticipating Uncle Stan's surprise. Then, glancing up and spotting her, he would smack his forehead and holler, his socks flying right off his feet and landing in a banana tree.

I wondered if Aunt Betty would leave before I had my first communion in May. As the cold spring sun melted the snow and the chill breeze dried the runoff, the countryside emerged brown and gray. This was the only season I didn't like. It was as though winter and spring fought over Minnesota. The sun shone weakly but determinedly; the cold wind blew kitty-corner down across the Dakotas. For two or three weeks you stopped believing in spring altogether. The year was stuck in the slowly drying mud.

Then one day late in April you walked home from school, carrying your jacket. Your heart grew light at the certainty that winter had been beaten back into the north. It was time to break out the roller skates and jump ropes and hopscotch chalk, to put away the long cotton stockings, the garter belts, and long underwear, the snowsuits and heavy mittens and scarves!

It was nearly time for First Communion.

But First Communion meant first confession. When that knowledge came over me, unexpected, while I tied my new brown oxfords or gathered pussy willow branches outside of town along the tracks, the air grew cold again.

I studied early and late. Sally and Beverly and I went over the lessons twice a week, once at Sally's on Tuesday; the second time at my house on Friday.

April zipped out of sight as if on greased skids, and then it was the first week in May.

"Sally, 'What sins are we bound to confess?' " I read from the *Baltimore Catechism*, slouching on a chair in the Wheeler kitchen.

" 'We are bound to confess all our mortal sins, but it is well also to confess our venial sins,' " she responded.

Sister was going to test us randomly on Saturday on all the chapters pertaining to confession and communion. Communion was also called the Holy Eucharist. Holy Eucharist was the name of the wafer you were given that must not be chewed, but must be allowed to slide down your throat without hindrance since it was the body of our Lord Jesus. You wouldn't *chew* the body of your Lord, would you? If you stopped to think about it, you probably wouldn't put the body of your Lord in your mouth at all.

One time I made a joke to Papa. He said he was going to play euchre with the boys over at Mr. Navarin's station after closing, and I told him he was a Holy Eucharist. At first he laughed hard, but then he got mad and told me never to say that again, that it was blasphemy. I still thought it was funny.

Sally and Beverly and I had been studying for half an hour now, and hadn't seen Mrs. Wheeler, although I could hear someone upstairs, pacing back and forth. Sally's parents' room was directly above the kitchen, so it must be Mrs. Wheeler. We rarely saw her anymore, but I was always aware of her, as if she were hiding in the corners, not in a sneaky way, but like a frightened animal. And yet there was a streak of courage in Mrs. Wheeler, if one remembered her saving Hilly from the men in the car.

"Lark." Beverly sat with her left elbow on the table, head resting on the palm of her hand, and read from the catechism book, " 'What is the Holy Eucharist?' "

"Somebody who plays euchre every Sunday."

She looked at me dumbly, then the light of comprehension came on, and she slapped her knee with the catechism and laughed with her head thrown back. "Godsakes. Ha ha ha ha. Godsakes."

Sally stared as if we'd gone mad. I was laughing, too. It was impossible to see Beverly laugh without joining her.

"Doncha get it?" Beverly said, and again broke into wild guffaws. She slipped off her chair, onto the floor and lay laughing in a heap. After a while we forgot what we were laughing about, but we couldn't stop.

Sally looked away as if we embarrassed her. But there was more in her expression. A wariness. As if she didn't trust such uncontrolled reactions.

Beverly gasped, "Uncle Eddie plays euchre every Sunday afternoon. Ain't that somethin'? He does, I swear to God." She hooted.

"Stop laughing!" Sally shouted. "Do you hear me?" She was out of her chair and standing over Beverly. "Go home then, Beverly. If you can't stop, go home."

No one my own age, not even my best friend, was going to tell me I couldn't laugh. I was running out of steam and about to wind down when she got upset. Now I redoubled my laughing, although it was no longer real. She gave me a dark, wild look, as if she wanted to slap my face. "You're crazy," she snapped at me, shoving me so that I would have fallen off the chair but for the edge of the table. "I don't want you ever to come here again." Whirling, she ran past me out of the kitchen. I heard her pounding up the stairs to her bedroom.

"Godsakes, what's wrong?" Beverly questioned. "She turning into a crybaby or something?"

"She wasn't crying," I defended, although I, too, was bewildered. And a cold little hand of meanness grabbed my heart, its voice whispering in my ear, "Let her go. Let her cry up there in her room. Serves her right."

"Let's go to my house, Beverly." I began gathering my things. "Maybe Mama will let you stay for supper."

Loudly, so that Sally might hear, Beverly answered, "Yeah, let's go to your house, Lark. Your ma makes better cookies anyhow."

Out the back door we went, Beverly slamming it behind us. "She sure acted like a baby," Beverly exclaimed as we minced across the muddy backyard to the street.

Glancing back as we reached the corner, I thought I saw Sally at her bedroom window, standing behind the dimity curtain, watching us depart.

"Where's Sally?" Mama asked.

"She couldn't come."

Mama's typewriter was on the kitchen table, but she carried it into the living room. "I nearly pounded the keys off that machine today," she told us. "I can type forty words a minute now."

Beverly and I sat down at the table and took turns reading and answering questions while Mama scrubbed baking potatoes, greased the skins, pricked them and popped them into the hot oven. I noted that she included one for Beverly. Nudging Beverly under the table, I nodded.

But, for all our seeming insouciance, our bad consciences held our noses to the catechism, and we did not let up until Papa came in to supper.

Papa and Beverly enjoyed a strange relationship. There were levels on which Papa did not approve of Beverly. She was not "womanly" in appearance or behavior. And she came from a distinctly "low-class" situation. While he himself derived from the hardworking poor, he greatly mistrusted the ragtag and bobtail who lived in the shacks south of the junkyard, suspecting them of the criminality and moral decay to which he might sink, were he in their place. Papa was never sure I ought to be associating with Beverly.

On the other hand, Beverly was in many ways the son for which he secretly wished. She could catch a softball or shinny up a telephone pole. Fearless and brash, she was a daredevil with a hearty laugh and the confident swagger of a self-made man. Her "Godsakes" he found both naughty and irresistible, and he laughed as though it were a joke between them. Had I said "Godsakes," he would have slapped me or grabbed my arm, leaving bruises, asking me who did I think I was, taking God's name in vain?

Mama did not interfere between Papa and Beverly. If it was on this basis that Beverly could come to our house with Papa's blessing, then Mama would go along, but she never treated Beverly in that manner herself.

"Time to get out the fishing poles," Papa observed at supper. "You fish?" he asked Beverly.

"Sure," she said, cramming a spoonful of baked potato and gravy into her mouth.

"You got a pole?"

"Sure." She wiped her mouth on the back of her hand. "I made it myself."

"That so? Catch anything?"

"Godsakes, I got twelve bullheads once last spring."

Papa laughed, as if at a sparkling witticism.

After supper Mama said, "I'll take Beverly home on my way to bridge club."

"Bridge club?" Papa said, as though this were the first he'd heard of it.

"Don't pull that," Mama warned. "I told you at lunch."

Beverly jumped down from the table and ran in the living room, settling herself in the red leatherette rocker Santa had brought me. Beverly was simple-minded over my red rocker. Sometimes I got peeved when she plunked herself down in it, rocking hard enough to wear the rockers down to a sliver, but Mama said it was an opportunity to practice my generosity.

"I'll be back," Papa said, going next door to the office.

"I'm leaving for bridge at quarter past seven," Mama told him.

When the time came for her to go, taking Beverly with her, Papa hadn't come home yet. We could hear his typewriter on the other side of the wall.

"If he's not here in ten minutes, Lark," Mama said, "you pound on the wall." We sometimes did that to let him know it was time to come home.

After Mama had kissed me good-bye, and she and Beverly had departed in the truck, I undressed and pulled on my nightie.

Easing the sin notebook out from under the mattress, I found a pencil in the kitchen and climbed into the crib.

What Beverly and I had done to Sally that afternoon must be a sin. If it weren't, I wouldn't feel so crummy about it. I sat for a long time over the notebook, trying to decide which commandment we had broken.

The list of my transgressions went on for page after page. Some I had entered in great detail, some were one word: "sassed" or "cussed." The notebook contained more than a year's worth of sin. The old ones from when I had first started the entries, were getting blurry and smudged. I went over some of them now, wetting the lead on my tongue and sharpening up the hazy printing so I would be able to read it in the confessional.

How embarrassing it was going to be, kneeling in the confessional, reciting this endless litany of evil. I would be mortified. After my first confession, I promised myself, I would never sin again. I couldn't endure this worry and disgrace a second time.

A week from tomorrow. That was the day of first confession. Then I could throw the notebook away. In the meantime, confused about my sin against Sally, I wrote: "hurt Sally's feelings." Outside the bedroom window the sky was light. In the trees alongside the Harvester Arms Hotel, birds were noisily bedding down for the night. Beverly was probably out playing kick-the-can with the other kids who lived south of the junkyard. I put my head down for a minute to listen to the birds and the rhythmic pounding of Papa's typewriter.

The next thing I knew, I was awake and shivering. I'd fallen asleep without pulling up the quilt. But that wasn't what woke me, I soon realized. It was Papa, standing beside the crib, terrible emanations of disgust and humiliation rolling out from him in scalding waves.

"What is this?" he demanded, sounding physically ill from the shock of what he had found.

"What?"

"This!" He held up the sin notebook.

"No!" I jumped up to snatch it from him, but he was too quick. He held it high above my head. "Papa, please! Give it to me," I cried. "Please, Papa. You're not supposed to read it."

"I've already read it," he told me, each word an indictment.

"No, Papa! Please. It's mine." I climbed down from the crib and fastened myself at his waist. "Please give it to me! Sister said no one should see it. It's just to help us confess."

"You're going to confess all of *that?*"

What was he saying? That I should withhold some of it?

"We have to, otherwise we can't go to heaven," I wept.

"Do you really think you're going to heaven?"

I was no longer sure. "Sister said. If we're really sorry . . ."

Unfastening my arms from his waist, he asked, "What kind of kid are you? Where did you come from?" Tossing the notebook into the crib, he turned and walked out of the bedroom and out of the house.

☙ 38 ☙

SALLY WAS NOT speaking to Beverly or me. For that matter, she spoke very little to anyone. I believe she would not have come to my house to study catechism on Tuesday, but Mama was sewing communion dresses for Sally and Beverly as well as for me, and she had to pin Sally's hem on Tuesday. She told me to tell Sally and I did. Sally didn't answer yes, no, or maybe, but she headed for my house after school, walking half a block behind Beverly and me.

As we sat around the kitchen table answering catechism questions, or took time out to slip into our white dresses and stand on a chair in the living room while Mama pinned up our hems, Sally did not speak one word of conversation. She didn't act mean. She acted quiet.

I had some idea how she felt. Since Papa read my sin notebook on Friday night, I had not felt like talking to *him.* I had got over my anger. He did not believe that, and he kept teasing me and tickling me and winking at me and doing other things to make me smile, but I didn't feel like smiling.

Mama was so busy sewing the communion dresses, she didn't notice, or if she did, she assumed I was being quiet so as not to bother her.

Wednesday morning as I was leaving for school, Papa came out of the depot office and called to me. "Wait!"

He hurried across the platform.

"I have to go," I told him. "I'll be late for school."

"I'll give you a ride."

I didn't want him to give me a ride, but I climbed into the truck.

"You know that this is a sin, don't you?"

"What's a sin?"

"Treating your pa like this. You're supposed to honor your father and mother. Didn't the sisters teach you that?"

I nodded.

"Well?"

I didn't know what to say. I guessed that he was probably right.

"Well?" he repeated.

"Well, what?" I asked. What should I say? I hated when he wanted me to say something and I didn't know what.

He threw on the brakes, sending my lunch pail and school things flying onto the floor. "Get out!" he yelled.

I grabbed up my things as fast as I could and jumped down from the cab.

"You're going to hell, little girl." He gunned the engine of the old truck and spun away, leaving me standing in the street a long way from school.

Thursday afternoon after school, Mama took me to Lemling's Photographic Studio to have my picture taken in my communion dress and veil, holding my new white prayer book and my new, white seed pearl rosary. Later she was to say of the portrait, "Doesn't she look pretty? A little sad, too, like a saint." A saint?

On Friday, as on Tuesday, Sally, Beverly, and I started legging it home from school to the depot, with Sally hanging half a block behind Beverly and me.

"Godsakes," Beverly complained, "I thought she'd forget by now."

"Should we tell her we're sorry?" We turned around and started running back toward Sally. Sally stopped, backed up a few steps, then whirled and ran as fast as she could. Beverly was more fleet than I. She left me behind and chased Sally all the way to the playground, where Sally tripped on the bicycle rack and went sprawling on the gravel, skinning her knees and tearing her dress.

"Go away," she screamed. "Leave me alone. Look what you made me do." She held up her torn skirt. She was crying.

"We was going to apologize," Beverly explained.

"We're sorry we laughed the other day," I told her. "We want to be friends again."

"I don't want you for my friends!"

She began gathering up her catechism and two or three workbooks that had scattered when she fell. Some arithmetic and spelling papers were snatched by the breeze and tossed in different directions. Beverly and I ran to fetch them.

"Leave my things alone."

Sally pulled herself up and hobbled on her skinned legs, desperate to get her papers before we did, as if she didn't want us even to *touch* her things. We handed her what we had retrieved.

"Don't come to my house anymore," she wept. "Understand? I don't want you in my house ever again." She limped away. "You both think you're so good."

"No, we don't," Beverly called after her, but Sally didn't turn around or answer. "You got a real pretty house," Beverly added. "Prettier than mine."

"And you're nicer than me," I called.

Mama and I drove Beverly home after supper. The street outside Beverly's house was not paved. There was still runoff in the deep ruts. Mama pulled the truck up on the forlorn bald area that was the front yard so that she and Beverly wouldn't have to jump down into a puddle. Mama's heels made a hollow, knocking sound on the boards that were laid down loose for a sidewalk.

The house itself, covered all over with tar paper, was about the size of the waiting room in the depot. Inside, the wallpaper, once pink and blue, was mostly brown from age and soil and leaks in the roof. Several pieces of linoleum, no two matching, covered the floor.

In the back there was an outhouse, and over to one side of the front yard, a pump for water. When I played at Beverly's house, which wasn't often, she let me pump water while she put her head under the spout and drank.

Mama saw Beverly to the door, carrying the communion dress, all pressed and hung on a hanger, ready to be worn. Charlie opened the door. Mama said something and disappeared inside for a minute.

Then, "I'll see you Erhardts tomorrow," Beverly called out the door as Mama teetered down the unstable board sidewalk to the truck.

"Well, I hope the dress stays clean till Sunday," Mama sighed, pulling herself up into the truck. "That'll be a miracle."

"Did Mrs. Ridza pay you?"

"Beverly's dress is a present." She started the engine. "I'm buying my way into heaven," she said with a laugh, "a few cents at a time. Don't wrinkle Sally's dress." Turning the truck around in the middle of the washboard street, Mama headed across town to the Wheelers'.

At Sally's, Mama waited a long time on the front stoop. There were no lights on downstairs. She rang the bell a second time. At last the door was opened by Mr. Wheeler. He took the dress from Mama, thanking her.

"You'll be at church for the First Communion?" I heard Mama ask.

"Yes. Oh, yes." He nodded, backing away, slowly closing the door. "Oh, yes."

While I was dressing for bed, Mama made popcorn.

"Are we going to study for confession?" I asked, standing in my nightie beside the stove.

Mama shook her head. "We're going to read a story."

"Can we look at a house book instead?"

We curled up on the couch with a couple of house books, one of them the same as that from which we'd cut out our Cape Ann. Beginning with the first plan in the Cape Ann book, we paged through, explaining aloud to each other what features were appropriate for us and which were silly or costly or ugly or simply inexplicable. Reaching #127—The Cape Ann, we exclaimed, "Isn't this a darling house?" and "We could live in this one, quite nicely," and "Here's where we'd have a bed of lily of the valley."

When Mama turned out the bedroom light, the great stone weight of confession settled down on my chest.

39

I WAS AWAKE, rehearsing confession in my mind, when Papa came home from playing cards at Mr. Navarin's house. Mama was asleep. After the ten o'clock news on WCCO, she had gone to bed, leaving a small light burning in the living room.

Papa came into the bedroom, smelling of beer and cigarette smoke. I liked the smell. It reminded me of Boomer's Tavern and other happy places. I lay perfectly still, feigning deep sleep.

Papa stood for several seconds beside the crib, hands resting on the rail. At length he whispered, "Good luck, kid," and tiptoed out to the living room, where he sat down on the couch and read the morning paper.

I resumed rehearsing confession. There was so much to remember. Sister said that if you forgot one little sin, it would be all right, if you really tried hard to remember and make a good confession. But, she'd added, you couldn't leave something out, pretending to yourself that you'd forgotten. If you did that, your soul would be blacker than before, and you wouldn't be able to take communion. And if you took communion *anyway*, you were in the worst trouble of your life.

But how could you be sure that you'd sincerely forgotten the omitted sins? How could you be sure you weren't doing such a good job of kidding yourself that you'd made yourself believe you'd forgotten when you hadn't? I tossed restlessly and began again, "Bless me, Father, for I have sinned."

During catechism class we practiced confession. Sister sat in the priest's cubbyhole. The class lined up in the pew outside, and one by one, quailing and scratching and pulling our knuckles, we slipped into the cubbyhole on the opposite side of the partition. It was dim inside. In the wall between Sister and me was a little hole maybe a foot square or less. Sister slid aside the door covering the hole. On the other side, she was indistinct, a hulking shadow. I thought, what if that isn't Sister? What if it's the Devil?

"Well?" she said impatiently. "Well?"

"Bless me, Father, for I have sinned. This is my first confession.

I have committed these sins." I hesitated. I wasn't supposed to tell *Sister* my sins, was I? This was only a rehearsal.

At long last and somewhat irritably she whispered in a voice audible halfway to Main Street, "Say fifteen Our Fathers and fifteen Hail Marys for penance. Now say an Act of Contrition."

I broke at once into an impassioned Act of Contrition. No one was ever so contrite as I, pledging, "Oh, my God! I am heartily sorry for having offended Thee, and I detest all my sins because I dread the loss of heaven and the pains of hell, but most of all because they offend Thee, my God, who art all-good and deserving of all my love. I firmly resolve, with the help of Thy grace, to confess my sins, do penance, and to amend my life. Amen."

"When you say it for Father, don't say it so loud," Sister told me.

Wasn't she a good one to talk, I thought, pushing aside the curtain of the confessional and heading toward a pew near the altar. Genuflecting, I slid in and knelt down. Fifteen Our Fathers and fifteen Hail Marys. Sister must think I'd been pretty wicked to give me that much penance.

Halfway through the Hail Marys, I realized that I hadn't actually confessed. I had it all to do over, and this time with my unending and heinous list of crimes included. Quickly I rattled off the remaining Hail Marys and left, as Sister had said we might when we had completed our penance.

Passing up the aisle, I noted that Sally had left. She hadn't spoken to me or looked at me this morning. Beverly, paste white around the gills, was waiting to enter the confessional. Her eyes were glazed, and she did not see me.

Following lunch, of which I ate almost none, I dug my sin notebook out of the bottom of the wardrobe where it was hidden under Mama's shoes.

Papa was in the kitchen eating blueberry pie. He might remain there for some time; it was never busy in the ticket office on weekends. I tucked the notebook inside the bodice of my dress and crossed my arms over it.

"Where are you off to?" Mama asked when she saw me heading to the door.

"Outside."

"How come you're walking so funny?"

"Stomachache."

"Maybe you should lie down for a while."

"I think I should walk."

"Suit yourself. Just remember, you have to be back at church at three."

"I'll remember."

"Wait a minute," Papa said.

I pushed the screen door open with my elbow.

"I said wait a minute." He thrust his chair back and turned to me. "I thought maybe you'd like to sit on my lap and help me finish this pie and ice cream."

"No, thank you, Papa."

" 'No, thank you, Papa'? Since when do you turn down pie and ice cream?"

"Let her go, Willie. She said she had a stomachache."

"You stay out of this. This kid got mad at me the other night, and she's been holding a grudge ever since. I don't like people who hold grudges and neither does God. I just want to make sure she tells Father Delias that she's been holding a grudge against her pa. Don't forget to confess *that* when you're tellin' him the other two thousand sins," he told me.

"Shut up, Willie."

"I told you to stay out of this."

"I'm not staying out. She's my kid as much as yours. Go on out and play, Lark."

"You stay right where you are, if you know what's good for you," Papa warned.

Mama was greasing an iron skillet before putting it away in the cupboard. She stopped running her fingers over it and held it in front of her, never taking her eyes off Papa. "Go on, Lark."

Papa stood, throwing back his chair. "What the hell is this?" he screamed. "It's always you two against me. If people in this town knew what I put up with, you wouldn't walk down the street like a goddamned duchess."

He stood looking at Mama, the skillet in her hands. Then he swept his plate and coffee cup off the table. They flew across the narrow kitchen, the coffee taking off, out of the cup, landing on Mama's skirt and running down her legs.

Absently, Mama reached down and brushed the dripping coffee from her leg, her eyes still fixed on Papa.

"I work damned hard and you know it!" he went on. "But does

anybody around here ever thank me for it? Hell, no. I'm just the damned fool who brings home the bacon for you to squander on presents for an idiot and . . . and a lot of fancy clothes I can't afford." Papa started to cry. "One of these days I'll kill you. But first I'm gonna tell people what you're like so they won't blame me."

In a voice I could barely hear, but whose intensity seared the air, Mama told him, "You get out of here, you sonofabitch, before I kill *you*." She slowly raised the iron skillet.

Through his tears, Papa cried, "That's right. Turn the kid against me and run me out of my own house."

Mama made a menacing gesture with the skillet, and Papa twisted away, pushing me aside and rushing blindly out the door. The sin notebook fell onto the floor at my feet.

"Bless me, Father, for I have sinned. This is my first confession."

From the pocket of my dress, I pulled the folded sheet of paper on which I had earlier compiled my list of sins, according to commandment. After Papa had hurled out of the house, I had hiked a mile into the country on the railroad tracks, and sat down in quiet and privacy to prepare the list from which I now began reading, twisting sideways to catch the meager light that filtered in around the confessional curtains.

"I don't think I broke the First Commandment, Father. I think I broke the Second Commandment about twelve times." It was hard to say precisely. I knew I'd whispered the Lord's name in vain a number of times when I was angry. Usually I said it into a pillow.

"I broke the Third Commandment twice." I could remember distinctly two occasions when I'd feigned a headache to stay home from church.

The Fourth Commandment was a real snake pit. "Honor thy father and thy mother." I had labored long over my list, pulling together as much as I could recall of Papa's criticisms, as well as my own recollections.

"I broke the Fourth Commandment about a hundred times, Father."

Father Delias cleared his throat. "Could you tell me one or two examples?"

"I bit my fingernails when Papa had told me not to."

"And did your papa punish you for that?"

"Yes."

"In what way?"

"With the brush."

"Were you sorry to have upset him?"

"Yes."

"I understand. Go on."

"Sometimes I can't stop being mad at Papa."

"When has that happened most recently?"

I told him about the sin notebook, and about Papa reading it.

"When your papa read the notebook, you felt like you'd let him down?"

"Oh, yes, Father."

"I understand. Go on to the next commandment, child."

I hesitated.

"It's the Fifth Commandment," he prompted. " 'Thou shalt not kill.' Have you been angry and fought with family or friends?"

"Yes, Father. About two hundred times."

"Go on to the next commandment."

"Father, I haven't finished the Fifth Commandment." I hurried on before I lost my nerve, blurting out, "I killed a baby."

There was silence on the other side, except for Father's breathing.

"Did you hear me, Father?"

"Yes. I'm wondering what makes you think you killed a baby."

The story came pouring out in a tumbling torrent of words and tears: how I had set myself to watch for the stork and catch the baby when it fell, as the baby in my dream had fallen; how I had lollygagged around that field behind Aunt Betty's house, failing to watch *all* the sky; and how the stork then had dropped the baby.

When at last I came to the end of the story, Father said, "There is such a bird as the stork, but the stork does not deliver babies. You recall that there was no mention in the Bible of a stork flying into Bethlehem with the baby Jesus."

"Then who does bring babies?"

"Before they come into the world, babies grow in the safest, warmest place that God could find for them, a place that makes them feel loved even before they are born."

"Where's that?"

"Inside the mother. That's where Jesus grew, and that's where Baby Marjorie grew—inside your aunt's body."

That was why Aunt Betty's belly was so fat. Why hadn't any-body told me? "How do they get out?"

"There's a small passageway. One of these days your mama will tell you about all of this. In the meantime, you mustn't worry. God has designed it all, and you must trust Him."

"Why did Baby Marjorie die?"

"I don't know. God knows. He has the plan, and we must have faith in His wisdom. Let's proceed now to the Sixth Commandment."

The remainder of the confession was over in a wink. When I thrust aside the curtain and left, my feet were as weightless as I imagined Fred Astaire's to be. I floated down the aisle in a gauzy haze of light and lightness. In my life I had never felt such disencumbrance. If I lifted my arms, I would float up to the dark beams and along the ceiling, and my new innocence would hold me aloft. This was how angels felt.

❧ 40 ☙

WARM, SCENTED, ten o'clock air hummed with the sound of bees in the lilac bushes beyond the church windows. One of the bees had got inside the church and was buzzing around the lilac branches massed in vases at the feet of Mary and Joseph, on either side of the altar.

The morning was unusually warm, and since the paper fans for summer had not yet been furnished, some worshipers were fan-ning themselves with missals or with the list of first communicants that had been passed out by the ushers in the vestibule. Men had dragged out their large white handkerchiefs to mop their brows and bulging pink necks, while ladies held dainty, scented hankies to their temples and blotted their noses and throats.

I knew neither heat nor discomfort as I waited in the front pew with the other first-time communicants, all of us starched and pressed, curled and combed, scrubbed and talcumed, more clearly and intimately connected to God in our impeccable innocence than we would ever again be in this world.

I thought that maybe I was beginning to understand God a little. Surely the most important thing about God was forgiveness. Yesterday he had forgiven me my sins, and I had become a brand-new girl. I had felt my brand-newness inside and out. Outside I was light and feathery; inside, blindingly white. If you looked inside me now, it would be like looking directly into the head of a flashlight.

The white, lacy dresses we girls wore, and the boys' white shirts, were not so white as the blaze of light inside us. If I opened my mouth wide, you could see the light shining up.

Sisters Mary Clair and Mary Frances stood. It was time for the class to stand and march to the communion rail. Hands clasped, white veil stirring in the current of air moving invisibly, like God, among us, I followed Lavonne Swenson to the altar.

Father Delias spoke but I didn't hear. Assisted by an altar boy, he moved along the rail, raising the communion wafer, blessing us, placing the wafer on our tongues. Thin as mica, magic wafer.

Very dry and utterly without flavor, it absorbed the saliva in my mouth and cleaved to my tongue. We must not chew it or allow it to get into our teeth, as some minute part of it might then be lost, brushed away by the next brushing of our teeth, some tiny bit of Jesus's body would go down the drain or, in my case, into the slop pail.

When we were back in the pew, kneeling and praying, I began swallowing, carefully working the wafer back to my throat. It wasn't easy. When it got as far as the soft palate, it wanted to stay there. But I summoned all the spit I could muster and gave it one final shove, sending it down to my soul, to feed the fire of love.

Before yesterday I had not understood how you could love God. Respect Him, yes. And obey Him. But love? But His forgiving me had engendered love. I trembled with the intimacy of God.

Soon we were standing in the sun outside the church, having our picture taken, the whole class together, the Sisters standing at either side, like dark bookends.

Then our parents claimed us and fussed over us and laughed, releasing their nervousness. We had made it. We were one of them. More than confirmation, First Communion brought us into Christ's circle of light, a circle our parents had known for so long, I wondered if they hadn't grown used to it.

Mama threw her arms around me, laughing and nearly losing her pretty, little navy blue straw hat with the pink roses growing on it. "You looked so beautiful, Lark. Like an angel. Didn't she, Willie? Didn't she look like an angel?"

Papa was ill at ease in the midst of my celebration. He thought Mama was talking too loud. He turned away to remark on something to Harry Mosely. From out of the crush, Father Delias appeared, and he was laughing and shaking hands and telling funny little stories about the bees and the communion wine, or something like that. He gave me a hug and held Mama's hand, and exclaimed over my catechism scholarship.

"She'll make a fine bright woman, she will," he declared, swinging around to include Papa. "You hear what I'm saying, William. You've got a fine girl." Papa smiled obligingly and said thank you.

I loved Father Delias. It was he, as God's surrogate, who had forgiven me, who had made me light, so light I could probably tap dance if I were at home. I looked down at the full-skirted organdy dress and the new, white patent leather shoes which had been sitting beside the crib when I woke this morning. Yes, if I were at home, I could tap dance, skirt billowing out from my legs, veil lifting and whirling around my head.

I grabbed Father Delias's hand and kissed the back of it.

"What on earth are you doing?" Papa demanded.

"She's kissing my hand, William," Father Delias explained, and he bent and kissed mine.

41

THE SUMMER of 1940 was like a movie starring Joan Blondell (as Mama) and Shirley Temple (as me). The first week in June, before the Majestic Movie Theater closed for the hot summer months, we went to see *Goodbye, Mr. Chips*, with Robert Donat and Greer Garson. Nearly everybody in the country had already seen it. We were always late getting anything that wasn't produced by Republic Pictures, Mama commented to Bernice McGivern when we met in front of the theater.

Mama and I were feeling unaccountably festive when we left the depot that night to walk downtown. Mama said we couldn't afford popcorn or candy, only our tickets, so we dressed with particular care. Mama wore a pair of homemade white sharkskin pants, which made her feel like Marlene Dietrich (and which Papa said only a chippy would wear on the street), and a silky-looking white top, trimmed with kelly green. I had chosen my navy-blue-and-white sailor dress with the big collar and red tie, and I was carrying my old red patent leather purse, from which the shininess was peeling. I had a Myrna Loy feeling as we stepped along, Mama humming, luridly off-key, "You Must Have Been a Beautiful Baby."

Before we left home, Mama had stuffed a hanky into my purse. "Just in case," she said. Mrs. Chips's death took me by surprise, and I completely wet that handkerchief and started on the hem of my dress. When the curtains closed and the lights came up, I was caught with my skirt to my face. The owner of the Majestic, Mr. Belling, short and pale and with an unnaturally smooth and uncreased look, as if he'd been made by a taxidermist, glided quickly down the aisle and onto the forestage. Mama admonished me to put my dress down.

"Ladies and gentlemen, as you know, tonight is Bank Nite at the Majestic, and some lucky person will win our grand prize for the year 1940!"

Realizing full well that it was Bank Nite, everyone had remained in his or her seat, ticket stub in hand. Only the blue, adult ticket stubs were eligible for the drawing, Mr. Belling reminded us.

Trailing his father down the aisle was Jimmy Belling, Mr. Belling's son and chief usher, toting a revolving wire basket filled with blue tickets. Sixteen-year-old Jimmy, like his father, was exceedingly pale, and he observed the world with worried, protuberant, skim-milk blue eyes.

"I need a volunteer from the audience to come up on stage and draw a ticket out of the basket," Mr. Belling requested.

From the third row, where children usually sat, Sheila Grubb, owner of the nasty Pekingese who had bitten holes in my shoes, and buyer of a new living room suite with Papa's poker losses, jumped up and squeezed along to the aisle.

"Mrs. Grubb," Mr. Belling greeted her, bowing slightly.

Sheila Grubb inquired, "If I draw my own ticket, I still win, don't I?"

"It's never happened," Mr. Belling told her, smiling.

"Yes, but I still win, don't I?"

Mr. Belling looked uncomfortable. "I . . . I suppose that would be the case."

"All right, then," Sheila Grubb declared and turned to Jimmy. "Spin the basket."

"Now, ladies and gentlemen," Mr. Belling began momentously, "it is time for the first big spin. There are three prizes tonight in our final Bank Nite of 1940. The owner of the first ticket drawn will receive a lovely set of fine china donated by Lundeen's Dry Goods. Several pieces of this china have been on display in the lobby, where you have been able to admire them. Spin the basket, Jimmy."

The younger Belling gave the basket a vigorous turn, and it whirled round and round. When it finally came to rest, Jimmy opened the little door and Sheila Grubb, closing her eyes dramatically, reached in to retrieve a ticket, which she handed to Mr. Belling after first checking the number against the stub she had in the breast pocket of her dress.

"Our first winner tonight, winner of the fine china, is number 10389." He repeated, "Number 10389."

"That's me!" cried Magdalen Haggerty of the Loon Cafe. Running down the aisle holding her blue stub aloft, she kept assuring us, "That's me!"

Wouldn't Papa be pleased to learn that his friend Magdalen Haggerty, whom he'd often promised a ride in the Oldsmobile that we no longer owned, had won a set of china?

Mr. Belling verified her number. "Ladies and gentlemen, we have a winner of the fine china: Miss Magdalen Haggerty of Harvester!"

We all applauded her good fortune and Mr. Belling continued, "If you will wait on stage, Magdalen, until the drawing is concluded, Harry Bjornson from the *Standard Ledger* will photograph all three winners." Turning again to the audience, Mr. Belling heralded, "The winner of the second number drawn will receive either a man's suit with two pairs of pants and vest, or a woman's complete outfit—dress, shoes, stockings, hat, handbag, and gloves—from Barnstable's Department Store in St. Bridget." A hum of approval ran through the audience.

Again Mr. Belling addressed his son. "And now, Jimmy, if you will give the basket another spin."

The number drawn this time was 10301. "10301," Mr. Belling called out. "Is there anyone here with that number? 10301."

"By God, it's me, Blanche," a heavy male voice boomed from the balcony.

We all craned to see who it was. I didn't recognize the rubicund giant in gray overalls, blue flannel shirt, and red-and-blue-figured tie. A couple of minutes passed while we waited impatiently for the winner to come downstairs. When at last he mounted the three steps to the stage, he towered over the others.

Proffering the stub, he shouted, "Here's the ticket!" His voice must have been plainly heard across the street at Lundeen's Dry Goods.

"And you are?" Mr. Belling inquired after verifying that the stub was indeed the winning one.

"Ernest Fraker from over near Red Berry." The man laughed as though this information were hilarious. And we all laughed, so infectious was Mr. Fraker's exuberant manner.

"You are the winner of a man's suit with two pairs of pants and a vest, provided by Barnstable's Department Store in St. Bridget." Mr. Belling handed the beaming winner a certificate of some sort, motioning him to stand beside Magdalen Haggerty.

"I can use it," Mr. Fraker told us candidly, taking his place next to the waitress from the Loon Cafe.

"And now . . ." Mr. Belling proclaimed with a small flourish of his stubby arm, "it is time for the Bank Nite grand prize." Pause. "Provided by the management of the Majestic Movie Theater." Pause. "Two hundred and fifty dollars!"

While we had all known for weeks that the grand prize was going to be two hundred and fifty dollars, a choking thrill ran through us. Two hundred and fifty dollars was as much as some men made in three months.

"Jimmy, will you please spin the basket?"

Jimmy gave it an extra flick, so that it seemed to take forever to come to rest. Our eyes were fixed to that revolving basket of fate. I was chewing on the strap of my purse.

Finally, the basket gave a slow, concluding toss to the tickets, and stopped. For the last time until the Majestic reopened in September, Jimmy unhooked the little door.

Sheila Grubb closed her eyes, bit her lip, and reached her painted fingernails into the wire basket, pulling out the number of the grand prize winner. Checking it against her stub, she gave a little stamp with her foot, and passed the ticket to Mr. Belling with a pretty pout.

After first reading the number silently and waiting what seemed hours, Mr. Belling declared, "The winning number is . . . 10375. 10375. Who is the lucky patron of the Majestic holding number 10375?"

Beside me, Mama stood up, leaning on the seat in front of her. I wondered if we were leaving before we knew who the winner was. I got up to follow her out.

"Mrs. Erhardt?" Mr. Belling called. "Do you have the winning number?"

Mama nodded.

"Ladies and gentlemen, Mrs. Erhardt seems overcome by good fortune. Could someone give her a hand?"

Bernice McGivern, who'd let out a whoop when she realized that Mama held the winning number, stood up excitedly now, laughing and "oh-mying" and guiding Mama, who moved like a sleepwalker, out into the aisle and down to the stage. Bernice stayed with her until Mama was up the stairs and beside Mr. Belling.

"Ladies and gentlemen, I think we can say that we have a happy and surprised grand prize winner in Mrs. Willie Erhardt of Harvester."

Dazed, Mama looked around as if unsure where she was. Mr. Belling removed a check from the inside pocket of his jacket and handed it to Mama as Harry Bjornson, holding the flash above his head, snapped their picture.

"Thank you," Mama told Mr. Belling weakly. "Thank you," she repeated, turning first to Sheila Grubb and then to Jimmy. "Thank you," she told the audience. Eventually she thanked Magdalen Haggerty and Mr. Ernest Fraker as well.

Mr. Belling led Mama to the other winners. Their pictures were taken together for next Thursday's *Standard Ledger*, and the audience all clapped before filing slowly, silently out. Bernice McGivern and I waited at the foot of the stage, as did Mrs. Fraker, who was crying happy tears.

When Mama drifted down the stairs, still stupefied, walking as if on eggs, she stammered, "I'm going . . . I'm going . . . into business."

*   *   *

The day after Mama won the grand prize money, she bought a little white Ford coupe secondhand for a hundred dollars. It would fall apart before a week was out, Papa assured her, and anyway, what did she need with a car of her own?

She needed it for Erhardt's Typing Service, she pointed out. On the front page of Thursday's *Standard Ledger* were pictures of Mama accepting the check for two hundred and fifty dollars, and Mama with Magdalen Haggerty and Ernest Fraker, all of them looking vacant and slightly inebriated. Inside was an ad for Mama's typing business. She would do expert business and personal typing, it said. For assignments totaling a dollar or more, she would pick up and deliver anywhere in St. Bridget County. If the customer desired, Mama would compose the business or personal correspondence for them. Satisfaction guaranteed.

"You had to wear those pants," Papa complained, seeing the pictures on the front page. "You'll be the laughingstock of the county," he added when he saw the ad on the inside back page.

Mama ran the same ad in the *Red Berry Shopper* and the *St. Bridget Bugle*. But she did not wait for customers to come to her. She had business cards printed, typed up sample letters, and took to the road in her Ford coupe. During the summer months, she took me with her.

In the morning after breakfast, Mama and I picked up the house, then she went immediately to her typewriter. She bought a typing table at the junk shop for a dollar, and made a little space for it in one corner of the living room. Each weekday morning, whether or not there was paid work to do, she typed. If she didn't have paid work, she typed letters to relatives or more samples to show prospective customers. "Typing is like playing the piano," she told me. "You have to keep practicing between performances."

While Mama typed and waited for business calls, I roller skated, or took a long walk past the hobo jungle out into the country, or played with Beverly. I didn't see much of Sally. Her Grandmother Elway came for an extended visit, and Sally stuck close to home. She was no longer mad at me, yet the distance between us widened inexplicably.

As soon as Papa had his lunch and the kitchen was clean, Mama and I cast off, venturing forth into the wide world in the Ford. Like a little day-sailer, the coupe plied the waters of St. Bridget County, tacking back and forth, from Red Berry to Hazelton, Deer Crossing to Inlet, Bradbury to Dusseldorf, St. Bridget to Harvester, and so on. Some of these were villages of less than five hundred people. No matter. Mama visited every café and gas station, creamery and grain elevator, describing her services, leaving a card, and telling them that she could be reached every morning at the number on the card. In emergencies they could call in the evening.

During the first two weeks of business, Mama had only two assignments: a dunning letter for the P & V Plumbing Company of Red Berry, and a long letter to her daughter from a very old woman in St. Bridget who had seen Mama's ad in the *Bugle.*

"You're spending more money on gas for the car than you'll ever take in," Papa pointed out.

"I'm spending my own money," Mama answered.

"We could have put that money down on another Olds."

Papa was peeved about the way Mama had handled the purchase of the coupe. Instead of coming to him and asking him to find her a car, she'd simply walked into Johnson's Chevrolet and Buick, and asked if they had any decent cars they'd taken on trade. The sale was in cash and in Mama's name.

"I'm not losing this one to gambling debts," she said.

Week by week, Mama's business picked up. Customers found her efficient yet sympathetic to their needs and problems. Mama was full of clever notions about how they could improve their businesses, or in the case of the old woman in St. Bridget, how she could better things between herself and her daughter in Iowa. Mama always found a way to couch these suggestions so that they appeared to be the *other* person's idea. It was amazing, they all noted, how much shrewder they were when Mama stopped by.

Summer rolled so merrily along, I regretted having to leave Harvester for a week's visit to Grandma and Grandpa Erhardt in New Frankfurt, and a two-week stay with Grandma and Grandpa Browning in Blue Lake, but Mama insisted.

"It's not good for you to be in the car every day. You need to go swimming and fishing and lie around reading books. Or, you can help the grandmas put up preserves. And maybe they'll teach you to bake. I never seem to have the time anymore."

All that sounded fine, but I was having a grand time in the car, traveling up and down the county, waving to farmers and counting pheasants. Papa always wanted to know how many pheasants

I'd seen and where their nests were. In the fall during hunting season, he'd know where to hunt.

Sometimes I accompanied Mama into P & V Plumbing, which was in Mr. Peete's garage, behind his house, or into the Dusseldorf Feed and Grain, at the end of Main Street in Dusseldorf. At other times Mama left me at the school playground or the town park, if there was one. St. Bridget had a municipal swimming pool, so I took along my swimsuit and brushed up my skills while Mama spent the afternoon calling on St. Bridget customers. I was able to swim across the pool now, so the lifeguards let me swim in the deep end and jump off the diving boards.

One day we took Beverly along to St. Bridget. The lifeguards there frowned on people swimming in their underwear, so Beverly wore my old, red polka dot suit, which barely covered her necessities, Mama said. I was half-dying to show Beverly how I could jump off the end of the low diving board and swim to the side of the pool. The first thing Beverly did was climb up the high board and dive off. If it had been anyone else, I'd have said she was showing off, but Beverly never noticed whether you were watching or not. Besides, she was always willing to teach you whatever she knew. Beverly just liked a good challenge. Like Mama.

By the end of August, when I returned from visiting the grandparents, Mama was typing all morning on assignments, with never a spare moment just for practice.

"By Christmas I'll have made back what I spent for the car," she told me. "Think of it, Lark, I'm going to make enough money next year for a big down payment on the house."

"The Cape Ann?" I asked, not daring to believe.

"When you're in the fourth grade, in the spring, we'll start building the Cape Ann," she promised.

I was entering the third grade in a week. In a year and a half, two years at the outside, I would have my own room. It seemed forever, and yet very near, very tangible. I imagined myself in a real bed, with no bars, stretching my legs and not being able to touch the foot.

I imagined Hilly and me in the garden, watering the flowers and sampling the sweet, baby peas. Whatever was happening to Hilly's brain, a garden could not fail to make him happy.

❧ 42 ❧

"WHO IN HELL'S wearing the pants in this family?" Papa asked at dinner one night in September. "I want to buy a new car this fall, I tell you."

"No," Mama repeated. "We're saving for the house. We've gotten along without a new car for more than a year. It won't kill us a while longer."

"Since you started that business, nothing's the same," Papa told her. "Suddenly *you're* making the decisions. By God, I'm putting my foot down. I'm buying a car."

"You buy a car, and that's that for you and me, Willie Erhardt."

What did Mama mean, "that's that"?

"I work, too," Papa reminded her. "And I make more money." He pushed his emptied plate away. "I should have some say around here."

"It's got nothing to do with who makes the most money," Mama said. "Don't you see that Lark can't go on sleeping in a crib, for God's sake? She's almost eight years old."

"Well, get one of those daybeds or whatever you call them, and put it in the living room."

"How can you be so selfish?" Mama asked. "How can it be more important for Willie Erhardt to have a new car than for his daughter to have a decent home?" Mama got up and went to fetch the applesauce cake.

"You're not going to make me the bogeyman," Papa told her. "You know what a car means to me. You've always known."

"I won't pay for it, Willie. I'm saving my money for a house. The money I earn is in *my* name, and so is my car. I won't sign for a new car for you and lose my own car if you can't make the payments. If that's what you've got in mind, forget it."

"I'm just the poor sucker who supported you all these years," Papa wept, and he shuffled into the bedroom and pulled a hand-kerchief from the bureau drawer. Mama went on eating her cake.

"Do you believe it?" she said at dinner several nights later. "I was offered two jobs today, two different, full-time jobs. The Ford garage over in St. Bridget wanted me to come to work for them, and Barnstable's Department Store said they needed somebody like me to reorganize their office. What do they know about me, except that I can type?"

"What did you tell them?" I asked.

"I said no. I said thank you very much, I'm flattered, but I like my independence. They looked so surprised," she said, and laughed. "I don't suppose they get a lot of turndowns from women. I can't tell you how . . . strong it made me feel."

"You're getting real good at saying no to people," Papa said.

"You don't understand what I mean," Mama said.

"What am I, too dumb to understand the English language?"

"Willie, there's no need to get steamed up," Mama said. "It made me feel strong to say no because I've worked hard getting my little business started, and now that it's succeeding, I feel confidence, real confidence in myself for the first time in my life. Doesn't that make you happy, just a little, Willie? Can't you be a tiny bit proud of me?"

But Papa turned the tables. "Have *you* ever been proud of *me?* I've had a decent job as long as you've known me. When other men were going on relief, I provided for you and the kid. You never worried about your next meal. Were you ever proud of me?

The following day when Mama came home from the road, she had a present for me. "I should have saved it for your birthday," she said, "but I've seen all those pictures you've been cutting out." She handed me a big scrapbook with a red leatherette cover and red cords, like shoelaces, tying it together, so that you could add more pages if you ran out. "It's your Cape Ann scrapbook," Mama explained, "for the pictures of rooms and gardens you're collecting."

I hugged her so hard she said I nearly broke her gizzard. The scrapbook was another proof that we were going to build the house. It was a pledge. Mama was not a person who went back on her word. I danced around the house with the book in my arms.

How quickly the days escaped. I was very busy. When I got home from school in the afternoon, there was a note on the table from Mama with a list of chores: set the table, empty the slop pails, turn the oven on at four-thirty, scrub three potatoes, etcetera. I felt important being assistant to the president of the company, as Mama had titled me. And Mama paid me well for my help. Fifteen cents a week. That was a nickel more than Katherine Albers got.

One evening after supper, along toward Thanksgiving of 1940, Mama phoned her best friend, Bernice McGivern. Papa had gone back to the depot office, and I was sitting at the kitchen table, pasting pictures in the scrapbook.

"I had a letter from Blue Lake today," Mama told Bernice. "It's got me upset." I heard her unfold Grandma's letter. "The first part's about the weather and Papa putting up the storm windows and Cousin Carrie from Marshalltown coming to visit. But then she says"—here Mama lowered her voice—" 'I'm worried about Betty. It seems pretty clear to all of us that Stan isn't going to send for her. There's been one excuse after another: He needed a new car. He needed a new place to live. He wrecked the new car.

'It's been nearly a year and a half since he left. We've told Betty to get on a bus and go out there. She's got the money saved, but I tell you, Arlene, the spirit's gone out of that girl. I think she's afraid of getting out to California and seeing the truth with her own eyes. She doesn't care about anything anymore. She won't even go to the pictures with the other girls from the dime store.

'I shouldn't say it, Arlene, and I want you to burn this letter right away, but I'm afraid Betty's going to get herself into something she shouldn't with that Mr. Miller that owns the dime store. He's married, with two young ones. It worries me half to death, but she won't talk so I'm helpless. What can we do?' "

Mama was silent. Bernice was talking.

"She ought to get a divorce is what she ought to do," Mama said.

Next to *death*, *divorce* was the most final and frightening word I knew. I listened sharply.

"I know you don't believe in divorce," Mama told Bernice, "but I don't believe in lying down and dying at age thirty-two."

Silence.

"Well, Betty's a convert, Bernice."

Silence.

"It'd damned near kill Mama and Papa, but they'd just have to get used to it."

Silence.

"What do you mean, do I feel guilty about sending Stan to California? Of course not. He couldn't make a living here. My sister was starving. It's not my fault if he turned out to be a four-flusher."

They went on talking for a long time, but I had heard the

shocking theme of it. Closing the scrapbook, I put it away in the top drawer of the buffet, and went to bed. It was a long time since I'd stepped into the cottage garden on the banjo clock. Tonight I was glad to have a cozy place to go.

I strolled through the cottage with its low, beamed ceiling and wing chairs drawn up beside the hearth. Out the front door, I continued, down the stone path and across the lawn to the cottage next door where I heard a baby goo-gooing.

Angela Roosevelt had married Earl Samson, and they had settled down in the cottage with their new baby, named after me. They were the happiest couple I'd ever seen.

43

IN THIRD GRADE we learned Palmer Method penmanship. I spent hours each week scratching hundreds of *m*'s and thousands of *o*'s in lines across the paper, like worms and eggs crawling and rolling from one side to the other. By the end of the year, I was grounded in the basics required to function in the adult world of business and family (reading, writing, arithmetic, and diplomacy), and I wondered if the other nine years of school might not be superfluous.

In kindergarten I'd learned to negotiate for what I wanted, and to listen while other people said things I wasn't interested in hearing. In first grade I'd learned to read. Learning to read and First Confession had been the two most important events in my life so far.

Second grade had been more prosaic than first. I'd learned to add and subtract. In a purely objective way, I was happy to have the skill because I would need it, but numbers were not as thrilling as words.

Now, in third grade, I'd learned to write longhand. I wasn't as adept as I had hoped. As was the case with tap dancing, mere desire did not make you graceful.

A remarkably parallel situation was occurring in Hilly's life.

Mrs. Stillman was reeducating Hilly in writing. When Mama heard this, she said, "Lark, I want you to write Hilly a note."

"What should I say?"

"Tell him that you're reading *Heidi*. And I'm sure he'd like to hear about the tap dancing lessons at Martha Beverton's Tap and Toe."

There wasn't anything to say about the tap dancing lessons at Martha Beverton's except that I was the worst pupil in the class, worse even than the little kindergarten dancers, so I told him that. Mama said that people enjoy hearing about other people's failures. It gives them hope.

But most of the letter was about *Heidi*, which I'd read through twice and enshrined in a hallowed niche in life, like *Happy Stories for Bedtime*.

Mama fixed a stamp to the envelope, and I mailed Hilly's letter on my way to school on a crackling cold morning in February. "It should come to him through the mail," Mama explained, "because it's exciting to receive real mail. It makes you feel important. You are *someone* if you get mail with your name on it."

A few days later, when I stopped at the post office on the way home from school, I found, in addition to the envelopes addressed to Erhardt Typing Service, one for Lark Ann Erhardt. Mama was right. I felt like *someone*.

I didn't rip it open then and there but tucked it away, along with Mama's mail, not showing it to Beverly, who was walking home from school with me.

When we reached the depot, Beverly hung on and on, talking about school and her mama's new job as cook at the Loon Cafe. I thought Beverly didn't want to go home because it was too cold there to take off your coat unless you got into bed, so I asked her to come in and study with me.

"I have to do my chores first," I told her, hiding the letter among the pages of *Happy Stories for Bedtime*, and piling Mama's mail on her typing table.

"Did you know Sally's pa's working in town now?" Beverly asked while we set the table.

"How come?"

"Guess he got tired of traveling."

"I bet Sally's glad."

"Godsakes, yes. Wouldn't *you* be if you had a ma like hers?"

"She's got a nice mama."

"She's got a spooky ma, if you ask me. You ever see her any more? What's she do all the time?"

"She worries a lot, I think."

Beverly stayed for supper and Mama drove her home in the coupe, which Beverly thought was grand and in which she liked to be seen riding. It was one of her few airs and graces.

The moment they were gone, I climbed into the crib and tore open the letter. My hands shook, and I lay the piece of lined notebook paper on the quilt.

> Dear Lark Ann Erhardt,
>
> I was very happy when I received your letter.
> Sometimes I am happy. I was happy when you told me about Heidi. In the mountains I think I would be happy.
> I am sad sometimes. There is war in the *Life* magazine. I don't want to see that.
> I read many books now. Mrs. Stillman my mother has bad eyes so I read to her. Do you remember that you read to me? I remember Peggy and the pansies.
> Please write.
>
> > Your friend,
> >
> > Hillyard E. Stillman

Hilly's Palmer Method was messy because he had the same problems with the pen that I had. But the letters were fat and round, like plump babies playing on the floor. Except for the signature, which was cramped and tiny.

Hilly and I began corresponding once a week. But when Mama and I called on the Stillmans, Hilly never mentioned our letters. He remained the shy, silent person he'd become when sanity began overtaking him. Yet, in his letters, he thanked me for visiting and sometimes spoke of the story I'd read or the picture I'd drawn for him.

I always composed my letters on Sunday, reviewing for him the previous week's events. Mama, seeing me at work on the letter, would say, "Don't forget to tell him about ice skating on Sioux Woman Lake," or when I'd been home in bed a week with tonsillitis, "Don't forget to mention how the doctor painted your throat."

In her travels around the county, Mama kept an eye open for anything that might amuse Hilly. "He's so cooped up," she'd say, but he wouldn't come out for a ride anymore. A circus that set up tent on the outskirts of St. Bridget was the source of a big poster, red and yellow and blue, with lions roaring and elephants rearing. The Methodist rummage sale in Dusseldorf yielded a copy of *Robinson Crusoe.*

Mama's business was growing. "I've created a monster!" she'd sigh, not displeased. She wasn't getting rich, but she was paying expenses, putting a little in her account each week, and "learning how the world works."

But Mama was worried about Aunt Betty. There were long letters back and forth. She burned the ones from Aunt Betty after reading them, and told me not to tell Papa.

In August of 1941, Mama took a week's vacation from Erhardt Typing Service. She gave all her customers fair warning that she would be away, then packed our bags, piled me into the coupe, and raced for Blue Lake as if the road in that direction might be closed the next day. She had her reasons, but she did not share them with me. When I asked, she said, "It's grown-up problems. Nothing for you to worry about."

I let it go. I would keep my eyes and ears open, and someday I would understand. I simply had to be patient and remember the details. Detective Erhardt of the FBI.

One thing I understood: Papa had had about all he could stomach of Mama's success. It was suffocating him. I saw it on his face as Mama talked business to us breakfast, lunch, and supper.

"Mr. Bracken, the manager of Barnstable's over in St. Bridget, said I should hire a bookkeeper to handle accounts for small businesses. I might do that after the first of the year," she'd say.

Or else, "That brochure I put together for the Harvester Businessmen's Association? . . . Mr. Loken told me it was 'top-notch.' That's the word he used—'top-notch.' "

"After the first of the year I'm going to invest in a portable typewriter. There are times when I need to throw the typewriter in the car and go, like that," she explained once, snapping her fingers, "and I can barely lift that thing I've got, much less throw it.

"Also, I'm going to get an instruction book and teach myself shorthand. I can take dictation plenty fast with my own system, but I'd do a lot better if I knew real shorthand. What do you think? D'ya think it's a waste of time?"

Papa sat in stony, unheeded silence. It galled him that *his* name, Erhardt, was on the business—Erhardt Typing Service— soon, perhaps, to become Erhardt Typing and Bookkeeping Service.

While Mama and I were in Blue Lake, maybe Papa would cool down. If he had a good time with Mr. Navarin and Sonny Steen and Herbie Wendel, he might be jolly and indulgent when we returned. He needed to go fishing and to hear not a word about Erhardt Typing Service the entire week.

Papa bid us a sullen good-bye as Mama and I drove off in the coupe at ten o'clock Saturday morning, August 16, 1941, the day after the celebration of the Assumption of Mary into heaven. Papa did not wave, though I turned and knelt on the seat, and waved to him through the rear window. He may not have seen me waving. It wasn't a very big window. He stood unsmiling, arms folded across his chest, eyes narrowed as if he were deep in speculation. Did he suspect a secret about our going, something afoot to which he was not privy?

Mama hit the blacktop running and took off for Blue Lake "flying low," as Papa described her driving. At high, hot noon on a dog day that was as still as a stagnant pond, we coasted into Blue Lake.

Grandma had laid the table with sliced watermelon, potato salad, deviled eggs, sliced tomatoes, and sliced cucumbers in cream and vinegar. We each had a tall, sweating glass of iced tea beside our plate. The electric fan on the sideboard swept back and forth over the table and over Grandma, Grandpa, Mama, and me. Aunt Betty was at work downtown at the Ben Franklin Five and Dime.

I was the only one eating much. Grandma and Grandpa asked about Mama's business. How many hours a day was she working? Was she home when I came home from school? What was she doing with me during the summer when school was out? They turned to me. What did *I* think of Mama running around St. Bridget County like a crazy secretary who'd escaped from the state hospital?

I liked it, I told them. "I'm learning to cook and keep house,

and if I'm good, next year Mama's going to teach me to type."
More than almost anything, I wanted to know how to type with
all ten fingers.

"Arlene, are you sure this child is having a proper childhood?"
Grandma questioned.

"For God's sake, Mama . . ."

"I don't like that kind of talk," Grandma interrupted.

"*You* worked when *I* was a kid," Mama reminded her.

Grandma and Grandpa had once been farmers. After the World
War, when crop prices went bust, they lost the farm and moved to
town. While Grandpa was getting established in the tinsmithing
and repair business, Grandma sold baked goods from her kitchen.

"That was different," Grandma pointed out. "I wasn't away
from home."

"Mama's working so we can have a house," I told Grandma.
"Would you like to see a picture of it?" I started to get down from
my chair.

"Later, child."

"Lark's right," Mama told them. "We've got a plan picked out,
and I've talked to Mr. Rayzeen at the lumberyard. I'm adding to
the nest egg from Bank Nite, and next spring the carpenters'll start
building our house. Next spring!"

This was the sort of talk Grandma and Grandpa understood,
although they didn't see why Mama couldn't buy a house that was
already built.

"I bet you've got enough for a down payment on an older
house," Grandpa speculated.

"I want *my* house, Papa. I want it the way Lark and I have
planned it. With a breakfast nook, and a downstairs powder room."

"Powder room!" Grandpa laughed. "That's a new one on me.
What in hell's a powder room?"

"Don't talk that way, Jim," Grandma admonished. "It's a toilet
and sink." She turned to me. "Do you want some ice cream,
child? There's vanilla and chocolate. Get yourself a dish and take
it outside."

This was my cue to leave them alone to discuss what was really
on their minds. Probably Aunt Betty. I let the kitchen screen door
slam so they'd know I was out of range. Sitting down on the back
step, I inclined an ear toward the dining room. Grown-ups forgot
how acute a child's hearing was.

"You've got to do something, Arlene," Grandma blurted tearfully. "I'm useless. Betty won't talk to me. I don't know what's going on."

"Do *you* know anything, Arlene?" Grandpa asked.

"Anything about what?" Mama sidestepped.

"About Betty and this Miller," Grandma huffed, suspicious of Mama's loyalties.

"No, Mama."

"If you do, you've got to tell us. I can't hold up my head downtown anymore. This will kill me."

"It won't kill you," Grandpa told Grandma.

"It *will*, I tell you. Our own flesh shaming us, right here in Blue Lake."

"How do you know she's shaming you?" Mama asked.

"It's all over her face. She can't look me in the eye anymore." Grandma broke down again. "I'm too ashamed to go shopping. I order groceries over the telephone so no one will see me."

"Well, that's just plain silly," Mama told her with a touch of impatience.

"That's what I keep telling her," Grandpa agreed.

Ignoring them, Grandma continued, "You raise a child up and you think you've put the right ideas in their head. You think your work is done and you've earned your rest. And then, something like this happens, and you don't know where you're at. I pray for the Lord to take me now, Arlene. I'm too old for this."

"Oh, Mama, stop that," Mama sighed. "You want me to start playing 'Nearer My God to Thee'?"

Grandma put her head down on her arms and cried. "Fouling her own nest, that's what she's doing."

Fouling her own nest? What did that mean?

❧ 44 ❧

WHEN I WAS little and had an accident in my sleep, Grandma used to talk about fouling the sheets. But, no, that didn't apply to Aunt Betty. No. But what could be the problem then, that Grandma was so ashamed she couldn't go downtown to buy groceries?

It was a quiet, humid, buzzing afternoon, cicadas whining away like tiny machines among the vegetation. There was a new municipal swimming pool. I asked Mama to take me.

"Not during dog days," Grandma said. "You'll pick up infantile paralysis, like the Yates boy did last year. He's paralyzed from the waist down. They say he'll never be able to farm."

So I put on my bathing suit and ran through the hose, which was not at all the same. But it was cooling. Afterward, when I was dry, I lay down on a narrow bed on the sleeping porch for a nap.

I loved Grandma's porch. Wrapped around the front and one side of the house, the screened porch held a couple of twin beds, one double bed, a wardrobe, a pair of rocking chairs, and a tall wooden cupboard full of Grandma's home remedies.

All three beds were covered with heavy, white cotton bedspreads. I thought the three beds looked like a little hospital ward I'd seen in *A Farewell to Arms* last summer at the penny movie. They showed old movies outdoors once a week during the summer when the Majestic was closed, and *A Farewell to Arms*, with Gary Cooper and Helen Hayes, was one of last summer's offerings. Gary Cooper was very handsome, though not so much to my taste as William Powell.

Past Grandma's bed was the tall cupboard containing remedies—powders and dried herbs in brown glass jars, and little brown paper bags with penciled identifications: "tansy," "camomile," "mint," and "catnip," and so forth.

When the door was opened, the mixed scents rolled out in an aromatic wave. It was a heady experience. There was an element of mystery about the cupboard which intimidated me, even as Maria Zelena's remedies had. And Grandma had warned me not to poke around in there, especially not among the jars on the top shelf. When I was small, I imagined a little brown gnome living behind the jars, who would bite my fingers if I got too nosy. Even now, if I sneaked a smell of the cupboard, I did so down low where he couldn't reach me.

When I woke from my nap, it was nearly time for Grandpa to come home. Grandma's big, silver-colored alarm clock sat ticking loudly, not far away, on the straight-backed chair beside the double bed. Five-fifteen, it said.

Wandering into the kitchen, I asked Grandma, "What time does Aunt Betty get off work?"

"Not till after nine on Saturday."

"Where's Mama?"

"She went downtown to have supper with your aunt at the Kitchen Kafe."

"Are we going downtown in the car tonight?" We always went downtown in the car on summer Saturday nights when I was staying at Grandma's. Grandpa went to the hardware store and the pool hall, while Grandma visited Ames Dry Goods and the dime store. After that we bought bags of popcorn and sat in the car, talking to friends strolling by, until the stores closed.

"This is little Lark?" people would ask, leaning on the car, foot resting on the running board, "Arlene's little girl? My, isn't she getting big, though. It doesn't seem possible."

Putting their heads into the car and addressing me in the backseat, where I sat eating popcorn, they'd ask, "Remember the time you and your mama was visiting, and you come to the birthday party for Hazel Willett?" Then, "Well, of course you don't remember," they'd remind themselves. "You were only a baby. You were the *best* baby. Not a peep out of you."

"We're not going downtown tonight," Grandma told me.

"Why not?"

"There's nothing we need at the stores."

"Can't we just sit and eat popcorn and talk to people?"

"Not tonight."

"Why not?"

"That's enough talk," she said with finality, slicing thin slices from a cold ham and laying them on a small platter. "Set the table now. Grandpa will be home before we know it."

Grandma was enduring me. She did not want to deal with my questions or with the meal she was gathering for the table. She worked absently and without enthusiasm.

Supper was an almost wordless meal. Grandpa announced that

he was going down to the pool hall to shoot the breeze for a while later on.

"I don't know how you can go downtown," Grandma told him.

"I haven't done anything wrong," he said.

"Well, if you're going downtown, bring home some chocolate ice cream," Grandma said with a weary, almost indifferent tone. "We're nearly out."

When the table was cleared, the dishes done, and Grandpa had driven off, I asked, "Do you want to play rummy, Grandma?"

"No, child."

I sat at the table and paged through seed catalogs. Grandma sat in a rocker with her eyes closed, hands folded across her middle. When I had looked at all the seed catalogs, with an eye to what would be pretty in the garden of the Cape Ann, I found a deck of cards in the drawer of the sideboard and played solitaire for half an hour or so.

"Isn't Mama coming home?" I asked.

"She'll probably stay downtown till your aunt gets off work."

I didn't beat the deck once, so finally I gave up, returned the cards to the drawer, and felt my way into the darkened living room, pulling the chain on the floor lamp by the piano.

There was new sheet music on the piano, pieces Aunt Betty had bought at the dime store where she worked. "I'll Never Smile Again," "All or Nothing at All," and "It Never Entered My Mind." I couldn't read music, so I looked at the pages as if I could, and hit any old keys on the piano. After a few minutes of this, Grandma said, "Why don't you turn on the radio and see if there's any music?"

Grandma had the dial of the big console radio set to an Omaha station that broadcast her daytime stories. I flicked the button on. An orchestra was playing "I Concentrate on You."

"That's nice," Grandma said, so I left it.

When Grandpa came home smelling of cigars, he and I each had a dish of chocolate ice cream. I had soda crackers with mine because I liked the sweet and salty together. Then Grandma said, "I'm going to bed. Lark, are you sleeping in your underpants?"

"I guess. Mama didn't unpack our suitcase."

"Well, come along then. You'll sleep on the porch."

"Where's Mama going to sleep?"

"I don't know."

"When's she coming home? Aren't the stores closed now?"

"She'll be along now soon, I'm sure. Come to bed."

After Grandpa read the Minneapolis paper, he came to bed, first extinguishing all the lights except the one on the back porch and the tiny night-light on Grandma's electric stove. Undressing in the dark, he climbed noisily into bed, turning several times like an old dog before finding a comfortable position. Grandma sighed intolerantly and gave her pillow a punch.

I liked to sleep on the porch because there were so many windows, it was like sleeping outdoors. I hoped that Mama was planning to sleep in the other narrow bed while we were visiting Grandma, so we could whisper before we fell asleep at night.

I had had such a long nap that afternoon and so little activity, I was not sleepy. I lay listening to crickets cricking and cars purring along in the dark, coming and going from interesting doings. Several times a car drove by on Cottonwood Street. Each time, I thought it was Mama in the coupe, but it wasn't.

Grandpa fell asleep quickly and snored softly. Grandma lay awake for a long while, sighing and punching her pillow. Once she reached for the clock and peered at its luminous dial. From where I lay I could not see the face of the clock, but I thought it must be midnight. I wished that Mama would come home before I fell asleep.

"Married women, both of you!" was the first thing I heard the next morning. Grandma, speaking low and intense, was standing beside the other narrow bed, giving Mama a piece of her mind.

"Oh, Mama, we just drove out to the ballroom to listen to the music. Even married women can listen to music."

"You can come home and listen to the radio," Grandma told her.

"Mama, you're not my boss anymore. I'm twenty-seven years old."

"While you're in this house, I'm your boss. I have to hold my head up in this town."

"Well, we didn't do anything scandalous," Mama said, and turned over as if to go back to sleep.

But Grandma wasn't through. "Keep your voice down. We don't need to wash our dirty laundry in public."

"If you'd let me sleep, we wouldn't be washing it at all."

"Did you dance?"

"What?"

"At the ballroom. Did you dance? Did Betty?"

Grandpa was already up and sitting at the dining room table, reading the Sunday paper. The bell at St. Matthews tolled people to seven o'clock Mass. Would Mama and I go to nine o'clock, or barmaid's, Mass?

"I danced, Mama. Betty danced."

Grandma collapsed into a rocking chair. "Have you lost your minds?"

Mama gave up. She pulled herself up so that her back rested against the iron bedstead. "We didn't run off to Rio de Janeiro, Mama. We only danced."

"Married women, without their husbands. What must decent people think? That you're a pair of loose chippies."

"Now don't start on your 'loose chippies' sermon, or I'm packing up and leaving for Harvester this morning. There's not a thing wrong with dancing."

"There is if you're a married woman without her husband," Grandma averred.

"Betty has been a married woman without a husband for *two years*," Mama pointed out. "Even married women have to have some fun."

"They didn't when I was a girl. Anyway, there's nothing to prevent your sister from going to California and joining her husband."

"Except that he hasn't asked her."

"Since when does a married woman wait for an engraved invitation to join her husband?"

"Oh, Mama." Mama's voice softened suddenly. "You know what I mean. If Stan wanted her out there, he'd say so. He'd send her a ticket."

Grandma started to cry. "I don't know what's wrong with that man. What's to become of her?"

"I told her to see a lawyer."

"What for?" Grandma asked anxiously.

"A divorce."

"Oh, my God, you didn't."

"I did."

"How could you?"

"She's been deserted."

"No, she hasn't. He writes and he says he loves her. It was her losing the baby the way she did. He can't face her."

"He's too weak to take hold."

"He just needs to grow up."

"Grow up, Mama? Stan is thirty-three years old."

"I won't have a divorce in this family. There's never been a divorce in this family." Grandma pulled her hanky from the neck of her dress and cried into it. Then, through her tears, she inquired, "Was Miller at the dance?"

"How should I know?"

"You've got eyes, I suppose."

"I don't know him."

"You didn't meet him when you picked your sister up from work?"

"Oh, *him*."

Grandma waited.

"He was only at the dance for a few minutes, just to see who was playing," Mama told her. "Then he left."

"Was Mrs. Miller with him?"

"I didn't see her."

Grandma made a little grunting sound of disgust. She did not believe Mama's innocent answers, or at any rate, she suspected that there was more to be known which she was not likely to learn.

"I'm a prisoner in this house, Arlene. I don't even go to Circle." Circle was Methodist Ladies Aide.

"Mama, that's just plain foolish. You brought us up right and sent us to church and to Sunday school, and taught us what was what. You can't blame yourself and neither can anybody else. If you're in prison, you put yourself there. Nobody else did it."

"That may be," Grandma said, "but what's the difference if I can't get out?" She pulled herself up from the rocker. "I'm going to get breakfast on. Your papa's hungry."

Mama sat, playing with the hem of the sheet and looking thoughtful. No, more than thoughtful. Troubled.

The temperature rose near a hundred and five that day. Grandma did not go to church. She said it was on account of the heat, but I never knew her to stay away from church in the past. When Mama and Aunt Betty and I came home from barmaid's Mass, we were dripping sweat.

"Look at me, Grandma. The bodice of my dress is all wet from sweat," I said.

"*Men* sweat," she told me. "*Ladies* perspire. But you're right, you're dripping wet. Better get out of that fancy dress. Do you have something cool?"

"Put on your seersucker sundress," Mama instructed.

The green-and-white-striped seersucker sundress was my favorite that summer. Mama had made it, and she'd appliquéd bright orange carrots on the bodice and at the pocket. It was the gayest sundress I had seen.

"Would anybody like to go for a ride out in the country?" Mama asked when I was dressed.

"Me," I told her.

Mama turned to Grandma. "You like to ride in the country."

"Not today."

"Oh, come on, Mama."

"No, Arlene. I would rather stay home."

"Well, don't ever say you weren't invited. Betty?"

Aunt Betty was removing her hat at the sideboard mirror and regarding herself strangely in the mirror. "I'll go," she said languidly. "Let me change first."

"I think I'll ask Papa if we can use his car. It's too crowded in the coupe on a hot day," Mama explained. "This is like the old days, when we were girls, Betty, only *you* drove the old car and I rode along."

"It's nothing like the old days," Grandma said to herself, but loud enough for us to hear. "In my worst nightmares, I would not have dreamed any of this in the old days."

So we drove into the country, Mama at the wheel, Aunt Betty beside her, and me in the backseat. Although it was immaculate, the inside of Grandpa's car smelled like the seats on the train, dusty and ancient. It was a smell as reassuring as the odor of talcum or fried onions.

Before leaving town, Mama pulled in at the all-night café and jumped out. "I'll be right back." Minutes later, she returned with three strawberry ice cream cones. "Hold mine till we're on the road," she said, handing two of them to Aunt Betty and one to me. "Lark, try not to get it on your dress." She slid in behind the wheel. "Roll down all the windows, ladies, we're heading for the country!"

Merrily the car jounced over the countryside, past heat-sleepy farm yards, where windmills stood silent and farm dogs lazed in the shade, too warm to chase the car. Dust from the gravel rose up behind us and hung in thick suspension, even as we disappeared over a far hill.

For half an hour we drove across the rolling prairie, then Mama pulled off and parked beneath the shade of a stand of cottonwoods, beside a dried-up creek bed. We piled out of the car and sat on the dusty grass. Except for the whining of cicadas and a lone meadowlark, there was absolute quiet, as if we were a thousand miles from anywhere. Occasionally the cottonwoods shook their shining leaves, not from the encouragement of any breeze but from a kind of impatience with the heat.

"Take off your dress, Lark, and lay your head down on it," Mama said. She could see that the day and the ice cream had made me drowsy. And I had not slept well last night, trying to stay awake until Mama came home.

Aunt Betty got to her feet and began to pace slowly up and down. "What time will we leave in the morning?" she asked Mama.

This was the first I knew of their going anywhere.

"Quarter to six."

"That early?"

"It's four hours to Minneapolis, or nearly, and we have to leave time to find the address."

"What are you going to do, Mama?" I asked.

"We're going shopping."

"Can I come?"

"Not this time."

"Why?"

"We're driving up and back in one day. There won't be time to worry about an extra passenger."

"You won't have to worry about me."

"Not this time, Lark," Mama silenced me peremptorily. "Do you have enough money . . . for shopping?" Mama asked Aunt Betty.

She nodded and turned her back, as if looking far off down the creek bed.

"Have you changed your mind?" Mama asked her.

"No," she said without turning around. "I wish I could, but I can't."

My eyes would not stay open. The day was humming me to sleep. But I was sure that Aunt Betty was crying. And then I thought I heard her say that she was afraid. Why would a grown-up be afraid to go shopping?

☙ 45 ☙

"I DON'T SEE why you have to go shopping today—and in *Minneapolis*," Grandma complained. "Taking off work! I never heard of such a thing." Grandma was standing in the kitchen doorway, still in her nightgown.

Mama was dressed and at the sink, finishing a cup of coffee. Aunt Betty, wan and silent, sat on a kitchen chair, her white summer purse on her lap. "I want to look for a winter coat," Mama said. "I won't have time once I'm back at work."

"But why does Betty have to go?"

"She needs a day off."

"She had one yesterday."

"Oh, Mama," Mama sighed with filial impatience. "Lark, give Mama a kiss. I'll see you tonight. Mind Grandma and I'll bring you something from Minneapolis."

Out they hurried, me behind them in my underpants, standing on the back stoop, waving as Mama backed out of the drive. She tooted the horn lightly and swung down the alley and into the street.

There were a few fading, decrepit toys in a box in the front hall, among them a rubber baby doll, her body grown hard as steel and dusky, as if she were changing her race. In the backyard, beside the tall lilac bushes, I spread an old cotton blanket and played house all morning with the mulatto doll.

Grandpa came home for lunch when the town whistle blew at noon. His blue work shirt was wet down the back and under the arms. "Over a hundred again today," he said, washing his hands and face at the kitchen sink before sitting down. Drying himself on the heavy, linen roller towel, he revealed, "Grandpa Whaley passed on, of the heat, they say. Collapsed in the garden pulling weeds."

"What was he doing in the garden with the heat over a hundred? That daughter of his must be simple, letting him do that. Why, it's criminal."

"They say she was cleaning the attic."

"Can you beat that?"

"Where's Arlene?" he asked, sitting down at the dining room table. He had left the house at five.

"Gone to Minneapolis and Betty with her, to look for a winter coat, she said! The hottest day of the year, and she runs off, dragging her sister, to try on winter coats. Sometimes I don't think either of them has good sense."

Grandpa shook his head. "I expect they'd clean the attic while I pulled weeds if the day were over a hundred and five." He chuckled, shaking his head some more.

After Grandpa had left again and the few dishes were washed and put away, Grandma said, "I'm going to take a lie-down now. I want you to do the same." She suffered vague, exhausting worries.

"I'm not tired."

"Then read your book, but do it in bed." She led the way to the sleeping porch.

Sitting on the edge of the bed, I pulled off my sandals. The smooth, gray painted floor was cool beneath my bare feet. I ran them lightly back and forth across the boards.

"Stop stalling and get into bed now. You can sleep on top of the spread."

I lay down with *Happy Stories for Bedtime*, and before long I drifted into a breathless, sticky sleep of fragmentary dreams. In a dim attic I tried on heavy, winter coats.

Grandma was in the kitchen pouring a glass of iced tea when I found her. "Is Mama back yet?" I inquired, picking sleep from my eyes.

"It's only half past three. They won't be back till after supper."

"I forgot to write to Hilly yesterday. Do you have paper I can use?"

"There's a tablet in the middle drawer of the desk."

Sitting down at the dining room table, I wrote, telling Hilly of our trip and the heat wave and Grandpa Whaley (who was a stranger to me) dying of the heat while pulling weeds, and his daughter cleaning the attic. I asked if it was hot in Harvester. The Stillmans' apartment was very close on warm summer days, as I recalled. I cautioned Hilly to drink plenty of water.

Grandma handed me a prestamped envelope and I addressed it: Hillyard Stillman, Harvester, Minnesota. I knew how to spell those words without help. On the back flap I drew a little heart. If Grandpa drove me to the depot after supper to mail the letter, Hilly would receive it tomorrow.

Grandpa seemed happy to get into the car after supper and drive us across town. The depot agent said that he'd see the letter went out that very night. Instead of heading immediately for home, Grandpa drove around the perimeter of town and out past the fairgrounds where men were setting up tents for the county fair, which opened on Wednesday. I knew because Grandma had remarked pensively that she wasn't entering anything this year, not even her strawberry-rhubarb preserves.

Before turning the car toward Cottonwood Street, Grandpa pulled in at the all-night café and bought me an ice cream cone. I didn't think there were many children around who had had two ice cream cones in as many days.

"Have you heard anything from the girls?" Grandpa inquired as we strolled into the house.

"I don't expect them before eight-thirty," Grandma replied, glancing up from her crocheting.

"What're you making, Grandma?"

"Edging for pillowcases." She yanked more thread from the ball. "In the past two years I've edged everything in the house except your grandpa's drawers," she said with a sardonic little smile. "It calms my nerves."

Grandpa, gazing past Grandma out the window, said, "I believe that was Arlene's Ford that went by." He turned toward the back door. I was at his heels, and Grandma, thrusting herself out of the chair so abruptly that the crochet thread went flying, pushed past both of us to reach the screen door first.

The white coupe pulled up beyond the gravel drive, up close to the back door onto the grass, before Mama braked and turned off the engine.

Aunt Betty's head leaned against the seat, and her face was whiter than the moon that hung over the garage. Grandma was at the car door, pulling it open.

"My, God, Betty, what is this!" she exclaimed, staring down at Aunt Betty's skirt, which was soaked with blood. "Fetch the blanket beside the lilacs," Grandma told me. I ran to get the thick cotton blanket on which I'd been playing house.

Somehow they got my aunt out of the car and wrapped the blanket around her hips. Grandpa carried her into the house and out to the sleeping porch.

"Fetch the rubber sheet from the closet in the bathroom, Lark." Grandma gave me a shove toward the stairs.

"What *is* this?" Grandma was demanding of Mama when I returned with the rubber sheet, which she spread out on the bed.

As if she were a sleeping baby, Grandpa lowered Aunt Betty tenderly onto the sheet, and Grandma began undressing her. "What happened today?" Grandma interrogated as she and Mama pulled off Aunt Betty's dress.

"She started hemorrhaging all of a sudden. She's anemic, I think. She got her period and it just gushed. She's got on three pads."

"Lark, find your aunt's nightgown upstairs and bring the box of pads from the bathroom." As I sped away, Grandma said to Mama, "You're lying to me."

I was frightened of the blood. There was so much of it. I didn't see how any one could lose that much blood and live. Aunt Betty looked dead. She wasn't. Now and then she moaned, and each time I was relieved to hear it. I wished that she would make more noise so that I could be sure that she would go on living.

Grandma and Mama were busy with my aunt. They didn't notice me in the twilit corners of the room. Mama was in a state as close to panic as I had ever seen her. She thrust herself here and there, now sitting on the edge of the bed, then bethinking herself and jumping immediately up again; now standing at the foot, regarding Aunt Betty with frightening intensity as if she could will her well, then swooping around the bed to brush Aunt Betty's hair back from her damp forehead. Mama behaved as if she were responsible for Aunt Betty's being sick.

"Stay with her," Grandma told Mama. "I'm going to make tea."

"*Now?*"

"Not for *us*," Grandma said. "For her. If she starts to hemorrhage bad again, come get me."

Mama nodded. She held her sister's hand, though Aunt Betty seemed unaware that Mama was there.

Grandma disappeared around the corner, into the dim shadows of the other arm of the sleeping porch where the cupboard of strange smells stood. She hurried to it, extracting three small Mason jars, which she carried into the house to the kitchen.

At the stove she measured a teaspoon of whatever was in each jar into a saucepan of water and began heating it, stirring it with a spoon. As the water started to simmer, it gave off a peculiar and pleasant odor. I thought there was some mint in it, but I couldn't identify the rest, and when I sidled past Grandma to have a look at the jar labels, she suddenly took note of me.

"What are you doing up?" she asked. "Get to bed. Up in your aunt's room tonight. She's in your bed," she told me as if I were not aware of this.

I didn't want to upset her further, so I slipped back out to the sleeping porch and climbed onto Mama's bed. There were no lights on except in the kitchen and dining room. Some small illumination filtered through to the porch, but mostly we saw by the faint light of the lavender late evening sky.

"Why don't we call the doctor?" I asked Mama.

"Because there's nothing he can do but make trouble," Mama said. She sat on a chair now, beside Aunt Betty's bed, holding the other woman's cold white hand.

Grandma emerged from the deeper shadows at the opposite end of the porch, a big cup held in both her hands, its rich potpourri preceding her, dispelling the doomsday odor of blood in the air.

"I think it's cool enough to give her," Grandma said. "Get the pillows from my bed and put them under her head."

Not moving, and barely breathing, I watched as Grandma spooned tea into Aunt Betty. From the backyard came the smell of a cigar. Grandpa was sitting there, out of the way.

The individual hours became lost in the dark. Certain moments flickered like fireflies. Mama said, "We're out of pads." Grandma said, "There's a length of cotton flannel in the sideboard." Later, I think, Aunt Betty sighed, "Stanley, is that you?" Mama whispered, "Sweet Jesus." Grandma did not reprimand her for using the Lord's name.

When Grandma went to the kitchen to reheat the tea, Mama whispered to Aunt Betty, "Don't die. You did the right thing." Then Grandma was there beside the bed administering tea.

I was reminded of Maria Zelena and her magic. I had wronged Maria Zelena. She had tried to tell me about the baby's death, and

I wouldn't listen. My knowledge of the universe was so small. How would I ever learn enough to survive? Aunt Betty was thirty-two, and she did not seem to have learned enough.

⚛ 46 ⚛

IN THE MORNING Grandma was asleep in one of the rockers, Mama in the other. I was in Mama's bed, fully clothed, the bedspread pulled over me. Grandpa, also in his clothes, was lying on top of the spread on the double bed, snoring and giving off vile fumes of cigar mouth.

Aunt Betty lay in my bed, with her arms straight at her sides. But she was breathing. Though it was nearly imperceptible, the white, ripple-weave spread *did* lift and settle, lift and settle. Was she going to live?

"She's not out of the woods yet," Grandma said later. The bleeding had abated, but Betty was running a slight fever. That meant there was a trace of infection, Grandma explained.

Mama called the dime store and told Mr. Miller that Aunt Betty was home with German measles. "I don't like telling lies, Lark," Mama said, "but this one time it's necessary. You mustn't tell anyone anything about this, not about the bleeding or . . . anything."

Our sweltering vigil continued. Aunt Betty was hotter than any of us. Grandma removed the covers from her and bathed her body with cool water, and sometimes with alcohol.

"I thought you were supposed to keep a person warm when they had a fever," Mama observed.

"I don't believe in that," Grandma responded tartly.

When they weren't bathing Aunt Betty, they were forcing liquid into her. "Keep her kidneys going," Grandma told us. "The kidneys carry off the poisons." That was what Maria Zelena had said.

It wasn't easy work. Aunt Betty was suffering awful pains in her belly. Even when she was half out of it, she'd pull her legs up and clutch herself and groan. The sweat poured off her till the sheet beneath her was soaked. The electric fan was brought out from the dining room, and Grandma filled a couple of hot water bottles with ice, applying them to Aunt Betty's arms.

At four o'clock Grandma said, "Arlene, you'd better call your papa home from work." The way she said it made me shudder. Still, Grandma would not let up on the liquids. Now it was ice water.

When Grandpa arrived, he sat on the bed, holding Aunt Betty in his arms while Grandma dribbled ice water into her mouth.

"Can't you leave her alone now?" Grandpa wept.

"No."

At six, the phone in the dining room rang. "See who that is, Lark, and remember what I told you about the measles."

"Hello."

"Hello. Who is this?" a man inquired.

"This is Lark Ann Erhardt."

"Is your mother there?" he asked.

"She's busy."

"Well, this is Mr. Miller. I was wondering how Mrs. Weller was feeling. Everyone missed her at work today."

"She's still sick with the measles, Mr. Miller. I don't think she'll be in tomorrow. She has more measles than anyone's ever seen before."

"Tell her we all said to take care of herself."

Mama snorted when she heard. "Sonofabitch."

Mama felt the ice packs. They were getting warm. Grandpa took the glass of water and the spoon. "Look how her mouth is getting sore, here at the corner, from the edge of the spoon," he pointed out.

"Better that than convulsions," Mama said, and she took the hot water bottles to the kitchen to fill with fresh ice.

Aunt Betty was retching. I held the pan and wiped her nose and mouth. "No more water," she moaned.

"Don't stop," Grandma commanded.

As twilight lengthened, we were shadows moving among shadows. Late in the evening Mama began to cry. She didn't sob, but I saw her brush tears away, and heard her sniffle and blow her nose.

"One more day of this and she'll be gone," she said to no one.

I lay down on Grandma's bed, not meaning to fall asleep, but it was as though someone closed a door on me. Hours later, I heard Mama say to Grandma, "Wake up! Betty asked what day this was. She's cooler, I think."

Grandma was on her feet and at Aunt Betty's side, running her hands along my aunt's arms and legs, then her face. She pulled the sheet up around Aunt Betty.

Weak as water and puffing as if words were a great exertion, Aunt Betty whispered, "If this is heaven, I bet there's ice cream."

Grandpa was awake now. He began to laugh. We all laughed. The birds woke up and set to chattering and singing and flying from tree to tree. I thought they were laughing, too, to see a porch full of crazy people laughing and eating ice cream at dawn.

≥ 47 ≤

AUNT BETTY gave up her job at the dime store. "If I went back, I'd be in the state hospital by Christmas."

"Come stay with us," Mama told her.

"No. Willie'd have a fit."

"What do I care? You're my only sister. You can help me with the business. Till you know where you're at."

Grandma packed a lunch for us, and we left after church on Sunday, Aunt Betty still weak and ashen, but anxious to get out of Blue Lake. "To think that I used to be somebody with a place of my own," Aunt Betty said to Mama.

"Do you see, Betty," Grandma told her as we were leaving, "this is God's way of telling you to go to California?"

"I'll never be able to have a baby now," Aunt Betty told Mama on the ride from Blue Lake to Harvester.

"Don't be silly," Mama said.

"It's true. I know it."

"You're no doctor," Mama reminded her.

"I know what I know."

*   *   *

Papa didn't throw a fit in front of Aunt Betty. He was as cordial as you could hope. But when he got Mama alone, down at the freight room, he wanted to know, "What the hell is this all about?"

"You can see she's in poor health, Willie. She needed to get away."

"Well, I don't want her staying, do you understand? A week, that's it, you'll have to tell her."

Aunt Betty slept on the davenport and lived out of her suitcase, except for two or three dresses on hangers which hung from a peg beside my crib. She stayed through the fall. It was close quarters, but Mama said that was all to the good. Maybe Papa would realize how much we needed the new house. "We can't go on living here, with Willie and Lark and me all sharing the same bedroom."

With Aunt Betty to help, Mama didn't need to hire another girl for the business. And Aunt Betty came up with an idea for adding to their income: letters from Santa. Aunt Betty was Santa. A discreet ad ran in the county papers, and as the holidays drew near, requests poured in for the letters. Aunt Betty cleared fifty dollars. It wasn't a fortune, but it pleased her.

After Mass on the first Sunday following Thanksgiving, Aunt Betty sat down at the kitchen table to write Santa letters. Papa was reading the paper in the living room.

"Betty, for heaven's sake, you can take a day off from that," Mama admonished.

"I'll get behind if I do."

Mama poured her a cup of coffee.

"Santa letters have to be written by hand, you know," Aunt Betty told Mama. "Santa wouldn't use a typewriter."

Mama sat down at the table. She was bursting to say something. Finally she confided in a low voice so Papa wouldn't hear, "I've got enough for the down payment on the house."

"Oh, my God, that's wonderful," Aunt Betty exclaimed.

"I'm going to talk to Mr. Rayzeen at the lumberyard this week, and then I'll go to the bank."

"What about the lot?" Aunt Betty wanted to know.

"Ben Albers is selling me a lot, a block east of the Catholic church. It's beautiful. Nice trees. A hundred wide by a hundred and fifty deep."

"Can I tell Beverly and Sally?" I asked.

"Wait a couple of weeks. Then you can tell *everybody*. When I own the lot, you can put it in the paper, for all of me."

I started dancing around the kitchen. Mama put a finger to her lips and nodded toward the living room.

Wednesday afternoon Mama came in from the road early and stopped at Rayzeen's to get the figures to take to the bank. At supper Papa said, "Saw you going into Rayzeen's when I was delivering freight."

"I'm thinking of putting up shelves in the living room," Mama said, passing him the platter of meat loaf. Papa looked at her closely, but she set the ketchup bottle in front of him and seemed not to notice.

I couldn't wait to tell Hilly. Mama said that since he went nowhere and spoke to no one, it would be all right, providing I swore him to secrecy. Saturday night I sat down at the table and wrote:

Dear Hilly,

I have a *wonderful* secret to tell you. You must not tell anyone, except your mama, until after next week.

Mama is buying a piece of land east of the Catholic church. As soon as the ground thaws in the spring, the builders will dig the basement for our new house! Next fall you will be able to visit me in my new house and help me decide what flowers to plant in the garden.

Do you believe it's really happening, Hilly? I've told you so *many* times that you could work in the garden with me. But now we have gotten down to brass tacks. That's what Mama says.

I'm so happy, Hilly. I'm shivering all over while I'm writing this.

I know you don't go out anymore, but you will like sitting in my new backyard. We can sit and look at the flowers, and no one can see us or bother us. I promise.

Your friend forever,

Lark Ann Erhardt

PS: I like sweet peas very much because they smell so nice. I think we should have a whole row of sweet peas. Do you know how to make chicken wire stand up, so sweet peas will climb on it?

I had meant to tell Hilly that God does answer our prayers, the new house was proof. I thought Hilly needed to know that, but I forgot. I would remember in my next letter.

In the morning, on the way to Mass, Mama swung by the post office, and I ran in and mailed the letter. When I came out, I waved in the direction of Hilly's bedroom window, which faced on Main Street. If he was there, looking down, he'd know I had mailed his letter.

Father Delias's sermon was about Advent being "The Giving and Forgiving Season." As the year drew to a close, he said, we remembered Christ not only with our gifts to Mother Church and our fellow man, but with loving hearts that wiped clean the slates of grievance and misunderstanding. We must celebrate the Christ child's birth with hearts cleansed of reproof and filled with love for all men, without reservation.

After church I rode home with Papa in the truck. "How about a movie this afternoon?" Papa asked.

"You and me?" Papa almost never went to the movies. Generally speaking, they were too feminine.

"You and me and *Sergeant York*."

"Is that about war?"

"About the World War. Sergeant York was a big hero. I remember hearing about him."

"You weren't in the World War."

"I was only nine when we went to war."

"That was lucky, Papa."

"I guess."

"Do you wish you'd been old enough?"

"Everybody wants a chance to be a hero."

We stopped at the Loon Cafe for coffee and doughnuts. Mama and Aunt Betty had already arrived in the Ford and were sitting at one of the booths by the window. This was a rare treat, rarer even than Papa going to a movie. Father Delias's sermon had put us all in a Christmas mood.

An hour later, when we piled out of the café, Mama and Aunt Betty were laughing about Sheila Grubb's fur piece. "Did you ever see so many heads and tails and little feet hanging on somebody's neck?" Mama squealed.

Then the town whistle blew. Aunt Betty looked at her watch. "It's a little after one," she said. "That's strange. It must be a fire."

But it didn't sound like a fire whistle. It was very long blasts. None short. And it continued.

The grown-ups exchanged uneasy glances. Papa and I climbed into the truck and headed for home. We all arrived at the same time, no one laughing or talking now, as the whistle continued blowing.

"The phone's ringing."

Mama ran into the house and straight to the living room. "Hello?"

Papa and Aunt Betty and I pulled off our coats and threw them on the bed. "Don't throw your hat on the bed, Willie. It's bad luck," Aunt Betty told him.

"Jesus Christ," Mama swore, motioning us to be quiet. "You sure it's not a mistake, Bernice? Yes, we'll turn on the radio right now. Willie, turn on the radio. It's awful." Her face had gone white around the lips. Somebody must have died. No, it couldn't be that. If somebody in Harvester died, it wouldn't be on the radio. "What does this mean, Bernice? It can't be. I've got to hang up, Bernice. I can't think. I just can't think." Mama sat down on the couch, still in her hat and coat, purse clutched under her left arm.

"What is it?" Aunt Betty asked.

"Shhhhh." Papa, tuning the radio, shushed us.

". . . about seven this morning, Honolulu time," a quiet, disbelieving masculine voice on the radio was saying. "I repeat, planes of the Japanese air force have bombed Pearl Harbor in the Hawaiian Islands early this morning. We have few details at this time, although it is known that the United States has suffered heavy losses of ships and airplanes. Please stay tuned for further details and developments."

Mama switched off the radio. "What's it mean?"

"It means we're in the war," Papa said.

"How far is Hawaii from California?" Aunt Betty wanted to know.

"Oh, Betty," Mama sighed. "It's a long way."

"What's going to happen now?" Aunt Betty asked.

"They'll start drafting men to fight," Papa told her, "and they'll have to build a lot of airplanes and ships, from the sound of it."

"What about Stan?" Aunt Betty pursued. "Will they take him?"

"I don't know," Papa said. "I think they take the younger men first. By the time they get to us old guys, the war'll be over, don't you worry, Betty."

❧ 48 ❧

"ONCE THE JAPS hit Hawaii, I wonder why they didn't keep coming, and knock out San Francisco and LA," Papa observed the next night at supper. "Although I don't know if LA has much of a harbor."

"Willie, do you have to talk like that in front of Betty?"

"Sorry."

We were eating the fried chicken that Mama hadn't cooked the day before. "The news took all the starch out of me," she told Bernice McGivern. "We had bologna sandwiches and didn't eat much of those."

"Did you call Stan," Papa asked Aunt Betty, "to see how they're taking it out in California?"

"No."

"Don't you think you should?"

"No."

"You know," Papa said, changing the subject, "if they *did* take me, they'd use me in the signal corps as a telegrapher." He poured gravy on his mashed potatoes. "I'm one of the best in the country. That's what they tell me. They're going to need good telegraphers to send coded messages."

It was true. Papa had a reputation down the line as one of the best and fastest telegraphers on the railroad. He was a whiz at sending messages, tap-tapping at the key like a magician, and he could receive messages off the wire just as fast.

Sometimes I'd wander into the depot office when he was sending, and afterward I'd ask, "What'd that say?"

"It's confidential."

"I won't tell."

"It said, 'Come at once. Stop. Grandma dead. Stop. Funeral Wednesday. Stop.' "

"Really?"

"That's right."

It was even more mysterious than Mama's touch-typing.

All day Monday no one talked of anything but the war. Congress had officially declared it, and President Roosevelt had said

282

that December seventh was a day that would live in infamy. Mama said that meant it would go down in history as an awful, tragic day.

There was a terrible excitement in the air. Everybody's adrenaline was pumping, and people didn't know whether to laugh or cry. It was very sad, of course, the lives that had been lost, but there was something about adrenaline that made people garrulous and almost merry, even when they were sad and worried.

Wednesday night we all went to see *Sergeant York*. Papa said it was our patriotic duty. Mama didn't want me to go.

"Lark has school tomorrow, and she's big enough to stay home by herself now," she said. "Anyway, I don't think this is a good show for a child to see."

"If she's big enough to stay home by herself, she's big enough to know about fighting for her country," Papa said.

"That doesn't make any sense at all, Willie." But Mama ended up letting me go.

Half the county had the same idea, and we ended up having to sit near the back. Papa held me on his lap so I could see. But before the movie even got started, Mr. Belling played a record of Kate Smith singing "God Bless America." That was something new. Everybody stood up as if it were "The Star Spangled Banner." And some people were wiping tears from their eyes when we sat down. I was at once moved and embarrassed.

Thursday night after supper, Mama and I called on Mrs. Stillman and Hilly, only we didn't see Hilly.

"He won't come out of his room, even for meals," Mrs. Stillman told us. "Not since he heard the news. I told him he doesn't have to go to war again, but that doesn't ease his mind. He can't turn off the pictures, he says."

"Did he get my letter?" I asked.

"Oh, yes. I read it to him. That was after the news had come, of course. I thought he'd be happy to hear about your new house. He said, 'There won't be a house. They'll bomb it.' "

"I haven't thought what effect the war will have on the house," Mama said. "What do you think?"

"I don't know about these things."

Before we left, I knocked on Hilly's door. "Take care of yourself," I told him. "Write to me. Remember that God answers your prayers."

That night a frightening thing began happening to me. Actually, it began the night before, after we'd seen the Movietone newsreel that accompanied the *Sergeant York* movie. It had shown Hitler's army marching down cobblestone streets, on parade, goose-stepping and turning their heads sharply to salute the Führer.

I started hearing the sound in my head, the clock, clock, clock sound of boots on cobblestones. It was dim, as if they were a long way away, across town. But it was menacing, too, because they seemed to move ever so slightly nearer. Maybe I was becoming like Hilly, I thought, and I hadn't even seen any real war yet, only pictures. I didn't tell anyone. They might send me to the state hospital.

The one good thing was that I heard the sound only at night when I went to bed. When everything was quiet, was it possible to hear boots in Europe if there were enough of them? Maybe ten thousand boots marching made such a thunder that it could be heard, in the night, on the other side of the world.

Mama and Papa and Aunt Betty made no mention of hearing the boots. Were my ears better than theirs? Did they not want to frighten me? Or was I crazy?

"Do you think the German soldiers will come here, Mama?"

"Of course not," she said. But of course she would say that, being a mother.

Saturday morning Mama and I drove downtown to Rabel's Meat Market to buy a roast for Sunday. It was snowing, big, soft, heavy flakes that had covered the ground and were accumulating in poufs on the fenders and hoods of parked cars.

"Do you want to come in?" Mama asked.

"Can I walk down to the Majestic and look at the coming attractions?"

"Don't wander off."

We parted, Mama hurrying into the market, me scuffing my galoshes through the fluffy white blanket, speculating about Christmas even though there was a war on.

I had begun studying the pictures of Maureen O'Hara and Walter Pidgeon in *How Green Was My Valley*, the next feature at the Majestic. I was thinking that Walter Pidgeon was probably as handsome as William Powell, but he didn't have William Powell's . . .

In the corner of my eye I saw Mama, leaning against the window of Rabel's Market. She held the roast by the string wrapped around the package. It hung at her side, nearly brushing the snowy sidewalk. What was wrong?

I ran. Was she sick?

"Mama, what is it?"

She looked very small. I'd never noticed before what a diminutive woman Mama was.

"Mama."

She looked at me and shook her head. The roast fell from her hand.

"Are the Germans coming?" I asked, bending to retrieve the roast.

She started walking away as if she'd forgotten I was there. I followed her down Main Street toward home.

A procession of two, we walked into the kitchen, paying no mind to the snow on our boots.

"What is it?" Aunt Betty whispered. "What's happened?" She looked to me.

I shook my head.

"Arlene." Aunt Betty shook Mama. "Tell me!"

"Hilly." Mama's face collapsed, and she sobbed like a child. "He's dead."

49

IT'S WORSE than the Germans marching on Harvester. That's all I could think when Mama told us that Hilly was dead.

I took off my mittens and scarf, my coat and cap and boots, and went into the bedroom. Slipping out of my dress and petticoat, I pulled on my flannel nightie and climbed into the crib. There lay *Happy Stories for Bedtime* and *Heidi* and *The Secret Garden*, all reminding me of Hilly.

"How did he die?" Aunt Betty wanted to know.

But it was some time before Mama could talk. Aunt Betty put the kettle on for tea. I heard it clank against the burner. The thought of tea made my stomach turn over. I pulled up the quilt, gathering it over my shoulders, and faced the wall. For once I couldn't cry, I who wept at the death of ladybugs. My body was as heavy as a locomotive, but my mind was as vacant as an empty boxcar. Nothing was worth thinking. I didn't want to think anymore.

The phone rang. Aunt Betty answered. "This is her Aunt Betty, Beverly. Lark has gone to bed. Yes, we heard about Hilly. I'll tell Lark you called. Thank you."

Aunt Betty came into the bedroom. I heard her throw my coat and Mama's across the bed, then leave again. "Sit down, Arlene," she said. "You need a stimulant. I'll make extra strong tea. Is there a hanky in your pocket?" Chairs slid out from the table.

Mama was trying to talk. She kept breaking down. "He . . . he . . . oh, Betty . . . he . . ."

"Here's a cup of tea. Calm yourself."

After a good long while, Mama blew her nose and cleared her throat. "He shot himself," she said in a husky voice. She began to cry again. "I can't stand to think of him so sad and scared. He went out on the landing at the top of the stairs and put the gun in his mouth. He didn't want blood in the house," Mama interpreted. "It was snowing. He fell down in the snow." Her voice became a little, squeaking mouse sound as she broke down again.

"Where did he get the gun?"

"From . . . from . . . from the war."

"And the bullet?"

Mama blew her nose again. "She had them hid."

"But why would she have them around?"

"She told me once she couldn't bear to throw any of it away. He had paid such a price for it, she said. It was all he had to show for what he'd given. But she kept the bullets hid."

"Don't you want the tea?"

"I'm sorry."

"It's all right. Do you want some whiskey? There's a bottle up in the cupboard."

"A little. Just a little to warm me. I'm cold. I'll put it in the tea." She coughed a bit after swallowing some whiskey tea. "She heard the shot in the middle of the night. One o'clock or so."

"Who told you this?"

"Mrs. Wall. She was in Rabel's. If Mrs. Wall hadn't been there," Mama said indignantly, "I wouldn't even know about Hilly. Old man Rabel wouldn't have told me. Can you believe it? Silent as a tomb. He doesn't want people thinking about it happening outside the meat market. Goddamned money grubber. See if I ever go in there again. I'll buy my meats at Truska's." The whiskey was warming her.

"Who's Mrs. Wall?"

"You know. The constable's wife. Somebody called him when they heard the shot in the middle of the night that way. I didn't hear a thing, did you? I . . . I . . . I wish I had. I'd feel . . . like I had been . . . oh, I don't know. Like I'd been with him, sort of." She added, "He was brave."

Brave. That was the word. All his life he had been brave.

That afternoon, while I slept, Mama called on Mrs. Stillman. When she returned, she was so angry, her voice woke me. I thought she was fighting with Papa.

"I can't believe it," she screamed, and threw something across the kitchen. "I can't believe it." She shoved a chair hard against the wall, and the flimsy panel trembled. "What is *wrong* with this world?" she cried, lifting the chair and beating it up and down on the floor in fury.

"What's the matter?" Aunt Betty, who was, I think, lying on the couch, came running.

"Get me a whiskey, Betty. I can't believe this world."

"What is it?"

Mama rarely took whiskey, and now she was having it twice in one day.

"The priest. The goddamned priest won't bury Hilly!" Mama screamed so loud that Papa beat on the wall. I guess they could hear her in the depot office.

"Go to hell," Mama screamed. Then, to Aunt Betty, "I'm so angry, I want to choke someone. And I'm going to start with that priest. That goddamned fair-weather-friend priest."

"Why won't he bury Hilly?" Aunt Betty asked, pouring whiskey.

"Because suicide is a mortal sin." Mama was so overcome with disdain, she could barely force the words from her mouth. They marched large, separate, and distinct.

"What's going to happen?"

"I'm going to the Methodist minister, that's what's going to happen. And if he won't bury him, I'll go to the Lutherans and the Baptists and the Holy Rollers, and everybody else till I find somebody worthy of Hilly. What time is it?"

"Three."

"I better get going."

"Brush your teeth."

"What?"

"I don't think you should breathe whiskey on the Methodist minister."

We were sitting down to supper when Mama came in. Her cheeks, above the turned-up coat collar, were rosy and her eyes shone with combat. "The Methodists said yes," she announced, pulling off her boots. "Tuesday. I stopped to tell Mrs. Stillman is why I'm late. Don't wait for me."

The only conversation at dinner was Mama's monologue about the Catholics not burying Hilly. Papa didn't approve of the things she said, but he sensed that she could go off like a bomb, so he kept quiet through most of the meal. Over the canned peaches he observed, "I doubt you'd make this much fuss if it were me."

After dinner Mama made phone calls, lining people up for the funeral. Getting pallbearers was the hardest part. Normally the American Legionnaires could be called on for a former comrade. But Hilly being strange and blowing his brains out made them quite punctilious. However, Dr. White agreed, as did Bill McGivern, himself a veteran of the war. Bill lined up Mr. Navarin, Mr. Navarin's son Danny, Sonny Steen, and a man from Red Berry who owed him a favor. That's what he said. Mama said she thought Bill McGivern paid him. No matter. The man had a dark suit.

Papa refused to have anything to do with the funeral. "I always told you the man was dangerous," he said. "Now he's in hell. All this fuss is sacrilege." I held my breath, waiting for Mama to throw something, but she only looked at Papa for a minute, then picked up the receiver and gave the operator Bernice McGivern's number again.

"You're sure you want to do that, Bernice? That's awfully nice. Betty and I'll bring pies and cakes and Jell-O salad. Let's see, what else . . . ?" They made lists and plans and arrangements, and half an hour later Mama hung up. "People are coming back to Bernice's after the funeral," she told Aunt Betty.

"People?" Papa asked. "How many people? You and Bernice and a couple of strays looking for a handout?"

"You'd be surprised, Willie." Her voice was light and patient. Nothing was important just now except Hilly.

❧ 50 ❧

I WASN'T hungry the next morning. Everything tasted like a cotton pillowcase.

"Eat," Papa said. "You'll be hungry before Mass is over."

"I'm not going."

"What d'ya mean, you're not going?"

"I'm never going to that church again."

"The hell you're not."

"I'm not going. I don't care what you say, Papa."

"You want a slap in the face?"

"I don't care. I don't want to hurt your feelings, but I'm not going there."

"You'll go if I have to drag you kicking and screaming."

"Leave her be, Willie. Maybe she should stay home today," Mama said.

"Oh, no, she shouldn't. No sniveling eight-year-old's going to quit the Church, not in *my* house."

When it was time to leave for Mass, Papa said, "Get on that coat."

"No."

He slapped me across the face, and I grabbed his hand and bit it as hard as I could. I couldn't stop. Finally he slapped me with the other hand, and I let go.

"You damned brat." He cradled his hand. "Get the alcohol, Arlene." Mama stood in the bedroom doorway, surveying the scene. "Did you hear me?" Papa yelled. "She bit me down to the bone."

Mama got the rubbing alcohol from the cupboard. "Keep your hand over the sink," she told Papa, pouring disinfectant on the wound.

Over his shoulder, Papa said, "Get your coat on or I'll beat you till you can't sit down for a week."

Aunt Betty had my coat. She motioned me into the living room while Mama swabbed Papa's hand with iodine.

"Put your coat on," my aunt directed, not unkindly.

At last I put a hand into a sleeve. I would rather have put it into a pit of vipers.

In church I sat as far from Papa as possible, next to Aunt Betty. I didn't take part in the service but sat, intransigent, huddled in my coat, staring at Father Delias. For refusing to bury Hilly, I hated him. And I hated the altar and crucifix and candles and carpeting and statues and music and Latin words.

I studied the worshippers in their heavy coats and scarves. I hated them for coming to this place that refused to bury Hilly, for kneeling and mumbling words whose meaning they did not even know.

Only one old woman sat between me and the side aisle. I waited until the communicants left their pews and made their way toward the altar for the sacrament. Not for me ever again this communion.

In the confusion of the procession, I slipped from the pew, keeping the shuffling line between me and Papa's vision. Heading toward the main doors at the back, I was into the vestibule before Papa spied me.

He would be only seconds behind me, however, expecting me to run out into the street. Instead, I took the descending stairway and let myself into the closet under the stairs, where folding chairs and tables were stored. There was a single, small, dim, basement window. Climbing onto a folding chair, I peered out.

There was Papa, standing at the curb, surveying the street up and down. He ran a few steps to the right and glowered into the near distance, checked beneath parked cars, then ran back again.

Now he tramped away, across and down the street to the truck. Yanking the door open, he searched for me inside. Slamming the door hard, he glanced into the back. I was not there. Where had Mama parked the Ford? he wondered, and contemplated the street once more. There it was, half a block farther on. Away he marched in that direction, but of course I was not there either.

Back to the truck he went, climbed in, and started the engine. He would drive home and see if I was hiding there, under the bed or behind the couch. What a thrashing I would get then.

I let myself out of the closet, hurried up the stairs and into the street, not hesitating for a moment. I covered the four blocks to Hilly's apartment before Papa could conclude his search through the meager nooks and crannies of our house.

Up the wooden steps I pounded, beating on the door as if the Devil were nipping my heels. As I waited, I thought: This is where it happened, right where I'm standing. In the snow. And who cleaned up afterward?

Mrs. Stillman opened the inside door, then the storm door. "Lark. What is it? Is something wrong?" She led me inside and closed the door.

I was startled half out of my wits to see Stella Wheeler, Sally's mama, sitting in the green wicker chair. And she was startled by my wild entrance. My knitted cap, with the pom-pom and earflaps that tied under the chin, had come half untied and was hanging down my back. My cheeks were wet with tears from the cold air rushing into my face. And now I stood bent over, like an old woman, pressing my side where it pinched sharply from the running.

"Sit down," Mrs. Stillman said, "before you fall over."

Not until I had assurances. "If Papa comes, don't tell him I'm here. Please." It was a lot to ask of grown-ups. They always stuck together.

"I won't tell," Mrs. Wheeler said without hesitation. She herself looked as if she were on the run from something or someone. Her beautiful hair, like Sally's only with some gray in it, was loose and unkempt. The fine bones of her face were sharp beneath the skin, which was as thin as ivory-colored tissue paper. The clothes she wore were not Sunday clothes, but an old, wrinkled brown wool skirt and a sweater missing a button, with a ladder near the hem where it was unraveling.

I turned to Mrs. Stillman, who wore a plain, dark blue dress of light wool, a church dress normally, a mourning dress now. She was very serene.

In the calm voice of one who has nothing left to fear, she said, "I'll tell him you were here and left." She smiled a little. "That's only half untrue. Give me your boots, and I'll put them in the kitchen." When she had carried away my outer garments, she said, "You'll have tea and milk and some of the nice Fig Newtons that Mrs. Wheeler brought."

She disappeared into the kitchen. I sensed that I had interrupted something. Stella Wheeler's look was even more tentative and distracted than usual. Mrs. Stillman came in with a plate of cookies and tea. "Mrs. Wheeler was telling me a sad story that you might not want to hear. Would you like to sit in Hillyard's room for a few minutes? You can watch the street from his windows."

I nodded and followed her into the bedroom. I wanted to hear the story, and I was fairly sure that, unless she whispered, I would be able to hear Stella Wheeler's voice from Hilly's room.

Mrs. Stillman set the plate on top of the bookcase and left. I looked around. I liked Hilly's room. It was plain but cozy, with homemade rag rugs on the floor and a patchwork quilt on the bed. The circus poster Mama had given him was tacked to the wall over the bed, and in the bookcase were books I recognized: *Stories for a Rainy Afternoon* and *Robinson Crusoe*, and others Mama had found for him when she was on the road. Above the bookcase hung the gilded wooden key which the mayor had presented Hilly. The gilt was tarnished to a warm brown.

I crossed to the windows to check for Papa's truck. One window looked on Main Street and the post office opposite; the other, because this was a corner room, looked onto the side street. On neither did I spy the truck.

On the lamp table beside Hilly's bed lay an open tablet, the kind on which he wrote his letters. "Dear Lark Ann Erhardt," was written on the exposed page.

"Oh," I said and started. It was as though Hilly's voice had spoken.

Dear Lark Ann Erhardt,

It is Sunday today.

My mother Mrs. Stillman brought me *Heidi* from the library and I am almost done. You liked it and I liked it. Sometimes it was sad. When Heidi had to leave Grandfather. But it was happy when she came back.

I wish I could live in the mountains. High up by the clouds. It is good that I can read about the mountains. I am a most . . .

There it stopped. He had never finished. The Hawaiian Islands had been bombed that day. I put the tablet down.

In the next room, Stella Wheeler's voice had risen.

"The world is wicked," she said. "What happened was the most terrible wickedness."

"Don't distress yourself," Mrs. Stillman said.

"It was just before Memorial Day. I should have told you then. They were chasing him down the road with the car. There were two young men in the front seat. They didn't see me. Hilly had on a shirt. That was all he had on. They . . . they had hurt him." Her voice was sliding up, out of control. "Then they saw me, and they stepped on the gas. But I saw the man in the backseat. I knew him. It was Axel Nelson. From the hotel."

"It's all right, Mrs. Wheeler. Hillyard is happy now. Don't cry."

"I've thought about it so much," said Stella Wheeler. "I know I should go to the hotel and kill Axel Nelson. But I can't. What is wrong with me?"

❧ 51 ❧

"SHHHHHH. Shhhhhh. Shhhhhh." Mrs. Stillman hushed and comforted Stella Wheeler. "You mustn't talk about killing. It was killing that broke Hillyard's mind. We don't want that to happen to you."

"But the wickedness—"

"God will punish the wickedness."

"I'm not sure He does that anymore."

"Then maybe it's punishment enough to live in the darkness where wicked people live." She spoke simply, as if she were talking to Hilly. "You're a kindhearted little soul. Hillyard would not want you to involve yourself with wickedness on his account."

I lay down on Hilly's bed and watched the snowfall, which had begun again. Big, heavy flakes drifted past the window. If Hilly was in hell, as Papa said, I didn't want to go to heaven. It must be a cold place, the opposite of hell, which was a hot place.

When I woke, a shawl lay over me. It was nearly dark outside. The street lamps were lit, and the deep, growling of snowplows came from Main Street below. How long had I been asleep?

I got out of bed, keeping the shawl pulled around me, and made my way to the living room. "Mrs. Stillman?"

"You're awake. Are you hungry? I've made dinner."

Was I hungry? I was still half asleep. "Yes. I'm hungry."

"Good. Sit down there on the davenport and look at magazines while I get the food on." She rose from the green wicker chair where Mrs. Wheeler had sat. Sally's mama had left. "Your mama came by while you were asleep. We had a nice visit."

"Does Papa know where I am?"

"He knows that you're safe."

A few minutes later we sat down to boiled potatoes, canned corn, and hamburger patties.

"Your mama brought a beautiful applesauce cake for our dessert," Mrs. Stillman told me. She left to fetch ketchup. "Would you like to stay with me tonight? I'd be grateful for the company."

"I've got school tomorrow."

"Your mama left clean clothes in case you decided to stay. She'll call on the telephone later to see what you want to do."

While we were clearing the dishes, I asked, "Are you sad?"

Wringing out a cloth to wipe the table, Mrs. Stillman paused. "Yes. I'm very sad because I'm lonely. But I'm happy for Hillyard because he's in heaven. Some people say that suicide is a sin, but I have never believed that. I say it's God's way of calling certain folks home early. It's much nicer than an awful accident, where the rest of us are left wondering if the person really wanted to go. I'll be lonely without Hillyard," she concluded, "but that's better than his being lonely without me."

We had our cake and tea in the living room, and when we were done, she asked, "Would you read me a story? That was always very soothing to Hillyard."

I slept in Hilly's bed. There was a smell of Cashmere Bouquet on his pillow. I was close to him and dreamed that he stood at the foot of the bed, wearing his Army uniform.

❧ 52 ❧

AUNT BETTY walked to school the next afternoon and met me as I slouched out of the central door.

"Thought you might like some company," she said, pushing her gloveless hands deeper into the pockets of her old green coat.

"See you tomorrow," Beverly and Sally called.

The gray-white sky hung a few feet above the water tower. The air was warm and hushed. It wanted to snow again.

"I've been baking," Aunt Betty told me.

When grown-ups were making conversation with me, I felt obliged to respond, whether or not I was in the mood. Also, Aunt Betty suddenly looked down-at-the-heel. The nap was entirely worn from the cuffs and collar of her coat, and she was wearing an old pair of Mama's boots, one of which was missing the tab that closed it, so the boot slopped loosely up and down, threatening to come off as Aunt Betty walked.

"What'd you bake?"

"Chocolate cake with fudge frosting," she said, waiting for me to say something.

"Mmmmm. That's good."

"And two mincemeat pies."

"Mmmm." Actually, I wasn't very fond of mincemeat. I only ate it if there was no other kind of pie around.

"And a couple of loaves of nut bread."

"That's a lot."

"It's for after the funeral."

"What time's the funeral?"

"Ten." She reached down to pull up the boot that was trying to stay behind. "Did you leave anything at Mrs. Stillman's that we should pick up now?"

"No. I've got it all in this paper bag." Including the letter Hilly had started to write. Mrs. Stillman had folded that and put it in the bag. Mama would keep it in her bureau drawer, along with Bub's pocket watch, given to him by his mama in 1923, and the letter from Earl Samson to his brother-in-law, Bill.

"How is Mrs. Stillman doing?" Aunt Betty asked.

"She's doing pretty good. She says Hilly is happy in heaven. She says it's better for her to be without him than for him to be without her."

"That's true."

"Do you think Hilly's in heaven?"

She didn't answer right away. Finally she said, "I don't know."

The only thing pleasing about that answer was that Aunt Betty was treating me like a grown-up. Still, I would rather she had said yes unhesitatingly.

"Why don't you know?"

"Because it's a terrible sin to kill yourself. You can ask the priest." Aunt Betty's Catholicism was a link to Uncle Stanley.

"Maybe the Catholic Church is wrong," I said.

Aunt Betty looked startled. "Well, I think it's in the Bible that suicide is a sin."

"If you ever met Hilly, you wouldn't think he was in hell. If you met Hilly, you'd say the Bible is wrong and so is Father Delias. Anyway, if it's so terrible, how come the Methodists are burying him?"

"For Mrs. Stillman's sake."

We plodded along in silence. The snowplows had piled the snow on Main Street in the middle of the road. I could barely see the top of Beverly's wool cap as she opened the door next to the Loon Cafe and let herself into the cramped stairway there.

Mrs. Ridza had a job cooking at the Loon now, and the Ridzas were living in the apartment over the café. Mrs. Ridza considered the job a step up from cleaning people's houses. And the rent on the apartment was real cheap if you worked at the café.

The Ridzas didn't have much furniture, but the apartment surely was an improvement over the shack. At least they weren't going to freeze to death.

Mrs. Ridza wasn't crazy about working with Magdalen Haggerty and Dora Noonan. "A couple of Crucifix kissers," she called them. "Confession every Saturday. Communion every Sunday. But I wouldn't trust either of 'em with my husband. If I had a husband." Still, it was worth it to have a real job and a decent roof over their heads.

Beverly's baby sister, Delores, who used to go with Mrs. Ridza when she cleaned houses, was now in afternoon kindergarten. That made me feel very old, as though Delores were pushing me

out of childhood. Would Mama and Papa love me as much when
I wasn't a child?

"Is Papa still mad?" I asked Aunt Betty.

"I'm afraid so. But he won't stay mad."

"No. But I will."

"What does *that* mean?"

"I'm not going back to church."

"You have to."

"I'll run away."

"Where would you run in the middle of winter?"

"I don't know. Just away."

"He'd find you at Mrs. Stillman's."

"I'd run away out of town."

"How would you do that?"

I shrugged. "Maybe on a freight."

"If you talk that way to your papa, he'll spank you."

"I don't care."

"That's what you say now."

"I really don't care, Aunt Betty. I'm as stubborn as a mule."

"Well, that's too bad. I feel sorry for stubborn people."

"Why?"

"Because they cut off their noses to spite their faces."

"Grandma says you cut off *your* nose to spite your face because
you won't go to California."

"Don't be smart."

"I'm sorry."

"Turning your back on God is very serious," she warned me.

If I told Aunt Betty that I loved Hilly more than I loved God,
she'd be shocked. I didn't want everybody on the outs with me, so
I just concluded, "Well, I'm not going to the Catholic Church
and that's all."

At supper Papa didn't speak to me. He thought he was punishing me, and it would have been better if he'd been pleasant, but
not talking to me was far better than a spanking. He did talk about
me, however.

"I'm going to have a talk with Father Delias," he told Mama.

"Oh?"

"About Lark."

"Why is that?"

"Because I'm afraid for her soul." He buttered a piece of bread. "If she died now, she'd go right to hell with her good friend Hilly Stillman."

"You think Hilly went to hell?" Mama asked.

"People who commit suicide go there automatically. Everybody knows that."

"The only people who know that for sure, are the people who commit suicide."

"That's sacrilege, what you're saying. No wonder the kid's the way she is. The Church tells us that people who commit suicide go to hell. Are you telling me the Church is wrong?"

"I don't know what I'm telling you. I just know that Hilly didn't go to hell."

"I guess I'd better talk to Father Delias about you, too."

"You do that, Willie."

Papa turned to Aunt Betty. "Betty, am I wrong? Does the Church say that people who kill themselves go to hell?"

Aunt Betty squirmed and looked from Mama to me. "No. You're not wrong, Willie. But, Hilly was—"

"You're damned right I'm not wrong," Papa said, dipping his bread into the Swiss steak gravy. "You're damned right I'm not wrong."

"Do you mind if I don't go to Bernice McGivern's tonight?" Aunt Betty was wiping dishes.

"You stay home with Lark," Mama said. "I'm only going long enough to help her pick out a tablecloth and lay out the dishes. And I thought I'd leave our baked goods there tonight. That way we don't have to worry about them tomorrow."

"You sure you don't mind?"

"I don't mind. You baked all day."

"You were on the road all afternoon."

"Being on the road's *fun*." Mama handed Aunt Betty a wet plate. "Joe Navarin says the war may ruin my business. He says the government's going to start controlling the amount of gas people can buy."

"Did they tell him that?"

"I don't think so, but he says the army's going to need the gas."

"It's so frightening, the war. I can hardly sleep at night."

"Do you hear soldiers marching at night?" I asked. Maybe that was why Aunt Betty couldn't sleep.

"What?" She looked at me blankly. "Soldiers marching?"

"Nothing," I said quickly. "I was thinking of something else."

"After Betty and I finish these dishes, I want you to carry the slop pails," Mama told me.

I nodded.

"And I want you in bed early tonight. Tomorrow will be a long day. Aunt Betty's going to see to it that you're in bed by eight."

"What will you do if you can't get gas?" I asked Mama.

"I'll think of something."

When I carried the slop pails across the tracks, I saw a man pulling himself up into an empty boxcar. I kept going, pretending I hadn't seen him. Technically, the hoboes weren't supposed to be in the cars. But he would freeze down in the hobo jungle tonight.

After putting the slop pails under the sink and washing my face and hands, I slipped into my nightie and climbed into the crib. I was getting so big for the crib that it felt like a cage. Still, I did like the bunnies painted at either end. I would miss them when we moved into our new house and I had a real bed.

From the living room Aunt Betty said, "I think I'll get ready for bed, too." A minute later she was brushing her teeth at the sink. As she rinsed her mouth, someone knocked at the door.

I jumped down from the crib and ran into the kitchen.

"Get back in bed," Aunt Betty told me. "I'll get it."

I retreated to the far side of the table.

"Yes?" she asked, opening the storm door.

A man stood on the step. I was sure it was the hobo. He had on an old, red plaid wool jacket, frayed at the bottom, a beaked gray wool cap with the earflaps down, faded black twill work trousers, and big, heavy shoes, like workmen wore.

"Ma'am? I don't mean to frighten you."

"Yes?"

"I'm sorry to bother you," he said, "but . . . I'm hungry. I'd pay, but I run out of cash."

"Step inside. On the paper." Aunt Betty closed the door against the cold and turned on the burner under the coffee.

The man nodded to me.

"Where you going?" I asked.

"Someplace warm."

"California?"

"If it works out that way. Maybe the gulf."

"Do you know a man named Earl Samson?"

"I can't say I do. At least not by his name."

"He's a friend of mine. You might meet him sometime."

"He riding the boxcars?"

"Yes."

"I'll keep an eye out."

"If you meet him, will you tell him something?"

"If I can remember."

"Tell him Angela Roosevelt is on the radio in Chicago. Can you remember that?"

"Angela Roosevelt is on the radio in Chicago."

"You can have a seat there for a minute," Aunt Betty told the man, setting a cup of coffee on the table.

He removed his cap and sat down. "Thank you."

"You can only stay a minute, because my brother-in-law who works in there"—she nodded toward the office—"might come any time."

"Yes, ma'am."

Aunt Betty buttered two slices of nut bread, set them on a plate, and placed it before the hobo. "I'll wrap the rest of it up for you," she said, and went to tie up the remainder of the loaf in wax paper, then slip it into a brown bag. Pouring milk into a fruit jar, she put that in the bag as well.

"Is there any chores I can do for you?" he asked. "I saw the little girl carrying pails across the tracks."

"No. There's nothing."

"Excuse me." Aunt Betty left for a moment. I heard her digging in her purse. Returning, she handed the man a quarter.

When he had gone and Aunt Betty was preparing to wash his dishes, I said, "You were really nice to him."

She sat down. "Didn't you think he looked like Uncle Stan?" she asked, and she put her head down on her arms.

I didn't think he looked one bit like Uncle Stan.

After the westbound freight had groaned away, pulling with it the empty boxcar with a Missouri Pacific emblem on the outside and our new friend on the inside, Papa came in for a cup of coffee. I heard him poking around in the bread box, searching for the nut bread.

"Betty?" he said, but when he walked into the living room, he saw that she was asleep. "Damn," he swore, and settled for saltine crackers with jam.

After he had snacked, Papa came in the bedroom to get a handkerchief from the drawer. "You're supposed to be asleep," he told me.

"Aunt Betty said I could read my book for a while."

He was ready to leave again when it occurred to him that this was an ideal time to get something settled between us. Sitting down on the edge of the big bed, he said, "You know that you make me very sad."

"Are you going to talk about Hilly again?"

"I'm going to tell you how sad it makes me that your ma and I'll be in heaven and our little girl'll be down in hell. What'll we tell people?"

"Tell 'em I went to hell," I said, lying down and pulling the quilt up.

"You don't care how sad I am," he said as if his heart would break.

"I care, but I don't want to talk about hell."

"No, I wouldn't either if I was going there."

"Maybe you will," I said, "maybe we'll be together."

"Well, that's the damnedest thing I ever heard of a kid telling her pa," he said, rising. "We'll see who goes to hell." He turned and fled back to the depot office.

53

PAPA DIDN'T attend Hilly's funeral. He was taking no chances with his immortal soul. And, as he pointed out two or three times between Saturday and Tuesday, he had been no friend of Hilly's in life. He would be no hypocrite in death.

One problem between Papa and Hilly was that, however touched Hilly might have been, he'd been a bona fide war hero. Unless

our shores were overrun by Huns and Nips, Papa would never be
called on to defend his country. He resented Hilly's fame.

The number of villagers who did attend the funeral was not
legion. Mama and Aunt Betty and I sat in the front pew of the
First Methodist Church, next to Mrs. Stillman. Across the aisle
were Bernice McGivern, Bill, and Bernice's sister, Maxine, who
was Doctor White's assistant. Dr. and Mrs. White sat beside them.
And in the pew behind were Mr. Navarin, his son Danny, Sonny
Steen, and a man I didn't recognize who turned out to be the
pallbearer from Red Berry.

Behind Mama and me were Mrs. Wheeler and Sally. And
beside them, Beverly and Mrs. Ridza. In the back pew on our side
sat a graying, red-faced man in the uniform of an officer of the last
war. Dignified and distant, he was not familiar to me, or to Mama.

Over Hilly's closed casket was draped an American flag, and on
that stood a photograph of the young Hilly in his uniform. It was
the portrait from the table in Mrs. Stillman's living room. The
sweet, open, far-off gaze made me feel right with myself.

The minister's sermon was chaste and succinct, giving offense to
no one and not much comfort either. The comfort lay in his giving
Hilly a Christian burial. For that we were all immoderately
grateful.

At the cemetery the red-faced officer and Bill McGivern
folded the flag ceremoniously and presented it to Mrs. Stillman.
But the officer failed to show up at the gathering at Bernice
McGivern's house. Who had he been?

"I never laid eyes on the man before," Bill McGivern confessed to Mrs. Stillman, who sat in the place of honor, the best
chair, in the bay window of the McGivern living room. "A
captain, he was."

Mrs. Stillman shook her head. She had not recognized the
officer. "He had a fine bearing," she noted.

" 'I never laid eyes on him before.' That's what Bill McGivern
told Mrs. Stillman," Mama relayed to Papa at supper. "And Bill
McGivern knows nearly every legionnaire in the state. Isn't that
interesting, Willie?"

"That Bill McGivern knows every legionnaire in the state?"

"No. That he *didn't* know this mysterious captain."

Papa shrugged. "How many people came to the funeral?"

"About twenty-five, I guess. And they all came to Bernice's except the officer." She reaffirmed to Aunt Betty, "I don't care what anyone says, it was mysterious."

"Yes, it was."

"Mama, when are you going to talk to Mr. Rayzeen again about the new house?" I asked. I thought that it would be wonderful if we had a bay window in the living room like the one Mrs. Stillman sat in at Bernice McGivern's.

"Saturday. I decided to wait till Saturday because that way I don't have to hurry back in from the road to get there by closing."

"Could you ask him how much it'd cost to have a bay window in the living room?"

"All right. I'll ask."

"I saw a fabric in a magazine that'd make beautiful living room drapes," Aunt Betty told Mama. "It was an off-white background with cabbage roses and peonies in different shades of pink, from real pale to real dark—almost red—and then lots of forest green leaves spread all over. It was stunning."

"Wouldn't those be pretty on either side of a bay window, with lace curtains in between?" Mama responded.

"And the walls could match the off-white in the background of the fabric."

"Is there going to be dessert?" Papa demanded.

Mama rose to fetch the remaining pie and cake she'd hauled home from Bernice McGivern's. Bernice had said, "You take this home. Bill and I'll never get around all this food." There were three pieces of chocolate cake and two of mincemeat pie.

"Is there any of that nut bread?" Papa inquired.

"You mean the kind we had at supper last night?"

"What other kind would I mean?"

"Lark, see if there's any in the bread box," Mama told me.

"I looked in there," Papa said. "There's none in there."

"Then I guess we don't have any," Mama said.

Aunt Betty was giving me a keen look. She could have saved herself the trouble. I wasn't going to tell.

"Mighty damned funny how that disappeared so suddenly," Papa complained.

"You like chocolate cake, Willie. Why don't you have a piece of that?"

"I had my mouth set for nut bread," he demurred.

Aunt Betty poured coffee. "That was a beautiful cloth Bernice McGivern had on her dining room table."

"I picked it out," Mama said. "She was going to use one that had a lot of cross-stitch on it. And I said, 'No, Bernice, you don't want to do that, with all the different platters and plates that'll be laid out. It'll look too busy. Use the ecru damask,' I told her."

"You were right. It had a rich look to it."

Papa pushed back from the table, rattling the cups and spilling coffee into the saucers. "It's like sitting with three cackling damned hens. I am sick of hearing about your tablecloths and houses." He put his knuckles on the table, bending close to Mama's face. "Where in hell will you be, lady, if I refuse to cosign?"

"You can't stop me, Willie. I've got the down payment. I'll get my Papa to cosign."

Papa shoved the table, knocking the ketchup bottle over. "There's no room left for me in this family. Where's the respect due me?" He turned and flung himself out the door. After slamming the inside door, he tried to slam the storm door. But it's difficult to slam a storm door because of the air that's caught between the two doors. He had to come back and give it an extra bang with his fist.

"Lark, get to your homework," Mama said, as if she were upset with me. "You missed a whole day of school. You get that made up now."

Mama and Aunt Betty remained at the table. Aunt Betty stood the ketchup bottle up. "It's my fault, Arlene. Because of me you're crowded."

"It's not your fault. We were crowded before you ever came. Answer me this, Betty, why is Willie so against the new house? Can you tell me that?"

Aunt Betty considered. She placed a paper napkin under her cup to absorb the spilled coffee, and then she said, "Willie thinks you love the new house more than you love him."

Mama looked at Aunt Betty for a long minute. Abruptly she broke into an odd, wild laugh, and abruptly she stopped. "Lark, I told you to get to your homework," she said. "What're you doing here?"

An hour later Mama came into the bedroom. "Would you like me to read you a story?" she asked. It had been a very long time since she'd done that. "What would you like to hear?"

I handed her *Happy Stories for Bedtime*.

"My goodness. You still read these stories? I'd think you'd be tired of them by now. Which one do you want?"

" 'Peggy Among the Pansies.' "
"Why that one?"
"It reminds me of Hilly."

When Mama turned out the bedroom light, I lay thinking about
Hilly in his casket in the ground. What did his head look like
where he blew his brains out? Could he still think? Did people
think after they were dead? When their brains turned to dust, what
did they think with? Their souls? Were their souls like beautiful
brains that never died? Yes, I thought they were.

I wished that I could look inside the casket to see if Hilly opened
his eyes. Did he open his eyes and find himself in a casket? Or did
he open them and find himself in heaven? Or did he find himself
in two places at once?

Maybe he would come and tell me. I wouldn't be afraid if Hilly
came and told me about dying and heaven. Grandma Browning
was once visited in a dream by a dead cousin she'd known well in
childhood. The cousin stood on a cloud, bathed in golden light,
and told Grandma that it was time for Great-Grandma Davis to
come to heaven. And the very next week Great-Grandma Davis
passed on of a stroke. But even if Hilly came to me as a real, live
ghost, instead of a dream, I wouldn't be afraid of him.

I asked God to let Hilly come to me and tell me how he was
doing. But maybe God wouldn't listen anymore, since I'd given up
the Church.

54

WHEN MAMA pulled in from the road on Friday, she brought a
Christmas tree, an enormous spruce that half-filled the living
room. The man at the American Legion tree lot had tied one end
of it to the hood ornament on the Ford, and the other end to the
trunk. Mama had to drive home with her head out the window to
see where she was going. "Lucky I didn't have but three blocks to
come," she exclaimed.

"It smells so good," Aunt Betty said, "I'm glad I sleep in the living room."

Papa was going to a railroad meeting in St. Bridget that night, something to do with seniority rights and "bumping" privileges, he said. "You girls have the tree all finished when I get home," he told us cheerfully, pulling on his heavy brown jacket and good leather gloves. Like Mama, Papa was in a good mood when he was going out for the evening.

"Be careful," Mama warned. "The roads over that way are as slick as glass. I nearly went off, coming around that curve right outside of St. Bridget."

"Don't worry. I'm a big boy."

Mama made buttered popcorn for us to eat, and then she filled the canning kettle with unbuttered for me to string for the tree.

When we had rearranged the living room furniture to accommodate the great tree, Mama and Aunt Betty, with a flashlight to show them the way, hurried down to the freight room at the opposite end of the depot to find the ladder, the boxes of Christmas tree ornaments, the lights, and the tree stand, which were stored on a high shelf, separate from the boxes of freight.

"I was going to buy tinsel in St. Bridget today and I forgot," Mama said, returning with the boxes in her arms. "Willie likes tinsel. If we don't have enough left from last year, we'll get some downtown tomorrow."

I sat on the couch, stringing popcorn while Mama and Aunt Betty set the tree in its stand and arranged the lights. "Next year we'll be putting the tree up in our new bay window," I said.

"*If* a bay window isn't too expensive," Mama reminded me.

"Think of it, Arlene—Christmas in the new house." Aunt Betty had caught house fever from Mama and me.

"And you will have the downstairs bedroom," Mama told her.

"That's your sewing room," Aunt Betty reminded her.

"I've decided to put the sewing room in the basement by the washing machine. It's more convenient for mending."

This was the first I'd heard of it.

"Next year everybody's presents to each other will be things for the house," Aunt Betty speculated. "What are you going to have in your room, Lark? Besides a bed and bureau?"

"Well, I've got my red leatherette rocker. Even if I'm too big for it then, I'll keep that because it's my favorite Christmas present. And I've got my doll chest of drawers that was Mama's when she was little. And Mama is going to make me a dressing table from orange crates. She said she'll make a real frilly skirt for it, like the movie stars have."

"What colors did you have in mind for your room?" Mama wanted to know.

I loved to talk like this. The house came near, so near I could smell its new-house smell under the aroma of the Christmas tree. And Mama and Aunt Betty were conversing with me as if I were an equal whose thoughts interested them. I felt seventeen years old and pretty and popular, like Bonnie Bostwick, who sometimes babysat me.

"I can't decide, Mama, whether to have pink and green, like Peggy Traherne's bedroom, or red, white, and blue for victory. What do you think?"

"Who's Peggy Traherne?" Aunt Betty wanted to know.

"She's a character in one of Lark's storybooks," Mama explained. " 'Peggy Among the Pansies.' "

Aunt Betty searched for the dead bulb, which was causing one string of lights not to work. "I like the patriotic idea," she said. "You could get a little flag and hang it over your bed. On the other hand, pink and pale green are very feminine."

"Either one is nice," Mama agreed.

"I can't believe we're at war," Aunt Betty sighed, stepping back to regard the placement of the lights. "In our lifetime, Arlene."

"The last one was in our lifetime," Mama said.

"Yes, but I was just a child, and you were hardly more than a baby. You don't remember the last one, do you?"

"No."

"I hardly remember it myself. I was about Lark's age."

"Did you think the German soldiers were going to march over here?" I asked. I was still hearing the marching at night.

She stopped to recall. "No. I don't think it ever occurred to me. Europe seemed like it was on the moon."

It didn't seem that way to me. It seemed like Europe was just beyond New Frankfurt, where Grandpa and Grandma Erhardt lived.

"I think it's getting chilly in here," Mama said. "I'm going to get the other scuttle of coal." She returned in a moment, weighted down with the heavy scuttle. "My God, it's cold out there. But beautiful. The stars are like Christmas tree lights. There's red ones and green ones and blue." She carried the coal to the stove. "Open the door, Betty."

Mama dumped part of the coal into the stove, then poked at it and arranged it with a little shovel. "There. That should do us," she said, slamming the stove door. "Now we'll be cozy." She looked at her hands. "I'm all filthy," she complained and went to the kitchen to wash. "Shall we sit down and have popcorn before we put the ornaments on?"

Aunt Betty sat beside me on the couch. "I worry about Stanley," she said, staring at the colored lights.

"Why on earth would you worry about him?" Mama asked. "Worry about the little children in the Philippine Islands. They say the Japs are going to take the Philippines." Mama sat in the armchair near the stove.

"I suppose I shouldn't say it, but Stanley has always needed a strong hand. Now that he's not living with Cousin Lloyd and Marlis, I'm afraid he might enlist."

"Could be the best thing that ever happened to him," Mama observed.

"It's easy for you to say that. He's not *your* husband."

"Betty, can't you get it through your head, he's not yours either?"

"We're not divorced," Aunt Betty retorted.

"As good as."

"No. There's still hope. If he asked me to come back."

"You mean you'd go?" Mama couldn't believe her ears.

"I might."

Mama shook her head.

"I married him for better or for worse," Aunt Betty said. "I had the worse. Now I want the better."

"Then you should find a better man. That's what I'd do."

They were turning over old ground, but Aunt Betty never tired of speculating about Uncle Stanley. It made her feel more married.

I helped hang the ornaments. Mama and Aunt Betty decorated the high branches; I did the low. I loved the delicate glass ornaments, especially those with special shapes—teardrops and diamonds and round pillows.

"These real pretty ones come from Germany," Mama pointed out. "We won't be getting any more for a while. Handle them with kid gloves."

It was eleven by the time we finished. Mama piled the empty boxes by the door to be carried back to the freight room in the morning.

"We need a highball, Betty," Mama said, reaching down a bottle of whiskey from the cupboard. "There's a bottle of Coca-Cola in the refrigerator. Do you want your whiskey in Coca-Cola?"

"How are you having yours?"

"I have mine in plain water with ice cubes."

"Oh, I can't drink mine in plain water. I don't like the taste. Put it in Coca-Cola, and give me some ice cubes, too."

"Lark, get your nightie on, and I'll give you a little Coca-Cola," Mama told me.

"In a highball glass with ice."

When we were settled in the living room with our drinks, Mama turned off all the lights except those on the tree. We sat in the glowing shadows, staring at the tree as if it were a flaming hearth or a crystal ball.

"To the three witches," Mama toasted, raising her glass and smiling at Aunt Betty and me. Aunt Betty and I raised our glasses. "To victory," Aunt Betty said.

55

I WOKE in the middle of the night. The light was on in the kitchen. The banjo clock said ten past three.

"I know he's in a ditch somewhere," Mama said. "The roads are terrible."

"Should we take the car and go look for him?" Aunt Betty asked.

"I don't know."

"I think we should go look."

"Let me wake Lark and tell her," Mama said.

"I'm awake."

"Aunt Betty and I're going to look for your papa. He might have gone off the road. But he'll be all right. Don't worry."

"Can I come?"

"No. We need you here to answer the phone. If we don't find him on the road, I'll check the hospital in St. Bridget and call you from there to see if you've heard anything." Mama looked at her watch. "We won't be back much before five," she said, "so don't worry about us. Why don't you go to bed on the couch now so you'll hear the phone."

Mama and Aunt Betty dressed as if they were going to trek across the Yukon. "Look at the frost on the window," Mama pointed out. "It must be twenty-five below." She poked up the fire in the stove and added a little coal. "If it gets real low, put in the rest of this," she advised me. "But make sure it gets going good and doesn't smoke."

It took a long time to start the Ford, but at length I heard them drive off. I got up and plugged in the Christmas tree lights and found the rest of the buttered popcorn. Stuffing my face with popcorn and mesmerizing myself with the colored lights, I considered Papa and where he might be. The more I worried, the more I ate, until I was as bloated as a dead fish.

If he was in the ditch, he might freeze to death. If he stayed in the truck and the heater was working, he would probably be all right. In an hour there would be creamery trucks coming by, and he could catch a ride. If Mama didn't find him. But if he were hurt . . . I prayed to God to look out for him.

At a quarter past four, the phone rang. "Lark, it's Mama. Is Papa home?"

"No."

"Did he call?"

"No."

She said something to Aunt Betty.

"Wait a minute, Mama. I heard the truck, I think."

"Look out the window," she said.

Through the delicate tracery of frost, I saw the headlights pull up beside the depot and wink off. Then the truck door slammed, and in a moment, Papa opened the storm door, then the inner door, in a tentative manner, as if the kitchen might be booby-trapped.

"Mama, Papa just came in."

"Put him on the line," Mama said in an angry voice.

"Papa, Mama wants to talk to you on the phone."

"Where's she?" He leaned against the doorway.

"In St. Bridget at the hospital."

"Wha's she doin' there?"

"Looking for you."

He pulled off a glove with his teeth and threw it down. Making his way overcarefully across the room, he said, "'Lo," into the phone.

Mama's voice crackled at the other end.

"Boys had a li'l party afterwards."

He hung up the receiver while Mama was still talking. "Can' even have a li'l fun."

I added the remainder of the coal to the fire, then found the old flatiron and set it on top of the stove. While it heated, I fetched a brown paper sack and a towel. When the iron was hot, I wrapped it in the bag and then in the towel, and tucked it under the quilt at the foot of the crib. Papa was sitting on the couch, still in his brown jacket, wearing one leather glove. Pulling the plug on the tree lights, I climbed into my crib, put my feet against the warmth of the iron, and fell asleep.

I didn't hear Mama and Aunt Betty return. Nor did I hear Mama later, after the sun came up, when she rose, dressed, and let herself out of the house. When I woke, Aunt Betty was asleep in Mama's bed. Papa had slept on the couch.

Now his unshaved face was puffy and gray as he sat at the kitchen table cradling a cup of reheated coffee, not drinking it, only holding it and staring at the wall.

I poured a bowl of cereal and carried it into the living room. Someone had refilled the coal scuttle. The morning paper lay on the sideboard, unopened. I got it down and, spreading it on the floor, knelt on all fours to read the funny papers.

In the kitchen, Papa scraped his chair back, got up, and dumped the coffee down the sink. Setting the cup on the drain board, he stood, palms on the rim of the sink, leaning heavily against it as if he hadn't the spunk to stand by himself.

"Where's your ma?" he asked after several minutes.

I didn't understand him because his voice was strained and thin, as if he had something caught in his throat. "What did you say?"

"Where's your ma?"

"I don't know. Are you sick?"

"Never mind." He turned and walked to the door, opening it and pushing the storm door open.

"You going next door?"

"Huh?"

"Are you going next door?"

"Why? What difference?"

"You don't have a coat or cap. It's real cold. Look at the windows." In fact, a blast of air swept in through the open door, armed with a thousand needles of arctic ice.

He turned away and left, as if he hadn't heard, and closed both doors behind him. I ran to the living room window. Maybe he was going across to Mr. Navarin's Sinclair station. Or maybe he'd drive downtown for coffee at the Loon Cafe. Sometimes he did that on Saturday morning. But he was walking along the tracks, just walking, not going anywhere. There was nowhere much to go in the direction he was headed. Not even the hobo jungle.

Aunt Betty padded out of the bedroom, clutching herself. "It's cold in here."

"Papa just went out," I explained.

"Where to?"

"Nowhere. Just walking. And he didn't even take a coat or cap."

"Must be going *somewhere*," she said.

"Just down the tracks."

"Going to check something on a siding."

"Not in that direction. Nothing on the siding down there."

"Your mama make coffee?"

"No."

Aunt Betty dumped out the little that remained in the pot of yesterday's coffee and began preparing a fresh pot. "Is there a fire in the coal stove?" she asked. "It feels like it's gone out."

"It's going. It's the kitchen that's cold. Turn on the oven."

I folded the paper and carried the cereal bowl to the kitchen. "Papa's going to freeze."

"Maybe you better get dressed and go look for him. Where's your mama?"

I lifted my shoulders. "Out someplace. She got up early, I guess."

"Is the car here?" Aunt Betty asked.

I nodded.

"Then she hasn't gone far. Maybe to Truska's for milk or something."

It was a strange morning, I thought, pulling a dress over my head. It felt as though I had wandered into somebody else's life. Normally Mama was up making breakfast on Saturday morning. She liked preparing breakfast on the weekends, when she didn't have to hurry off to her typewriter. Usually Papa stayed in bed, head under the pillow, until Mama called him to the table. After breakfast he had another cup of coffee and a Lucky Strike while he read the sports section of the Minneapolis paper. The smell of bacon and coffee and Lucky Strikes spoke of ritual Saturday morning indolence.

Not this morning. Papa was out wandering in twenty-below weather. Mama was God-knew-where, not even leaving a note on the table. I had a tight, expectant pain in my stomach. I wanted to climb into the crib, and scramble up into the banjo clock. But it was my place to go after Papa.

When I had pulled on my boots and coat and mittens and cap, and Aunt Betty had tied the cap under my chin and wound the long scarf around my face below my eyes, I tramped out into the virgin air. It was so clear and calm that I felt like a monster laying waste to its purity. Shlump, clump, shlump, clump, down the rail bed. People could hear me down the line in Hazelton, I thought.

When I came abreast of the last of the grain elevators, I saw Papa standing in the sharp, blue morning shadows, between the last elevator and its nearest companion. He was leaning against the great, high wall, looking at his feet.

"Papa, come home."

He paid no attention. I shlumped across the rows of tracks. "Papa, it's freezing. Come home. Aunt Betty wants you to come home." At length he looked up. He glanced at me as if I were Beverly or Sally, someone else's kid. "I'm not supposed to come home without you," I told him, "so if you don't come, I have to stand here till I freeze." I reached for his hand and pulled. "Come on. It's cold."

He followed docilely. What was the matter with him? I was worried. Was he sick? Crazy? Where were his brains? I led the way into the house and closed the doors. Aunt Betty poured Papa a fresh cup of coffee and helped me out of my heavy things. "What's going on, Willie?" she asked.

He shook his head and wouldn't look at her. We remained in place, as if waiting for an actor whose entrance was late. The door opened, and Mama dragged into the kitchen. She passed us, saying nothing, and went into the bedroom to take off her coat. She had forgotten to remove her boots. I was shocked. What terrible thing did this portend? What else could happen? We were already at war. And Hilly had died.

"Mama, what is it?"

I don't think she realized that I had spoken. She was sitting on the bed. She pulled her arms out of her coat and let it drop behind her.

"Mama, take off your boots!" I cried.

Papa came into the bedroom. "How did you find out? Who told you?"

Mama stared at him.

"I was going to tell you as soon as you came home."

Still she was silent, with a wondering look on her face.

"We were drinking boilermakers. I shouldn't've. I shoulda stayed with beer. But you know what them bastards are like. 'God hates a coward, Willie.' That's what they say, 'God hates a coward.' So I drank boilermakers with 'em.

"I never meant to lose the money, Arlene. I wasn't even going to play, but you know how they are. They think you're not one of them if you don't play."

Papa knelt on the bedroom floor and grasped Mama about the waist. "I'm so sorry, Arlene," he sobbed, and tears gushed from his eyes and washed his cheeks.

Horrified, I climbed into the crib. This was the day the world ended, I thought.

"I know how bad you wanted that house. We'll build it, you'll see. Only we can't build it right now. I'm going to need that money. How much is there, Arlene? Is there five hundred dollars? There's nowhere else I can turn." Through his sobs, he pleaded, "Don't turn your back on me. I'm at the end of my rope."

Except for Papa's crying and the twittering of a family of snow buntings on the roof, the town was quiet. No engine growled, no mother called, no foot fell overhead in the Bigelow's apartment.

At last Mama said, "You didn't have to lose the money after all, Willie—Mr. Rayzeen says by spring there won't be any home building. The government needs the materials, he says."

"You think I lost it on purpose?" Papa cried.

Mama didn't answer. She stood up, pulling away, and drifted into the kitchen, leaving Papa weeping beside the bed.

"Lark and I're leaving for California in January, Betty. You want to come along? I'll pay for your ticket."

"I can't go to Los Angeles."

"Then we won't go there. We'll go someplace else. There's lots of towns in California."

"For a vacation?"

"For good."

Now the world *had* ended.

🌿56🌿

"WHERE'LL YOU get the money?" Aunt Betty asked Mama.

"I'll sell the car. Willie can get tickets for Lark and me." Being family of a railroad man, Mama and I rode on passes. "If we put your fifty dollars together with what I get for the car, I think we can make it."

"You think I'm gonna get tickets for you to leave me?" Papa asked, barging into the kitchen, grabbing Mama's arm.

"Do you want the five hundred dollars, Willie?"

"What is this, blackmail?"

"Yes."

"I'm not gonna let you do this to me."

"Then you'll never see the five hundred dollars, Willie."

"Well, you're not taking the kid, I'll tell you that. I'll see a lawyer."

"Do that, Willie. Tell him about the five hundred dollars. Tell him how we lost the Oldsmobile. Tell him all of it. You'll end up without me, Lark, *or* the money."

"I don't see how you can just walk out like this, all of a sudden, without any warning. You never said a thing."

"No, Willie, you never *heard* a thing."

"I've been a good husband, better than most, given you every-thing you ever wanted. I've gone without so you could have the nice things you wanted, expensive things."

"You mean like this dump we live in?"

"I'll get you a house."

"It's too late."

"You won't have a friend left in this town if you leave me. They all know what I put up with."

"God, Willie, you believe your own bullshit. You disgust me."

"No!" he cried. "Don't talk like that. I can't stand it. I love you. You know that. Don't talk to me like I was dirt." Papa lowered himself onto a kitchen chair, pulling a handkerchief from his back pocket. "You'll put my folks in their graves, you know."

"I'm sorry about your folks, Willie, and I'm sorry about mine, but I'm leaving."

Mama sat down. "I'm leaving in January, so order the tickets. For Lark and Betty and me, to—where did I tell you the Huemillers moved, Betty?"

"Long Beach, I think it was called."

"Long Beach. We want to go to Long Beach. I'll pay for Betty's ticket."

"How are you going to feel in Long Beach when you hear that I killed myself?"

"I'll think it's strange. You told us Hilly went to hell for doing the same thing."

Papa was like a wild thing, stung by a hornet, flailing his arms and sending the cups flying. He bellowed and stumbled to his feet, pushing the table halfway across the room. "You never cared!" He grabbed the bread knife from the cupboard. "Why do you think I've done the things I have? Because I knew you didn't care, and it was driving me crazy."

"Willie, don't!" Aunt Betty screamed. I jumped from the crib and ran into the kitchen. "Don't! Please, don't!"

"Get out of the way," he yelled, pushing me aside. Aunt Betty grabbed me.

Papa looked like a bear, reared onto his hind legs, one great, huge claw on his right paw, wild pain distorting his face.

Mama was on her feet, putting the table between herself and Papa.

He lunged across the table, and Mama sidestepped. The knife scraped a gash down the wall. "I'll kill you before I let you go!"

Mama stood still then, and dropped her arms. "All right, Willie. Come kill me." She was crying, too. "I'd rather die than stay."

Every day thereafter, Mama asked Papa if he'd ordered the tickets. "When I see the tickets, Willie, you'll see the five hundred dollars."

Papa didn't answer. There could be no acceptance of our leaving, no admission that his life had split in two and half of it was going to California. He went silently about his days, selling tickets, sending telegrams, delivering freight. I heard him laugh and joke, as he always had, to Art Bigelow and the trainmen and the passengers who waited beside the depot coal stove for the train to pull in. But as soon as he stepped through the kitchen door, he closed himself up.

"Why do we have to go, Mama?"

"Because I can't take any more, Lark."

"I don't want to go. I want to stay here, even if we live in the depot."

"If you want to stay, you can. I have to go."

I felt as though she had pushed me out into the cold. She was supposed to say, "No, I won't hear of your staying. You're coming with me." She was not supposed to make me decide, and she was not supposed to act as though she could get along without me.

Life was flying at me like trash in a wind storm. Mama was leaving Papa, going to California to find work. Aunt Betty was leaving, too, starting over. California was the place to be, everybody said that. Thousands of jobs were going to open up there.

Who would Mama become in California? It frightened me to think that she might change. And yet she rushed toward change as if she would perish without it.

Mama was not joyful exactly. There was too much worry and tension for that. But she was keyed up, expectant, breathless. She rushed around, winding up the affairs of Erhardt Typing Service and packing our things, hers and mine, into cardboard boxes, most of them to be sent on to us when we found a place. Each time Mama tried to explain these matters to Papa, he would fling himself out of the house, slamming the door.

Christmas was a desolate little occasion, over which the glittering tall tree, the best we'd ever had, stood ironic and aloof. Mama sent back some of the things she'd ordered from Monkey Wards (I wouldn't need ice skates and a new snowsuit), exchanging them for things I'd need in California: a new raincoat and galoshes. "It rains a lot in winter, they say."

We didn't have many presents under the tree. "It's just more to pack," Mama explained. "We'll have Christmas in February when everybody else's having Valentine's Day!" It sounded half-baked and forlorn to me.

Besides the raincoat and galoshes, I got some coloring books and new Crayolas ("For the long train trip"), a deck of playing cards with a basket of puppies on them, and a Nancy Drew mystery.

Every time I thought about moving to California, I cried until Mama got mad. "Don't I have enough to worry about?" What did I care that she had enough to worry about? That was her choice.

One afternoon during Christmas vacation, I dragged myself

downtown to Beverly's apartment above the Loon Cafe and told her my troubles. "Godsakes, what're you crying about?" she asked. "I don't have no pa and you don't see *me* crying. *I'd* sure like to go to California on the train. You stay here and be Beverly, and I'll go to California and be Lark." To Delores and Charlie, who were hanging around, she explained, "It's warm all the time in California, and they got orange trees all over. Alls you have to do is go outside and pick yourself an orange when you feel like it."

"But we're not going to build our new house," I cried, breaking down. Delores was thoroughly mystified by my tears, and Charlie disappeared in a dudgeon of disgust.

"Even if you stayed here, you wouldn't build your new house. That's what Mr. Rayzeen told your ma."

"But maybe we'd *buy* a nice house, one like Katherine Albers'."

"Thhhhhhhlllleeeeech," Beverly pronounced with distaste at mention of perfect Katherine Albers, with her perfect teeth and perfect pitch. "Who wants to live in a house like *hers?*"

"You don't understand, Beverly."

"You tell your ma I'll go to California with her."

There was no sympathy to be had from Beverly. "Let's go see Mrs. Stillman," she suggested. "Maybe she'll give us tea and arrowroot cookies." And sympathy. There was always sympathy at Mrs. Stillman's.

"I'm so pleased that you girls came by this afternoon," Mrs. Stillman told us. "I was sitting here by my lonesome, thinking wouldn't it be nice if someone stopped for a cup of tea."

When I explained to Mrs. Stillman that Mama and I were moving to California, she said, "I'll surely miss you and your mama. You have been my closest friends. And what would Hillyard have done without you?" She stirred half a teaspoon of sugar into her tea. "But you'll have a fine adventure there, Lark."

She spoke soberly. These were not cheap words with which she dismissed a child's fretting. "We have to be ready for the adventures life throws down in our path. Everything difficult or painful that we can do with a merry heart, gives us . . ." She searched for the word. Squaring her shoulders a little, she pronounced, "style." An uncharacteristic word, I thought. "And character. Yes, style and character. Mr. Roosevelt has style and character, don't you know. And Mrs. Roosevelt, too."

She went on, "I have a third cousin on my papa's side who lives in California. She and her little family are the last of my relations. They live in a small place on the coast. Oxnard. It's nearly forty years since I've seen her, but she writes every Christmas. I have a letter arrived the other day." Mrs. Stillman rose from the green wicker chair and went to the table in the corner, where Hilly's photograph was displayed. An envelope lay beside it. Picking it up and removing the enclosed sheets of lined paper, Mrs. Stillman scanned its words, searching for a particular line or paragraph. "Here it is," she said, turning to us, as though she'd already agreed to reveal part of the letter's contents.

" 'We were sorry to hear of Hillyard's passing, but now you are free to travel,' " she read. " 'Mary Ann is grown up and with her own family, and I am alone again. I would welcome a visit from you when you feel up to it. Who knows? Maybe you'll decide to stay. There's plenty of room, and we would be company for each other.' "

She folded the letter, returning it to the envelope. Slipping it into her pocket, she said, "I couldn't leave Hillyard so soon. But in another year I might go." She poured more tea into our cups.

"For good?" I asked, not believing that she would abandon Hilly.

She shrugged. "I'd have to see how my cousin and I got along. If we fit together like a pair of old shoes, I might leave here for good."

I was dumbfounded. How unsentimental old people were. If Hilly were my son, I could never pull up stakes and leave him behind.

"Hillyard is gone, Lark," she said, answering my thoughts. "What is left of him on this earth is in my heart and in yours."

No. No. No. He wasn't gone. He was in that grave. I was not so certain about heaven anymore. I had not come to any conclusions about that since leaving the Church. Maybe heaven and hell were both a lie.

"Will you write to me when you're settled?" Mrs. Stillman asked, moving effortlessly forward into my future in a way that I could not.

I nodded.

"I sure like these cookies," Beverly said somewhat obviously.

"Please have some more," Mrs. Stillman offered. "I hope that you'll come visit me when Lark has left us. We will miss her, won't we? Maybe you can keep me company now and then, and we'll read Lark's letters telling us all about California and the Pacific Ocean and the movies. Maybe she'll see William Powell and Myrna Loy there. I think they're her favorites."

How it hurt me to hear Mrs. Stillman talk about me as if I were gone.

"Can I look at Hilly's books, Mrs. Stillman?"

"Maybe you'd like to take some with you."

I was embarrassed. I hadn't been hinting. It wasn't Hilly's books that called me, but his room. "No. It's all right. I just wanted to look." I fled to the bedroom, closing the door. It was plain, warm, ordered, and unchanging. I should stay here, in this room, and Mrs. Stillman should go to California.

Withdrawing *Stories for a Rainy Afternoon* from the bookcase, I sat down on the bed, reaching out for Hilly, in the grave or in the sky, or wherever he'd gone.

❧ 57 ❧

"HER COUSIN?" Mama said, drawing the two words out in a wondering, remembering way. "Why, that must be the cousin who got pregnant while she was working for Mrs. Stillman and had to leave town. No one knew where she went. California. Isn't that a coincidence? A lot of people seem to end up in California, don't they?"

"Most of 'em running away," Papa said.

Mama was at her typing table, preparing the last of the bills to be sent out by Erhardt Typing, for services rendered. At the kitchen table Aunt Betty was writing a long letter to Grandma and Grandpa Browning, outlining our California plans.

Papa, in the chair by the stove, had been reading from the newspaper the account of the fall of Manila. "MacArthur's withdrawn his forces to the Bataan peninsula and declared Manila an open city."

Mama shuddered. "Where's it all going to end?"

"It could end with the Japs invading California," Papa asserted.

"You go there and you could be living under the Emperor of Japan in a few months."

"I'll take my chances," Mama told him.

During that brief period—a month it was, only—between Papa's losing the five hundred dollars and the middle of January, it seemed to me that we all spent a great deal of our time looking sideways at each other, sizing up one another's true intentions. Wouldn't you think, after all those years together, that we would know each other better than that? We were dumbfounded to learn what strangers we were.

Would Mama leave? Papa wondered. No. Despite her big talk, when it came down to it, it was too big a step into the dark. At the last moment, she would find a graceful way of backing out.

Mama studied Papa. What would Willie do? Lock her up? Kill her?

Aunt Betty contemplated both of them, changing her mind daily about the chances of moving to California. Was Arlene all brave talk? Would she cave in to Willie? What if Willie went berserk and killed them all?

Like Papa, I chose to believe that life would return to normal. It must. Someplace out west lay the edge of the world that I recognized and understood. When the train reached that divide, I would fall into the chasm of Beyond Here.

A week after New Year's, Papa presented Mama with the three tickets to Los Angeles. She was at the stove, browning a pot roast.

"I'm putting them here on the table," he said.

Mama turned to see what he was talking about.

"Your tickets," he said. "They're here on the table."

He smiled. Once her bluff was called, she would begin backing down. He was not an old poker player for nothing. He would try hard to be forbearing and tolerant. Wasn't that the manly thing to do?

"Thank you, Willie. I'll put them away so they don't get lost." She covered the roast with a lid, wiped her hands on her apron, and carried the tickets to the bedroom. Returning, she said, "I'll get the five hundred out of the bank tomorrow."

When we sat down to dinner, Mama told Aunt Betty and me, "We're leaving on the sixteenth, that's a Monday."

Papa did not comment on that, but mentioned the story in the news about the navy pilot who dropped a depth charge on a Japanese submarine and then radioed the succinct message: "Sighted sub, sank same." "A man of few words," Papa said.

Mama looked askance at Papa. Was there a hidden message in his words? After Papa returned to the depot office to wait for the westbound freight, Mama advised, "We'll pack our suitcases and keep them under the bed, ready to go."

There were two farewell parties for Mama during the next week, one at bridge club, the other at sewing club. Everyone was shocked at her leaving and many disapproved. But it was exciting, nevertheless, and what were they to do, ignore her going? No, they would fete her on her way. Who knew what life held for any of them, with the war tossing everything topsy-turvy?

My last day of school was Friday, the thirteenth. Wasn't that a sad omen? Mrs. Borgen organized a party with cupcakes and Kool-Aid and word games. Katherine Albers presented me with going-away presents—a diary and an autograph book which everyone had signed. Then the bell rang, and they all filed out except Beverly and Sally and Mrs. Borgen.

I cleaned out my desk, packing into a brown bag all that was mine to take: notes and Smith Brothers cough drops, papers, an empty pencil box, and my workbooks and an ink-stained hanky and two hair ribbons.

I didn't want to leave. I liked the fourth grade room, which was on the second floor, looking down on the main entrance and off toward Main Street.

At last I said good-bye to Mrs. Borgen. "Write to us when you get settled, Lark. Tell us about California and your trip."

I still thought there was a good chance I'd be back in class on Monday. That would be embarrassing, but I could live with a little embarrassment.

From the Ridzas' apartment, I called Mama on their new phone to tell her that Beverly had invited Sally and me for day-old pastries from the Loon Cafe. "It's a going-away party, Mama."

We sat at the kitchen table drinking reheated coffee and eating glazed doughnuts. At any rate, I ate doughnuts. Beverly ate chocolate cake, and Sally, lemon meringue pie.

"D'ya think you'll ever come back?" Beverly asked.

I shook my head. "I might run away, though. I might run away to my Grandma Browning's."

"All the way from California?" Sally asked.

"Sure. I could get a map and figure out the way."

"I'd like to live in California," Beverly said, as she had before.

Wiping away chocolate frosting from around her mouth, she said, "Maybe you'll get to be in a movie with William Powell and Myrna Loy."

"Oh, Beverly, that's stupid. How would I get to be in a movie? We're not going to live around Hollywood. That's where Uncle Stan is, and Aunt Betty doesn't want to run into him."

"Well, if you get to be a movie star, will you send me a ticket to come visit you? And one for Sally, too?"

"If I get to be a movie star," I said, humoring Beverly, "I'll send tickets, and you can both come live with me and be in the movies with me."

"And you'll have a party and invite Mickey Rooney?"

"Yes. Whoever you want."

"Do you promise?" Sally said, and it surprised me that she was so serious about it.

In her excitement, Beverly nearly climbed on top of the table. She was sprawled half across it, waving her hand in Sally's face. "And we'll ride in taxicabs. Everywhere. Even just to the grocery store."

Sally's face was suffused with a soft light, like an angel's, as she listened. Sally, too, wanted to go to California. Why? She lived in a nice house. And she was pretty, prettier even than Katherine Albers. She was much nicer than Katherine Albers. Sally could be the most popular girl in Harvester someday. Why would she want to give all that up and go to Hollywood?

"We'll each have a hundred dresses," Beverly decided, "and a hundred pairs of shoes. I'm going to live in a mansion with a hundred rooms. I'll do everything by the hundreds."

Once, when I was wishing for Christmas to come, Grandma Browning warned, "Don't wish your life away." Beverly and Sally were wishing my life away—wishing me to California, wishing me into the movies. I wanted them to stop. I wanted them to tell me that they would miss me and that I should hurry back.

On Sunday afternoon Papa asked me to go for a drive in the truck with him. "A farewell tour," he explained. Apprehensive, I didn't want a farewell tour. I wanted to believe that if we left tomorrow as planned, I would be back again so soon, a farewell tour was uncalled-for.

"Go on," Mama told me.

Up and down the streets we rode, Papa very quiet. The town was bedraggled in the cheerless gray light. Leafless black trees, twisted and painful-looking, were outlined against dirty snow. Small and shabby and huddled together was how everything looked. And in need of me.

"I don't think you should worry," Papa finally said. "I don't believe your ma is going to leave."

"Really?"

"You wait and see," he said. "At the last minute she's going to get a migraine headache or lose the tickets or something. I've lived with her a long time and I'm telling you, she's too fond of her bridge club and church work and all her cackling hens to give it up and light out on her own."

We pulled up in front of Anderson's Candy and Ice Cream. "What're you hungry for?" Papa asked.

Nothing. I wasn't hungry for anything in the world. But Papa was waiting, wanting to please. "Butter brickle."

He laughed as if at a great joke and opened the door of the truck.

The next morning Papa went to work as usual, winking at me as he closed the door behind him. If Mama was going to get a migraine, she'd have to do it soon. The westbound passenger train was due at one. We were scheduled to travel as far as Blue Lake today, stay over with Grandma and Grandpa until Wednesday, then get back on the train and head for California.

Mama spent most of the morning cooking things for Papa to eat and writing notes to remind him. When a lunch was packed for the trip and our suitcases were set beside the door, she sat down at the typewriter and typed several letters, stuffing a few dollars into each.

"What's that about?" Aunt Betty wanted to know. "Aunt Carrie?" she asked, reading the address on one of the envelopes. "Why are you sending her money?"

Mama stopped typing. She didn't look at Aunt Betty but stared at the typewriter, about where the word "Royal" was, and explained, "These are the last of the payments to people who loaned Stan money to go to California."

"Why on earth should *you* pay them? This is craziness. Have you been doing this all along? This makes me upset, Arlene.

These are Stan's debts." Aunt Betty sounded as though she were about to cry. We were all on edge and needed little to start us blubbering.

"It was my idea to ask for the money. I wrote the letters. I can't walk away, leaving these debts. I won't be free of here if they're not paid. Anyway, it's only a few dollars. Most of 'em are already paid. I don't want you upset. None of this was your idea."

"Are we going to have enough money? We could pay these after we get settled, Arlene."

"If we're careful, I think we'll be okay. I've still got a little money coming from some of the typing accounts. I've asked them to send it general delivery to Los Angeles."

"Why Los Angeles? I thought we were going to Long Beach. You're not interfering again, are you, Arlene?"

"I told them Los Angeles because it's central. What if we decide against Long Beach? We have to go where the jobs are. I'm doing the best I can, Betty. Don't be so damned suspicious. I've got a lot on my mind."

"I'm sorry, Arlene, really I am. You're doing your best," Aunt Betty cried, throwing her arms around Mama.

At ten minutes before train time, we set our grips out on the platform. "You've got the tickets?" Aunt Betty asked.

"Yes," Mama assured her. "I've got everybody's. I'll take care of the tickets."

Papa came out of the office carrying the mailbag, which he set beside the tracks. Then he rolled the freight wagon out onto the platform. I wasn't going to see him do that again, I thought. In the distance the train whistled as it approached a railroad crossing east of town.

I ran to Papa. "I don't want to go, Papa. I don't want to leave you. Please tell Mama not to go."

He laughed. "Don't worry. She'll have a nice visit with her folks in Blue Lake and enjoy giving me a little scare, and on Wednesday she'll get back on the eastbound and come home. You'll see." He lifted me, although I was getting big, and carried me toward Mama and Aunt Betty. I clung to his neck, trying to believe, as he did.

"Well, ladies," he said jauntily, as the train appeared, "write if you get work." He laughed.

The engine ground to a screaming halt and spat steam at us. The conductor lowered the steps. Papa hugged me and handed me up, smiling as I turned to wave. Mama shook his hand. I couldn't hear what she said, but she was crying. Papa kept smiling. He shook hands with Aunt Betty and helped the conductor with our grips.

As the train pulled away from the depot, Papa waved until we were out of sight. I waved back, trying to memorize everything: Papa, the depot where I had lived for eight years, the Harvester Arms Hotel, the grain elevators, the hobo jungle.

As soon as the train was out of town, Mama handed the tickets to Aunt Betty and hurried back to the rest room. We did not see her again for twenty minutes, and when she returned, her face was red and swollen.

58

"IT'S NOT RIGHT," Grandma proclaimed. "To pull up stakes, just walk out, dragging a child across the country to God-knows-where, is not right."

Mama and Aunt Betty and I sat at the dining room table, facing Grandma. Grandpa had fetched us from the depot, dropped us at the house, and returned to work. All around the dining room our grips stood as if this were a depot waiting room.

"I just thought you'd understand everything I've put up with," Mama said. "Most mothers want a home and security for their children. I want that for Lark."

"Looks to me like you're turning your back on a home and security."

Mama laughed derisively. "If that's your idea of a home, I'd hate to see your idea of a dump."

"It's a roof over your head."

"Is that all I can hope for in life, a roof over my head?"

"Yes." Grandma was dead serious. "Haven't ten years of this Depression taught you anything?"

"They've taught me that if I want a home and security, I've got to depend on myself for them."

Now it was Grandma's turn to laugh derisively. "You poor fool. You think all there is to marriage is a home and security?"

"No. I think there's love and respect and working together to accomplish something."

"And did you love and respect Willie?"

Mama got to her feet, moving restlessly to the window, where she stood gazing into the late afternoon darkness and the fresh, heavy snowfall which could turn to a blizzard if the wind blew down from Saskatchewan.

"I tried to," she said.

"I was against your marriage from the first," Grandma pointed out. "Your papa and I pleaded with you to wait. You and Willie were never suited. And there was the religion. But you *would* have him. Your papa and I were old fogies, trying to spoil your happiness. Now we're old fogies again, trying to spoil your happiness because we don't believe people should break up a ten-year marriage, especially when there's a child, and run off to California."

"Why don't you tell me that I made my bed, now lie in it," Mama sighed. She rubbed her arms as if she were cold or imagining herself out in the storm. "I came here so we could spend some time saying good-bye. I don't know when we'll see you and Papa again. But it was a mistake. You don't understand or care that I've been miserable."

"I understand all right, and I care," Grandma told her. "It's in the cards that we'll all be miserable part of our lives."

I stopped listening to them and concentrated on the rhythmic creak, creak of the rocker. Forward and back I swayed to keep it moving, my hands on the arms, pushing, pulling.

"For God's sake, Lark, stop that," Mama cried.

I got down from the rocker and crossed to the window. Out in Cottonwood Street cars drove slowly, wipers brushing aside snow, cleaning the window for more. Headlights illuminated the feathery fall. "The old woman's plucking her goose," Grandma usually said of such a snowfall. She didn't say that today.

"The old woman's plucking her goose," I said.

No one paid any attention. Tire chains made muffled, clinking sounds in the deep drifts already accumulated in the streets.

When Grandpa came in from work, he stamped his feet on the rug beside the kitchen door. Thick, wet snow clung to them, and to his jacket and cap. His eyebrows and lashes were dusted with flakes, and as the snow melted, it ran down his face as if he were crying. "Don't know if I'll be able to get the car out in the morning," he announced, breathing hard. "May have to walk to work."

"Get out of those wet things," Grandma told him. "Hang them by the radiator, but not too close."

Grandpa glanced around, trying to determine how far the family conflict had progressed. Were they going to be able to talk sense into Mama, or was she going to go off half-cocked to California?

Under the yellow light of the dining room chandelier, supper and the ensuing hours inched forward in stubborn slow-motion, as if the evening were an awkward and heavy burden which we must pull up a long, difficult hill.

Mama tried to make conversation unrelated to our trip. Grandpa had tacked a world map to the back of the dining room door, and Mama asked him where Hong Kong was, and Wake Island, both of which had recently fallen to the Japanese.

"There's Japanese all over California," Grandma told her.

"American Japanese, Mama."

"What difference?"

Aunt Betty stood at the window and watched the snow falling beneath the streetlight at the corner. "Good thing we don't have to get to the depot tomorrow morning," she said. "I don't think there'll be a car on the street. It's filling in again as soon as the plow goes through."

"Well, you know," Grandma pointed out, "the weather isn't perfect in California either. Cousin Marlis says it rains, sometimes for weeks, in the winter, then gets dry as dust in the summer. And she says it's real cold at night in the winter. She's got a heavy coat, and she says she *needs* it."

"I don't suppose it's like *this* in Los Angeles more than once or twice a year," Mama observed dryly.

"You can make fun of me if you want," Grandma chafed, "but it's damp along the ocean, it stands to reason. And Lark's going to have tonsillitis, wait and see."

"Would anybody like to play a game of five hundred?" Mama suggested. Five hundred was a game somewhat related to whist and extremely popular with Grandma and Grandpa Browning, who played one or two nights a week with friends or cousins.

Mama's suggestion put Grandma in a quandary. On the one hand, she would enjoy a few hands of her favorite game, but on the other hand, it seemed a frivolous thing to do in these serious circumstances, like dancing at a wake.

"Well, then," Mama said to Aunt Betty, "would *you* like to play honeymoon bridge?"

"I didn't say I wouldn't play five hundred," Grandma fumed. "Papa, are you up to a game?"

But even five hundred, a pastime ordinarily filled with laughing and joking and good-natured teasing, failed to lighten the atmosphere. And Grandpa called Grandma a fool for bidding nine hearts and going down one, while Mama kept losing track of the unplayed trump cards, a thing she never did.

While Aunt Betty shuffled and dealt in her turn, Grandma observed, "I don't know how poor Willie is going to get along. He can't keep house. He'll take to drink, Arlene. You'll have that on your conscience."

"Poor Willie," Mama snorted. "The first time I ever heard *you* call him poor Willie. You never had a good word for him before I married him. He hasn't changed."

"He's Lark's father. I have to feel differently about him because of that, and so should you."

"Well, I can't," Mama said, picking up her cards. "That fellow—what's his name?—Mussolini, he's somebody's father, too, I read."

Mama sent me to bed at half past eight. She and I and Aunt Betty were sleeping in the big upstairs bedroom that held two double beds—the room with sloping ceilings, under the eaves. If you got out of bed on the side closest to the wall, you had to duck your head so as not to hit it on the ceiling. I always slept next to the wall since I was short.

Leaving the hall light burning, I climbed into bed and pulled the feather bed over me. It was still snowing and showing no signs of letting up. Maybe it would snow so much the trains wouldn't get through on Wednesday. That would provide an extra day for Grandma and Grandpa to talk Mama out of California. So far, she seemed determined.

But Papa had assured me she would change her mind. I had put my faith in him. And there was still tomorrow. But, if she persisted, I would have to work on the plan to run away. In the spring when it was warm, I would come back. I knew quite a bit about railroads, and I thought I could find my way. Except for Mama, everything I loved was here, in southern Minnesota. All my memories, and all my plans. In California I would be nobody.

I rubbed my feet together to warm them. The upstairs was always cold in winter, except the bathroom. The radiator was left open there. The feather bed would soon warm me, however. I curled down until it covered my ears.

Would Papa remember to bank the fire in the stove before he went to bed? Mama usually did that. Poor Papa. How lonely he must be tonight. And probably cold. I should have reminded him to bank the fire.

My own feet were beginning to warm. When Mama came to bed, she would put her feet against mine, calling me her portable heater. Outside, two snow plows met at the corner, great behemoths, backing, turning, lumbering forward, like a pair of disgruntled tyrannosauruses. Growling, they passed, one prowling north, one east, combat declined.

The street grew quiet again. And now I heard the marching boots. Even here in Blue Lake, the sound reached me.

Mama and Aunt Betty climbed the stairs at ten-thirty. They were twenty minutes in the bathroom, preparing themselves for bed.

"God, it's cold in here," Aunt Betty whispered, pulling the covers up.

"My portable heater has this bed warm," Mama told her.

When they had turned this way and that, arranged and rearranged the pillows, and finally settled down, Aunt Betty asked, in a stage whisper, "Are we doing the right thing, Arlene?"

"I don't know, Betty. But right or wrong, I'm doing it."

❧ 59 ☙

"LOOK OUT the kitchen window," Mama told me after breakfast.

Snow was drifted against the north side of the garage, as high as the roof.

"It's the same in the front of the house," she said. "It's drifted up over the porch windows."

In the night, after the snowplows had come through, a north wind had descended from Saskatchewan, bringing more snow and driving it up against the sides of buildings. The plows might almost have saved themselves the trouble of clearing the streets. All their work had been undone.

Trees and bushes bent with the weight of great dollops of snow. Roofs were concealed beneath deep blankets. In the street and in drives, cars left out were buried. And, above, the sky hung heavy, inches from the treetops, waiting to throw down another batting on top of that already covering us.

No cars were moving. A profound, underwater hush enveloped the town. I cocked my head and listened, then ran to the back door and flung it open, and the storm door as well. Sticking my head out into the lush stillness, I listened. There wasn't a sound.

"Close the door. Do you want to catch your death?" Mama said.

"It's not cold, Mama."

"Well, it's getting cold in here."

"How did Grandpa get to work?"

"Goodness only knows," Grandma said. "On foot. He couldn't get the car out of the garage. Must have been snow up to his armpits in places."

Later Mama and Aunt Betty attacked the drifts outside the back door with snow shovels, beginning a path to the alley and another around the side of the house to the street. The entire morning was spent clearing the narrowest of passageways.

At noon the plows returned, and when they'd passed, the two women had to reopen their corridor to the street, as the thrown spume from the plows had filled it in once more. They laughed and squealed as they labored, lifting and tossing the heavy snow. Exertion rouged their cheeks, and tendrils of hair escaped their woolen caps. They looked like snow princesses. The laughter, muted by the swollen drifts, came to me as if from a distant afternoon of happiness.

At lunch Mama announced, "Betty and I are going downtown."

"Why on earth would you do that?" Grandma wanted to know. "It'll take you an hour to get there."

"That's all right," Mama said. "We don't mind."

Mama could not tolerate being boxed in. Cabin fever seized her the moment the exits were blocked. "We need to get out and move around."

"I thought that's what you were doing all morning."

"That's different," Mama said.

"Can I come?" I asked.

"You stay and keep Grandma company. I'll bring you a package of gum from downtown."

"The snow's so deep by the garage," Aunt Betty pointed out, "you can make a snow cave there."

And that was what I did for the better part of the afternoon. I carved out a cave with a living room, bedroom, and kitchen. It was warm inside, and quiet and snug. Was this what it was like in the satin confinement of Hilly's casket?

As the afternoon crested and declined, and the street lights winked on, Grandma called me into the house. The trembling black hands of the electric clock above the stove read ten to four. The crimson second hand sped nervously on its rounds, humming in the watery silence of deepest January. I sat down on a chair and pulled off my boots and snow pants.

"Don't get snow all over the kitchen," Grandma warned, calling from the dining room. "Your mother and Betty are taking their sweet time downtown. What could they be up to, do you suppose?"

When I had hung my coat over the back of the chair to dry and laid my mittens on the radiator, I reached the box of coconut-covered marshmallow cookies down from the top of the refrigerator. I made less noise than the clock, but Grandma said, "Don't fill up on cookies before supper."

Removing two, I returned the box.

"Get yourself a glass of milk and pour me a cup of coffee from the perk," Grandma told me.

I poured two cups of coffee, adding milk to mine.

"When will I see you again?" Grandma wondered aloud, studying me as I ate cookies, keeping my head over the table so the crumbs would not fall on the rug. "I think your mama should leave you here, at least until she finds a place." Grandma turned her cup this way and that. "Where will it end? Where will *any* of it end? Your mama, Willie, the war . . . I thought I knew the world, and I thought I knew your mama. Now it's all strange. I'm a stranger, looking in and not understanding what I see."

Mama and Aunt Betty flung open the back door, panting and stomping and creating a commotion, yet at the same time giggling intimately, bearing with them, at the center of their noisy entrance, a secret, a surprise perhaps.

Grandma and I waited. Aunt Betty appeared first, pulling off the scarf wound around her head and looking from one of us to the other.

"What do you think? Isn't it glamorous?"

She'd been to the Blue Lake Beautee Shoppe and had her hair done. The pinkish gold around her face was pulled back in two rolls that framed the upper face, the rest of the lovely pale red hair fell free, billowing out in fluff at her shoulders. She looked like Carole Landis in *I Wake Up Screaming*.

Aunt Betty stepped aside, like a model making way for another model, and Mama advanced, her scarf removed. Mama's shorter hair had been pulled back from her face into a froth of short curls at the back of her head, sort of like Norma Shearer's in *The Women*. But the most notable change in it was not the style. Mama had had her hair hennaed. The henna had taken a firm hold of her hair, shining brilliantly red even in the twilight of the dining room chandelier. Mama smiled and struck a couple of poses.

"My God," Grandma breathed. "What have you done?"

"Had my hair hennaed."

"My God," repeated Grandma, who normally didn't take the Lord's name in vain twice in a year. She seemed unable to venture further, however. Her right hand flew to her breast as if to quell violent upheaval there. Presently the left joined it, but to no avail, for her breast heaved as though a volcanic eruption were building.

Mama, in dumb innocence, waited to be complimented.

At last Grandma exploded, "You look like a Minneapolis streetwalker!"

Mama glanced wildly from Grandma to Betty to me, then back to Grandma. The starch went out of her, and she seemed to shrink two inches in height.

I ran to her. "Mama, it's beautiful. You look like Norma Shearer." But she didn't hear me.

"And the expense," Grandma went on. "You two girls can't afford a pot to pee in, and off you go to the beauty parlor to throw your money away. Then back you come, looking like Mrs. Astor's horses, and wonder why I'm upset."

"You can go to hell," Mama screamed, and ran upstairs, slamming the door behind her. I followed. At the top of the stairs, she turned. "Leave me alone, all of you." She hurried down the dark hall. "If I never come back to this place, it'll be too damned soon," she swore.

I sat down on the top step. Beyond the closed door at the bottom, Grandma's muffled voice implored, "Why did she do it?"

"She wanted to be a redhead for her new life. What's so awful about that?"

"She looks like a trollop."

"Everybody at the Beautee Shoppe thought she looked like a movie star."

"I don't doubt it," Grandma retorted. "I think half the stars in Hollywood were floozies before they got into the movies."

"What do *you* know about movie stars?"

"I know about people. And I know your sister is leading you across the country by the nose. And in the middle of a war."

"It wasn't long ago, you were begging me to go to California," Aunt Betty reminded her.

"It was right for a woman to follow her husband. It's wrong for a woman to run off, like a wild horse, not knowing why."

Mama didn't come down for supper. She closed the bedroom door behind her, and even Aunt Betty's coaxing wouldn't bring her out.

"Why would you do a stupid thing like that?" Grandpa asked Grandma when he heard the story of the henna. "On her last night?"

Grandma's eyes filled. "Because I'm beside myself with worry, old man. Now leave me be." A few minutes later she pointed to me, advising him, "Take a good look at this child. You may never see her again."

"They're not sailing for Tokyo, Hattie. They're taking the train to Los Angeles."

The next morning we were pious and regenerate. A gentle snowfall had built the drifts higher and rounded them into whipped cream mounds, but it was not enough to interfere with travel, and several cousins from around Blue Lake stopped for coffee and Grandma's caramel rolls.

Grandma didn't mention Mama's hair. Cousin Millie said, "Now you and Betty are both redheads," and that was all that was said. The cousins assumed that Aunt Betty was going to California to be reunited with Uncle Stan, and that Mama and I were merely accompanying her. For Grandma's sake, Mama did not disabuse them.

"If we tell them everything," Mama observed to Aunt Betty in the kitchen, "they'll have nothing to speculate about."

By two o'clock our grips were lined up by the back door, and Grandma was weeping, although we would not leave for an hour. "Come sit by me, Lark," she said.

We were ranged around the dining room table, the last of the cousins having departed. I dragged my chair close to Grandma's, and she put an arm around me. Mama and Aunt Betty cleared the remaining dishes and began washing up in the kitchen.

"You'll be a good girl and help your mama, I know," Grandma said.

I nodded, smelling the English Lavender cologne that drifted up from the hanky tucked between her bosoms.

"And show respect to your papa. Write to him."

Again I nodded.

"Sometimes when two people quarrel and break up, a child can get them back together. You might think about that." She gave me a tight squeeze and kissed my cheek. "Do you understand what I'm saying?" she asked quietly, not wishing Mama to hear.

"I understand."

"Good." She rose then, saying, "I'd best start packing food for the train. If you look in the china cupboard, you'll find a bag of jelly beans and a couple of packs of Black Jack. You put those in your purse."

Since the front porch windows were still covered with snow, the living room was nearly as dark as night, with only a spill of yellow from the dining room showing me the way. I sat on the davenport and secreted the candy and gum in my old red patent leather purse. If Mama knew I had the candy and gum, she would want to keep it, doling it out in little rewards throughout the trip.

When the treats were stashed, I sat in the dark, mulling over Grandma's words: "a child can get them back together." Grandma was telling me that there were yet things I might do to restore life as it had been. But what were they?

I heard Mama climb the stairs to prepare her face for the train. I followed, knocking on the bathroom door. "Can I come in?"

"It isn't locked."

She stood at the mirror, adjusting the collar of her blouse, critically eyeing herself this way and that, complimenting the newly red hair with the touch of her hand.

Opening a tube of lipstick, she freshened her lips with coral-red color, then blotted them with toilet paper. "Do you need to go to the toilet?"

"No."

From her purse she extracted a box of Lady Esther face powder, patting her nose and chin and forehead with the cloth puff it held. "Did you want something?"

"I . . . I . . ." What words held the magic to keep us in

Minnesota and carry her back to Papa? Time ticked away and I stood dumb.

Mama picked up her purse and dropped the box of Lady Esther into it. "It's almost time to leave. If you have something to say, say it."

"If we go to California, I'm going to die," I blurted. Her face held the stunned, accusing look of someone who's been slapped. "Don't go, Mama. Please, please, please, please." I fell on the floor, weeping and pleading.

"Don't make it harder for me," she said flatly, pulling me to my feet.

I yanked myself free from her grasp, anger detonating in me. How dare she be calm! Lowering my head, I struck out with my fists, rapidly, mechanically, feeling release and reward when blows struck firm flesh. "I hate you!" I cried, and that felt as good as anything I'd ever said, including confession. "I'll run away!"

Grandpa closed the shop to come home and drive us to the depot. Because there were so many grips to load into the car, Grandma didn't come with us but said good-bye at the back door, crying and hugging each of us, then hugging us again, withdrawing the hanky from her dress and wiping her face, waving it as we drove slowly away.

Though Grandpa drove with care, now and again the car slipped sideways in the snow-clogged streets, wheels spinning. Once, when the back end slid into a snowbank, we were stuck for several minutes while Grandpa got the shovel and a box of furnace cinders out of the trunk, and spread cinders under the wheels. The car pulled away from the snowbank and we were on our way again. Because of the delays, we drew up to the depot with only minutes to spare. Everyone grabbed a couple of grips and hurried with them to the platform.

"Want any of those checked?" the agent inquired.

Mama pointed to several, and they were tagged. The others we would carry on board. The door to the waiting room opened and Papa rushed out onto the platform. "Papa," I cried, and ran to him. I would stay with Papa.

Mama stood stiff as a fence picket, holding her purse tight in her two hands as if to prevent herself from doing mayhem.

"When you didn't show up on the early train, I jumped in the truck and came highballing down here, seventy miles an hour all the way," Papa told her. "I want you to come home," he pleaded. "Please, Arlene. I'll change. No more gambling, I swear to you. Don't go to California. I'll go crazy." He tried to reach for her hand, but she would not be touched. "I've been talking to Dick Mellin about finding a house. He tells me the old Linden house is up for sale. He says it's in good shape. The old woman took real good care of it. Only the best. Four big bedrooms, he says. Also a back parlor downstairs for your office. He thinks we can get it for a song if we make an offer this week."

Several blocks away, the train was tooting and bearing down on the station, overtaking us. Papa put his hands on Mama's shoulders. Her face was a clay mask, lacking all expression.

"Arlene, say something. This is what you wanted. I told Dick Mellin we were interested, and he should let me know right away if anybody came asking about it. You remember the yard? It's two lots—a hundred and fifty feet wide by a hundred and fifty deep. Lots of lilac bushes, he says, and roses and peonies. Beautiful trees. Elms all the way around, and remember the willow you were always pointing out? Now it can be *your* willow."

"Mama, let's go home. I want to live there. Please." If we lived in the Linden house, we'd all be our best selves, I knew it. It was that kind of house. A big, open porch wrapped around it where you could sit on warm evenings, reading the newspaper until the sun went down. And out in the middle of the side yard, on a tall pole, like a flagpole, perched an enormous white birdhouse made to look just like the Linden house.

There was a little widow's walk on the third floor, which *must* mean there was an attic. I could have a playroom up there. I was resigned to never having perfect pitch, but with a playroom under the eaves, I would be as confident as Katherine Albers, and if my pitch wasn't perfect, I would at least have the courage to sing.

"Mama, please."

The train was slowing, puffing, laboring, screeching, demanding we pay attention. "Please, let's live there."

One time, when I had ventured across town selling bazaar tickets, old Grandma Linden had invited me inside because it was cold, and she didn't want the door standing open. "Stand there, on the rug," she'd said to me, leaving to fetch her purse.

I had stood in the front hall, peering around. There was a big, open stairway on the right, a stained-glass window at the foot of it.

To the left were open double doors leading to the living room, and beyond that, the dining room. A real dining room, not just an ell.

Except for the ticking of a clock, the house was still and serene and self-possessed, without being arrogant. It was not a mansion, yet it was a house that proclaimed from every clapboard and gingerbreaded eave, "I am what I am, and that is enough." If we lived there, we would one day be able to say that.

I had hold of Mama's arm, imploring her to consider Papa's offer. Our grips with tags on them were carried off to the baggage car and handed up. Freight was off-loaded onto a freight wagon.

"Mama, there are hollyhocks by the garage, I remember. And you could have two tables of bridge in the dining room alone. Three or four in the living room, it's that big."

"Lark, get your grip," Mama ordered.

Papa grabbed me. "You can't take her, Arlene."

Papa and I would live in the Linden house.

"Betty, give the conductor our grips," Mama said, without looking away from Papa. The conductor tossed the three bags up into the car and waited for us to board. Shifting her purse onto her arm, Mama took my hand. "She's going with me, Willie." Now they both had hold of me. "I don't wish you any bad, Willie. You can visit Lark in California, and she can visit back here, but we're leaving."

"You don't love me at all," Papa said, as if believing it for the first time. He looked at Mama, waiting for her to respond, but she said nothing. The train tooted impatiently, anxious to be on its way. It was needed. People waited for it in other places, on down the line.

Papa pulled me into his arms, hugging me and crying. "I love you, Lark. Forget the bad times. Just remember the good ones. Remember the time we went hunting night crawlers in the rain? Didn't we have a good time?" He squeezed the breath out of me.

Mama pulled me firmly away. Grandpa Browning, who had been standing to one side, picked me up and told me, "Be good to your mama. And don't worry, d'ya hear? I bet you'll be back here before next Christmas." But his voice lacked conviction. He was trying to steal the edge from my fear. "You let us know what you want for Christmas so we can be all ready." He held me with his left arm now. "Reach in my right pocket of my jacket," he told me.

There was a little paper bag. I pulled it out.

"I know how you like gumdrops," he said, and the rims of his eyes grew red.

"We've got to board," the conductor told us.

Grandpa set me down, and Mama and Aunt Betty gave him hugs and promises to write.

"You can call collect when you get there," Grandpa offered. "It's all right."

Papa was crying, and he gave me another painful hug before Mama shoved me toward the conductor, who handed me up to Aunt Betty. In the end, I was going with Mama. "I don't see how you can leave like this," I heard Papa say as Mama mounted the steps. The conductor waved to the engineer, then tossed the portable step onto the landing and climbed up into the car.

Aunt Betty led the way, choosing a seat where she could wave to Grandpa, who stood apart from Papa, frowning to keep from weeping. The train gave a jerk and the couplings clanged and the great iron wheels cried sorrowfully.

I sat opposite Aunt Betty, waving to Papa and Grandpa, and feeling my heart being pulled out of my chest. Mama stood between Aunt Betty and me, frowning like Grandpa. Papa ran alongside the train, on the shoveled platform, calling, "Come back. I'm going to buy the house. Come back!"

Gradually the movement of the train smoothed as we picked up momentum and began rolling purposefully forward. Papa lost ground. Still running, he receded until he was a lone, dark figure against the snow, waving from the last margin of the platform.

⚑ 60 ⚑

HAVING USED the toilet and washed my hands in the brushed metal bowl, I dried them and searched beneath the candy and gum in my purse for a comb. There was half of one, and I extracted it.

Removing the barrette from my hair, I combed all that I could see, front and sides. The back would have to wait. My hair needed

. . . something. Maybe a henna, like Mrs. Erhardt's. Maybe a more sophisticated style, like Mrs. Weller's. *Something.* I sighed. It was a 1930s style in 1942.

Returning the comb to my purse, I dug into the bag of jelly beans and came up with two reds, a green, a yellow, and a black. I dropped the yellow and one red back into the bag, and sat down on the toilet lid to enjoy the remaining three, eating the red first and saving the black for last. Black was my favorite. The most sophisticated flavor in jelly beans, someone once told me.

The train swayed around a curve as I left the rest room, and the heavy door slammed metallically behind me. I stood in the narrow passage between the two rest rooms, savoring the taste of black jelly bean that lingered on my tongue. Far up the aisle Mrs. Erhardt and Mrs. Weller, each beside a window, faced one another, staring intently out at nothing.

I made my way toward them. "Mrs. Erhardt. Mrs. Weller. I don't know anyone else on this train. Are you going a long ways?"

Mrs. Erhardt stirred and stared at me, as if trying to place me. "Mrs. . . . ?"

"Brown."

"Oh, yes, Mrs. Brown. It's been a long time. Yes, we're going all the way across the country, to California."

"That's where I'm going. And so is my little girl, Myrna Loy."

"Mr. Brown? He didn't come?"

"No."

"How is Myrna Loy?"

"Sad. She misses her papa. He thought the world of her. He always said she was the holiest child he'd ever met."

"And pretty, too, if I remember."

"Her papa said it was lucky we named her Myrna Loy, since she looked like a movie star."

"What grade is Myrna Loy in now?"

"She'll be in the fifth grade next fall."

"Oh, my, is she that old already?"

"She's reading Nancy Drew mysteries. Sometimes she reads *Happy Stories for Bedtime,* because it reminds her of her childhood."

"It seems like only last year that she was in kindergarten. I'm sure she's going to like her school in California."

"I don't think so. She doesn't have any friends there. And her best friend at home died."

"Oh, dear."

"He was a great war hero. Also a prince."

"A prince?"

"He was in . . . what do you call it when you can't live in your own country?"

"Exile?"

"He was in exile. But they followed him. They caught him once and took off his clothes and tortured him."

"Oh, dear God."

"It's true. Every word. I heard it from an eyewitness. A Mrs. Wheeler."

Mrs. Erhardt regarded me sharply. "That's terrible."

"Yes. A war hero and a prince, and he wasn't even safe in exile. He blew his brains out on his front doorstep."

Mrs. Erhardt was a sympathetic listener. Her eyes were moist, and she groped in her purse for a hanky.

"Don't cry, Mrs. Erhardt. He's happy now."

"Yes, I suppose."

"He *is* happy," I said. "He's in heaven. Jesus sent angels to carry him to heaven. And angels to play harps and . . . ocarinas along the way." I opened my purse. "Would you like a jelly bean or gumdrop, Mrs. Erhardt?" She took an orange gumdrop.

"God was going to send the Prince to hell because he committed suicide. But Jesus got mad. He said, 'I want this man with Me.' Then God got mad and roared around heaven, scaring everybody. Fathers are sometimes too strict—God is like that—but we have to love them anyway. Jesus said, 'If the Prince can't come to heaven, I'm leaving. People with good hearts should be with Me, even if they're babies who haven't been baptized or war heroes who blow their brains out.' "

Mrs. Erhardt wondered, "How do you know all this, Mrs. Brown?"

I had to think. How *did* I know it? "I have amazing hearing. I can hear the Germans marching, all the way across the ocean. At night I hear them before I fall asleep. I think that's because it's daytime where they are."

"And you heard Jesus talking to God?"

"I think I heard Him in my sleep. I know it happened the way I told you. I'm not a liar, Mrs. Erhardt."

"I know that," she assured me, reaching for a second gumdrop. "Not many people can hear God talking," she observed and popped the gumdrop into her mouth. "Have you told anyone else what happened between God and Jesus?"

"Heavens, no."

"There are some things that people simply won't understand."

"Yes."

"Sometimes I let people think the worst of me because I can't explain the truth."

"I do that sometimes, too." I was amazed to hear this about Mrs. Erhardt. "What don't people understand about you?" I pressed.

"Well," she said, wiping sugary fingers on her hanky, "people don't understand how I could drag my little girl, Lark, off to California."

"Yes. I'm sure people don't understand that."

"But being married was like having a hippopotamus sitting on my face, Mrs. Brown. No matter how hard I pushed or which way I turned, I couldn't get up. I couldn't even breathe."

I had felt like that after Baby Marjorie died.

"Hippopotamuses aren't all bad. They are what they are. But I wasn't meant to have one sitting on my face."

I nodded. All I understood of this was her sincerity, which was like an open wound—painful to look at but impossible to ignore.

"I love my little girl, Lark, the way you love your daughter, Myrna Loy. And I know that she is very partial to hippopotamuses. You can see what a problem we have."

I wanted to tell Mrs. Erhardt that for Myrna Loy's sake I would live with a hippopotamus on my face forever. However, it was easy to *imagine* doing painful things. Before music class, when I was a child, I always imagined that I would volunteer to sing a solo. When the time for solos came, like Mrs. Erhardt, I couldn't breathe. I couldn't move at all.

"I don't know how to solve the problem, Mrs. Brown."

I told her, "It's a long way to California, Mrs. Erhardt. Maybe we'll think of something."